Citadel of the Fallen

Rebirth of the Fallen | Book One

JR Konkol

Black Rose Writing | Texas

The author grants the final approval for this literary material.

First printing

This is a work of fiction. Names, characters, businesses, places, events, and incidents are either the products of the author's imagination or used in a fictitious manner. Any resemblance to actual persons, living or dead, or actual events is purely coincidental.

ISBN: 978-1-68433-546-6
PUBLISHED BY BLACK ROSE WRITING
www.blackrosewriting.com

Printed in the United States of America
Suggested Retail Price (SRP) $19.95

Citadel of the Fallen is printed in Georgia

*As a planet-friendly publisher, Black Rose Writing does its best to eliminate unnecessary waste to reduce paper usage and energy costs, while never compromising the reading experience. As a result, the final word count vs. page count may not meet common expectations.

Map courtesy of Maureen Harkin

Kelly,

It isn't enough. How can it ever be? Not a day passes where I don't think of the trials you faced... the horrible cards you were dealt. You worked so damn hard, but at every turn, you faced nothing but hurdles and complications. Eventually, you got too exhausted to keep jumping those hurdles, but you never stopped trying... ever.

I didn't thank you enough for that. Now, although it feels hollow and ashen to me... thank you so very much. Thank you for fighting as hard as you did. You touched so many lives, whether you knew it or not.

Hopefully, you can live on here, in this fantasy world, through all the characters you helped to craft and shape.

Love,
Jeff

Shiver Tusk
The Black Scar
The Citadel
Grotto Web
The Citadel
and
Serpent River Basin

Citadel of the Fallen

1
Cedric

Cedric slapped at the stinging ant, but it was no use. The damn thing was beneath the plating of his armor. The air was hot and wet as the summer sun beat down on the thick canopy of leaves above, adding a yellowish glow to the lush green foliage of the rainforest floor. Sweat stung his eyes, and his lungs burned from the effort of keeping up with teenagers who seemed to revel in their ability to move through the foliage with ease.

Cedric was miserable, but it was only a few weeks until harvest. The work would be hard until then, but there'd be plenty of leave after. Still, he knew this assignment would be awful the moment he'd gotten it. Chaperone the Commander's sons and their classmates to gather herbs. The fact that Liam and Conner were involved meant that there would be no chance of traveling without his armor. No, Duncan would expect him to set an example of the perfect soldier for his eldest, Liam. Cedric was afraid it would get back to the Commander if he so much as complained.

He could hear them all giggling and arguing. The whole damn forest probably could. Attia, the girl who was tasked by the Pathfinders to guide them through the rainforest, long since stopped trying to shut them up. She was the only one he liked. At fifteen harvests, she was the second oldest of the group. Only Liam was older. Attia was lithe with long, raven black hair and a deep tan. She reminded him of his daughter, Kara.

Kara was much younger. She was quiet and confident. Kara didn't need to call attention to her actions. She let her actions speak for themselves. He likened it to how Attia kept her curved, wooden practice sword on her back where it belonged, unlike the other kids who preferred to swing sticks at trees, stumps and each other.

Cedric was responsible for eight of them. A few hours ago, he might've attached names to faces for most of them, but the afternoon heat took its toll. He knew his wife wanted to have more kids. Maybe it was time, he thought. A few moments later, he was reminded why he was opposed the idea when he nearly stumbled over one of the youngest, a small red-headed girl. She ran across his path without even looking. She crouched down, pointing at a grouping of plants with leaves crisscrossed by faint, milky yellow veins.

"You guys, right here!" she insisted. "We need to collect nectar from these."

"Are you sure, Ellie?" asked Conner as he darted out from behind a nearby bush. Conner was Duncan's other son, and it was well-known that he wasn't his father's favorite. Conner was a few years younger than Liam, and he had a very slight frame. He was quite ill as a child, and as a result, he was forced to spend a good amount of time with the healers. During that time, he developed enough of a familiarity with their crafts that it seemed to be the obvious direction for his studies.

"Of course, I'm sure," she quipped back. "Here. Watch as I give them a shadow," she said while cupping her hands above one of the larger leaves to shield it from the dispersed sunlight. The glowing veins on the leaf slowly faded out in response to the loss of light. Within seconds, there was no evidence they'd ever been there. She shielded the leaf for a few moments longer before pulling her hands away with a dramatic flourish. A few breaths later, the golden veins started glowing again in response to the sunlight. "See?"

"Okay, okay. I believe you, Ellie. I just still remember..."

"Oh, would you stop bringing up the stupid Prickling Ivy!" she snapped, cutting him off. "No one's perfect."

"Actually, I'm pretty close," called Logan as he bounded over from back down the game trail they'd been traveling. He saw where Eliana was crouching and rushed to join her, catching his foot on a clump of roots in the process. He crashed through the plants, landing in a heap next to her.

The forest came alive in that moment. A pair of brightly speckled Yen that were nesting deeper in the thicket of plants, frightened by the motion of the clumsy boy falling, spread their webbed wings and darted up into the air. Other branches and leaves started moving as many unseen forest creatures fled the noisy pack of children.

"Liam! Get back here, and bring the others," called Cedric. He looked around nervously, uncomfortable with how loudly he just yelled. With all the noise and motion, though, he couldn't see any harm in it. He needed everyone close and accounted for.

"On our way, sir," he heard shouted from ahead in the distance. How did he let everyone get so spread out? He swore under his breath as he took a few steps forward and reached down and helped Logan to his feet.

Eliana was working to pluck leaves from the plants in front of her. She moved with practiced hands, taking each leaf from the nearest node to minimize damage to the plant. She tucked a dozen of the large leaves in her leather belt-pouch before Liam led two other children out from a shady patch of nearby trees.

"Here, sir," Liam said with a salute. The boy was nearly full grown. He looked so much like his father. His hair was a sandy brown and his face and neck both seemed wider than they should be. He was wearing a form fitting chain tunic. Both the sword that rested at his side and the shield he carried across his back were metal.

"Only three of you? There should be four!" spat Cedric. His panicked tone betrayed a touch of his own guilt. He didn't know the students well enough to identify which one was missing.

"Tessa spotted a Pelan nest in the clearing. She wanted to see if she could bring one down with her bow. She isn't far, sir."

Cedric started to reply, but was cut short by Attia's upheld fist, and the sharp hissing noise she made. In all the commotion, Cedric hadn't even registered the noises of the forest. He heard birds, frantically calling, and he saw a small pack of monkeys leaping from branch to branch overhead. Attia's eyes, though, were focused on a pair of Yen flying past them.

Why did she care about the Yen? The two they scared up earlier flew further ahead. Then it dawned on him. These were the same birds! Something chased them back this way. "Everyone behind me, now!" he shouted as he took a step forward. His heart raced as he let his shield swing off his shoulder, slipping his arm through its sturdy leather straps. He felt subtle magics responding to his adrenaline and heart rate. His battlemagic wasn't strong, but it would help him perform better. "Defensive spells," he called. "If any of you know 'em, you'd best use 'em."

The boy he just helped up staggered backwards and fell with a bit of a shriek. The rest seemed to maintain their wits as they took positions ten feet down the path behind him. He saw the Pathfinder girl flank out into the foliage to his right, next to a sturdy tree. She nodded to him and pointed up and ahead. "See the trees?" she said, pointing at how the branches of the canopy were shaking in the distance. "Whatever it is, it's big."

"Liam, flank out to my left. It doesn't get past us," Cedric said, trying to mask his fear. He took another couple of steps forward, hoping to make himself the easiest target to get to. Cedric glanced down at the ground and made a mental note of how the roots were positioned. He couldn't afford to be tripped up. The rustling of the trees got louder, and now beneath it, there was a deep, raspy breathing like a slow drumbeat. He scanned the trees in front of him. The sun ducked behind a bank of clouds, and the shadows beneath the canopy all grew deeper and darker. How can something this big be hard to see?

Cedric saw its eyes first. Sickly and yellow. It saw him too, pausing for the merest of moments to sniff the air before emerging from the shadowy forest on to the game trail perhaps fifty feet away. It was a wild boar, but the proportions were all wrong. The boar was enormous. Its massive head rested on its shoulders at a height of a normal man's, and it was nearly as wide as it was tall. The thing's frame was bigger than anything he encountered before. It had to weigh three tons. Its breathing was labored, and Cedric saw that one of its tusks hung off to the side of its snout. That wound was an old one, as scar tissue and sinew grew to hold it in place. The tusk shivered like a loose tooth as the beast breathed.

"No, fire and smoke, no! What is it?" whimpered Logan as he noisily scrambled to his feet. Cedric heard the boy stumbling away behind him. "Be still!" Cedric hissed, but it was too late. The boy already started running, and the boar's gaze immediately shifted to the moving target. It made a loud, guttural call before bounding into a full charge down the trail toward them. Cedric set himself with his shield forward and his feet at an angle. He couldn't take the charge head on, but he needed to slow it down. He saw Attia creeping closer, her heavy wooden practice katana in position.

Time seemed to slow as the beast got closer. Cedric could smell the foul rot and infection coming off the thing, and he could see huge, leaking sores along its flanks and across its back. He saw countless black, chitinous legs and body segments of giant ants crushed and smeared into and around the beast's body. It'd been swarmed and stung into a near frenzied madness, and now he was in its way.

It was on him before he knew it. Adrenaline coursed through him, bringing with it magic to help absorb the bone crushing impact. His shield ripped across his body as the boar clipped his shoulder, and he felt white heat as bones and tendons gave way under the strain. He caught a glimpse of Attia spinning low and wide, driving her heavy weapon into the beast's ankle, right above its hoof. Her timing was good. As Cedric was falling to the ground, so was the boar.

"Get up!" he shouted to himself as he rolled to his stomach and got to his knees. He saw the beast righting itself. It turned in Attia's direction, but she wisely leapt back after her attack. If it charged, she'd be able to make it behind a tree in time. Cedric winced as he regained his feet. His heart was beating even faster now, and he used the magic it provided to numb the pain in his shoulder.

The giant boar pawed the ground, ready to charge at the girl, but Cedric was on it before it could, driving his sword into its back. The beast bellowed as the blade bit into a swollen sore left by the ants. It whipped around toward Cedric, impossibly fast, catching him in the side with its body mass. His heavy plate armor stopped his ribs from shattering, but the force of the blow was enough to send him spinning off balance. The beast quickly completed its turn and centered itself before charging at the dazed soldier. Cedric got his shield in front of his chest to deflect part of the blow, but with no sense of balance to begin with, he found himself knocked backwards into a tree. His legs gave out and his vision blurred.

He watched in horror as the boar lowered its head and readied itself again. If it charged, it'd kill him. He thought about his wife and daughter and knew he couldn't let it end this way. Cedric winced as he tried to roll to the side, but there were too many branches blocking his path. He could see Liam moving behind the boar now. Come on, man, I need you! Just hit the damn thing, he thought. His vision blurred more, but then he heard clanging and shouting. Liam was trying to get its attention.

Arrows started flying from somewhere behind Liam, and they were hitting their mark. Liam backed away and settled into a lower stance as the boar turned to confront its attackers. It lunged forward into Liam's shield, knocking him back a few feet. Liam swung his sword at its head, but his angle was bad, and the blade harmlessly deflected off the boar's thick skull. Another arrow flew past, missing the mark as the boar charged forward again, this time whipping its massive head into Liam's legs, knocking him to the ground.

Cedric shook the fog from his head. He cried out in agony as he used the tree to work himself back to his feet. Blood was running down the side of his neck from where he got slammed into the tree. He felt his wounds starting to overcome him. In desperation, he let his magic overcome him instead. Giving in to the rage and the heat of battle, he worked himself into a frenzy. His anger blocked out his pain. His bloodlust replaced his fear but took his reason in return. The frenzy was upon him. There was nothing left, but him and the beast.

He charged forward, hurling himself into the broadside of the boar with a shout. He started stabbing. The boar bellowed in pain, and once again rolled around toward its attacker. Cedric caught that sideways tusk in his side. It impaled him, but he kept stabbing. Even as the beast lifted him off his feet and whipped its head from side to side, he kept stabbing. Long after he should've been dead, he kept stabbing. There was a sensation of vertigo as the boar buckled beneath its own weight. It whipped its head one more time as it lost its balance, driving him into the ground with incredible force as it fell.

Cedric heard a staccato cracking as countless bones in his face and neck all shattered in succession.

And then there was no more...

2
Attia

Attia watched in horror as the boar swung its head. Cedric's body whipped around as he was driven face first into the ground. His neck snapped and the tusk split his side open as the boar fell onto his lifeless body. The beast's own lifeblood gushed out from the sea of stab wounds Cedric delivered before his death. Its breathing got slow, wet and sputtering. It was dying.

Attia expected its eyes to glaze over, but a strange light shone in its eyes instead. The light grew in intensity until the boar's eyes smoldered with brilliant emerald fire. That fiery light spread out from the beast's eyes, pulsing through its body for a moment before vanishing as if it hadn't ever been there. The boar's breathing returned, clearer and calmer. No! It wasn't possible, she told herself. The deep wounds were still there, but many of them stopped bleeding. Her heart raced as she saw the monstrosity roll back to its stomach and start to slowly rise. It was dying! How can it get back up?

Attia bit back her terror and took a shaky breath. She needed to clear her head and remain calm. She needed to be an example for the younger ones. Liam was back on his feet, but he looked shaken. He must've seen its wounds heal. Tessa darted off to the side, hiding behind a tree. She was nearly in position to take clean shots again. Conner was moving toward his brother, but the rest of them were wisely spreading out amongst the trees.

She moved in, deciding that her best bet at this point was to stay behind the boar and work at its legs. Liam regained its attention by cutting it deeply along the neck. She used the opening to swing her heavy wooden sword into the back of the thing's knee, just as it lunged forward.

The boar buckled under its own weight for a second, and Liam danced in and cut it again. The boar sprung back up far more quickly than something of its size should, though, and it caught Liam in the gut with its snout. The wind went out of him, and Attia feared the worst. Fortunately, it seemed to glance with its tusk. Liam fell to one knee. She shouted and swung again, this time at the other leg just as Tessa found her mark with another arrow. The beast buckled again, giving time for Liam to get back to his feet and for Tessa to sink yet another arrow into its side.

The boar whipped around, thrashing wildly. Attia saw its body turn and swing her way and she relaxed, letting her own magic guide her. She moved in concert with the boar, falling back as it crashed into her, gently landing a few feet to the side. She felt a wave of fatigue wash over her in response, telling her that her graceful dodge was more a result of magical energy than her own skill. Still, the boar was getting slower. Another arrow landed in its side, and the boar fell back to the ground. Blood poured from its sides from a multitude of wounds, and this time, there was no emerald glow in its eye. Liam stood over it now, able to take his time to line up his blade before sinking it deep.

There was virtually no sound. The beast didn't cry out or struggle. The life simply went out of it. When it did, a cloud of white mist burst forth from it in all directions. It was like a shockwave, but it passed through trees and foliage as if they weren't there. No one was knocked over or even moved by the strange spectral wind. It was there and gone in a single breath. It travelled out far enough to have touched all the children within sight of the fallen boar.

"What... what was that? What just happened?" called Malcolm from behind a tree.

"We can't worry about that now. Attia, will you help me get Liam on his back?" said Conner as he rushed to Liam's side.

"I'm fine, little brother."

"No, you're not!" he spat. "I need you lying down before the shock wears off." Conner looked to Attia pleadingly. He had one hand on his brother's shoulder and the other was near where the boar gored him. She could see the dark red stains bleeding through where Liam's chainmail was cut open along his side.

"Liam... I want you to listen to your brother," she said while walking to him. She held his gaze as best she could to keep his attention. Soon, she had an arm behind his back, and between her and Conner, they got Liam comfortably to the ground.

"Let me see how bad this is," Conner said as he gently worked the bloody chainmail up past where it was torn. Liam's stomach and ribs on the left side already turned an ugly mix of brown and yellow and there was a nasty, deep gash all along his side from where the boar's tusk cut him. Had it not been for the armor, it would've impaled him. There was so much blood, and it showed no sign of stopping soon. Conner shouted for Eliana.

"I'm right here," she replied.

The entire group had made their way over to Liam. Everyone except Logan. Attia registered the absence with a sigh. "We must move soon. Get him ready—"

"We are not moving him," Conner interrupted. "The Citadel knows where we are. Father will send someone for us."

"Not in time," growled Attia, her anger rising. She hated dealing with other people. She was used to spending time out in the forest alone or with other Pathfinders. Verbal communication wasn't a skill she prioritized.

"Look, I don't really care," Conner said a little too dismissively. "He needs a proper healer before he can make the journey."

Attia didn't have time for any of this. She and Liam were the oldest. The rest needed to respect that. She didn't have time to teach them all the things they didn't know about the forest. "Let me make this clear," hissed Attia as moved down the path to where the boar came from. "The thing we just killed... it's not from this region. It tore itself a path through the woods to get here." She could hear herself getting louder but found herself powerless to stop it. "It broke branches. It trampled plants. It uprooted trees. It chased predators and prey out of their hidey-holes and gave them a nice clear path!" She started walking back to them, stopping a few feet from the dead boar. "Ending here. With stinking rotting meat," she said as she looked down at the boar for a moment before looking back up at the rest of them. "But then there's all this fresh meat to be had."

"Stop, you've made your point," said Liam weakly. He was starting to feel his injuries. "You do what you can for me, Conner. I believe in you, little brother."

"You need to be ready to move in five minutes. I'll see if I can find Logan." With that, Attia took off down the path at a light jog, following the trail of a terrified little boy. She was worried for both Liam and Conner. That wound was deep. It wasn't going to stop bleeding without healing, which meant Conner would have no choice but to treat it. The poor kid was constantly doubting himself, especially when it came to his older brother. She sighed. It was a people problem. Not something she was equipped to help with.

Logan's trail was easy to follow. He was clumsy and scared. His footprints were deep, and he was careless enough to break several branches along the way. She found where he tripped, fell, and scrambled back to his feet. Why hadn't this kid slowed down? She scanned the canopy above. There was a lot of activity. He probably thought something was chasing him. Maybe something actually was?

She followed the path until it went over a ridge and dipped down into a gulley. It wasn't all that steep along the path, but steeper off to either side. She saw where Logan slipped off the path and tumbled down to one side. He tumbled fast enough to trample down a thick patch of nettles. Torn pieces of his tunic were caught in the thorns. If she looked hard enough, she knew she'd find blood.

She carefully scanned the gulley below for signs of the boy, but there were none. Something felt wrong about the gulley's contour. It seemed to funnel to one point. It wasn't a natural formation, and it wasn't something she should carelessly investigate.

Already tired from the battle, she knew she wouldn't be able to rely too heavily on her magic. Unlike Cedric and Liam, her chosen path was balance. It centered her and helped her to move smoothly and efficiently. She drew on it more, letting the magic lighten her footsteps. Fatigue once again washed over her, but it wasn't bad enough to truly concern her. There would be time to rest later.

She worked her way down the side of the hill and was immediately relieved to have taken precautions. The soil beneath the groundcover was a slick clay. It would be easy for one to lose their footing here. She carefully worked her way down closer to the bottom until she could see well enough to understand.

A fine, translucent silk shimmered on the ground in and around the carefully formed funnel. She could see small rivulets in the muddy ground where she suspected poor Logan tried to stop himself from being pulled into the nest.

Attia felt sick. She knew what she'd find, but she had to be certain.

She climbed back up the hill a good distance until she found a fairly large downed tree branch. She tossed it down the hill into the web. The thing that came out moved with eerie fluidity. It sprung forward, its many legs neatly spreading out over the tree branch. It disappeared quickly, taking the tree branch with it. She estimated it was the size of a large goat. Trapdoor spiders of that size were not unheard of in the rainforest. She'd heard of some the size of bears, but none this near the Citadel.

Her eyes stung. It was all too much. "Keep it together," she muttered to herself, but the tears were already flowing. Poor Logan, she thought. It would've been a horrible way to go. There was nothing she could do about it now. The spider had him in that nest for minutes. What was she supposed to do? She couldn't save him. Her, alone with her damn wooden sword? What was she going to do if she did somehow get him out of there and he was still alive? The paralytic venom would eat him from inside, dissolving him so the spider could drink, and poor Logan couldn't even scream. She couldn't get the image out of her head! The tears came faster as she started to openly sob. It was all too much. She wanted to run home. She wanted to be back at the bonfire where someone older would tell her it would be all right. The others still needed her, though. She was already gone too long. What would happen if they came looking for her and something happened to someone else?

"Sorry, Logan," she whispered through her tears as she turned, made her way back to the path, and started her run back to the others.

3
Conner

Conner was never good enough. His older brother was always the center of attention. Liam was always the one they asked about. His accomplishments were what they celebrated. Liam lived at home with Father, while Conner lived in the Monastery, only spending time with his father a few days a week, and occasionally during an evening meal. They told him it was what Mother wanted. That she wanted balance in the family. She wanted one son to take the path of the soldier, and the other to take the path of the healer. Maybe that would've worked out if she was still alive.

"Ivy Glue won't keep this wound sealed. I can protect it from infection with herbs, but you'll have to stop the bleeding." Eliana was sorting through a selection of acorn-sized balls of herbal blends, each neatly wrapped in leaves of various colors that identified the contents.

Just what I need, thought Conner, a chance to rise to truly new levels of disappointment by failing to stop his brother's bleeding. He pictured his father's face wracked with sorrow and disappointment. The thought of it made him nauseous. His hands started to sweat and tremble.

"Conner," Malcolm said as he lightly laid a hand on his shoulder. "He's losing blood fast. You can do this."

Conner felt the hand on his shoulder more than he heard the words. He knew it was Malcolm, and knew his friend was trying to encourage him, but it wasn't helping. It wasn't foolish to be nervous. Novices could hurt or even kill themselves by attempting magic beyond their skills. The more complicated the spell, the more the magic needed to be held and manipulated. His teacher described it like a spring. The tighter you wind and compress it, the more damage it might do to you, should you slip and lose control.

Healing was more like a catapult than a spring when it went wrong.

Step one, find my focus, he thought. Liam was fading in and out of consciousness now. There was no more time to waste. Conner placed his hand over the bloody wound and gathered his thoughts. He started to feel a sympathetic pain in his own side. It was a simple trick he learned in the Monastery. He nourished that pain until it was almost intolerable before starting to let stronger energies coalesce in his body. He used the pain in his own side to guide him as he worked to gently close the wound.

He made a few missteps. He lost his focus enough to let thoughts of his father's grief and disappointment back into his head, filling him with self-doubt. He gasped as the pain in his own side snapped him back into focus. Thank the stars he had the foresight to establish that sympathetic link before starting his work.

He saw skilled healers fix wounds of this magnitude in a matter of seconds, but it took him more than a minute to finally close the wound. There'd be a lot of scarring in the areas where he messed up, but in the end, he stopped the bleeding. Slow and steady wins the race, he thought. His brother would live. He smiled to himself as he closed his eyes and slumped over.

The moss felt nice against the side of his face. It was cool and damp, and a nice contrast to the hot, sticky air. Conner didn't remember falling over. He felt exhausted and breathless, like he ran until his body gave out. He could see Russell and Tessa helping Liam back to his feet a little ways away.

"Hey, I think he's coming to," called Malcolm from right behind him. He felt an arm on his shoulder as he was gently rolled to his back. Malcolm was kneeling close by, looking down at him with concern. Malcolm's hair was blond and wispy. His complexion was nearly as pale as Conner's. He leaned in close. "You all right, buddy? That was beyond your skills. I'm pretty sure your well went dry." He spoke softly enough that the others wouldn't be able to hear.

Conner considered for a moment before nodding. He was taught about it. He even saw it happen before, but this was the first time he experienced it. When a person works with more magical energy than they're able to manage, they often pass out from it. Some of the professors described it as a well going dry. Now that he felt it, he had to agree with the characterization.

"Is he going to be able to walk?" asked Eliana. "Little miss temper-tantrum has been gone a long time. We better be ready to go when she gets back."

Conner sat up. He was tired, but he felt all right. "I'll be fine," he said as he turned to face Eliana. The body of the monstrous boar was behind her. Blood continued to drain from it. There was so much blood that small pools formed everywhere its hooves cut into the ground during the fight. Cedric's dead body was a small distance from the beast, his head bent at an extreme angle from landing on it.

Conner felt like he would pass out again. He was just getting ready to celebrate his fourteenth harvest in a few weeks. He shouldn't be seeing this. He shouldn't be out in the forest, fighting for his life. He shouldn't need to save his brother from bleeding out. He shook his head as he climbed to his feet.

"I can walk," Conner said, but he didn't think he would be fine anymore.

"So," said Russell as he finished helping Liam. "No real great way to say this, but... what we do about Cedric?"

"Please show a little respect," replied Liam.

"I'm trying to. It needed to be brought up—"

"I know," interrupted Liam. "I just..." His voice trailed off as he considered the situation. "I just thought we would be more honorable about it. He saved our lives."

"So, do we bury him? Do we just leave him?" Russell waited a moment for Liam to answer. He looked as if he would say more but thought better of it.

After a few tense moments, Liam answered. "His armor is Attuned to him by runecrafting. No one else can wear it. So, we leave that. We take his sword and shield with us, and as much as it sickens me, we leave the rest."

Liam walked over to Cedric's body and regarded it for some time. Conner wasn't close enough to hear what his brother was saying to the fallen soldier, or if he was saying anything at all. He didn't know how well his brother knew Cedric. He didn't know if Cedric was one of his instructors, if they practiced with each other, or if they ate meals together. He didn't know, and because of that, he didn't feel he had any right to know how Liam said goodbye.

"Russell. If you would be good enough to carry his sword and shield, I would appreciate it," Liam said when he was done paying his respects.

"Everyone just about ready?" came a call, shouted from down the game trail. Conner turned and saw Attia jogging toward them. He really appreciated the girl, despite how abrasive she was. She stumbled upon him one day while a group of kids were bullying him. Nothing serious. They were just knocking books out of his hands and messing with his clothes, but she wouldn't have it. All three kids got a pretty strong beating. He heard that she was punished harshly for it, but she never gave any hint it bothered her. What was obvious in this moment, though, was that Attia was seriously troubled. Conner knew her well enough to know that some of the moisture on her face might not be sweat from her jog.

"Attia, is everything all right?" She flashed him a serious look. Her eyes were almost pleading.

"I followed Logan's trail. He was running the whole time, but he was sticking to the game trail. I guess we'll see him back at the Citadel," said Attia.

Conner knew she was lying. Her words were far too practiced and smooth. As she got closer, he confirmed his suspicion that she'd been crying. He met her gaze for a moment. Something bad happened to Logan. He didn't think they'd ever find him back at the Citadel, but she wasn't ready to talk about it. He sighed and nodded to her and she looked relieved. Maybe this was a way for him to protect her for a change. He'd get everyone moving and try to keep anyone from questioning her until they were safely home.

"Okay everyone," Conner called. "Attia will set a slow, but steady pace. We follow her down the trail back toward home. We should make it by nightfall."

4
Malcolm

Malcolm felt old. It was a strange feeling to process for someone who only saw fourteen harvests, but it was how he felt. His mother died when he was a small child. He had a few faded memories of her to hold on to and cherish, but not much else.

Malcolm's father was killed last year while the Citadel was undertaking preparations for the annual Black Tide. Each year, around this time, the forest floor became a raging river of giant ants as they migrated south, stripping the land of food and resources to take back to their towering anthills. It always happened during the annual harvest time, and the Citadel was constantly forced to send dozens of expeditions to quickly claim its valuable crops before the ants came and swept them away.

Last year was a particularly bloody one. Many of the foraging teams were attacked by forces from the demon city of Nerreka. Malcolm's father was unfortunate enough to be with one of the teams that was hit the hardest.

Malcolm was alone ever since.

The Citadel moved him out of his family chambers and into a small, but nice room of his own. It was heartbreaking to be moved from the rooms he grew up in, but it was necessary. A symbolic step into a new life, they said, although he later suspected that it was more about repurposing the space than anything else. Still, everyone was encouraging and helpful, and he was given a choice of many different paths of study for his new life. He was too old to be adopted by a new family, and yet too young to provide for himself. There was no easy way to handle it. Ultimately, he threw himself into his studies, taking comfort in the more arcane sciences.

"Try and keep up, we don't want to make Attia slow down," said Eliana as she turned and waited twenty feet farther down the trail from him. "You know how she gets." Eliana was a few years younger than Malcolm. Her skin was deeply freckled, as was common for red-headed girls, but she at least had the sense and the skills to protect it from the sun. She offered to show him the proper mixture of plants and how to apply them a few times before. His own pale skin burned in the sun. He decided to take her up on the offer at the next opportunity.

"Sorry. I just have a lot on my mind." Malcolm hadn't realized he was lagging behind so much. He lightly jogged to catch up with her and resolved to pay more attention to where he was. Fortunately, Attia was moving at a slower pace than normal, and no one seemed overly concerned as he and Eliana caught up to the rest of the group.

Perhaps it was the events of the day, or perhaps the skies above the treetops were getting overcast, but the rainforest took on a much darker feel. The canopy in this area was thick, encouraging the growth of nettles and other thorny plants that flourished in the shade. It was the hottest part of the day, and the thick foliage acted as an oven, allowing the sun to filter through without permitting the heat to escape. Malcolm's head hurt and his mouth felt dry.

There was something else, though. He couldn't quite put his finger on it. Maybe his eyes were playing tricks on him, but he swore he was seeing moving shadows as he walked. He had to partially close his eyes just right, but when he did, he could see wispy shadows, flying or rather floating in the air. They followed behind the group, but never got too close. He turned around and stopped to watch them and was surprised to see many of them stop in response.

His eyes were starting to sting, and no one else seemed to have issues. His mind had to be playing tricks on him. Maybe he just needed water and sleep?

"What are you looking at?" Once again, Eliana was waiting for him farther down the path. "I mean, if you were looking at the ground, trying to find me Camphor Berries... well, that would make perfect sense. In any case, Conner said I now must hold your hand so we don't lose you. Everyone is up around that bend, taking a rest. There's a dangerous part of the path going down a hill soon. We will move through as a group."

Malcolm walked with Eliana, feeling unnerved. He still saw the moving shadows when he tried to. It was a distraction he really couldn't afford right now. He felt a bit of relief as he rounded the bend and saw his friends. Maybe staying closer to them and engaging in a little light conversation would keep the shadows at bay.

"Okay, now that we're all together," Attia said in a tone that very much demanded attention, "I want us all walking down this hill together. Stay on the game trail and you'll be fine, but the ground on either side is slick. We can't afford to have anyone fall here."

Attia didn't leave anyone time to linger. She started moving down the trail until the rest of the group followed. She stopped right where the path made a very slight turn, and there was indeed a bit of a drop-off had one missed the turn. She carefully guided everyone past that point.

Malcolm was the last to move by, and he couldn't help but look down into the gully as he passed. His breath caught in his throat as he saw a dark shadow coalescing right above the very bottom of the gulley. It seemed human in so many ways, and eerily, it very much looked like it was watching him. He felt a chill in his bones. It was almost as if he knew it, and it knew him. Malcolm distinctly heard a voice. A whisper from right behind him, or perhaps within him.

"*A brand-new shade, from a very recent death.*"

Malcolm jumped in surprise. He started to lose his balance, but Attia caught him and moved him back on to the path. "What's wrong?" she asked with a mixture of concern and annoyance.

"I... I think I just saw a ghost."

"Where?"

"At the bottom of the ravine." Malcolm saw the color drain from Attia's face.

"We need to get going. You've been lagging behind ever since we started home. You almost fell just now. You need to stay with the group the rest of the way back."

Malcolm nodded. He shivered as he turned away and walked down the path. The hair on the back of his neck tingled as he imagined the shade at the bottom of the ravine watching him go. Was he going mad? He was seeing things none of the others were seeing, and now he was hearing voices? Should he talk to someone about it? No, he thought. A good night of sleep and a warm meal will set everything right.

"All right, everyone," said Attia as both rejoined the waiting group of children. "I think we've passed the only risky parts of the journey. The trails from here on out are pretty well traveled by the Pathfinders.—"

"The place where we were foraging was supposed to be safe too," said Eliana before Attia could finish.

Attia started to answer, but Liam cut her off. "Eliana. None of that was supposed to happen, but it did. Father wouldn't have knowingly sent us into harm's way. Right now, we need to follow our guide and get home safely." Liam's voice was strong and clear as he took charge of the situation. "Attia. Would you care to get us moving again? The sooner we make it back to the Citadel, the better."

Attia nodded and started back down the trail without another word. The group followed along behind her. Malcolm found the pace slow enough where he could keep up with relative ease. At times, when the group stopped for a bit of a breather, he squinted again. He saw more of those wispy shadows each time he did. He practiced a little, and in time, he could shift his vision back and forth fluidly enough where he could take occasional views while on the move without slowing down.

They traveled this way for two hours, occasionally stopping for water. At one point, Eliana found a bed of herbs she needed for a project and she forced a stop to harvest some, but other than that, the travel went smoothly.

It was a few hours from dusk when Attia started making bird calls. Her calls went unanswered at first, but soon enough, Malcolm heard distinctive answers to her calls. Those answering calls got louder and clearer until a short woman stepped on to the trail. She was wearing tightly fitted leathers, dyed to a mottled pattern of dark greens and black. Her face was painted with more patterns of green, and she had a few strands of leaves woven into her long black hair. This woman would be nearly impossible to see in the forest if she didn't want to be seen.

"Attia. Did you intend to cry for aid, or do you need more training on your calls?" The woman's tone was playful.

"Pathrunner Felerin," replied Attia as she bowed her head in greeting. "My call is correct. We are in need of aid."

The other woman was already carefully looking over each of the haggard teenagers, taking note of Liam's bloody, damaged armor. "Tell me, how I may help, Pathwalker."

"We were attacked by a monster... a boar."

"Where?" asked Felerin.

"Nearly to Black Claw's log." Attia responded.

"Boar don't travel that region. Why was it there?"

"Ants, ma'am. It'd been driven mad from the stings. It tore its own path through the forest. It didn't travel a trail to reach us."

"Tore a path? How large was this boar, Attia?" asked Felerin with a touch of amusement, a smile on her face.

"Larger than a bear. Much larger. It was ancient. One of its tusks was broken or torn to the side."

The smile disappeared from the woman's face in an instant. Attia started to speak, but Felerin held up her hand, silencing her. "I know of such a boar, but it ranged far to the north. We were told it died long ago. I'll need to see for myself." With that, Felerin extended her hand out to the side in a fist. A man dressed in similarly camouflaged leathers emerged from the forest ten feet behind her. From the reactions of the others, Malcolm was sure no one had been aware of his presence.

"Pathrunner Arick," said Felerin. She never looked back to acknowledge the man. "Run and notify the Citadel that Shivertusk may have returned, driven from his home." She waited to hear the man depart before continuing. "Pathwalker Attia, what of the boar?"

"The boar is dead, ma'am. The soldier who was sent with us, Cedric, fell to protect us."

Felerin stayed silent for a few seconds. Malcolm didn't know why. Perhaps she was surprised, or perhaps she knew Cedric and was processing his loss. After a time, she quietly asked, "Did anyone else fall?"

Attia's back stiffened and she looked down at the ground. "Yes, ma'am. A boy named Logan. He ran when the boar attacked. He slipped off the path and down to a trapdoor spider nest. I marked the place on the path for you with—"

"You lied to us!" Liam's tone was unforgiving. "You said we would see him back at the Citadel."

Felerin took a step forward. "Be silent," she hissed to Liam before putting a hand on Attia's shoulder. She spoke again with a much gentler voice. "Are you sure, Pathwalker?"

"Yes. I crawled down and saw the trap. I saw... I saw where it pulled him in, and I tested it. I threw a branch into its web and the spider came out."

"Good job, Pathwalker." Felerin paused a moment before adding, "Your role, at that point, was to get the rest of them home safely. Telling them about the boy wouldn't have made your task easier." She looked at Liam pointedly for a few moments as if inviting an argument. "Now, finish your mission, Attia. You must hurry if you're to guide them home before nightfall. I need to see Shivertusk for myself."

Malcolm quietly processed what he heard. His head began to hurt again as he remembered the shadowy apparition at the bottom of the hill.

"*Yes. You did see a ghost,*" came that same whisper from before.

Once again, he couldn't quite tell if the voice was right behind him, or inside him.

5
Liam

The paths and game trails melted away. They traveled through crop-filled clearings now. Liam knew these clearings. They'd be home soon, and he still hadn't perfected his version of the story in his head. Liam felt sick.

Father would want to know what happened. Father would need to know how Cedric died, and how his eldest performed in the heat of battle. He'd want to know about the wound, and how they made it back safely, and about the other boy who died. No matter how Liam worked and reworked the narrative, he couldn't escape the chilling reality that he wasn't the main character. Cedric fought the boar. Attia got them home. Tessa and Cedric were the ones to kill the thing, and he only survived because of his brother's healing.

He hadn't done poorly, though. When push came to shove, he engaged the boar after Cedric fell. No one else could have done that. He wondered if that would be enough to earn his father's praise. The sounds of excited chatter behind him reminded him he wasn't alone. Everyone else seemed relieved to be home. Was he was the only one who wanted to throw up? On a whim, he called out. "Attia, a word please?"

Attia turned and nodded. Liam stepped forward so he was just a few inches from the girl. He spoke quietly so the others couldn't hear.

"Thank you for leading us home. I've had some time to think about it... the decision you made about Logan... It was the right call."

Attia didn't seem moved, but she didn't appear offended either. "My mentor already approved of my decision, but thanks for letting me know where you stand on it," she said tersely before softening. "It wasn't easy, Liam. I'm sure he was still alive when I found the nest, but what could I have done?" She bit her lip hard enough to produce a small trickle of blood. "Understand that, by the time all of you walked past him, he was already dead."

Liam started to respond, but something in her eyes stopped him. He intended to claim the mantle of leadership, and therefore take responsibility for the death. She wasn't going to let him. She made it clear it was her decision, and hers alone. She let the boy die. If Logan was already dead by the time he got there, and she actively deceived him regarding the boy's safety, what in the world could he have done? Liam smiled as he started to understand. He almost wanted to hug her. Attia effectively stripped him of any responsibility with respect to Logan. "Thank you, I understand."

"Good."

Liam turned to the others. They were standing a few feet away. He noted how they recognized his need for privacy, and that they granted it. It was good of them. "So, most of us saw what the boar did," he started. "The bright green light. The wounds that seemed to heal on their own."

"And that blast of white mist when it finally died," added Tessa.

"Yes. And the white mist." Liam always prided himself on being forthcoming and honest. This was hard for him. "I think we need to keep silent about all of it." He watched as the others quickly exchanged glances. "At least for a little while," he added. "I just don't want our parents and teachers to think we're making anything up."

"I plan on spending a lot of time in the library, researching what we saw," said Malcolm.

"That's a good idea. Let's give it a few days at least. We need to better understand what we saw before we talk about it." Liam spoke quietly, but with confidence. It drew his audience in. It was one of many leadership tools he learned.

He saw the others nodding to themselves as he spoke. He knew they were close to agreeing. They just needed a little push. "We can talk about it again in a few days. Maybe then we'll know more, but for now, we keep quiet."

"We need to keep moving," Attia said as she turned and resumed walking. Liam let her get a few steps ahead before he slowly followed.

"Do you need anything for the pain? Your color isn't so good," said Eliana as she caught up to him. "I have a lot of different herbs that might help," she said as she rummaged in her belt pouch.

"No. I'll be all right. It hurts when I take a breath, and I guess it itches?" Liam smiled at the girl and tried to lighten the mood. In truth, his side was aching to the point of distraction. He felt burning sparks of pain as the wound moved with every step and every breath. His vision went blurry. He was taught about how the body responds to battle, trauma, and healing spells. His symptoms were all within the normal range as far as he could tell, but it was still troubling. "We'll be home soon enough," he said, more to calm himself than Eliana.

The sun sank down beneath the tree line. Had they been back in the rainforest, deep beneath the canopy, it would be getting dark, but here amidst the expansive clearings there was ample light. Liam saw a family of farmers off in the distance to his left, tending to their fields of rice. Part of him wanted to go and ask to borrow a skiff. It would be nice to let the river's current carry them the last mile, but it would take too long. It was already getting dark.

Attia led them along a path that moved from clearing to clearing, never getting too close to any of the farmers, but never remaining in the forest's darkness for too long. It made sense to Liam. The Pathfinders would want to move quickly and easily on their patrols. At the same time, they wouldn't want to be a distraction to any of the farmers. This method of skirting the edges of the clearings made that possible. He tried to pay attention to some of the landmarks hoping to be able to follow part of this route in the future, but he knew he'd never manage it. The Pathfinders started training for the trails when they were young, often before seeing their sixth harvest. Still, the mental exercise passed the time and kept him from worrying about his wounds.

They crossed a few more clearings this way until they eventually spilled out into an open field. The sun was fully set, and stars were just starting to appear in the darkening twilight sky. The field itself was peppered with close to a dozen bonfires, each hosting a loose collection of tents. Pathfinders and visiting farmers normally stayed in the small tent cities. Liam always wanted to spend a few nights out beneath the stars at one of the bonfires simply to experience it, but with all his studies, he hadn't found the time.

He saw the river off in the distance. The Serpent, as they called it, was quite wide here. It snaked its way through the rainforest from the north, picking up size and speed from the countless small streams and tributaries that fed it along the way. The river was the lifeblood of the Citadel. Farmers set up all along its banks during the dry seasons, using its waters to flood their rice fields. The Citadel itself was built directly over several carefully engineered river channels so that clean water could be taken from some, while waste could be sent away through others.

Liam was getting more and more nervous as they made their way through the clearing towards the enormous wood and stone structure that was the only home he ever knew. The Citadel was built on top of a series of massive stone pylons that were sunk deep into the ground. The elevation kept it safe during the rainy seasons when the Serpent often escaped her banks. It had four levels on the inside that Liam was aware of, and although some children told tales of secret libraries and hidden floors throughout, Liam was pretty certain of the dimensions. Each level was roughly a square, 350 feet on a side, filled with living quarters, classrooms, kitchens, and crafting spaces. A tower and several storage buildings rested on top of the structure. All told, nearly two thousand people lived out most of their lives within the walls of the Citadel.

Liam and his father shared quarters on the third level, close to the blacksmiths. The halls often rang with the sound of hammers on metal, and despite the well-constructed ventilation systems, Liam normally woke each morning to the light sting of smoke in the air. His father's position could have afforded them larger and much nicer quarters but being close to the smithies had advantages, especially for one who spent his life leading heavily armored soldiers.

Liam suspected that the real reason they lived where they did was so they could be close to Conner. The forges were directly below the Monastery, where the healing students were stationed. The healers relied on large volumes of hot water to keep the sick and injured clean, so, they engineered heating vents into the forges to redirect excess heat to the Monastery's water tanks. The design was simple, yet elegant. It was an aesthetic that was common throughout the Citadel. Each room or area served more than one purpose whenever possible.

Attia stopped ahead of Liam, signaling for the others to stop. A pair of armored soldiers were approaching. Liam thought he recognized one of them, but he couldn't quite remember the name. It was something he knew he needed to improve on if he ever wanted a command of his own. A commander must live the lives of all who serve with him, his father often said. His dad practiced what he preached, regularly telling Liam detailed stories about the lives of the men and women he commanded.

The soldiers stopped a few feet away. One of them held up a hand in greeting while the other studied the group of students. "Liam," the man started. "You and Conner are to go to the Monastery. The Commander will find you there when he can. Does anyone else have injuries that need treatment?"

Attia moved to the side, allowing Liam to step forward. A part of him wondered if she was deferring as a favor to him, but it was more likely that she just didn't want to deal with the conversation. Liam turned and looked back to his friends for reassurance. He didn't think any of them were wounded, and no one seemed to be calling attention to themselves. "No, sir. I'm the only one with wounds."

The soldier regarded him for a moment. He looked like he wanted to ask a question but thought better of it. "The rest of you are to report to Dean Maye's quarters."

Liam was nervous about that. The Dean was an ornery old woman. She was the one who generally administered discipline to students who were guilty of serious infractions. "The Dean? Is everything all right?"

The soldier shrugged. "I guess you'll find out," he said with a chuckle. "Now come along. We'll walk you back."

6
Eliana

"Would you be so kind as to describe what happened again, Malcolm?"

The group was seated on one side of a long wooden table. Dean Selandra Mayes sat on the other side, partially hidden behind stacks of books and scattered papers. She looked tired and she wore a disapproving look on her face. She continued to take notes as Malcolm gave her a summary of what happened when they encountered the boar. Eliana didn't understand why the Dean only wanted to hear from Malcolm. Ever since his dad died, Malcolm studied runes with the Dean personally, but that shouldn't matter. That would be favoritism, and Eliana definitely didn't approve. Perhaps the Dean would ask each of them for their recollection of the events? That would be very thorough. That's how she'd do it.

Eliana tried to distract herself as Malcolm droned on. She didn't want to listen to his rather poor retelling of the events. After all, it might distort her far more accurate account. She decided to pay attention to the room itself, instead.

The space was lit by bowls of glowing, milky yellow liquid. Liquidlight potions. Those were made with the same nectar she was harvesting right before the beast found them. She'd have to add that to her report. The nice lighting highlighted the fact that the room was rather messy. There were two enormous pillows and some bedding piled up against one wall. Shelves dominated the long wall behind the Dean's table, each stocked with an assortment of plants, liquids, and containers of colorful powdered dusts.

The dusts were required for runecrafting, alchemy, and an assortment of other arcane arts. She loved how the magic of the land expressed itself in so many ways. It blossomed in certain plants and fruits. It bubbled up out of the ground in natural springs, but it was strongest in gemstones. Eliana liked to think the magic inside was what made gems shine. When those gemstones were crushed, new magic could be built and stored in the gem powder.

"Hmmm. I see," the Dean said as she continued making notes. "You're absolutely certain that its right tusk was ripped to the side, and that it came out at an angle?" The Dean paused, her lips pursed. "Malcolm? Malcolm, I asked a question."

Eliana looked over to see Malcolm's eyes distant. It was obvious he hadn't even heard the question. It reminded her of how he behaved on the journey back. It was very inconsiderate. He ignored everyone most of the way back. He hadn't even taken her suggestion to look for Camphor Berries. Something was definitely wrong with him.

"Malcolm!" Dean Mayes was getting insistent. Eliana raised her hand as she always did in class. When the Dean didn't immediately acknowledge her, she cleared her throat, as she often needed to do in class. That almost always worked!

"Miss?"

"Bodenbrum. Eliana Bodenbrum, ma'am." Eliana smiled. It worked again!

"Yes, very well." Dean Mayes made another note before looking up impatiently. "You have something to add, I trust?"

Eliana nodded as she stood up. She really wished she had a slate board to write on. A diagram would be far more accurate, but she'd just have to make do. "First, we are absolutely certain about the tusk. It was the right one, and it was off to the side. It was strong enough to break through armor before the boar fell."

"Right. Well, the Pathfinders will recover the remains, so we'll be certain soon enough." The Dean put down her quill and folded her hands neatly in front of her. She looked amused. "Seeing as you are standing, and evidently eager, what else can you tell me?"

"Well," Eliana started, pausing a bit to make sure she had everyone's attention. "It was a very hot morning out in the forest. I correctly identified the Dawnflowers we were sent to harvest. It makes Liquidlight, like the lights in this room—"

"Yes, Miss Bodenbrum. I'm well aware."

"Oh. I didn't know if everyone else was," she said as she gestured to her classmates.

"Let's move to the boar itself. Malcolm described it as covered in large sores which you all assumed were from giant ants," the Dean said.

"Yes, ma'am. There were some ants crushed into its body."

"Dean Mayes," Attia interjected. "I've seen dire bear and other large forest animals after being swarmed before. The sores were the same on the boar."

The Dean nodded to the young Pathfinder for a moment. "Did the boar do anything..." she paused, searching for the right phrase, "out of the ordinary? It was so far from its home, Attia. It makes little sense that it would come this far. Perhaps it fell to madness?"

Eliana's heart sank. The Dean was questioning Attia now. Why did everyone care what Attia thought? She blurted out, "No one mentioned the green light!" She immediately felt guilty after saying it. They'd made a pact to keep the details about the pulse of emerald light and the strange white mist to themselves until they could do some research on their own. Then again, she rationalized, this was the Dean they were talking to, and the Dean asked about anything out of the ordinary. Was there a better way to research the strange events?

"Green light? Please tell me this isn't another herbalism lesson." The Dean's tone was playful, but also weary.

"When the boar fell for the first time, we thought it was dying. There was a bright green glow in its eyes. The light went all over its body. Um... like if you were to splash one of the Liquidlight potions over yourself. It gets bright for a few moments, but then the Liquidlight dies out completely. It was like that, except it was green instead of gold." Eliana chewed on her knuckle nervously. She knew her friends would be angry with her for talking about this, but she was more nervous about her analogy. It wasn't very good. The green light on the boar wasn't really a splash. It was more like—

"Go on."

The interruption startled Eliana. "Oh, I was just thinking of a better way to describe it." She saw the Dean frown. She didn't want any of the others to talk, so she continued. "The boar's wounds healed."

"What do you mean? Healed? How?"

Eliana had her attention now. "It fell over on top of the man before the—"

"Cedric. His name was Cedric," hissed Attia.

"Sorry. It fell on Cedric. Then there was that wave of green light and a lot of its wounds healed."

The Dean stood up. She was tall and portly. The combination of the two made her quite an imposing figure. "Is this true?" She looked at each of them. Maybe she was expecting one of them to contradict the story, but none of them did. "Please continue."

"The boar didn't last much longer. The next time it fell, there was some kind of frost or mist that shot out from it, but none of us got wet or anything."

"Nothing moved at all from the mist," added Tessa. "I was crouching behind several giant frond leaves, trying to hide while I shot at it. Even tiny breezes move fronds. This mist didn't move them at all. There wasn't any frost either."

"It's because the mist was spiritual," said Malcolm.

"Oh, how nice of you to rejoin us," chided the Dean. "Are you all right? And exactly how do you know this?"

Eliana was behind everyone as she'd opted to stand for her presentation. She couldn't see Malcolm's face, but she saw the tension in his shoulders. "I'm fine. I'm just tired." Malcolm sighed. "Look, I don't know how I know it, I just do. It had a great spirit within it. When it died, that spirit shattered, touching each of us." He put his fingers up to the side of his head and started massaging his temple as if he had a bad headache.

Dean Mayes sat back down and grabbed her quill, looking at Malcolm the entire time. She only looked away after she started writing. All of them were quiet, not wanting to anger the Dean. Eliana felt a bit uncomfortable standing, so she quietly crept back into her chair and sat down. She quickly looked down at her hands, not wanting to look at any of the others. She felt foolish for breaking the pact. She regretted doing it. Eventually, she looked back up from her hands to watch Dean Mayes.

The Dean kept writing for what seemed like an eternity before finally placing her quill to the side. "It's a bit late," she said. "It'll likely take us a day or two to sort things out. I expect each of you to attend your classes tomorrow. None of you will speak of this with anyone other than me or the Chancellor. I'm sure Duncan will speak with his sons when he makes it to the Monastery, and that's acceptable." Dean Mayes paused, taking time to look at each of them. "Let me be crystal clear," she said slowly for emphasis. "Children gossip, and the stories will spread like fire in the wind. Your friends will ask what happened. They'll keep asking. Some may even be hurtful to you when you don't respond, but you WILL keep quiet." She paused again. "Have I made myself perfectly clear?"

"Crystal clear," replied Russell. "So, Eliana, that means we actually don't talk about the green light and the mist," he chided. "I just wanted to make sure you were clear on that this time."

Eliana felt her cheeks flush. She quickly looked down at her hands.

"Go back to your chambers and get some sleep, students," said the Dean. "You are dismissed."

7
Conner

"Well, let's take a good look at that wound," said Professor Eleanor Wells as she approached the bed where Liam rested.

Liam's armor had been replaced with a cloth robe. Conner sat next to his brother's bed, and he was nervous. Professor Wells was one of the more skilled practitioners of the healing arts in the Citadel, and she immediately understood what happened. Junior students were expressly forbidden from working with anything but the most basic of castings. He definitely violated that rule.

"Roll to your side, please," she said, opening Liam's robe so she could see the wound. She bent her face close to Liam. She ran her fingers along the contour of the wound and inhaled through her nose. Conner knew she was checking for infection and fractured ribs. Ellie's herbs would have cared for the infection. He corrected at least one fracture when he stopped the bleeding. The professor continued to examine Liam's abdomen and side for a time before asking, "You did this, Conner? Out in the forest, after the attack?"

"Yes, ma'am."

"This is quite impressive, but I have a few questions. How long did it take you?" she asked, her back to him.

"A minute. I think a little more."

"So, your spell failed. A few times even," she pointed out. "You needed to start and stop it, didn't you?"

"Yes, ma'am. Several times. I was trying to be careful. I knew there would be scarring..."

"Don't concern yourself with the scars. Tell me, what are your other disciplines?"

"Enchantment and balance, ma'am," Conner replied.

"There's a simple Shield spell in balance. Why didn't you protect yourself?" the professor asked.

"I'm not skilled enough to cast that Shield spell, ma'am."

"You weren't skilled enough to heal your brother's wound, either, yet you did. Tell me, young Conner, which backlash is more dangerous between the two disciplines?"

Conner felt sick. The professor was completely right. He took a dangerous and unnecessary risk. Failing with a balance spell, while painful, was almost never lethal. In the heat of the moment, he hadn't thought it through. He should have shielded himself before attempting to mend his brother's wound. "You're right. I was foolish."

"You're too hard on yourself, Conner," Professor Wells said gently. "Your brother was going to die. You risked yourself to heal him. I respect your heroism. I'm merely offering guidance."

"There was a lot going on out there," added Liam in Conner's defense. "My brother didn't have time or a lot of options."

Professor Wells made a disapproving clicking noise with her tongue as she continued to inspect the wound. "You were both very lucky. Your armor turned the blow just enough to keep it on the outside of your rib cage, Liam. And Conner, I suspect you aren't even aware that you dealt with three broken ribs, as well as the bleed." She closed Liam's robe and gently rolled him to his back.

"Everything is all right now though, right?" asked Conner.

Professor Wells nodded to Conner as she made her way toward the door. "Duncan, you can come see them now. Liam should stay overnight, but he can return to classes tomorrow," she said as she left the room and their father entered.

Their dad was a powerfully built man, standing just over 6' tall. His neck and shoulders were thickly corded with muscle, and his face seemed unnaturally wide. Liam shared all these traits with his father, while Conner shared very little. He hastened to the far side of the bed so he could see both of his sons, but when he spoke, it was clear to Conner he was only addressing Liam. "How do you feel, son?"

"Like a failure."

"Don't be so hard on yourself, Liam."

"It would have killed us all, if Cedric hadn't been there." said Liam.

"You don't know that. For now, tell me exactly what happened as you recall it. You too, Conner. I'm sure you both saw different things."

Liam went first. His retelling was incredibly detailed in terms of the position of everything. Conner added in a few details with respect to when Tessa joined in and where she was firing from, but little more than that. Neither of the boys included any details about the green light or the white mist. Their father was content to patiently listen until they finished.

Their dad waited in silence for a few moments before speaking. "There are Pathfinders already working to bring back the bodies. From what you describe, though, I think I know the boar you fought. Surviving it, let alone killing it... Stars above, that was no small feat! You both should be proud. Tell me though..." He paused for a moment as if he was searching for the right words. "Did the boar do anything outside of expectations? Did you find your blows turned aside at times? Was it faster than it should've been? Did its wounds heal on their own? Anything like that?"

Conner was dumbstruck. How did he know? Liam spoke before Conner could process whether to deny it or to come clean.

"Yes, sir. There was some kind of light. It healed itself."

Their father reached down and squeezed Liam's shoulder while he nodded to Conner. "I understand why you didn't mention it in your retelling. Do me a favor, and don't mention it in the future," he said as he pulled a chair over to the bed and sat down. "The boar you met earlier today has quite a story, and I think you two deserve to hear it. It began maybe a decade ago. The Pathfinders started reporting problems with a huge wild boar to the north. A small group of them tried to hunt it, you see, but they found it to be more than a match for them. The hunters were forced to return empty-handed. Other hunters made the journey, only to meet with the same results. Over the months, that boar grew into a bit of a legend. They named it Shivertusk."

"I'm not sure I understand, sir," said Conner as he tried to think through what his father was saying.

"Patience, Conner," he chided. "That year's Black Tide came and went, and when it was safe to venture north again, the hunts resumed. Things were different, though. Shivertusk grew wiser. He was harder to find. The hunters started staying out there to hunt for a few days at a time. That's when the boar started hunting them.

"Shivertusk first attacked in the middle of the night. It was a group of four Pathfinders. One was gored and another was trampled to death. Only two made it home. Weeks later, a larger group of five went out, hoping to avenge the fallen. We don't know how they died. They never returned. No bodies were ever found."

"But how did you know about the healing, Dad?" asked Liam.

"Well, Gunther and I decided that we needed to go see for ourselves. Neither of us are hunters, of course, but we figured if the two of us patrolled its lands long enough, we'd eventually run into it. So, we headed north. Shivertusk lived on the savannah, rather close to where the Serpent comes into the forest. Pathfinders can make it there in four days or so, but it took us a full week. It's quite a thriving region. There's this massive, sprawling colony of giant spiders to the north. Hundreds of giant spiders living in a mile-wide web are a strong deterrent for the ants. The Black Tide avoids the web, flowing around it to either side. It creates a safe pocket for the animal life to live and thrive within.

"We had to be one hell of a sight. Two men in full plate armor, covered with runes, no less, stomping around the savannah. The place was just teeming with wildlife. We moved ourselves in to one of the bomas a past hunting expedition built—"

"What's a boma, Dad?" asked Conner.

"A little fort made of limbs and branches. Nothing really secure, but enough at least to keep us from getting accidentally trampled. Does that make sense?" He waited until Conner nodded before continuing. "We slept in shifts during the day so we could stay up during the nights. Truth be told, we were taking so many Camphor Berries, we probably could've just ignored sleep all-together.

"Shivertusk came for us the third night. The moons were dim, and we could barely see ten feet past our fire. The boar likely started his charge from fifty feet or more away. Had we not both been in our armor, it might have been bad. He hit Gunther dead center, but Gunther has the finest suit of armor in the Citadel. The charge barely bruised him. He got knocked back into the campfire, though, and his beard caught fire. Oh, I teased him about that for years," their father said, laughing.

Conner was astonished. He never heard stories like this from his dad before. He felt jealous of Liam. Did Dad talk to Liam like this often? He considered what he saw the boar do to Cedric. It knocked him around with ease. It ripped right through his armor with its tusk, but Gunther took the charge easily. He'd heard other children talk about the runes they hoped to one day see written into their armor, but he never paid it much mind. Now he thought he finally understood.

"I circled around behind it to push it inside the boma," continued their dad after recovering from his laughter. "Gunther was so pissing mad… I remember he punched it in the snout before retrieving his sword. I hacked at the thing's haunches to see if I could get it to attack me instead of Gunther, but those two apparently bonded. It kept trying to gore him without doing any true damage, but it stayed so close that Gunther was having trouble swinging his stupidly large sword, and all the while, his beard was smoldering. So eventually, Shivertusk pulled back a way. I'm guessing he wanted to charge again. Gunther finally got his chance to really swing, and he delivered just a perfect strike towards its neck. And then it happened."

"What happened?" Liam prompted, his eyes wide.

"It was as if an invisible sword or shield blocked Gunther's attack. His blade just stopped in mid-air, inches from Shivertusk," their father said.

"But… how is that possible?" asked Conner, wondering out loud. At the same time, he witnessed that green light and he saw Shivertusk's wounds heal on their own.

Almost as if he were reading Conner's mind, their dad asked, "How is it possible for a dying boar to heal his own wounds?" He massaged his forehead for a moment, as if he'd suddenly developed a headache, before continuing. "I can't really explain it well. Perhaps the Chancellor will speak to you about it sometime. Understand that we barely fathom how this world works. We comprehend even less about how other worlds touch and interact with this one. I like to think Shivertusk had a friend watching over him. Perhaps a spirit that lived within him, and maybe the spirit could help him from time to time."

"And are there spirits living in other animals, monsters, or even people, Father?"

Liam asked the exact question Conner wanted to ask, but their father either didn't hear it or he chose not to answer. "What happened when Shivertusk died, Liam?" their dad asked. Conner wanted to press the question he thought was being ignored, but Liam spoke before he could gather his thoughts.

"There was a white mist. Kind of like a blast of air, but it had no weight or force to it."

Their dad stood and smiled. "Well, boys, I think I should let you two rest. You've both had a busy day—"

"Why did you and Gunther let Shivertusk live?" Conner realized he was getting closer to understanding. He knew his father was trying to get away without saying any more, but he needed more.

"After seeing Shivertusk deflect Gunther's sword, we just didn't feel right about killing him. We drove him off and tracked him as best we could the next morning. Shivertusk built himself a little nest, close to the giant spider hive. He even used some of the webs to hold all the branches together. It certainly explained why the Pathfinders were having a hard time finding him. We decided to let him be. If he made peace with everything in the region, including the spiders, he earned peace with us as well. When we returned, we told everyone that we drove him into the web and that we didn't think he'd be bothering anyone ever again. A few of the Pathfinders were angry. They wanted to see proof of his death, but none of them would go looking. If he truly went into the web, there wouldn't be any proof to find. The spiders seldom leave much behind."

Their father started walking toward the door. He stopped, turning to face the boys. "Now that I'm certain it was Shivertusk, I need to go back to that savannah and see for myself. If the Black Tide isn't forced to circumnavigate the spiders, it may take a different path. It might be here much earlier than expected."

"But you said it took nearly a week for you and Gunther to make it there?" Conner asked.

"Light magic, brother," said Liam.

Their father nodded. "I'm much more skilled than I was a decade ago. Once day breaks, I'll be there to see what I can learn. Hopefully, nothing's changed with the hive. It's possible, even likely, that something else drove Shivertusk from his home and into the path of the ants. I need to be certain, though, but first, I need rest. And so do the two of you. Liam, please sleep. Conner. A word with you outside?"

Conner's mouth went dry. His father's tone didn't seem harsh, but it was anything but gentle. He looked down at Liam as he got up out of his chair. His brother looked concerned. He must've heard the edge in their father's voice as well. Whatever the issue was, he wouldn't improve his situation by delaying. He quickly followed his father.

His dad shut the door once Conner left the room. He spoke quietly, but sternly. "I heard what you did out there. It was heroic, but that's not how to heal in battle. A soldier slows down and tires as he's hit. You need to be there, next to your brother. Had you refreshed him after the boar first hit him, he would've had the strength and speed to get out of the way. Instead, he almost got gored, and you had to risk your life to fix the wound."

It stunned Conner. He saved his brother. Was his father really attacking him for not saving Liam's life the right way? His eyes stung as if he were going to cry. It was so unfair! He wanted to say something to defend himself, but his tongue felt like it was wrapped in cotton. Why couldn't his dad understand? He needed to hear that he did a good job out there. He needed to be praised for saving Liam's life. Would anything he did ever be good enough?

"I understand you're not a soldier, Conner. I'll speak to Solen about giving you some private lessons on moving in combat like a balance fighter does. It's one of your areas of study already. It shouldn't be too difficult to build upon it."

Defeated, Conner simply nodded. "Am I dismissed, sir?"

"Yes. Get some sleep." His father started to leave, but stopped and said, "You did well out there today."

To Conner, it felt like an afterthought.

8
Tessa

"Please focus, students," said Professor Thompson from behind his lectern. "The Harvest is nearly upon us. I'm sure it saddens all of you to know that today will be our last opportunity to review this semester's material prior to your final exams." The professor paused as a few students giggled and another outright laughed.

Tessa Callinden finally decided. She hated this professor. He forced participation by constantly asking questions, and she was certain that he purposefully called on kids who didn't know the answers just to embarrass them. He teased kids when he didn't like their ideas, and he seemed to enjoy setting students against one another. Tessa was one of the students who giggled at the notion that anyone might be sad about this being the last class. She couldn't wait to be done with history classes for good.

"Well, since a few of you find it funny, I think we have our first volunteer," continued Professor Thompson. "You there... is it Russell Sorenson?" he said, looking down at his seating chart. "Yes, Mr. Sorenson, I'm sure you were only laughing because you've spent so much time studying the material that you hardly need a review. Tell me then, what is the central defining theme of our new history?"

Tessa looked over at Russell. It was only yesterday that they were in the rainforest together, fighting for their lives. He was short, and a touch overweight, but he had a somewhat flippant attitude that she couldn't help but admire. He looked over at her and rolled his eyes as he answered, "Ganna fruit?"

"Mr. Sorenson. This is a history class, not a comedy class."

"No, seriously. Try to go a day without eating or drinking something with—"

The Professor moved on quickly, cutting Russell off. "Miss Simmons. Would you be kind enough to provide a less childish opinion?"

The girl was sinking in her desk, using the students in front of her to try and hide. "Um... the formation of the Demonic city states," she answered timidly, her cheeks flushing red.

Professor Thompson rubbed his chin in a thoughtful fashion. Tessa sighed. This was yet another reason she hated him. He obviously knew what answers he wanted to draw out of the class, but he still went through the theater of acting like he was thinking about it. "I don't know if I'm comfortable with that answer, Miss Simmons. I mean, if whomever won the war determines history, then I'd have to agree with you. Maybe your answer will be correct in a few hundred years. Right now, though, humanity is still surviving."

He smiled at the girl for a moment before looking down at his seating chart. "Hmmm, Mr. Mitchell," he said, scanning the class until he could locate the boy in the back. "I contend that it's premature to surrender history to the demons. But if not them, who should we focus our attention on?"

The boy looked around nervously for a moment before meekly asking, "Humanity?"

The Professor slowly clapped as he said, "There, you see? No reason to be nervous Mr. Mitchell. You knew the answer all along." Tessa added the slow clap to her list of reasons to hate Professor Thompson. "We need to be specific. We spent a good amount of time this semester discussing some of the prevailing theories about why humanity's still here," he said as he looked around the class for his next victim. "You there, Miss Olson, can you tell me how many cities we're aware of?"

"Eleven, sir," she said smiling.

"That's correct. Let's leave Hammeron out of the discussion for now, as I think it's fair to say the question of who or what governs Hammeron is unsettled. How many of the remaining ten cities are considered to be human-governed cities?" The Professor kept his attention on Miss Olson.

"Three, sir."

Professor Thompson nodded. "Yes, three predominantly human-governed cities. Derregain, Vorrenkempe, and, of course, our home, the Citadel," he said as he tapped his lectern for emphasis. "Tell me, what do we know about the conditions of human life in the other cities? Miss Callinden, why don't you answer that question for us?"

Tessa flinched when she heard her name called. She was tempted to point out that Professor Thompson asked two questions, and then just answer the second one, but she knew that wasn't an option. "Humans are property. Bred as slaves and worked to death," she said quietly.

Professor Thompson frowned, but then sighed, nodding. "As far as we've been able to determine, that's certainly true for Nerreka. There are other cities, though, like Corinum and Istantinople, where humans are permitted to work and have limited property rights. Who here can give me the definition of a Demonocracy?" He scanned the class, finally pointing to the girl in the front who was raising her hand and clearing her throat. "Ah... Miss Bodenbrum. I trust that you have the textbook answer for us."

"Demonocracy," Eliana started. "A system of government where demons constitute the governing classes. They define the rule of law. They control voting rights and they control all significant means of production." Tessa was still angry at the girl for what she said in the Dean's office. Everyone agreed to stay quiet a few hours earlier, but brown-nosing Eliana couldn't keep her little mouth shut.

"Textbook, as expected," said Professor Thompson. "The important takeaway is that even in the demon city states, humanity still lives. In some cases, as slaves, but in other cases with limited freedom. To what purpose, though? Why has humanity been preserved?"

The professor looked around the classroom for a moment before continuing. "Philosophers might give an impassioned argument about duality, and the implied codependence within relationships where power disparities exist, but I reject the notion that humans suffer merely to provide something for the demons to oppress. No," he said as he tapped the lectern. "We must serve some kind of purpose to them. Are we here to provide simple slave labor? That makes little sense, given that they've enslaved orcs, goblins, ogres, and all manner of races that are better laborers than us."

"What about the demonoids?" asked a boy sitting a few rows behind Tessa.

The professor pursed his lips and scratched his chin again. "True, in the past decade, we have witnessed the rise of those half-demon, half-human creatures. Perhaps that's the purpose of humanity now. I'll concede, it's far more compelling an explanation than our value as a labor source. So, class, are we being kept alive to see if we can be bred with the demons into some new, perhaps stronger race? Discuss amongst yourselves for a few moments," he said as he waved his hands, indicating it was all right to stand and move about.

Tessa got up from her desk and looked for Russell. Apparently, he had a similar idea, as he was already heading over to her. She met him halfway, by a couple of empty desks to give them some measure of privacy. "So, are we going to discuss the purpose of humanity?" she asked as flatly as she could, hoping to convey how bored she was with the topic.

"Piss on that. Not interested," said Russell with a chuckle. "How long have you been working on your archery?"

Tessa grinned. She liked Russell. "Since I was a little girl. Pretty much since I was tall enough to hold a bow."

"You didn't get that good just from classes here?"

"Nope. My parents work one of the rice paddies south of here. Do you know where the Serpent splits into three?" She waited until Russell nodded. "They have a little shack off the Eastern fork. I go there and work the fields with them when school isn't in session. My dad has targets set up all over the place. He taught me."

Russell nodded and said, "Well, be sure and thank him for me."

Tessa felt good. It was nice to be appreciated. "We should get together later, Russ. All of us from yesterday, don't you think?"

"Agreed. Let me talk to Malcolm about it. He has his own quarters."

Tessa heard the professor call the class back to order. She looked around and saw other children returning to their desks. She sighed and quickly nodded to Russell before heading back to her seat. She learned from experience that Professor Thompson took great pleasure in taunting any students who were slow to get back to their desks.

"Class," the professor started, "from what I could overhear from your conversations, it seems that the general consensus is there must be something more. I fully agree. After all, if our only purpose was to be crossbred, wouldn't it be safer on their part to wipe most of us out and just keep a small population for that purpose?" The professor waited. Tessa could see some students nodding and she heard a general expression of agreement.

"I also overheard some discussion about the demons needing our blood," he said, continuing. "The theories about demons requiring human blood all stem from what little we've been able to learn about the magical art of demonology as it existed hundreds of years ago in comparison to how it functions now. In short, demon-summoning spells currently require human blood as a component. While there are dissenting opinions out there, most historians agree that human blood was never a requirement in the distant past."

A young girl sitting towards the front asked, "Doesn't that answer the question then?"

"Not entirely," countered Professor Thompson. "We know that blood is needed for summons, but if that was all they needed, they could just keep a small population of people in captivity to be bled. Some have speculated that even after crossing over into our world, demons regularly require human blood to remain here, but that hasn't been confirmed. In any event, students," he said as he organized the parchments on his lectern. "This is a mystery to all of us, and that's precisely why I wanted to close our semester with this discussion. You'll all be working hard during the harvest. Afterward, there will be time spent with family and friends. During that time, I encourage all of you to think about this question. Discuss it with your family. Discuss it with your friends."

Professor Thompson finished gathering his papers. He stayed up at the lectern for a few agonizing moments that seemed to stretch to an eternity before finally saying, "Class dismissed!"

9
Malcolm

Malcolm's head was pounding. He went right to bed when he made it back to his quarters last night, but he felt like he hadn't slept a wink. He woke to find his sheets soaked in sweat and urine. He was overwhelmed with a mixture of fear and embarrassment. What could have driven him to such a state?

He remembered constantly waking up throughout the night, his heart racing. He was having terrifying nightmares. They were so vivid during the night, but he was struggling to remember much of anything now. He knew he was dreaming of the dead. Malcolm could remember the stench of corpses rotting in the humid heat. He remembered feeling a horrible clammy chill throughout his body. He just couldn't picture anything.

"I've been evaluating your work all semester, so there is no need for an exam," Dean Mayes said. "By and large, all of you did quite well on your Enchantment Runes. This is to be expected. Increasing the speed or sharpness of a sword is tedious, but the runes themselves are easy to scribe. There were some missteps on the armor and shield runes, though, particularly in cases where runes needed to be layered to generate stronger effects. But in general, I was pleased with your work."

Runecrafting was the art of carving intricate magical symbols and words. Enchantment Runes were carved into objects, normally weapons or armor, while Binding Runes were chiseled into a surface of earth or stone. Once all the words were connected, they were filled with carefully prepared mixtures of gem dust and other components. That's what powered the magic.

Malcolm closed his eyes. The room was too bright. The darkness helped, and he thought the pounding pain in his head would be enough to keep him from nodding off. There were only seven students in the honors runecrafting class, and Dean Mayes was still angry at him for how he behaved the night before. He couldn't remember doing it, but Russell was concerned and pulled him aside afterward to tell him about it. Falling asleep certainly wouldn't improve matters.

"Your Binding Runes weren't as impressive," she continued, "but all of you did well identifying the different reagent combinations and what effects they generate. Understanding the concept is half the battle. Proper Binding Runes produce a field that is physically constrained by the runewords you write. What the field actually accomplishes is completely dependent on how you combine your reagents. Most of you have a good enough understanding of how to approach crafting successful recipes. I found the most problems in how the runewords themselves were written. You must understand, any point of weakness in a Binding Rune may cause it to fail. This can be catastrophic, especially when it comes to Runes of Protection."

He remembered the Runes of Protection versus Insects each of the students worked on this semester. His ended up being small. Just a connected line of words spanning across a stone work table. Other students tried to write runes that created barriers to block off doorways, while one student, Michael, carved enough to stretch his runes all the way across the room. When they were finished, the Dean tested the runes by placing crickets next to them. It was fun watching the magical fields snap into being to stop the bugs from crossing over them.

Malcolm began to feel off balance. He felt his elbows on the table, and his forehead resting in his right hand. He could still hear Dean Mayes talking. He knew where he was, but at the same time, he felt like he was falling. He could see a forest through his closed eyes. He once again smelled the awful stench of bodies rotting in the tropical sun.

"Michael. Your Runes of Protection versus Insects were stretched much too thin. Do you know what would happen if your runes were used against something like the Black Tide?" the Dean asked.

"The ants would eventually break through where my runes didn't quite connect, Dean Mayes." Malcolm half-heard the boy as he walked through the forest in his mind. It was a hot day, made worse by the sun beating down on his head. The trees were mostly cut down on the hill he was climbing, leaving very little canopy to shield him.

"No, Michael. Each Binding Rune is a complete spell. Once it breaks, in any way, the entire rune fails. You wouldn't have left a small opening. Your whole rune would have collapsed, allowing thousands of ants to flood through."

Malcolm tuned out the voices. Instead, he could hear his blood pounding in his ears, and his own raspy breathing as he struggled to climb. He found himself needing to use roots to help himself where it got too steep for him. It was harder than it should be. His body felt feeble and weak in this dream. The sounds of shuffling feet started to eclipse all else as he climbed higher. His legs buckled when he finally crested the top, not from fatigue but from what he saw below.

The hill overlooked a wide plain. There were no trees. They'd all been logged, probably decades ago. An ocean of human bodies stretched across the plain. They'd been peasants, soldiers, women, and children from all walks of life. He couldn't tell how long they'd been dead. Some were rotted to the point of being nearly skeletal, while others still had fresh wounds that barely festered. Most shuffled and walked, while others with misshapen or destroyed bodies were forced to crawl. There had to be tens of thousands of these corpses. They were marching, all in their own way, towards a city on the far, distant end of the plain.

His body suddenly grew very cold as he felt his right hand reach into a pouch and grasp an icy sphere. It barely fit in his hand. He looked down and saw what he held was a glowing orb. A miasma of swirling blue and white light danced both within and around the orb. A strange spectral mist started to pour out of it. The mist snaked around his arm, but as more and more of the translucent mist poured from the orb, it wasn't long before Malcolm's entire body was completely enveloped. He felt so very cold. He could hear his heart pounding now over the shuffling as he slowly sunk to his knees. Wait. That wasn't right. There wasn't any shuffling. Everything was deathly quiet.

Malcolm looked back down at the field. The dead were all stopped and every one of them was facing him. They each had a faint blue-white ember of light in their eyes, and those lights were enough to confirm his horrifying realization. They were all looking at him, and in fact, the lights in their eyes were growing brighter and more intense, by the moment, as they looked up at him. His stomach turned as waves of nausea washed over him. He wanted to run, or even fall back down the hill, but he couldn't get his legs to move. Everything was just so damn cold. It had to be the orb, he thought. His arm felt sluggish and heavy as he thrust the orb back into the pouch he pulled it from.

Warmth immediately flowed back into his body as he watched the sea of walking corpses all turn back and resume their shuffling march toward the city in the distance. They moved much faster now. They were somehow bolstered and revitalized. They were his army. Malcolm knew it in his bones. He was no longer sickened by the smell. He wasn't terrified anymore. In fact, he felt strong as he started to make his way down the hill towards the plains and his army of the dead.

"Malcolm!"

He heard a few voices. He tried to drown them out again. He wanted to ride this dream, but they just kept getting stronger. He thought he could hear his own voice in the conversation now. He was arguing with the Dean about runes.

"Malcolm, you don't know that," she said.

"Yes, I do," he heard himself respond. He almost made his way down to the plains to join his walking dead. He could just barely see armies moving to protect the city in the distance. Malcolm was excited, but he couldn't keep the voices from intruding anymore. He heard his own voice again, "...they work with runes as well. Don't you understand? They can disable ours with ease."

"I don't understand what's gotten into you. You aren't yourself anymore. Last night was bad enough, but now this," said Dean Mayes. "I'm concerned."

Malcolm opened his eyes. The Dean and most of the other students were staring at him. Some of them looked confused, but others were clearly trying not to laugh. The Dean looked frustrated and worried.

"I'm sorry. I don't know what came over me," said Malcolm quietly.

"Fire and smoke, Malcolm! You fought with me about material we haven't even covered. You called me a fool!" Professor Mayes rarely raised her voice, but she was close to shouting now. Malcolm decided to stay quiet and let her continue. "If it were only the odd behavior yesterday it would be one thing, but we just had a discussion." She corrected herself. "No, an argument, actually. Everyone in the room heard it. Everyone except you?" She stood up and retrieved her cane from the ledge behind her. "Come with me, Malcolm," said Professor Mayes as she walked out of the room.

10
Attia

The meaty sounds of wood striking wood rung out through the clearing. It was an overcast day, the sky filled with stifling layers of rolling clouds. It felt like rain, but Attia knew from experience, it rarely rained on days like this. You merely wanted it to. By afternoon, it would be chokingly hot and humid. She was glad her outside classes were in the morning today.

This combat class was among her favorites. Solen, the instructor, was also Attia's teacher for balance magic. It meant he understood her skills and abilities well enough that he could push her without risking injury. She had little doubt that the quality and intensity of Solen's lessons were the only thing that kept her alive against the boar. He was so proud of her after she described how the battle played out, but he made her promise never to try to hamstring a three-ton animal with a wooden sword again.

She got lucky and she knew it.

Class was different this morning. Conner joined the group today, no doubt at the order of his father. It would've made more sense to her if Conner brought a weapon, but she trusted her teacher. Solen wouldn't let him participate if he thought the training would have no value. Scanning the combatants for the day, Attia waited for her turn. She noted the mixture of weapons and styles represented, including an older, heavily armored boy with a sword and shield. She hadn't seen him before, which made sense. Armored students normally trained with the other armored students. Attia rarely practiced against a shield, let alone armor. She was excited for the opportunity.

Solen clapped his hands above his head to get everyone's attention. "Please divide up into groups of two or three for open sparring. Raehl," he said, pointing to the armored boy as a means of introducing him, "has been loaned to us for the morning. Fighting against strong armor and a shield can be frustrating. Jehlin, will you please pair up with Raehl for starters? Conner, please line up with Attia."

Conner looked nervous as he made his way over toward her. Attia was expecting someone to hand him a weapon of some sorts, but it didn't happen. "Solen," she asked. "What do you want me to work on with him?"

"He's working on movement today," Solen answered as he jogged over to the two of them. Her instructor was a short cheery man. What little hair he had left was silver, but he still moved with the speed and grace of a jaguar. "In particular," he continued, "he's going to learn how to move in battle to safely provide healing support for his brother."

Conner sighed. While Attia felt sorry for him, she understood the value of the training exercise. "For now, you can work with him on evading attacks. Give him the basics at least." Attia frowned. This wasn't how she wanted to spend her time. She didn't hide her reaction too well, though, as Solen quickly added, "Teaching another is often the best way to learn, Attia."

She didn't see any value in arguing. She wasn't very good at it, and Solen probably had a point anyway. "Okay, Conner," she started. "We're going to start very slowly."

"What good is that going to do?" he asked.

Attia drew her wooden katana into a full speed cut. She was a few feet away from Conner. There was no risk of hitting him, but the effect was the same. Conner looked scared and a touch stunned. She executed two more full speed cuts with her practice sword before she broke her stance and let her weapon hang loose. "Could you have moved fast enough to avoid any of those swings?"

"Stars above, no!" he spat back.

Attia knew this was going to be difficult. She understood that particular lesson right away when Solen did the same thing for her. Patience wasn't one of her endearing traits. She sighed and said, "There are people who could have dodged all three."

"Sure, with the balance Shield spell," he countered.

"Without magic!" She took a deep breath before continuing. Conner was a friend. "Yes, the balance Shield will move you out of the way of an attack, like what I did with the boar."

"I remember."

"That nearly exhausted me, Conner. We only have so much energy to spend. It took everything you had to save your brother. You wouldn't have had the strength if you'd been using it to protect yourself."

Conner paused for a long moment. "Okay, but I don't see how a person can move fast enough to dodge a sword."

Attia smiled. She finally got his mind moving down the right path. "If you wait for the swing, you can't. Instead, you anticipate the swing. You need to be moving before your opponent starts. Let me show you." She stepped back into her stance, and this time, exaggerated the body motions involved in setting up each swing. She still executed her cuts at full speed. She watched as Conner began making slight movements to be in better position to get out of the way of each cut. "Good. Do that, but trust yourself and do it more," she said as she inched closer to him.

She moved faster as she executed each of the three cuts in order, gradually moving closer and closer until he was actually dodging them. She slowed down before changing the order of her cuts, and was happy she did. Conner continued moving as if she were locked into the same pattern of strikes. He moved into her strike as opposed to out of the way of it. She hit him in the shoulder, but was able to check and turn her swing enough to avoid hitting his collarbone.

Conner winced and yelped. He took a step back, but then nodded for her to continue. Attia was proud of him. She was worried he might stop after getting hit, but he didn't. She started again. This time, more carefully. She chose the order of her attacks now, waiting just an instant before each swing to make sure he was moving correctly. They continued this dance for a minute or two before Conner started to breathe heavily. She decided it would be safest to stop.

"Good job, Conner," she said with a smile. "Let's watch Jehlin and Raehl for a bit. Keep an eye on how they move. Watch for patterns and think about how to move out of the way." Attia and Conner walked closer to get a better view, joining a growing group of other students on the sidelines.

Attia could immediately tell that Raehl had been training for years. He wore plate armor, and although she couldn't make out any runes carved into the metal, she knew the armor was at least Attuned to him. It fit too well and moved with a suppleness that was simply impossible for metal without magical assistance. Armor of that quality meant he was likely a senior student or a graduate. Both his sword and shield were metal, which seemed unfair against Jehlin's pair of wooden short swords, but Raehl was at least swinging with the flat of his blade. Even though they'd just started the round, she knew Jehlin was growing impatient. He was wasting energy on attacks that had little to no chance of landing past the shield.

Raehl, for his part, was playing on that frustration by angling his body behind his shield. His sword was longer than his opponent's weapons, so he could afford to have his own blade a little bit farther away. To make matters worse, Jehlin fell into a pattern with his movement.

Attia pointed out to Conner how Jehlin kept trying to draw Raehl to one side in order to flow around the shield the other direction. Raehl easily picked up on it. He started slapping Jehlin on the arm and even the hip sometimes with the flat of his blade at the end of each pattern. Frustrated, Jehlin broke off the fight, tossing his swords to the ground in anger. "This is impossible!" he complained.

Solen calmly retrieved the pair of wooden swords from the ground. "May I?" he asked Raehl.

Attia was surprised when the armored boy nodded an invitation to Solen, but didn't change his stance. "This will be quick. Jehlin fell into a pattern with his attacks, but Raehl defended it the same way each time. Solen will use that," she whispered to Conner as Solen started his attack.

He began much like Jehlin did, trying to draw the shield to the side, but he varied the heights of his swings, forcing Raehl to move the shield up higher. When Solen moved back around to the other side, he lowered himself. Raehl predictably tried to slap Solen with his sword, but he was off balance and slow, allowing the quicker man to get inside the swing. Solen jammed the inside of Raehl's arm, stopping his swing entirely while he drove his other wooden sword up into the boy's armpit. He followed with a quick strike to the back of the hand, which sent Raehl's heavy metal weapon out of his grip and into the ground a few paces away.

"An armored opponent will be slower, but more importantly, you must be faster," Solen said. "Swinging a light blade will do little but distract against strong armor. So, use it as a distraction. When you do strike, pick your targets carefully. There are always soft spots," he said as he retrieved Raehl's sword from the ground and returned it to him.

"Next drill," he continued. "Conner, you stand behind Raehl. Your job is to keep a hand on him, without making it more difficult for him to move. This will teach you how to better heal in combat. Raehl, your role is to protect both yourself and Conner. Finally, Attia, your task in this should be obvious. You score by landing blows against either of them. Please don't hurt the Commander's son, even if you do manage to get in position for a clean shot against him."

"Won't happen," said Raehl with a sneer. Attia didn't mind his overconfidence. It might prove an advantage to her.

"She's fast, Raehl. I saw her take the legs out from under a charging boar," added Conner in an attempt to be helpful.

"Quiet," snapped Raehl. "Just stay out of my way, boy, and we'll win."

Attia's cheeks flushed with anger. Raehl had no right to talk that way to Conner. Maybe these two knew each other? Raehl probably knew Liam, so maybe he was making an inside joke with his friend's younger brother? "Do you two know each other?" she asked.

Raehl frowned. "Nah, never met him."

"Oh." Attia knew she shouldn't say it, but she didn't care. "So, you're just an ass. Good to know."

There were a few scattered laughs from the group of students gathered to watch. Attia looked and it was clear most of those who didn't laugh were working hard to suppress their reactions. As she moved into position to start the drill, it became obvious that Raehl realized he was being laughed at. His lip was quivering, and she saw him flexing his fingers around the pommel of his sword. She'd seen this before. Battlemages needed to get the adrenaline of battle flowing to direct their magic, but this was just a training exercise. Surely that was excessive—

"Please begin," said Solen before she could finish pursuing her thought.

Raehl charged behind his shield, literally running the sheet of metal into Attia before slamming it full force across her body. She wasn't ready, and the initial impact caught her clean. Fortunately for Attia, Raehl hadn't timed his slam to land with his charge, so she was able to spin away from most of the impact of the slam. Raehl quickly turned, trying to intercept her, but Attia was too fast, and she deftly made it past him, closing the gap to Conner with ease. Instead of swinging, she pressed her wooden weapon into her friend and drew it as if she were cutting. It was a way to demonstrate victory without risking harm to Conner, or so she thought.

Attia finished her cut and took a single step back from Conner. She won the round. She assumed that they'd reset and start again, but Raehl seemed to have other ideas. She felt a massive impact as the armored boy crashed into her back. Attia saw stars and lost her wind as she was knocked forward into Conner, her forehead catching him in the mouth. They both tumbled to the ground.

"Stop," said Solen calmly, but with a hint of danger in his voice. "What do you think you're doing?"

"Saving the boy. Winning the fight," said Raehl.

Solen shook his head. "You lost that round. Rather decisively, I might add."

"Who's on the ground, huh?"

"Both of them. You crashed into Attia after she executed a full draw cut across his belly. She already disengaged. Your hit was far too late."

Attia rolled off Conner. He was bleeding from where a tooth cut his lip. Her back hurt and she was short of breath, but nothing was broken. She'd recover.

"Okay. Maybe I didn't understand the rules—"

"Silence," hissed Solen, cutting the boy off. "Conner is here to practice healing in combat situations. My intent was to let him practice his movement. If you misbehave again, however, I'll fight the following round against you. This will ensure that Conner gets ample opportunity to practice healing you." Solen paused and watched the boy. Attia, and likely most of the class, heard the threat loud and clear, but Solen continued. "Movement or healing. Your choice, but Conner gets his practice either way."

Attia rolled to a crouch and extended her hand to Conner. The look in his eyes told her he hated this, but there was no way to back out now. "Come on," she said encouragingly. Eventually, he took her hand and they both climbed to their feet.

"Let's try again," said Solen.

Attia took a few steps back, leaving space for Raehl to take his place in front of Conner. Even after Solen's threat, she didn't trust Raehl. The boy's face was flushed, his upper lip twisted into a sneer. His anger was obvious. Maybe she should have given him a straightforward fight instead of running around him in the first round?

She started carefully, using her greater range to test his reactions. Raehl angled his body behind his shield as he did before, inviting her to come closer. She stepped in and swung low, trying to hit his knee, but Raehl was quick enough to dance back a step. Conner to his credit anticipated it and moved back at the same time.

Attia wanted to retreat and force Raehl to engage her, but that wasn't the drill. She needed to close distance fast, so she leapt into a somersault, finishing on one knee with a strong strike against Raehl's thigh. The meaty crack of her wooden weapon against his armor made her think she hurt the boy, but he didn't even flinch. He stabbed down at her, forcing her to parry and roll backwards. His blade slid up along hers, and she just barely shifted her hands out of the way in time to avoid getting cut.

He tried to stab her, and he swept his blade across her parry, knowing that the practice sword lacked a hand guard. Raehl wasn't using the flat of his blade. He was trying to hurt her!

Attia quickly rolled to a crouch and waited for him. Damn the drill! Raehl waited for a few moments before getting impatient. He moved forward, Conner following behind on his shield side.

Attia sprung from her crouch. She started her attack as a swing, but checked it, changing it to a thrust right as Raehl moved his shield to block. She hoped to catch him in the gut, but Raehl managed to turn the thrust down. She ended up hitting him in the groin. Served him right, she thought, but Raehl wasn't even phased. His codpiece dispersed the impact easily, and his battlemagic probably took the sting out of the rest of it.

Worse still, the thrust brought her much closer to Raehl than she would've preferred. He bashed her with his shield again, and this time, made good contact. The impact sent her sprawling to the side, but she used the momentum to roll herself into a somersault.

Attia was back on her feet right as Raehl began his charge. He was no longer angling his body back behind his shield. It told Attia he was likely to swing. She slowed her breathing as best she could to calm herself. She didn't want to rely on her balance magic, but she didn't see a better way.

The swing came just as she predicted. It was wide and fast. She spun and lowered herself. The sword was faster, but she counted on that. She relaxed and let her magic pull her through the motion she already initiated, allowing her to cleanly evade the blow. She continued her spin, turning it into a strike. The backs of Raehl's legs were exposed, but she wanted to hurt him. He didn't deserve kindness. He didn't deserve respect! She raised the angle of her strike as she danced back up to her full height, her body spinning beautifully. Her wooden blade struck Raehl with tremendous force in the back, right at the very top of his shoulders, barely an inch below his exposed neck, her intended target.

Raehl coughed and gagged as he stumbled forward, his legs wobbly. Conner was right next to her, but Attia ignored him. She turned and gave chase to Raehl, bringing her sword behind her back in preparation for an overhead strike. She was just about to start her motion when she felt a strong hand on her shoulder. “I think that’s enough for today,” said Solen.

Attia took a deep breath and pushed her anger aside. Raehl was still trying to recover. He hadn’t even turned to face her. Thankfully, Solen was there, or the boy may never have recovered.

11
Eliana

Eliana was so proud of herself! She did well on her natural magic finals. Most students restricted their studies to a single element, freeing them up to study other disciplines. Eliana decided to fully dedicate herself to elemental magic and study all four elements. She had her doubts, but she exceeded every expectation during the exam. Eliana produced water from thin air. She made earth and rocks move on their own. She directed and strengthen the wind, and perhaps most impressively, she produced a flame with just the snap of a finger. She was exhausted from the effort. Fortunately, herbalism was her last class of the day.

Her parents would be proud too. She was looking forward to seeing them soon. They farmed a small Ganna fruit field a little less than a day south of the Citadel. Eliana was an only child, and she felt bad she wasn't there to help them with the harvests. They said it was more important for her to have the opportunity to learn and grow, but it didn't help with the guilt. The fact that her parents didn't have other children to help them with the farming meant their lives would get harder and harder as they grew older.

It helped guide her into her studies. Being able to literally direct nature to move and reshape the land would make up for everything. Her parents each knew some natural magic, but not enough. With her understanding of all four elements, Eliana could get the land to do almost everything for itself. And further, she planned to use her extensive knowledge of herbalism to develop recipes to make their Ganna fruit crop the strongest around.

"Go ahead and gather around the table, students," Professor Eilenhoss said as she organized various trays of plants. Eliana loved the loamy smell that filled the room whenever they collected all the materials for inventory and storage. It happened at the end of each semester. "Let's start by sorting by discipline, please," she continued. "Alchemy supplies to the right, runecrafting reagents to the middle here. Please wear gloves when moving the poisons. They go over to the left."

Most of the students did this before. They didn't need the guidance, but Eliana still liked it. It was a ritual of sorts. Organization was absolutely critical when working with herbalism. Every art needed different plants and herbs, each prepared in specific ways. Alchemy needed elaborate combinations of herbs to make the magic within their potions last, and runecrafting needed similar combinations to define and align the powerful magic written into their gem dusts.

But the plants were magical by themselves as well. She could do all sorts of things without needing runes or potions. She could combine herbs to cure poisons, treat wounds, keep a person awake, or heighten their senses. It amazed her how few students took to herbalism, given how useful it was.

There was a sharp knock on the door, but it was only a courtesy, as barely a moment later Dean Mayes entered the room. Her normal limp was more pronounced as she stepped forward, leaning heavily on her cane. The Dean looked exhausted.

"I'm going to need you to send everything you have for runecrafting down to Kromgor's lab, Lanara," said Dean Mayes.

"I don't understand," answered Professor Lanara Eilenhoss. "We paid our annual tithe for the upkeep of the protective runes a few months ago."

"We need more," said the Dean softly.

"Were there errors? Did some runes need to be rewritten? You know, it's precisely for this reason that we're to be notified if students are being permitted to practice on something important like this. We can grow more base herbs, but it takes—"

"That's not it," interrupted the Dean, agitation creeping into her voice. "I'm well aware of the requisition forms and their importance. I'm the one who instituted them in the first place!" The Dean's volume grew as she spoke. She tapped her cane against the ground nervously. She took a few breaths to calm herself before continuing. "The Black Tide has taken another path. We need to scribe more runes. We'll need supplies. This isn't a request."

There was a loud clanging as Professor Eilenhoss dropped the tray she was holding on to the desk. "Stars above," she gasped. "The Tide isn't riding the Black Scar?"

"No."

"Then," she started as she fumbled with the herbs that spilled out of the tray she dropped. Her hands were shaking. "What path, then?"

Eliana's heart skipped a beat as the reality of the conversation sank in. The Black Scar was a narrow path through the rainforest, devoid of trees, and nearly devoid of foliage. The giant ants of the Black Tide used this path to move through the forest each and every year.

"The Commander said they're following the banks of the Serpent."

"The Serpent? Dean.... Selandra." Eliana could see the color draining out of the professor's face. "They'll devour everything!"

The Dean took a few measured breaths before answering. "Duncan said they were moving very slowly. The forest is incredibly thick along the banks of the river. I've seen the Tide moving through the Black Scar before. It was horrifying how fast it moved, but the Scar is both wide and barren. Along the river, they'll be forced to crawl over one another. It'll be much slower for them."

"What about the Ganna farms and the rice farms? What about all our planting beds? What about—"

"Lanara!" the Dean interrupted. "This is neither the time nor the place. Now please, just do as I asked. We have time, but not a lot."

"Yes, of course," replied Professor Eilenhoss. "We'll gather everything, even those things I've been saving."

The Dean nodded before speaking in a strong tone, addressing everyone. "There'll be a gathering, a little over an hour from now in the

Great Hall. All will need to be in attendance. I expect that each of you will help your teacher for the next hour and then immediately head to the gathering."

Eliana felt sick. Her parents' farm was to the south of the Citadel, but the reality would be the same. If the ants continued to follow the Serpent past the Citadel, they'd find the farm. Her parents' land would be stripped to the bone. The modest shack that served as their home would likely be swept away. Everything would need to be rebuilt. She could picture it in her mind, and it was horrifying. The knot in her stomach and the tight feeling in her chest only got worse as her mind traced the path the Black Tide would take to her parents' farm. Continuing to follow the Serpent past the Citadel meant they'd inevitably have to wash over the Citadel itself. "They'll come right through us," she said without even realizing she was thinking out loud.

"Yes, Miss Bodenbrum, they will," replied the Dean as she turned to leave the room.

Eliana felt unsteady. She pictured an endless flood of ants, some nearly as big a small boy, mindlessly racing down the river towards them. Her heart was racing, and she felt dizzy.

She was terrified.

12
Liam

Falheart banged his wooden gavel against the lectern at the front of the Great Hall as he shouted for order. Liam sensed uneasiness and fear all around him. He was trained to look for all the signs, but he scarcely needed that training here. The tension was plain and obvious. Falheart banged his gavel and shouted again. That had to be the third or fourth time now, Liam thought, but people were finally starting to quiet down.

Liam never saw the Great Hall this full in all his life. The room's high ceiling took up space on both the first and second floors. It was positioned right in the center of the Citadel, with hallways and living quarters flowing around it on all sides. More than the function though, Liam admired the simple beauty of the room.

Each of the walls was adorned with a decorative pattern created from layered tiles of different hardwoods. Deep green tapestries hung from the walls. They matched and paired with the lighter green cloths lining the long dark wooden tables. The design was simple, but all the subtle nuances made it striking to him. It felt so very much like the rainforest outside. Simple when taken at its most basic level. A place filled with green and brown. Anyone who cared to take a closer look, though, couldn't help but be astonished by the vast, intricate complexity of how all the greens and browns came together into a cohesive mosaic.

"Now that we've achieved some semblance of order," said Falheart from the head of the room, his voice magically amplified, "I think it would be prudent if we got started."

Liam knew Falheart was one of the arcane sciences professors, but he knew little else about him. He scanned the room and found his father sitting at the head table. Gunther was next to him on one side, sitting literally a full head higher than anyone else. Silver sat on the other side of him, her trained parrot resting on her shoulder. From the embarrassed scowl on Dean Mayes face, a few seats away, it seemed that Silver's parrot was swearing up a storm like it normally did. Silver tried to date Liam's father a few times over the past couple of years. It never worked out, which suited Liam fine. He really hated waking up in the morning to descriptions of lewd sex acts, delivered by a parrot.

"We all know the Black Tide comes each year, like clockwork," said Falheart. "In almost all cases, the ants depart from their colonies, heading generally to the southwest. This carries them to a pathway through the forest we refer to as the Black Scar. The Scar runs down from the savannah, all the way clear to the swamps in the south. It passes us roughly one mile to the west. While we don't know what originally broke the trees and trampled the foliage to create this travel way, we do know it makes an excellent path for the Black Tide."

Liam looked for his friends. He caught Conner's eye and waved when they initially entered, but he wasn't able to sit with him. He saw Russell and Tessa taking seats in the very back, and Eliana was sitting a few tables ahead of him. Not surprisingly, she was taking notes. He hadn't managed to find Malcolm, though, which was troubling. Malcolm's classes were pretty much restricted to runecrafting and the arcane sciences. Those classes came down together in groups, and they were sitting together in those groupings. Malcolm wasn't with them. Something was definitely wrong with Malcolm.

"Over the years, the ants have stripped all meaningful foliage out of the Black Scar. Nothing but thick ground cover grows there anymore. It makes it the perfect pathway through the forest to get to the nutrient-rich swamps," the professor continued. "It's been this way for decades now, and it makes logical sense that it will continue that way for decades to come. As a result, we've structured our plantings, harvests and our very lives around this reality. Herbs and crops grown in or near the Scar are harvested early, while everything along and to the east of the Serpent can wait. Further, our defensive runes have been predominantly built and reinforced with the singular purpose of guiding insects to, and keeping them within the Black Scar."

Falheart paused for a moment, looking out across the assembly. A knot formed in Liam's stomach. His dad was worried the Black Tide might take another route. Falheart's entire speech seemed to be leading up to that. It had to be what this was all about, but what would it really mean? The ants could literally go any direction they wanted. Maybe they weren't going to come south at all.

"This year, regrettably, will be different," said Falheart. "The Black Tide isn't taking the Scar this year. It's currently moving directly south, following the path of the Serpent."

The room erupted into a myriad of anxious conversations. Some people shouted questions, and others soon began to follow suit. Falheart banged his gavel again, but he was losing control. Liam understood the fear and anger. So many farms depended on the Serpent for irrigation. The ants would destroy any land they crossed over. People would lose everything.

Gunther rose from his chair and pounded on the table. He was nearly seven feet tall, with long hair and a bushy beard, that in combination looked much like a lion's mane. "Hold your words!" he shouted, and people started to gradually quiet down. When others refused to stop shouting their panicked questions, Gunther glared at them and repeated his demand, "Hold your words!" One by one, he quelled each outburst, until Falheart was able to continue.

"Now, there's still time. The ants move very rapidly when travelling the Black Scar, but the foliage along the banks of the river is quite dense. There are fallen trees, and dozens of areas along the Serpent where tributaries enter and streams exit. The Tide will have to cross each of those water ways. This should slow it down even more. Further, just because the ants started their swarm by following the river doesn't mean they're going to continue the entire way. There are easily a half a dozen places along the river's path where it makes sense that the Black Tide might turn and take another route. Make no mistake, though, we must prepare for the worst. Duncan, if you would take it from here?"

Gunther, who remained standing, pounded the table again, preemptively. Liam's father rose to his feet but didn't move to the lectern. When he spoke, it was with the same magical amplification spell Falheart used. Liam knew of the spell, but he hadn't spent much time studying either the sonic or light schools of magic. His father always recommended he focus on mastering his sword and shield before anything else.

"Assuming the Tide doesn't change course, I estimate we have a little over a week… maybe as long as ten days. We have Pathfinders en route to monitor the ants as they make their way down the river, so we'll have more information in a couple of days. We're working under the assumption the Black Tide follows the Serpent all the way to the Citadel itself." Liam's father paused to give the crowd a chance to process what he said, but he started speaking again before any side conversations grew too loud. "We need to be efficient in how we organize our efforts during the time remaining. First, we've already dispatched Pathfinders to notify all the southern farms to harvest what they can and to gather at the Serpent's Tongue."

The Serpent's Tongue was a place where the river split into three. It wasn't too far south of the Citadel. Liam had been there a few times over the years. There were a number of farms along both the eastern and western paths of the river, while the central path turned into a small lake before splitting into dozens of tiny rivers that eventually bled into swampland.

"Once there, they'll meet up with the barges we're sending. We'll load as many crops as we can on to those barges and anchor them out in the middle of the lake, just south of there. That should be enough to protect the crops from the ants. We can retrieve the barges after the Black Tide has come and gone."

Liam's father cleared his throat and frowned. Liam knew this expression. It meant his father didn't particularly like what was coming next. "Second, we'll be dispatching groups north along the river. Each will be given a different farm to harvest. We'll be prioritizing Ganna fruit over rice, but we'll need rice as well. We'll send groups composed of

Pathfinders and soldiers to the farthest farms to rapidly harvest what we can, but we have more farms to harvest than we have adults to send." The crowd started to get uneasy and louder. "Because of that, we have no choice but to send students to harvest the closer farms..." Liam's father was forced to stop as the crowd got outright angry. Parents started shouting, while a few of the younger students descended into hysterics.

"Shut the hell up," Gunther shouted as he pounded the table, but it did little to rein in the spiraling chaos of the crowd. Falheart banging his gavel on the lectern only seemed to make it worse. Liam watched as a silvery white light began to flow forth from his father. A simple Light spell, nothing more, but it was enough to draw everyone's attention as he raised his hand and lofted a ball of brilliant light high into the air. The ball floated, weightless, for a few moments before it vanished. Some people gasped, while others covered their eyes, but most quieted down.

"I'd give all the stars in the sky to not have to send students, really, I would, but this is what must be done. Please understand, each group of students will be escorted. No one's being sent out unguarded. The farther from the Citadel we send our students, the more adults we'll send along with them. We want all the students back safely within a few days." Liam's father once again paused to give people a moment to process what he said. "The work won't stop once we've collected the crops. Everyone will be working double shifts. We'll need to process and store the Ganna fruit, paying careful mind to extract the seeds. A lot of farmers will be starting over from scratch next planting season, and we need to be prepared for that. We'll need to build bulwarks and magically reshape our clearing as much as possible. We need to direct the ants away from the Citadel itself. Most importantly, we'll need to bolster any defensive runes we already have in place around the Citadel and build as many new ones as we can as a last means of defense."

Falheart cleared his throat, but Liam's father held up his hand. "Just a moment, Falheart. I have more to say," he said. Liam's head was spinning as he processed everything he heard. It was just yesterday that he was out in the woods, messing around with his friends on an assignment to collect some useless plant or another, and now everything was at risk. The Tide was coming. In years past, even with the Black Scar being a mile away, he could hear the swarm as it passed. Now it was coming right toward them.

"I know you're all scared," said Liam's father, his voice ringing clear and confident throughout the Great Hall. "And you should be. What's coming for us could be the end of our civilization, but only if we let it be. We're survivors! Armies of demons have tried and failed to destroy this place, our home. After standing against that, are we going to let ourselves be swept away by a swarm of insects? No, we're not! We have time to prepare. We have the skills to protect ourselves, but most importantly, we have the courage to fight!

"You're going to be tired over the next few weeks, but you must fight through it. Each and every time you want to rest, picture the Black Tide. Picture an ebony sea of swarming ants, as far as the eye can see. Understand that's what's coming for us, and just keep working. We can and will survive this, but only if we sacrifice for it!" Liam's father let his words hang in the air for a few moments before nodding to Falheart.

"Thank you for those words, Duncan," said Falheart. "Everyone's assignments for tomorrow are being delivered to their quarters. Anyone who is on a harvesting expedition will be assigned a number. They are to report at dawn, outside in the clearing. Find the sign with your number and gather there. The rest of you will be split into teams with different tasks. Most will be digging or logging...."

Falheart droned on, but Liam wasn't listening anymore. He knew he'd be on a harvesting team, and he didn't care about the rest of it. He needed to talk with his dad. He wanted to know more, but he wasn't sure it was possible. Everything was happening so fast. He hadn't even been able to get the broken rings in his chainmail repaired. Hell, he hadn't even had a good night's sleep yet, and it didn't sound to him like he would get one anytime soon.

13
Chariden

Chariden let her gown fall to the cold stone floor. She felt the man's lust growing, crowding out any rationality. The pathetic, sniveling creature before her broke about an hour ago. He broke when she whispered the burning need into his heart to come to her and draw her a boiling hot bath. She didn't know who the man was, or where he lived, or if he had a family. Chariden didn't care. She'd wanted a bath. Her Desires poured out from her like a living thing. They danced across the streets of her city until they found someone, and that was that.

Nothing human in this world could resist her for long. Of all her powers, her Desires were her strongest. She could send them nearly anywhere in the world. Once they worked their way into a mortal's heart, they became an irresistible siren's song, compelling the person to seek her out and serve her.

This was her world!

She smiled at the man as she posed. Tears ran down his face as he witnessed beauty he couldn't conceive of. She looked down at the stone basin filled with boiling water. "Hmmm, just how I like it," she purred. "Test it for me. Reach in and fetch me one of the hot stones along the bottom."

The man nodded, his eyes glassy. There was no hesitation as he thrust his arm into the boiling water. He screamed as his skin blistered and bubbled, but he never turned away from the Demon Queen. She saw faint wisps of red start to color the boiling water as his skin started to split, break, and fall away, but he kept reaching. He looked so happy when he managed to pull a stone from the water. He fell to his knees, presenting it to her.

"Such a good boy," she teased as she looked down at the wretched creature. Humans were so worthless, she mused. Weak-willed and simple minded. It drove her mad that they still had a home in her world. It was more than three centuries since she shattered this world's Gaea spirit and yet humanity was still here, sharing her lands. Something was preventing this place from surrendering to her. Chariden knew it was only a matter of time. She'd find it. She'd destroy it, and then she'd finally purge the land of humanity and all its wretchedness.

"I suppose you've earned a reward," she said as she reached down and playfully patted the man on the head. "Leave the city along the eastern road until you reach the river, then follow the river to the south. You'll find a bush adorned with silver roses. Pluck one and bring it to me. It shouldn't take you more than a few hours, and when you return, I'll reward you with a kiss." She heard the man crying his thanks as he scampered to his feet, but he didn't matter anymore. "Run along now," she whispered as she stepped into her bath of boiling, bloody water.

She smiled as the man sprinted out of the room. He wouldn't return from his quest, of course. She wasn't sure if silver rose bushes even existed. If the man managed to survive his injuries long enough to make it out of the city and down the road, the spiders would surely claim him.

She agreed a few months ago to let the spider queen of the savannas establish a new hive outside of Nerreka. She hadn't initially liked the idea, but she grew to enjoy feeding them. It was a necessary evil. She'd wanted to send the Black Tide at the Citadel for quite some time. The deal with the spiders allowed that to happen. They hollowed out a huge section of their webs to allow the Tide a direct path through the savannah. In exchange, she provided them a safe new home under her protection.

It'd all be worth it to see the human settlement to the south finally fall. She hated the Citadel with a passion. Something about the place vexed her. It defied her! She faced its leaders in battle herself more than a decade ago. They gazed upon her perfection, and she knew of them, yet she couldn't seduce them. She tried again and again to send her Desires into their hearts, to make them yearn to crawl through the forest on hands and knees for the privilege of kneeling in her presence, but something always blocked her.

Chariden sent armies of demons to lay siege to their tiny city, only to have them return speaking of a barrier, or some kind of invisible field they couldn't cross. She finally sent her strongest agents, her Guardians, down to test. While they were able to cross, all three reported that it was tremendously difficult.

Only recently, she managed to get her Desires to worm their way into the leader's heart. The foolish mage was magically transporting to Derregain so frequently he became predictable. Without his precious Citadel to protect him, she snared him. Arronhelm was strong, though. So strong that she knew he must be El'orin, one who shares its body with a powerful soul. If she disabled the protections of the Citadel, though, he'd eventually surrender to her will. It was only a matter of time.

If the Citadel's leader was El'orin, it meant the city itself was protected by an El'ominae, a powerful territorial spirit. She suspected it all along, of course. El'ominae started appearing all across the world perhaps a century after she shattered the Gaea spirit. Chariden assumed it was this world's way of fighting back against her. She found and destroyed so many over the years she lost count, but when one fell, another would always rise. A powerful El'ominae could do many things to defend its region. She never thought one might be strong enough to block her abilities, though, let alone all but prevent demons from entering an entire region. It was a chilling thought. If such a thing existed, it needed to be destroyed.

And it would be. The Black Tide was following the Serpent. The river would lead the swarm right to the Citadel. Chariden smiled wickedly and stretched in her bath as she pictured it. They'd build their runic circles to try and redirect the swarm, but she'd already sent two of her Guardians south. Human runecrafting was like the babbling of an infant when compared to the runewords she and her kind could craft. It wouldn't take much for either Cinderhorn or Erranaekis to shatter a few Runes of Protection and allow the Tide to continue its deadly march.

Arronhelm and his kind were anything but weak. They'd call the elements and marshal their greatest spells to destroy the endless sea of ants, but nothing could stand against the Black Tide. It was nature's fury manifest. She pictured their pathetic soldiers, arrogantly trusting in their armor, falling one by one. The giant ants would swarm them. Hundreds would climb each of them until the sheer weight of insects suffocated and crushed them.

Chariden sighed, feeling her bath start to cool. As much as she enjoyed picturing them all being stung to death and carried along with the Tide to feed and grow it, she knew nothing was a certainty. The Tide, by itself, wouldn't be enough. It was merely a tool. She knew it was a risk sending two of her strongest servants down there, but it was necessary. She needed to have contingencies and options. The Citadel had survived for far too long, largely because she continually underestimated it. That was a mistake she was intent on correcting.

Chariden climbed out of the boiling water and stretched out her leathery wings to let them dry. She admired herself in the mirror for a moment. Most succubi were beautiful, and she was no different. They were demons of lust, after all. Her body, however, told a tale of incredible power. Her wings were large and strong, with each point coming to a razor-sharp talon. Instead of the soft curves that many of her demonic sisters wore, her body carried with it an incredible grace and balance. Most succubi chose to move through the world without their wings, their horns, or their tail. She embraced all of it. She was a Demon Queen, and she was proud of it.

The Citadel had defied her for too long. She was the Queen, and this was her world. She gave them ample opportunities to surrender to her will. They resisted for too long. Now they'd simply be destroyed.

14
Malcolm

The old man looked at him from across the table. His face was patient and still, and his hands were folded in front of him as he continued to calmly observe. Malcolm was uneasy. It felt like the Chancellor was looking right through him. What troubled him most, though, was it seemed like the old man expected the visit.

The door was already open when Dean Mayes brought him. He invited them in before the Dean announced herself. He nodded politely while she was describing the argument they had in runecrafting class. When she was done talking, he simply asked her to close the door on her way out. Malcolm never saw anyone be so dismissive to the Dean before.

The Chancellor cleared his throat before speaking. "I remember my earliest experiences with my spirit quite fondly, but I often wonder how it appeared to those around me. I'd like to think that I appeared completely sane... completely the same person as I was before, but that's entirely unlikely. It's not every day a person's forced to come to grips with no longer being alone in his own head," the Chancellor said with a wink.

"You... You understand what's happening to me, Chancellor?"

"Please, it's Arronhelm, and let's say that I have some level of understanding. Like me, your body is the home to a second soul. The similarity regrettably ends there. Each person has to make their own peace with their spirit, and I've known a few cases where that wasn't easy." He smiled and pushed an open hand across the table, palm up. "Take my hand, boy."

Malcolm's head began to hurt. He squinted as he'd learned to do in the forest. Arronhelm was wearing a heavy grey robe, so really, only his hands and face were visible, but Malcolm could see faint, wispy shadows dancing over the little bit of skin he could see. He felt nervous as he extended his hand. The Chancellor's hand was warm and soft, though. Not at all what Malcolm was expecting.

"You must have so many questions, young man. I'm afraid there won't be time to answer them all, but go ahead and ask a few," said Arronhelm.

"Why did this happen to me?"

"That's a rather poor question," chided Arronhelm. "Try again."

"What happened to me? Am I... am I possessed?"

"A much better question!" Arronhelm hummed softly for a moment. "Technically, yes, but I really wouldn't think of it that way. A powerful spirit now shares your body with you."

"Can we get it out of me?"

"Why for all the stars in the sky would you want to do that?"

Malcolm's headache got worse as he recalled the images from his dreams. Were those scenes from the spirit's life? He wasn't sure how much he should share but holding things back from the Chancellor seemed foolish. "I've been having dreams. Terrible dreams. And I can see ghosts or shades, or whatever they're called."

Arronhelm let go of Malcolm's hand and leaned back in his chair. He rubbed his temples and closed his eyes for a moment. "The dreams are almost certainly your spirit's way of introducing itself. My spirit speaks to me from time to time through dreams. When I dream, it's generally a vision of the future. Tell me about yours."

"I was walking through a forest. A rain forest, like this one, I think. It was hot, and I could smell rotting flesh. The smell was just horrible. It's the thing I remember most." Malcolm swallowed hard, as just remembering it made him want to gag. "I climbed a hill and on the other side of it there were all these dead bodies, but they were alive, or moving at least. They were walking and shuffling toward a distant city. There were thousands of them, and I knew... I just knew they were mine. I'd created them. They obeyed me. I've never felt so great in all my life." Malcolm hadn't intended to share so much, but once he started talking, he found it difficult to stop.

The Chancellor nodded. "An ancient necromancer. It's what my own dreams suggested to me. Your visions confirm it."

"Isn't necromancy forbidden? I mean, it's not taught in the Citadel for a reason, right?"

"No, we don't teach it, but I wouldn't necessarily call it forbidden, or evil, or any such nonsense. Necromancy is..." Arronhelm searched for the right words. "Necromancy is dangerous, and, well... messy. It's not for the faint of heart. It wasn't anything we wanted students dabbling with."

"So, I shouldn't learn it then?"

"Don't be absurd! Of course, you should learn it. I've already gathered what texts I could scrounge together on the subject." The Chancellor motioned toward a desk in the corner of the room, piled with scattered scrolls and books, lit by a globe of Liquidlight.

"This thing that happened to me, does it happen often? I mean, how many others are there like me? Like us?"

"It's tremendously rare, my boy," Arronhelm said with a smile. "I assume that in a short time, you'll actually have a better understanding of it than I do."

"Why?"

"Spirits rarely retain their identities for long after crossing over from our world to the Astral. The memories of their lives wash away. I suspect most lose all recollection of life within days, but some spirits are stronger than others. They find ways to hold on to who or what they were. They lose some of it, of course, but they keep enough to hold themselves together over the years, decades or even centuries."

Malcolm struggled to understand what he was being told. He pieced together that Arronhelm answered why it was rare, but not why his understanding would be greater. Spirits and the dead fell under necromancy, though, so that must be what he meant.

"Eventually," the Chancellor continued, "those spirits are left little choice but to find more permanent ways to protect themselves from the constant deterioration of their thoughts and memories. One way, I presume, is to find another soul to share a body with."

"Share my body?" Malcolm closed his eyes as his headache grew nearly blinding. "I didn't ask for this!"

'Let the man speak," a voice whispered in his head.

He took a deep, shuddering breath and tried to relax.

The Chancellor gave him a concerned look. "You're fighting with it right now. Remember how it feels and listen to this next part very carefully. Whether you like it or not, you and that spirit are together now, for better or worse. Your body is still your own, but your thoughts and ideas may not be entirely your own." Arronhelm once again paused to find the words. "Your spirit has its own memories, dreams, and desires. It will try to force those upon you. It's critical that you learn what it wants and needs. Headaches are just the beginning, Malcolm. It can get so much worse, and if you can't strike a balance, it absolutely will get worse."

"You say it's some kind of necromancer. I had dreams of leading an army of corpses, and it felt better than anything I've ever felt, yet you keep talking like this is some great gift? I'm becoming some kind of monster!" Malcolm saw stars as the pain and whispering in his head grew in intensity. He did his best to ignore it all.

"Oh, child. There is so much I need to show you, but all in its due course. For now, please trust me. In this place, at least, spirits are drawn together for a greater purpose. My spirit, in life, was a leader and architect of sorts. He strove to build great things that would endure so the generations that followed could flourish. He and I have worked with the others here to make this place much the same."

Malcolm looked at the pile of scrolls and books as he took in the Chancellor's words. "Wait, are you saying... are you saying that you called this thing... this spirit into me?" He was shouting, and his hands were shaking.

Arronhelm took a step back, surprised. "No. I don't have the power to call spirits. None of us do. The Painting.... Something else did that. Maybe even the region itself." Arronhelm waved his hands, obviously flustered by Malcolm's sudden flash of anger. "I started dreaming the future again, you see," he said with a wavering voice, sounding very much like an old man. The surprising change in demeanor and tone was enough to calm Malcolm down. "I dreamt of the new spirits. It was a few months ago, right after Aelith died. Her death made room for you." Arronhelm smiled sadly and sighed. "I dreamt of the next generation."

Malcolm took a few deep breaths to calm himself further. The Chancellor wasn't making complete sense. He needed to focus on the man's words if he wanted any hope of deciphering the meaning. Arronhelm was trying to convey something important without outright saying it. An architect who builds great things so the generations that follow could flourish, and then he referred to the new spirits as the next generation. The Chancellor said he only learned about the new spirits after someone died. So, the person who died must have had a spirit, Malcolm reasoned. It was making sense, but he needed to confirm one detail, even though he thought he already knew the answer. "There's a limit, isn't there?"

Arronhelm nodded.

"Does one spirit have to die before another can come?"

Arronhelm nodded again.

"But you dreamt of more new spirits than just mine, right?"

"Many more, Malcolm," he said as he made his way over to the desk with the collection of books and scrolls.

"So, others will be dying. Who are the others? Did your dream tell you how soon? What about the painting? I heard you say the word, 'painting'."

"We can speak on this topic again another time, but for now, you've work to do," said Arronhelm as he gestured to an empty chair. The old man seemingly regained complete control over his faculties and emotions. "Start your studies tonight. There are Camphor Berries to keep you awake. I will gather you some things for your journey in the morning."

"Journey?"

"No more questions please. There's so much to do, and so little time. Now, where's that book?" he said as he pushed a few scrolls to the side until he found an old, cracked, leather-bound tome. “Ah yes, this would be the best place to start.”

Malcolm sighed and walked over, accepting the Chancellor’s invitation.

“*I so very much look forward to working with you, Malcolm,*” came the voice in his head.

It sounded smug to him, but at least his headache was gone.

15
Russell

Russell yawned and rubbed his eyes as he shuffled out into the clearing. The morning air felt cool and damp. It was still dark, but the glow of the horizon above the distant tree line promised morning would arrive soon. He really didn't enjoy being up this early, but at the same time, he couldn't help but feel a touch of excitement.

He continued to rub the sleep from his eyes as he passed other groups of people forming up all across the field. His number was seven, which he guessed was farther away from the Citadel. Turning and taking stock of it all, he estimated there were twenty separate groups, each marked by a sign atop a pole. The numbers were painted on with an ink that glowed a deep purple. He actually learned to make that ink in his arcane sciences class. Wren blood, a bit of Liquidlight, an ounce of gem powder, plus water and sand all carefully blended together over low heat.

Russell yawned again as he approached the sign marked with a glowing seven. Many people were already assembled. He must've overslept. He expected to see almost everyone from the herbalism expedition yesterday but was surprised to see more people. There were a few students he didn't know, but his attention was drawn to a group of four adults.

There was a Pathfinder woman with a bow loosely strung over her back. Russell couldn't be certain, but he thought it was the same woman Attia called to the night they came back from the boar. Next to her was a young man with a plain brown robe. He was leaning on a short staff that must double as a walking stick much of the time. His head was cleanly shaven, which likely meant he was a healer from the Monastery. Russell heard Conner complaining about the head shaving a few times. He agreed. It looked stupid.

One of the other adults nodded to him and said, "Felerin, is that the last one? Are we about ready to get moving?"

Felerin shook her head. "I was told we have to wait for one more."

The man shook his head and mumbled something to himself. He and the man next to him were both wearing full plate armor, with shields strung across their backs. Russell heard plenty of whining from Cedric the other day about how hot and miserable it was to wear that kind of armor. He understood why they wanted to get an early start before the full heat of the day set in. The man nodded to the other armored man and asked, "Do these things ever start on time? Coulda slept longer."

"Nah. Don't reckon they ever do, Vincent," answered the other man. He was taller and a good deal older. He had a deep scar running from his temple all the way down to the bottom of his jaw, and it looked like his nose had been broken a few times.

"Morning, Russ," said Tessa as she skipped over to him and playfully slugged him in the arm. "Not a morning person, huh?"

Russell shook his head. The sun cleared the treetops, flooding the clearing with morning light. The way the sun highlighted Tessa's long auburn hair was breathtaking. The morning just got better. "Nothing like getting up before dawn to go on a forced march through the rainforest."

"With mules!" Tessa giggled. "Don't forget about the mules," she said as she pointed to a ragged pair of mules, yoked to a large cart off to the side. "And a cart, I guess."

"You know, I really think Professor Thompson owes me an apology."

Tessa looked at him with a confused expression. "What for? Well, beyond being an ass. He owes everyone an apology for that."

Russell grinned. "He pissed all over my answer when I said Ganna fruit defines human existence, yet here we are, at way too early an hour in the morning, getting ready to spend the next few days frantically harvesting Ganna Fruit."

Tessa laughed. Russell was happy she appreciated his humor. His dry sarcasm didn't make it easy for him to make friends. Few appreciated it, and many took offense. Tessa's laughter came at a price, though, as it drew the attention of Liam. Russell thought it was far too early in the morning to deal with a difficult person.

"Morning," called Liam as he walked over, physically forcing himself into the conversation. "Have either of you seen Malcolm? I looked for him in the Great Hall last night, and I'm pretty sure he wasn't there. He's not out here this morning either."

Russell hadn't even thought to look for him. He felt a bit guilty, but everything was moving so fast. It was hard to keep up. "No. I just know that he's been acting really strange ever since the boar."

Liam nodded. "Ever since. Those words make it sound like we're talking about something that happened months ago."

"Right," said Tessa. "It was just a couple days ago that we were gathering before dawn to go out on a different mission."

"More of us on this mission. A lot bigger escort too," said Russell as he looked over at the group of adults. The taller man with the smashed face noticed them and started walking over. "Know this guy, Liam?"

Liam turned and casually saluted the man. "What did you do to pull this assignment, Vargus? The Commander must've had a score to settle. I'm amazed that armor still fits you with all the double meal shifts you've been pulling."

Russell was taken off guard by Liam's tone. He hadn't seen this side of him before, but he liked it. He couldn't quite read Vargus's reaction. He was concerned that Liam went too far, but after a few moments of silence, the older soldier started laughing. It was a throaty, painful sound, like a wagon wheel in terrible need of grease.

"Nah. The Chancellor, believe it or not. Yer dad had a different group running protection for you. Chancellor changed the assignments for your group. He's sending you out to one of the farther Ganna farms, but he put both me and Felerin with ya."

Russell only saw the Chancellor on a handful of occasions in arcane sciences classes. He knew the old man taught some of the advanced wizardry students. Russell didn't fall into that category. The fact that their destination was changed worried him. After the boar the other day, he thought they deserved a safe and easy assignment.

"You think we're likely to run into trouble," asked Liam, suddenly in a less jovial mood.

Vargus shrugged and scratched at his scar a bit. "Dunno. Felerin was saying there's a goblin tribe real close to that field. There's trouble up there every now and then, from what I hear. With the Tide coming, the goblins will be on the move." He thought for a bit longer and frowned. "Don't mean to piss on your morning, but yeah, I reckon we might see a little action up there."

Russell wasn't happy with that answer. He could understand Liam, Attia, or even Tessa being out there, but what was he supposed to do? They barely scratched the surface of offensive wizardry spells in his classes this semester, and he never took the time to study a weapon. It had to be some kind of mistake. He thought about raising the issue with Vargus, but the grizzled soldier wasn't looking at him anymore. Vargus's attention moved to a pair of people walking out to them.

Russell turned and saw the two robed figures approaching, one old man and another much younger one. As they got closer, he realized that the young man was Malcolm, but he looked so different. Malcolm was wearing a tan robe that shimmered as the morning sun reflected off the tight script of runes written across the cloth. He was carrying a leather pack on his back, but it was more than just the clothes. Russell couldn't quite put his finger on it, but there was just a sense that something significant changed in Malcolm's life.

"Didn't expect you to come out to send us off in person, Chancellor," said Vargus. The Chancellor was a short, slight wisp of a man with a neatly trimmed beard, and a mustache of thin, white hair. His skin was rather dark, which seemed odd to Russell given how rarely the Chancellor was ever seen outside of a classroom or his own chambers.

"It's quite a beautiful day. I thought I might enjoy a little fresh air, and I needed to deliver Malcolm."

Russell noticed that everyone in their group, and most of the people in the neighboring groups, were paying attention now. The arrival of the Chancellor was something of an event. Russell could see kids and adults alike whispering to each other as they watched.

"I'll take good care of him, for ya, Chancellor," said Vargus. "But from the looks of it, you're already seeing to that a bit, aren't ya?" he said as he nodded towards Malcolm's rune covered robe.

The Chancellor waved a hand dismissively. "Just an old robe I had laying around from my younger days, nothing too extravagant. The color looks dreadful on me, and I was even shorter back then. We barely needed to hem it to make it fit." He turned to face Malcolm. "Now you must keep up on your reading, young man. Take advantage of every opportunity to practice, but most of all, be safe."

Malcolm nodded. The Chancellor, satisfied, took a step back and turned to the group gathered by signpost seven. "Young Malcolm is working on a very special project for me. I expect that he'll have little time for farming. I've added a few extra people to this expedition, so there should be no shortage of workers."

"Why we bringing him then?" asked Vincent.

The Chancellor frowned. "What part of 'working on a special project for me' did you fail to understand?"

"Just didn't know what kind of project--"

"Hold your tongue," hissed Vargus, cutting the other soldier off, but the damage was already done. The Chancellor strode over to signpost six and started speaking with a different armored man. A few moments later, both the Chancellor and the man walked back over to their group. The man had a thick, unkempt beard and a dirty look. He carried a long-edged spear of sorts. Russell couldn't remember what it was called, but it didn't matter to him all that much.

"You," said the Chancellor as he pointed to Vincent. "I've reassigned you to group six."

Vincent swore under his breath but didn't act out any worse than that as he walked over to the other group.

"Now that that's been sorted, let me introduce..." The Chancellor paused for a moment before sheepishly saying, "I'm sorry. I've already forgotten your—"

"Darach, sir," the new man blurted.

"Yes. Darach here will accompany you. Now, does anyone else want to annoy me with questions?"

Russell wanted to ask why he was being sent, but he suspected speaking out would just make matters worse for him. Then again, Tessa would be on this trip, so it might not be that bad.

"No questions then?" said the Chancellor before Russell decided whether or not to ask his question. "Excellent. Questions are rather bothersome anyway. Have a safe expedition." With that, the Chancellor waved, turned, and walked back toward the Citadel.

16
Felerin

Felerin was on edge. This was the largest group she was ever asked to lead through the forest. She was concerned about the amount of noise they'd make, but there was no helping it. They already needed to cut the brush back to allow the mules and the cart safe passage a few times, and they only made it past the first set of clearings, and into the forest proper, an hour ago.

She knew the paths up alongside the Serpent well. Once through this section of forest, they'd have to skirt along the edges of the rice farms for a few hours. It was far too soft and muddy in the rice fields to travel over that ground with a cart. On the bright side, the amount of noise they were making, pulling a cart through the forest, put the wildlife on notice. The large party moving through would create enough commotion to keep any snakes and poisonous frogs away, but she knew of two territorial jaguars in this patch of woods she wanted to watch out for.

Felerin turned to make sure everyone was keeping together. She stationed Vargus and Joshua at the back with the cart to make sure no one lagged behind. She also asked Attia to herd the group and keep them on the trails. Felerin watched the young Pathwalker perform her duties and sighed.

Felerin spoke with Solen after the gathering last night about Attia's anger issues. It weighed on her. Felerin tried for some time to soften Attia's edge in preparation of her receiving the katana blade the Pathfinders commissioned for her. It was a gorgeous blade, with a nearly perfect edge. She stowed it with the supplies in the cart a few hours before dawn, but Solen's concerns weren't without merit. If Attia were to lose her temper like Solen described while wielding a live blade, she might kill someone. On the other hand, had she given Attia the blade earlier maybe Cedric would still be alive. With the likelihood of danger ahead, she didn't think she could put it off any longer.

"Hey. We gonna take a break soon?" asked Glenn as he approached. Felerin met Glenn and his brother Caleb earlier when their parents walked them out to the meeting point. The parents were glassblowers who lived up by the forges in the Citadel. They gave her a tiny, but beautiful glass pendant necklace as a gift. It was their way of pleading for the safety of their children. A constant reminder that these kids had parents who desperately wanted them to return home safely.

"You can take a minute or two now as the group catches up."

"Oh," said the boy. "I was hoping to sit and rest my legs."

"Sorry, but I'm afraid that's not going to happen. We need to make it to the farm before dark. The earlier, the better. If it gets too bad, I can let you rest in the cart, but it'll be bumpy. We have a lot of distance to cover yet." Ordinarily, Felerin wouldn't push the pace with this large a group, but she had grave concerns about approaching the Ganna farm after dark.

A flourishing tribe of goblins lived in the trees less than a quarter mile west of the Serpent. Over the years, the farmers along the river built an uneasy truce with the goblins. The Pathfinders played a critical role in maintaining that peace. Every year, after the harvest, a group of Pathfinders stopped by each farm and collected seeds and surplus crops and left them in the goblins' territory as offerings. There were a few incidents of violence each year between farmers and goblins, but most of those could be attributed to individuals inadvertently wandering into a snare trap. The golden rule was that farmers never strayed from their farmlands at night.

Goblins, as a species, were nocturnal. They had excellent night vision, and sunlight dried and burned their skin. This restricted their daytime movement to the dense regions of the rainforest, where the canopy was thick enough to all but block out the sun. They could move with complete freedom during the night. Felerin suspected the goblins already knew about the Black Tide's new path through the jungle. It would destroy the ecosystem of the entire area. An uneasy truce couldn't be expected to hold in the face of that kind of terror.

"You look troubled, Pathwalker Felerin," said Liam as he approached. Most of the group reached her. She was only waiting on Vargus and Joshua.

"Pathrunner, not Pathwalker, Liam. Three ranks. Walker, Runner, and Maker."

"I'm sorry. I meant no offense," Liam said. He sounded sincere.

"Don't trouble yourself over it. Just call me Felerin," she said curtly. "But to answer your question, I'm worried about how the animals will react to the Tide and all these caravans disturbing their hunting grounds."

Liam looked at her for a few moments before saying, "This isn't the same as withholding a tragedy that can't be changed from a group of scared teenagers to get them to safety. Knowing what's really out there might help everyone be more prepared."

It stunned Felerin. How did he know? Vargus must have told him about the goblins, she reasoned. Still, she hadn't expected such a direct confrontation from the boy. Further, she was surprised that his argument was so good. He used the lesson she taught him the other night to highlight and make his argument for him. She nodded to Liam.

"All right, can everyone hear me?" she asked. She waited as a few of her group moved closer before continuing. "We will be travelling quickly for the next hour. If anyone gets too winded, they can ride in the cart until they recover. The goal is to make the next set of clearings within an hour. From there, we must weave in and out along the edges of those clearings. There are a few partially paved paths along the way. We'll try to take those as often as possible to help get the cart through, but if the cart breaks down or gets caught, we may have to leave it."

"What good are we to the farmers without a cart?" asked Conner.

"The farm will have its own cart. With any luck, we'll be returning to the Citadel with two full carts, but one's better than nothing. Under no circumstances will I let us get caught out in the forest at night."

"My mom gave me some Liquidlight. We can use it if we need it," added a young girl. Felerin was pretty sure her name was Claudia.

"That's very nice of you. Should we fail to make it to the farm before sunset, having light won't be our biggest problem." She wasn't an orator. She didn't quite know what words to use to make everyone feel safer, so she stopped trying. "There's a large tribe of goblins that live close to our destination. If we run into them after dark, I'm fairly certain they'll attack."

Vargus and Joshua arrived while she was speaking. She nodded to Vargus, hoping he would speak a bit.

"Right. Goblins," he started. "If they catch us out in the rainforest at night, all we can do is try to take cover. We'll have some kind of shelter, I'm sure. Other than that, we got two shields and a cart. Most of 'em will have bows or spears. If they can, they'll stay up high in the trees and pick us off."

"Those arrows will likely be poisoned," added Felerin.

"I have herbs for that!" chirped Eliana, a little too enthusiastically.

"Good. Keep them at the ready. I have some as well," said Felerin.

"Understand," continued Vargus, "even if its pitch black out there beneath the trees, they'll be able to see you. They can see in the dark. If you run, or wander off on your own, we won't be able to help you. If fortune takes a piss on us and something happens out there, everyone's gotta stick together." Vargus looked over to Felerin. "Anything else?"

"What about the necromancy?" asked Malcolm. The boy had been quiet the entire trip. His friends continually asked him questions about his time with the Chancellor, but he brushed their questions off. Few knew about the strange ritual magic the goblins practiced. It wasn't talked about, but Felerin saw it with her own eyes a few times in the past. She didn't understand how Malcolm knew, but she assumed it had to have something to do with the Chancellor.

Vargus frowned. "Bah. Old wives' tale—"

"No," Felerin interrupted. "It's true. I've seen it. It's just not something I understand well enough to warn you about."

Vargus shot Felerin a glare. It looked like he wanted to argue the point, but Malcolm started speaking. "They can call spirits," said Malcolm, his eyes unfocused and looking off to the side. "In the darkness, you probably wouldn't be able to see them. You might feel them though as freezing cold if they were to touch you or pass through you. They'll most likely send the spirits they call into the bodies of the dead, to reanimate them."

Felerin saw the children drawing closer together. It wasn't just Malcolm's words that were scaring them. It was the way he was saying it. His tone was even and distant, and he was looking off in a direction where no one was standing. It was just too disturbing.

"A dead body with a spirit inside it is dangerous. Stronger spirits make stronger living dead. They can still be killed again, but it's difficult. Damaging the body enough will force the spirit out of it," said Malcolm in that same distant tone of voice.

"Malcolm," said Liam as he tentatively approached the other boy. "We don't know what's been happening with you." He gently placed a hand on his friend's shoulder, and Malcolm startled. "We appreciate the information, and we believe you. We really do, but let's revisit it after we make it to the farm?"

Malcolm nodded to him, and Felerin felt relieved. As much as she wanted to know more, the fact that a strange boy was delivering it in such an odd way made it feel dangerous to her. "All right, we've rested enough. Everyone get moving," she said as she turned and reconvened the journey.

The group moved with difficulty at first. They needed to stop frequently to clear roots or branches to get the cart through, which meant they were moving faster than any of the other groups. She took comfort because the trails they were clearing would make things easier for the others that would follow throughout the morning. Most of the expeditions would finish their journeys at one of the several farms that made up the next collection of clearings. Only a handful of expeditions were being sent farther through the forest to the more distant clusters of farms.

Travel became easier once they made it to the first rice fields. The group could set a comfortable, but brisk pace as they snaked their way through trails and the dryer areas on the outskirts of the fields. The sun was hot and bright, and the warm light seemed to do a lot to lift the spirits of the group as they continued to make good time.

It was early afternoon when the group reached the end of the clearings, and the beginning of the next section of forest. Felerin monitored the movements of birds and wildlife throughout the day and felt reasonably confident they wouldn't face any issues from the animal life. There were six hours of daylight left, with only a little over three hours of travel to go.

"All right, everyone," she called. "Take twenty minutes. Rest your legs and get some lunch. We're making great time, so you've earned a little rest." She walked back toward the cart. "Attia, could you come here?"

Attia made her way over quickly. Felerin appreciated the girl's lack of hesitation in most aspects of her apprenticeship with the Pathfinders. She pushed back at times and made her opinions known, but almost invariably after completing the task at hand. Felerin moved a few packs and retrieved a tightly wrapped bundle.

"I think it's time you move on from your practice sword, Attia," Felerin said as she worked the wrapping blanket aside to reveal a curved wooden scabbard, decorated with finely carved reliefs of leaves and branches.

"I… I don't know what to say."

Felerin smiled warmly. "You needn't say anything. You earned this." Felerin presented the sheathed blade to the young Pathwalker, balancing it on the outsides of both index fingers, blade side up.

Attia bowed her head and reached out with one hand to accept the sword. Both women stood still, holding it for a moment before Felerin stepped back, leaving the weapon in the other's hand, nodding her permission. Attia's smile was radiant as she drew the blade from its scabbard in a single motion. The sword shone in the afternoon sun. A thin, tight line of runes ran the entire length of the blade, right along the edge.

"I think you'll be impressed with the craftsmanship. The balance is truly breathtaking. So much so, that a few of us came together to get the edge magically hardened with runes. We didn't want to risk such a fine blade dulling or rolling."

Attia took a few practice cuts in the air, but only a few. She quickly returned her new sword to the safety of its sheath and rushed in, wrapping Felerin in a tight hug. "Thank you so much," she whispered through her tears.

"No thanks needed. You earned it," whispered Felerin.

17
Eliana

Eliana grinned as she stepped out into the Ganna field. The sun was still high in the sky, which meant they had a few hours to organize and work before light would become an issue. She heard some of the others complaining about how long the journey was, and how few breaks they were allowed along the way, but she didn't care anymore. She spent much of her life working with her parents on the family Ganna farm. This one was much larger, but it still felt like home to her.

The farm fields were all contained within a single large clearing, roughly a hundred yards across in each direction. A few trees near the southwestern corner of the clearing were preserved to provide some shade for four shacks, clustered together. A cart and a pair of donkeys were tethered near the shacks. Long rows of Ganna trees dominated the rest of the clearing, separated from one another by narrow, but deep irrigation channels. The farmers planted their trees two yards apart from one another. She estimated that they had a few thousand trees on this farm to tend to.

Eliana moved out into the field while the rest of her group was gathering at the edge of the clearing. They probably needed to organize and decide how to proceed, but she wanted to see the trees. She smiled as she felt the water and mud from the irrigation trenches flood into her boots. It reminded her so much of home. The Ganna trees here were only four feet high, while nearly all the trees on her parents' farm topped six feet. She wondered if the high number of plants within this single field was causing the trees to compete for nutrients.

She made her way to the first tree and knelt down by it. A tight spiral of roots which fanned out in all directions from the tree, just beneath the surface of the mud, formed the trunk. The Ganna itself sprung up from those roots. Thick, thorny stalks held each piece of fruit a few inches above the ground, and the tight branches and foliage on the tops of the trees functioned as an umbrella of sorts to shield the fruit from the most intense hours of mid-day sun. Eliana counted the fruit. The tree she knelt by had thirteen roots, each producing three or four Ganna fruit. She smiled. It was a normal, healthy tree, just a bit shorter than what she was used to.

She reached out and carefully turned and rocked one of pieces of Ganna fruit free. There was an art to it. You needed to grip the stalk in just the right spot to separate the fruit from it without rupturing the fragile core inside. She'd done it all her life, so, it only took her a few moments. The fruit itself had a skin with a rich sapphire color. The core within glowed with a pulsing golden light. The combination of the colors gave the fruit a vibrant green color. She expected this farm to be breathtaking at night, given its thousands of trees. The fruit would glow enough to be emerald green points of light in the darkness, but they wouldn't be bright enough to provide any real illumination.

"Ellie, come on back," called Conner.

Eliana turned with a smile and walked back to the group. They were all spread out along the sides of the field from where the trail spilled out into the area, and both Felerin and the taller of the two soldiers, Vargus was his name, she thought, were off to the side, speaking with a man and a woman who clearly worked the farm. Eliana could tell just from the way they stood, and the layers upon layers of mud and soot worked into their clothes. The conversation was short, or perhaps she lost track of time looking at the Ganna tree, as both Felerin and Vargus shook hands with the farmers and returned to the group.

"All right, everyone, we have a little less than three hours of light left. The farmers here have been working all day, ever since getting notice early this morning from the Pathrunners we sent up this way last night. They said they have a lot of Ganna fruit to seal before they can be any help. I don't quite know what that means . . ."

"When you pick Ganna fruit, you separate it from the land. It leaves a wound. You seal it by taking some of the stalks and cutting them into small pieces. You wrap those in leaves from the trees and plug the hole, otherwise the magic in the core seeps out, spoiling the fruit." Eliana was happy that she was sent with this group. None of the others were Ganna farmers. She was critical to the operation.

"Okay, that's what it means, I guess," said Felerin with a smile. "They'll take our donkeys and cart back over by their shacks and load it with the Ganna fruit as they seal it. As I understand it, there are four farmers who work this farm. Two are resting, but when they wake, I think the plan is they'll join us in the fields and seal and load the fruit onto sleds as we harvest it."

"Don't we get to rest at all?" asked Caleb. "We've been moving all day with barely a break."

"We'll start taking rest shifts in a little while, but only after we get ourselves situated out in the fields. Don't expect to be comfortable, but we'll make a fire and set up as dry a camp as we can. We can let three or four rest at a time. Don't plan on getting more than a few hours of sleep, though."

Eliana brought a good assortment of herbs with her, including Camphor Berries for wakefulness, and a nice thick salve that she could burn in the campfire to keep the insects at bay. She started to offer them to the group, but the Pathfinder directed everyone to move towards a section of unharvested Ganna trees near the very center of the field.

It took them an hour to get everyone situated and harvesting. The brothers, Glenn and Caleb, didn't want to get their boots wet, so they made quite a show of avoiding the irrigation trenches. The young girl, Claudia, tripped over some roots and ended up getting tangled up in one of the trees. Eliana was most disturbed by Malcolm. He was constantly looking around, but at nothing in particular. His eyes were glassy and distant. Russell ended up having to walk with him to make sure he didn't trip and fall.

Teaching everyone how to pick Ganna fruit took Eliana another hour. This expedition was fortunate to have an expert like her. They ruined two full trees worth of fruit before she taught most of them the proper technique. Liam never got the hang of it, so Felerin put him to work building the camp and keeping a fire going. She didn't get to teach Malcolm. He wasted no time finding a dry place to sit and read whatever books were stowed away in his backpack. She wanted to force him to learn, but Felerin shot her a look as soon as she tried to teach him.

As everyone slowly found their spots and started plucking Ganna fruit, Eliana set herself up within earshot of Malcolm. Liam would be working near Malcolm building the camp around him. She knew he would eventually start asking Malcolm questions, and she wasn't disappointed. Her plan worked, and quite quickly. It only took Liam a quarter hour to start asking questions.

"So, Malcolm, what's been going on with you? You're spending time with the Chancellor now?" he started.

"He has me studying some other things. I mean, I just started last night, but I think he will keep working with me," answered Malcolm.

"All right. Mind me asking what you're studying?"

"I don't know how much I'm allowed to say."

Eliana saw Liam crouch down next to Malcolm and put a hand on his shoulder. "I guess we're all worried about you. You haven't been yourself ever since the boar. I just want to understand a little better. That's all."

Malcolm let the book drop into his lap as he rubbed his temples. "I don't know if I can explain it. It's not just knowing if I should share. I don't think I understand enough to be able to."

"All right. So, you were trying to tell us some things back on the trail. About the goblins, remember?" Malcolm nodded, so Liam continued. "I said that we'd revisit that conversation when we got to the farm. How about now?"

Malcolm continued to hold his head like it hurt. For a moment, Eliana was worried that he wouldn't speak, but eventually, he answered. "So, necromancers can call spirits. They can bring them across and pull them back into this world."

"Spirits of the dead? Dead people?"

"Not just people. I don't think it matters if the spirit was from a person, a monster, an animal, or whatever. They all just stop being what they were and become spirits. I don't know how that happens. Arronhelm said that sometimes it doesn't happen, or that it can take centuries."

Eliana's jaw dropped. Malcolm was on a first name basis with the Chancellor?

"Okay. I don't understand that, but I don't think I need to. So, the goblins can bring these spirits back into our world. What happens then?" asked Liam.

"They can direct and control them. Well, sometimes. I haven't read enough to understand. Sometimes when a necromancer opens the way for a spirit, a weaker or stronger spirit comes through, so they might lose control. But I think, in most cases, they can control the spirits they call."

"What can they do with them?" asked Liam.

"They can make them attack the living. From what I'm reading though, doing that can be really tiring to the necromancer. Keeping the spirit here without a body takes constant energy and effort. That's why they make the spirit enter a dead body. It's a lot easier."

"Why?"

"Maybe the body protects the spirit," Malcolm answered quietly. Something about him seemed to change in that moment. It looked to Eliana like whatever was hurting his head stopped. He put his hand back in his lap and his voice sounded eerie and distant when he started speaking again. "Souls exist in bodies, never being called by the Astral. It's only when a soul is outside the safety of its body that it's drawn into the Astral to be eroded and ultimately torn apart until nothing but a spirit remains. A necromancer who brings a spirit over must fight to keep the Astral from reclaiming it. Putting it in a body protects the spirit. A soul also can protect itself by entering a body. Do you understand?"

Liam rocked back on his heels. He ended up breaking his crouch and falling on to his backside. He was nodding. Eliana noticed Malcolm was also nodding. What was going on? She realized Malcolm must be working with the Chancellor to learn necromancy. She really wanted to see the books he brought. Maybe she could sneak a look after Malcolm went to sleep. Having watched that exchange, she thought Malcolm wasn't himself. He was nodding in answer to his own question.

"Damnit!" she heard shouted from the other direction. "Ellie, can you show me what I'm doing wrong?" called Conner.

Eliana frowned. She wanted to eavesdrop more. She climbed to her feet and moved away from Liam and Malcolm before answering, "Coming." As she made her way toward him, she noticed several others having trouble picking the Ganna fruit without damaging it. She sighed as she realized that she would need to spend more time teaching. This expedition was truly fortunate to have her.

18
Tessa

The sun already set by the time the farmers came out to join them with sleds for the Ganna fruit. The men, Jonin and Samuel, were both young and stocky. Tessa thought they were the sons of the man and woman they met when they first arrived. With a farm this size, it only made sense for the whole family to stay and tend it full time.

They farmed quietly as a group for a few hours as all vestiges of daylight faded. Tessa saw Ganna farms at night many times in her life, but this one was truly astonishing. Tens of thousands of bulbs of Ganna fruit, each glowing like a tiny emerald star on the ground below, and the deep indigo sky cascading moonlight and starlight down from above. It was too much beauty to take in all at once.

Felerin started sending small groups to rest for a few hours at a time as the night wore on. Both she and Attia appeared to be on edge. The chittering sounds of insects competed with the wind that picked up over the hours, forcing conversations to get louder as everyone worked. Felerin paced around the camp. Eventually, her agitation became so obvious that the younger of the two guards, Darach, mustered the gumption to ask the question that many were likely feeling.

"What is it? What's wrong?"

Felerin held up a hand but didn't turn. "We're being watched," she said. "Stalked even. Be discreet but wake the sleepers."

Tessa's blood ran cold as she watched Darach carefully make his way over to the campfire. Looking out across the field covered in darkness, she realized the vulnerability of their position. The noises of the night, coupled with their conversations, would've masked the sounds of any predator, and the field of short, squat trees provided endless cover. Fortunately, she had the foresight to bring her bow and quiver with her to each tree as she worked. She crouched down and slowly gathered them up, hoping not to be too obvious about it.

"We first noticed some of the lights of the Ganna fruit fading in and out, off in the distance," said Felerin as quietly as she could while still being heard over the wind and insects. All other conversations went quiet. "We've been tracking their movement that way for a while now. There's a lot of them, and they're organized. It has to be the goblins from the west. We hoped that they'd move on after seeing how many of us there were. No such luck."

Tessa's hands shook as she slipped the harness of her quiver over her shoulder. She saw others doing their best to discreetly prepare as well. Vargus crossed an irrigation trench over to the next row of Ganna trees. He set himself up in the gap between two of the trees, making an effective wall in front of the area where the group established the campfire. She turned and saw both Attia and Liam taking up a position behind her, facing out and away from the group. Both of them waited, weapons in hand. Were they surrounded?

"You sure, miss?" asked Jonin. "I been working this farm all my life. Never once had any of them goblins set foot in this field. We set fruit out for 'em down the trail a ways, and that's always been enough. Been that way as long as I can recollect."

"Yes. I'm sure." Felerin's tone was forceful. "Everyone needs to stay together. No one runs." She turned and surveyed the group and the placement of everyone. "Darach. You and Sam flip that sled on its side and brace it against those two trees back by Liam and Attia. Let's see if we can't build a little cover for that flank"

The farmer and the soldier rushed over to the sled and flipped it, spilling an hour's worth of Ganna fruit into the irrigation trench. There was a sudden chorus of whistling sounds as the men tried to wrestle the sled into position. Tessa yelped in surprise as a slender arrow thudded into the tree right next to her, and another splashed into the muddy water in front of her. She saw splinters as a few arrows shattered against Darach's plate armor, but she also saw one lodge in his shoulder. Samuel wasn't so lucky. He fell backwards to the ground, clutching his belly. Tessa saw three arrows sunk deep into his body. The man screamed as his blood spilled on to the ground and into the muddy water. Tessa screamed as well.

"Everyone take cover," shouted Felerin, though she was barely louder than the shouts and cries of everyone else. Tessa crouched as low as she could as two more arrows struck the fallen farmer. His screaming turned into a wet gurgling noise as one of the arrows hit him in the neck. Tessa's heart raced and panic threatened to overwhelm her. She crawled toward the campfire only to be nearly trampled by Glenn and his brother running away, out into the darkness.

"No one run!" Felerin shouted, but even as she did, Tessa saw the little girl, Claudia, run out into the field toward the farmers' shacks. "You must stay together," she shouted as she sprinted after the two running boys. Felerin moved with grace, but the boys ran far enough to be out of sight already. Tessa could only hope Felerin would find them before the goblins did.

"Help me, Liam," shouted Darach. The sled fell back down into the trench when the farmer was shot, and Darach was now struggling to wedge the sled into position against the trees.

"You go, I'll cover," said Liam to Attia as he crouched beneath his shield. Tessa watched, stunned, as arrow after arrow crashed against Liam's shield. Attia moved quickly and smoothly, running in a low crouch until she could dart behind the sled and help Darach maneuver it into position. Tessa crawled as fast as she could until she was behind the safety of the sled. She heard a few thuds as arrows struck it, but she felt a lot safer, at least for the time being.

"Conner! Malcolm! Over here!" called Tessa. She saw the two ducking in the other irrigation trench behind where Vargus was acting as a human shield. The bald man with the walking stick stood behind Vargus, with one hand on his back. She watched as arrows shattered against Vargus's shield and deflected off the trees to either side of him. It occurred to her that the goblins' arrows must be poorly crafted or made of a weak wood to be so ineffective against armor. It was something to be grateful for, at least.

"I think Russ and Ellie found some good cover in the trench over by the campfire," said Conner, pointing to a bridge of thick earthy mud that had developed between two rows of trees to cover the pair of children huddling in the irrigation trench beneath it. "She made the earth protect them."

Tessa smiled to herself, thankful that Eliana could use her skills to protect Russ. She used the thought to push away the terror and return to her senses. She saw a silvery light emanate from Vargus, spreading forth from him in all directions. He advanced behind his shield, Joshua remaining close behind him. Arrows kept striking him, but his shield or armor turned aside most. As he moved, the light moved with him, and it wasn't long before she could see where the goblins on that side were shooting from. She crawled past her friends and over to a tree for cover. She took her bow and carefully lined up a shot, but an arrow from somewhere behind her sunk into the tree not more than a few inches from her head. She yelped, her fear quickly returning

"I'll cover you, Tessa," said Liam from behind her. She heard arrows smashing into his shield as he got into position. She lined up her shot again, her heart racing. Things were clearer this time. Vargus and his magical light were closer to the patch of trees the goblins were situated in. She fired her first arrow, carefully watching to see how the wind pushed it. She missed, a little wide to the left. Tessa nocked another and, this time, got much closer. With Vargus approaching, a few of the goblins dropped their bows in favor of spears. She fired again and hit one in the leg. Having found her range, she started shooting more rapidly and struck another before the goblins appreciated they were being fired upon.

And then Vargus was on them. The first goblin lunged forward with its spear, but Vargus slapped the thrust to the side with his shield. He cut down and across in the same motion, catching the goblin in the shoulder, and slicing cleanly into its chest. Sickly yellow blood erupted from the wound as the dying goblin slid to the ground. Two more goblins darted forward with their spears, trying to keep the veteran soldier at a distance. A pair of them moved out to the side, working to get an angle to shoot at Vargus while he was engaged in melee. She took aim and started firing on them as they moved, hitting one in the chest, and forcing the other back into cover.

"You've got a few more seconds, no more," said Liam from right behind her. "The goblins on this side are giving up on their bows. Looks like they're advancing."

Tessa fired a couple more arrows at the clump of trees in the distance, mostly to keep the goblins from trying to flank Vargus again. Her breath caught in her throat as she watched the veteran soldier catch a spear right in the belly from one of the goblins. He didn't even seem fazed by it as he slammed his shield into the side of the little creature, knocking it to the ground. He stepped on it and pushed off as he jumped up and in between the Ganna trees the goblins were hiding within, forcing Joshua to dash forward to stay with him. Another goblin moved to engage him, but the others ran.

"Here they come!" shouted Liam. Tessa turned and moved back to the other side of the tree she was using for cover. She was confident that none of those on Vargus's side would take any shots at her. They were running away.

The light was poor, but she could still make out a group of six or so of the small creatures advancing at Liam with their spears. They were no more than four feet tall, with glistening green skin. All in all, they looked a little like giant frogs to her, although their heads and faces seemed more human than that.

Liam and Darach moved next to one another to provide a wall of armor for Attia, who followed close behind. It was a good thing, as a couple of arrows came whistling in, and one sank deep into Darach's thigh. He cried out in pain or anger as he sprung forward, swinging his pole arm in a downward arc toward the clump of goblins. They scattered to avoid the blow, but in doing so, lost whatever defensive advantage their formation provided.

Liam charged forward to engage a pair off to the right, while Attia followed him, drifting out farther to flank them. The goblins turned to face Liam but saw Attia too late. She swung her blade wide and low, slicing cleanly through one of the goblin's legs right above its knees. It tried to hop back, not even realizing it'd been cut. Instead, it fell backwards, wailing as its thighs separated and slid off its severed legs. The other goblin tried to back away, but Liam lunged, slicing it on the shoulder.

Tessa saw another arrow come whistling in towards Liam, but it missed its mark. She followed it back to where she thought the archers were firing from and took aim. It was too dark for her to see, but if nothing more, a few shots might be enough to make them think twice about shooting at her friends. She fired three arrows in rapid succession and heard a yelp after the third. It was the best she could do. She hoped it was enough.

Tessa was so focused on placing her shots, she didn't see the goblins break and run, but when she looked back, she saw Liam and Attia helping Darach make his way back to the safety of the overturned sled. In addition to arrows in the shoulder and thigh, another caught him in the stomach, but at an odd angle. Tessa didn't think it made it all the way through his armor.

"Everyone gather!" shouted Vargus. Tessa turned and saw the man walking back with Joshua still following. His brilliant silvery light was fading, and it was completely gone by the time he made it back to their makeshift camp. Tessa started to head over to him, but he shook his head. "You six stay by the sled," he said as he looked around and counted people, his eyes lingering for a bit on the dead, bloody farmer. "So, Samuel didn't make it. Anyone seen Jonin?"

"He's over here," said Russell as he crawled out the tunnel Eliana made to protect them. "He took an arrow in the chest. He's back against that tree," he said, pointing to a tree beyond the fire.

"Is he alive?"

"I think so."

"Joshua. Can you see what you can do for him?"

The bald man nodded and made his way over to where Russell pointed. Tessa saw the man turn and nod to Vargus after making it to the tree. He knelt and worked. She hoped it meant he could save the farmer.

"Should maybe a group of us find Felerin?" asked Liam.

"Nah. I think I see her on the way back now."

Tessa turned and watched. It took a few moments before she could make out the silhouette in the darkness, but the picture got clearer as Felerin came closer. She was leading one boy by the hand. She had another draped across her shoulder. Tessa was amazed at how easily the Pathfinder moved while carrying the weight of another. She assumed it must have something to do with balance magic.

Felerin released the boy's hand once she made it all the way back. It was Glenn, and he immediately fell to his knees and started sobbing. She knelt next to him and gently lowered the boy on her shoulder to the ground. Tessa saw the lethal puncture wound that went straight through Caleb's chest. It must have been from a spear. He probably ran right into it.

"I'm sorry, Glenn," Felerin said, gently placing a hand on his shoulder. If he heard her, he didn't show it. He just kept sobbing. She climbed back to her feet and asked, "Did Claudia ever return?"

Vargus shook his head, frowning. "She ran off towards the farmers' buildings. We'd best go check, but we move as a group."

"Right," said Felerin. "And this time, no one runs."

19
Malcolm

Malcolm watched the soul leave the farmer's body. It happened shortly after the arrow struck the man's neck. He could appreciate the subtleties more now that he had a sliver of an understanding of the nature of spirits. He saw the vibrant vitality of the soul fading almost immediately after leaving the body, and he could picture that if it kept fading and changing, it would eventually end up looking like the shadows he saw whenever he squinted now.

Those images dominated his thoughts as he walked with the others over to the farmers' small collection of shacks. Fortunately, Joshua was able to remove the arrow from Jonin's chest and treat the wound well enough to where the man could make the short walk with them over to the huts.

"Hold," hissed Felerin about ten yards from the shacks. She crouched down with her bow in her hand and nodded to Vargus. It was obvious things weren't at all right with the farmers' camp. Malcolm could smell the sweet coppery scent of entrails. He saw Russell and Conner wrinkling their noses, so, they smelled it too.

Vargus carefully walked forward, his shield held close to his body. A few moments later, he frowned and waved the group forward. "There's no good way to say this... it's a bit of a mess."

"Fire and smoke... No, please no," stammered Jonin, staggering forward, still weak from his wound. Joshua moved along next to the man to help him, should he fall, and the rest of the group followed at a respectful distance.

"Mom? Dad?" the man called, but there was no reply. The scene was horrific. Malcolm heard Eliana gag and retch as she saw what happened to the encampment. He suspected others were having difficulties as well. All four mules lay dead on the soft earth. They'd each been eviscerated, their intestines and viscera stretched and spread out messily. Both carts were overturned, and it looked as if their axles were damaged. The ground was covered with scattered Ganna fruit, and a soupy mix of blood and mud that was already starting to thicken as the gore dried.

The bodies of the farmers or little Claudia were nowhere to be found. There were tracks though, a lot of them, all generally leading back into the forest. Felerin crouched and studied them for some time before following them over to the shack where the farmers were sleeping when the attack happened. The door was smashed open. Jonin rushed past her into the shack, openly sobbing now.

"That's odd," said Felerin, running her hand over the door. Everyone could hear the farm boy crying inside the shack. Felerin paused for a moment, a look of concern on her face, before shaking her head and continuing her investigation. "There's no blood inside. Barely any struggle, it seems. And this door... it was smashed open from the inside."

Malcolm winced and his vision blurred. He felt the intrusive thoughts of the other. He relaxed and let them in, finding that the pain immediately faded.

"*I know what happened. Do you?*" the voice chided.

He didn't, but he didn't think the voice would tell him without him trying to understand on his own. He walked over to the shack, squinting so he could see the spiritual world as well. There were a lot of shadows. A lot more than he ever witnessed in one place at a time.

"*They gather whenever some are brought across, hoping to cross over themselves,*" the voice explained.

"What's he looking at?" asked Eliana.

"Just leave him be. Maybe he knows something we don't," said Liam.

Malcolm walked around the shack. There was a small glass window on the side of it. There was a thin sheen of moisture and fog on the window. He reached out and touched it and was surprised to find it was ice cold to the touch.

I think I know, he thought, wondering if the voice would answer him this way. To his delight, it did.

"*Then imagine it. Show me,*" it answered.

Malcolm considered it. Spirits were called. Two, maybe more. The spirits passed through the wall by the window. He imagined that whatever goblins were controlling the spirits wanted to or maybe even needed to see to provide direction. The spirits were used to kill the farmers. There wouldn't be any blood. There may not have even been a struggle. He guessed it depended on if the farmers were able to wake before the spirits froze the life out of their bones.

"*Good,*" the voice in his head whispered. "*Now what happened to the farmers?*"

Malcolm knew he was right. He didn't need the voice to validate his understanding of what happened. He spoke out loud, addressing the gathered group. "I know what happened here."

"All right, Malcolm. Let's hear it," said Felerin.

"They summoned spirits here. I don't know how many."

"Old wives' tale," muttered Vargus.

"Save it, Vargus. Let's hear him out," countered Felerin.

"The spirits passed through the wall right here. The window is still ice cold from their crossing." Malcolm paused as Vargus walked over and touched his hand to the window. The man grunted and nodded to the others. "Once inside, the spirits killed both the farmers. It would have been quick if the farmers were both sleeping. Then the necromancers forced those spirits into the dead bodies to reanimate them. They used the dead farmers to break through the door. I'm guessing they used them to kill the mules. When it was all done, they walked with them out into the forest."

Felerin listened with a horrified expression on her face. She went back to the door and studied as much of the tracks as she could before they became obscured by the gore from the mules. Attia moved over toward the forest. She crouched, studying the footprints for some time. "I think he's right."

"What are you seeing, Pathwalker?" asked Felerin as she moved over to Attia.

"Goblin footprints here. Footprints from the farmers here. And look at these, here. Smaller, but not goblin prints."

"Claudia's. They got her too, it seems," Felerin said as she moved back to the group.

"All right, what're we gonna do now? The whole point of being up here is to fill those carts with Ganna and get 'em back to the Citadel. The carts are probably shot. Even if they aren't, we got no mules to pull 'em," said Vargus.

"Aren't you forgetting the small army of goblins hunting us?" asked Russell.

"No. That's a different problem we need to solve. One thing at a time, though—"

"All right," said Felerin, interrupting. "I'll leave at first light or a little earlier. I'll be able to make it back to the Citadel quickly if I go alone. With any luck, I should be able to scare up another cart and some mules, and hopefully, some more help."

Vargus frowned but nodded. "All right. I don't like you going alone, but I don't see a better choice."

"I wouldn't slow you down at all, Pathrunner," said Attia.

"No need, Attia. I know the trails well, and I want you patrolling the forest around this farm tomorrow, when there's light. Goblins build snares and spring traps. I need you disabling those, so we don't have problems getting out of here. I also want you scouting for likely ambush sites and ways to avoid them."

"That issue's settled," said Vargus. "Now we need to worry about making it through the night. If you've got ideas on the matter, it's time to share 'em."

"I have one," said Jonin as he left his parents' shack, tears streaming down his face. "This farm's lost. I won't farm here again. My family's dead." He looked as if he might break down, but he was able to rein it in and continue. "We take this damn shack apart. Bring the walls out with us into the fields where we were. We set us up some cover so the little maggots can't just shoot us like fish in a barrel."

Vargus nodded. "All right. Let's get started on that. Who's got Camphor Berries, and anything else to help?"

Eliana eagerly reached for her pack. "I do!" she chirped as she knelt down and quickly sorted out her leaf-wrapped, blended herbal pouches. "We should really take some of these now," she said as she pushed a group of pouches off to the side. "Munitau Bark will help fight off any poisons. I have some Oranthinum Gum... maybe for whoever will be taking down the walls?"

Malcolm tried Oranthinum once and vowed never to again. It filled the body with energy. He heard soldiers often liked to chew it when going into battle or on long marches. All it did for him was make his heart race and his palms sweat.

"Good," Vargus said. "Give everyone the Munitau. Give me and Darach the gums. Attia, is that blade hardened?"

"It's magically hardened with runes, Vargus. It won't dull against metal, let alone wood," answered Felerin. She sounded proud.

Vargus whistled. "Well, well. Give my gum to Attia. Darach, you make sure the fasteners are found and removed. Attia should be able to cut that wall up pretty quick."

Malcolm had some herbs in his backpack. He was told to save them if he could for study sessions, but he thought getting slaughtered in the middle of a Ganna field would be more of a problem than fatigue. He laid his backpack down carefully before opening it and fishing out a small wooden case.

"Oh heavens! Look at all the Camphor Berries!" yelped Eliana as she saw the rows upon rows of tightly wrapped clusters of red berries in the case. She blushed and quieted down almost immediately.

Malcolm smiled. "We don't want anyone sleeping tonight, right?"

20
Attia

Attia scanned the field nervously, watching the green glowing Ganna fruit to track movement as she did earlier in the night. It took them the better part of an hour to dismantle the shack and transport the wall pieces out to their camp, but she was happy they spent the time. They took the beds and bedding as well. She cut each section of wall in half, which made them a convenient size to prop against the Ganna trees. They uses the walls to almost completely shield their work area from any direct missile fire.

All rest shifts were suspended until after dawn. Attia knew they couldn't afford to give her a sleeping shift the next morning without Felerin there to watch for them, so she'd have to stay up for the duration. It wasn't the first time, and it wouldn't be the last. One of the challenges to earn the title of Pathrunner was a continuous two-day patrol, without the aid of Camphor Berries. She and a friend started practicing for it together last year. She already could make it through the full duration without passing out.

They made the decision to take advantage of the Liquidlight Claudia offered to them on the journey out to the farm. She felt bad about using Claudia's things, but it wasn't like they could do anything to bring the little girl back. The combination of the Liquidlight and a pair of campfires granted enough illumination to make farming possible, but difficult.

About an hour after the group began farming in earnest, Felerin went out to scout the places where the goblins mounted their attacks from. It only took her a few minutes to run out to each location with a torch and investigate. When she returned, she reported that all the bodies of the slain goblins were gone. The footprints and marks suggested that they were dragged off by other goblins. It most likely happened while the group was investigating the farmers' shacks.

The thought of what the goblins might do with those bodies combined with the chill in the wet night air made Attia shiver. She felt like she was being forced to grow up overnight. At least she owned a real sword now. She remembered how easily it cut through that goblin's legs. The thing hadn't even registered the cut until it tried to move.

"Attia," came the call from Felerin. "Out there," she said, pointing.

Attia quickly scanned her direction for movement. None of the lights from the Ganna fruit were being blocked by anything moving in front of them, so she moved over to the other side of the camp to join Felerin. She immediately saw where the glowing fruit was being obscured, but she didn't need the lights to identify the threats.

There were two forms out in the field walking toward them. They were taller than goblins, and taller than the Ganna trees as well. They were making no effort to conceal themselves or their movement. Attia felt sick as they drew closer and the truth became unmistakable. "Stars above, it's them, isn't it?" she said. She didn't bother turning to Felerin for confirmation. She knew, deep down, that the walking bodies were the corpses of the farmer and his wife.

"Vargus, to me! Darach, guard the rear!" Felerin shouted as she reached for her bow. It looked like the forms would be on them soon. Felerin lined up her shot, but at this distance, she'd have no way to see the farmers clearly enough to know if they were truly dead. Attia knew in her heart that they were. She knew that Felerin was wasting her opportunity to pound arrows into their dead bodies before they reached the camp, but at the same time, she couldn't blame her mentor. What if it was just an old wives' tale after all? What if the farmers fought off the goblins and ran and hid or something and they were just now coming to the group for safety?

Vargus moved in front of everyone and settled into a defensive stance as the farmers shuffled toward them. The pair was only one tree away when there was finally enough light to see them clearly. There was no blood, and no visible wounds to mark them as dead, but they were dead, nonetheless. Their eyes were milky and sightless, and their bodies moved in a graceless shuffling manner. Worse still, their skin was faded and nearly white. The only exception was their hands, where their fingernails turned a rusty, sickly brown.

"What the hell?" Vargus whispered. He was held frozen for a moment as he saw them clearly for the first time. That moment of hesitation was all it took for the two corpses to lurch forward, closing the distance alarmingly quickly. The male corpse approached on Vargus's side and clawed and ripped at his shield. He failed to make it past it, but with the shield held, the other corpse passed Vargus's guard easily. It swung at the soldier's head and neck, tearing a deep cut across the already scarred left side of his face.

"So.... cold," the veteran soldier panted, and Attia saw thin lines of frost form on the man's face where the thing clawed him. Vargus swung his shield back and forth trying to dislodge the corpse while he desperately tried to push the farmer's dead wife away, but she was already too close.

Attia cried out and danced to the left of Vargus to find an angle. Her options were limited with the walking corpse holding on to the armored soldier, but she crouched low, and cut even lower. Her sword sliced into the dead woman's calf, biting into the bone, but not cutting cleanly through like she did so easily with the goblin. Something about this dead flesh was supernaturally strong.

The cut unbalanced the dead woman, and Vargus took advantage of it. He pushed as the dead woman's leg buckled, breaking her grip on him. He staggered back, pulling the male corpse that still clung to his shield along with him. Liam moved next to Vargus, shouting, "Flip around, I'll cover your back." Attia risked a glance back and understood. Tessa and Felerin were in position to fire. Once Vargus turned, both archers would have clear shots with little risk of hurting Vargus because of the position of his shield.

"Do it, Vargus," she shouted as she turned to face the dead woman she just cut, but she was too late. The farmer's wife slashed down at her with one clawed hand, tearing through her tunic and ripping a cut across her shoulder. Attia immediately felt an exhausting cold surge through her body. She tried to roll backward and away, but her muscles were sluggish and unresponsive. The cold was like nothing she ever felt before.

She looked up in horror as the corpse swung down at her face with both clawed hands, but the swing never finished. Liam dove, shield first, into the farmer's dead wife. Normally, a young man of Liam's size and weight would have easily knocked someone aside, but the walking corpse was stronger and faster than a body ordinarily could be. Liam knocked her back far enough that she wasn't able to complete her swing, but little more than that.

"Get up!" Attia shouted to herself as she forced her frozen muscles to move again. She made it up to a crouch just as the dead woman lunged at her again. She knew it would exhaust her, but she was too sluggish to dodge otherwise. Attia relaxed, completely surrendering to her balance magic. As the corpse swiped down and across with both hands, she fell to the side, letting her magic move her body where her muscles otherwise wouldn't. She concentrated on holding her sword even, edge out, and was rewarded as her magic spun her out of the way of the swipe, drawing her sword across the corpse's belly in a deep, clean cut.

The corpse staggered back a step. Liam regained his feet and advanced buying Attia the time and space she needed to recover. She felt waves of fatigue wash over her from using so much magic, but she didn't have time to think about it. She climbed back to her feet, turning towards Vargus in time to see the corpse of the husband slide off the veteran's shield and to the ground, a half dozen or more arrows sticking out of its back.

"Circle around, Liam. Force it to turn," shouted Vargus as he moved past Attia to form a wall. Attia understood immediately. The two soldiers would box the corpse between their shields so that the archers could shoot it like they had the other one.

Attia took a few steps back as both Felerin and Tessa fired arrow after arrow into the corpse of the farmer's wife. It fell to the ground after the fourth arrow, but each of them fired another for good measure.

Attia's sense of relief and joy quickly turned to terror, though. She caught a faint shadow of motion, near the two women sending arrows into the downed corpse of the farmer's wife. Something small and as black as midnight entered the camp. It was behind the two archers. They hadn't seen it. She saw Darach turning, having finally noticed, but everyone seemed to be in slow motion compared to the tiny dead girl, with skin as black as oil.

Attia screamed and watched in paralyzed horror as the ebony skinned dead girl leapt on Tessa, driving her to the ground. It immediately began ripping at Tessa's back. At first, it looked like it wasn't doing any real harm. Tessa's tunic didn't rip, but it slowly, inexorably started to turn red. Attia felt sick as the realization dawned on her. The creature's claws were razor sharp. The tunic hadn't ripped. The creature's claws sliced cleanly though the tunic and into Tessa's back.

"No!" shouted Russell from somewhere off to the side. "Please, no!"

Attia moved forward, shouting, "Do something, Darach!" The soldier was shocked, or in a daze. Perhaps the shout helped him to his senses, because he whipped his pole arm around in a wide arc designed to cut the creature clean off of Tessa's back.

The creature was oblivious to everything but the girl beneath it. It swept its claws across Tessa's back again and again, its arms moving impossibly fast. Darach's pole arm caught it squarely in the side, cutting deep. Amazingly, the little midnight dead girl wasn't knocked off of Tessa by the wide swing. Attia wanted to cry. A swing like that would have carved a goat in two, and yet it didn't even move the undead thing. She shouted and threw her body at the creature, drawing her magically sharpened blade in a diagonal arc.

She hit the girl right where the neck and collarbone met. Attia's sword cut into the thing, cleaving all the way to the sternum. The little girl's head and neck slipped to the side at an odd angle, but she kept ripping into Tessa. Attia was so close now. She could see the dead girl's features. It was clearly Claudia. Her face looked mostly like it had in life, the only difference being that her skin was pitch black.

Attia tried to pull her sword free, but it held fast, stuck in the dead girl's sternum. Rivers of blood flowed from Tessa's back onto the muddy ground. Attia knew that her friend was dead. Worse, the corpse of Claudia knew it too. It abruptly stopped tearing into Tessa and looked up. Attia's blood ran cold as it looked at her. Attia panicked and tried to free her sword, again to no avail.

"No!" shouted Russell. "Damn you, no! Burn, you bastard, burn!" he shouted. Attia's heart pounded as she let go of her sword and tried to crawl back away from the creature that just killed Tessa. It crawled after her, but as it did, it was struck in the side by a thick bolt of liquid fire. Its black, oily skin erupted into flame, but it kept crawling. Attia scrambled as fast as she could, desperate to get away as another bolt of thick molten fire slammed into the creature.

The corpse of Claudia smoldered and wailed as it continued to crawl after Attia, but the fires weakened and slowed it. Both Vargus and Liam moved in front of it, preventing it from continuing its chase. Darach was behind it now, with his pole arm held high, ready to impale it, but there was no need. Even though his own hands and forearms were burning, Russell was there, hurling yet another gout of flame into the dead body of Claudia.

The fires swelled and grew, and the body of Claudia finally rested.

21
Russell

Even as the bald man with the walking stick carefully worked on his burned and blistered hands, Russell couldn't get the images out of his head. He kept seeing that thing ripping and tearing at Tessa's back. The fiery bolts he conjured and sent into the corpse of Claudia were well beyond his skills. Had he been more skilled, those gouts of flame would've initially formed a few inches from his hands. The first blast of flame behaved correctly. He lost control of the second one, and it sprung into being on his hands. The third was even worse. It formed on his forearms and burned all the way across his wrists and hands before incinerating Tessa's murderer.

The burns were horribly painful, but the bald guy was a skilled healer. Russell knew the man's name was Joshua, but he also knew he'd eventually forget that. Bald guy was a name he'd remember. Conner was there watching and learning as the bald guy poured healing energy into Russell's charred skin. It felt cool and soothing as the magic coaxed the blisters to slowly drain back into his body and the angry red burns to fade. When it was done, Russell's hands were tender, but he'd live.

Tessa wouldn't. The corpse stripped most of the muscle from her back as it clawed through into her viscera. Russell saw it happen again and again in his mind's eye. It was all he could see when he tried to remember her now. Not her auburn hair, or her soft smile, or the music of her laughter. No, it was the sight of her bloody back being fileted, and it was too late now to take another look at her. After the group took what was left of her out into the fields and burned her, there was nothing left of Tessa's body to see.

Malcolm pored through the book he'd been reading since the moment they arrived at this accursed farm. He said he believed the farmers' corpses were ghouls, and that Claudia was a wight. There was something about stronger spirits leading to stronger living dead, and about how the necromancers who made these must have been very skilled. Russell let most of those details drift by him. Malcolm said both types of living dead were hurt by fire. That was the only detail that mattered to him. If he knew that a few hours ago, maybe he could have saved Tessa.

It took the Pathfinders and Malcolm time to sort out what happened. The ghouls approached carelessly, but the wight deliberately approached by walking up the irrigation trench that led to the camp. It hadn't been moving in front of any of the Ganna fruit so there were no points of green light fading in and out with which to notice it. Given how small Claudia was, and that the wight's skin was pitch black, Attia had almost zero chance of spotting it while it approached.

Malcolm surmised that the ghouls were probably just sent into the fields. Living dead literally see life and will naturally seek it out. As long as the necromancer could get far enough away and out of sight before releasing his control, he wouldn't have needed to take the risk of remaining during the attack. The ghouls would have seen living things and attacked with no need for direction. The wight, on the other hand, moved carefully and deliberately. Whatever necromancer animated it was likely following close behind it, controlling it.

The revelations of how the attack was coordinated, coupled with the fact that the goblins previously collected the bodies of their own dead, put an end to any serious thoughts of farming. They removed two of the wall sections and cut them into long poles and positioned them all around the camp as torches. If fire hurt the walking dead, having more of it around must've seemed appealing to everyone.

The night grew cold and still as the group struggled to master their fears of what might be out there, crawling in the darkness. Russell passed the time by observing how different people dealt with it. The Pathfinders shifted from standing and watching to a constant walking patrol around the camp, the thought being that the changing angles eliminated the blind spots created by the irrigation trenches. Malcolm thumbed through his books, looking for details that might be of further assistance. Conner, Eliana and the bald guy grouped together, visiting each person with magical healing and insect repelling herbal pastes for anyone who might need it. Glenn cried softly by the fire. The group burned his brother's body out in the fields, like they had with Tessa. Russell didn't think he was handling it all that well. In contrast, Jonin ignored everything and went back to farming Ganna. It made sense. It's what he did all his life. Russell guessed that it brought the man a little peace and comfort, given how much he'd lost. He decided that he liked Jonin.

Eventually, the darkness gave way to a gradual glowing light on the horizon, above the tree line. Everyone looked exhausted and ragged, but Russell couldn't help but notice the smiles and the tremendous sense of relief. They made it through the night, and within an hour, the sun would be overhead to warm them and hopefully wipe away some of the fear and dread Russell felt.

There was a large argument about whether the group should stay. Darach argued that they should abort the mission. He wanted everyone to pack up and leave now, and Russell agreed.

Felerin was concerned about the goblins ambushing them on the trails. There were many places where the canopy was thick enough to block the sun. For her own safety, she would take a different set of paths to go get help. Those paths were much harder to navigate and some climbing was involved. She didn't think the full group could travel that route.

Vargus was adamant they finish the mission. He said the Chancellor made him swear an oath that no matter how things went on the farm, the group must see the mission through to completion.

To the surprise of most, it was Jonin, not Vargus who made the strongest case for staying. He spoke about how his family dedicated their entire lives to planting and harvesting the magical fruit. He spoke about how important Ganna fruit was to their society, and how just a single piece of fruit provides a grown man ample energy for an entire day. He brought his argument home when he asked each person to eat one of the Gannas he harvested the night before. The sweet thick nectar of each bite was like ecstasy to Russell. He never tasted Ganna directly from the field like this. After everyone ate, Jonin reminded them that his entire family died so they could enjoy those pieces of fruit. Felerin and Darach gave up their arguments after that, and Russell decided that he no longer liked Jonin.

Felerin left after that with a promise to return before sunset with the best help she could find. The work began shortly thereafter. Eliana and Jonin supervised, helping by sealing the Ganna as they harvested it, while Attia patrolled the fields and the surrounding trails. Originally, there was the promise of rest breaks, and they allowed anyone who asked for one to sleep for a few hours, but with Malcolm's treasure trove of Camphor Berries to rely on, only Glenn and Darach took the opportunity.

The camp settled itself into an efficient rhythm. The group filled sled after sled with the vibrant fruit, and it soon became apparent that they needed some place to stack it. Vargus and Darach ventured over to the shacks around midmorning and braved the stench of the decomposing donkeys to see about salvaging the carts. By using axles from each, they made one cart functional. It was past noon before they completed the repairs and wheeled the cart out to a dry patch of ground along the edge of the field. It wasn't ideal, and there was some fear the cart might be difficult to pull clear of the mud once it was fully loaded, but no one wanted to store the harvest anywhere near a group of decomposing donkeys.

Felerin and another woman arrived with an hour of daylight left. They brought with them a slightly smaller cart than the one repaired earlier in the day, pulled by a team of three donkeys. They moved their cart and donkeys over to where the group positioned theirs, and everyone stopped farming and walked over to meet with them.

Russell envisioned more than a single person coming to help them, but as he got closer, He noticed a few things that reassured him. Based on the way she was dressed, she was obviously a Pathfinder. She was older and much more muscular than Felerin. Instead of carrying a bow, she wore a pair of slender swords. The way she walked and the way she held herself rang of confidence and experience.

"Vargus, this is Pathmaker Constance, one of the leaders of our order," said Felerin.

Vargus whistled quietly and said, "Pathmaker, eh. Pleased to have you. I trust Felerin had time to fill you in during the journey?"

Constance nodded as she studied each person. "Has the day been safe?" she asked.

Vargus scratched his scar. "Darach and I lost our breakfasts getting that damn cart free from a lake of maggot infested donkey soup, but other than that, we done fine." He grinned and pointed to the full cart of Ganna fruit, and the half dozen other piles on the ground ready to be loaded onto the new cart.

"Felerin, go pull your Pathwalker in from patrol," said Constance. "We have another hour of light. There are a lot of preparations to make, and little time to make them," she said as she retrieved a large pack from the back of their cart.

22
Liam

His father often said that every soldier had their own way of getting ready for battle. Some continuously sharpened their weapons or polished their armor. Some ate a special meal. Some stretched, while others sang songs. Liam never thought about how he'd prepare. His stomach was in knots and his hands were shaky. He was nervous and scared. He always assumed those sorts of rituals were what soldiers did to distract themselves from the fear. Now he understood it firsthand.

Constance wasted no time preparing their camp for an attack. She sent Attia and Vargus to cut more barrier walls from the other shacks. With the additional walls, she was able to make a larger defensive area for the main camp, with single entrance points on each side. There was enough leftover wood to place a small defensive wall out in the field, ten yards from each entrance. The goblins could take advantage of the walls too, but nearly all of them would have bows. Felerin was the only archer left in camp, so anything that provided cover would hurt the goblins far more than it hurt them.

Setting up torches throughout the field became a priority. Liam thought Constance did a good job placing them. The goblins could disable them easily, of course, but it meant there'd be no element of surprise. Either they'd be visible in the torchlight, or the group would notice as they extinguished the torches.

Constance also set up three additional fire pits within the camp so the work could continue after dark. Liam was pretty sure her decision was more about morale. Having the warmth and light of the fires brought people together and led to a few conversations.

No one knew when the attack would come, or if an attack would even happen at all, but the thought of sitting and waiting for it all night made Liam queasy. He was supposed to be a soldier and yet the fear was getting to him. Liam couldn't imagine how everyone else was dealing with the stress. He wanted to reassure his brother and his friends, but he didn't know what to say to make things better.

The more Liam thought it, through, the less convinced he was there'd even be an attack. It made little sense. The farmers coexisted in relative peace for years with the goblins up here. He understood, with the Black Tide coming, everything would change, but why was it so important to the goblins to continue their attacks? They killed the farmers already. If they just wanted the Ganna, they could have stolen what was in the carts instead of attacking. They wouldn't even need to do that, though. Come tomorrow morning, the group would be leaving. They could only harvest a small part of the field. There'd be plenty left for the goblins if that was all they were after.

Liam approached Malcolm and his brother, who were sitting near one of the fires. "None of this makes any sense. Why are they attacking? I mean, what do they want?"

Malcolm continued reading. Liam was used to that response from Malcolm lately, but Conner frowned and said, "Ellie and I talked about that earlier. It can't be about the Ganna. There's no way we're getting all of this out of here with just two carts."

"Maybe they think more carts and farming teams will be on the way, and they're trying to scare us away," said Liam.

Conner nodded. "That could be it," he said as he held his hands out to warm them by the fire. "That explains the first attack, at least. Maybe even the one with the risen dead. Stars above, I'm certainly scared."

Liam smiled. "So am I, little brother. Let's hope that's all it is, and they leave us alone tonight. We can pack up at first light, leave them the farm, and put this grisly matter behind us."

"I think they'll attack tonight," said Malcolm. His voice had that distant quality to it again. Liam was growing frustrated with what he was coming to equate as two different versions of Malcolm. Part of him just wanted to walk away, but much of what Malcolm warned them about came to pass.

Liam's father hinted at spirits living within other bodies, and Malcolm's sudden deep understanding of necromancy and the spiritual world couldn't just be from a night working with the Chancellor and a few hours of reading a book. Everything changed after Shivertusk and that white mist. Maybe the boar was possessed by something and when it died, the spirit possessed Malcolm?

"They're coming!" shouted Attia.

"Damn," spat Liam as he stood up and looked out into the field to the west. The goblins took great care to hide their approach the previous night, but Pathmaker Constance's placement of the torches throughout the field convinced them to abandon that tactic entirely. The goblins were organized into three groups, with roughly ten of them in each.

From this distance, it looked to Liam like the central group was the command team. A small cluster of four goblins with pale white skin shuffled along in front of them as a vanguard. Liam was certain they were ghouls, just like what the farmers were the other night. The six goblins behind them were much better armed than the rest. Instead of spears and bows, some carried halberds and others had traditional swords and shields. Each of them wore armor composed of carved wooden plates.

The teams to both the left and right of the command group were much more like the goblins they faced during the initial attack. Bows, spears and little more than loincloths for armor. They broke out into a jog, fanning out to either side as they moved closer. Liam thought he understood their strategy. They'd surround the encampment and try to fire arrows into the camp. If the defensive walls failed to keep the arrows off of the group, the fight would be over before it began. The group would have no choice but to run out into the waiting arms of the ghouls or back out the seemingly safe eastern exit.

Liam immediately understood. He turned and ran to the east and found Vargus and Joshua defending that opening in the wall. "Expect some action! They're trying to flush us out this direction." he shouted. The veteran soldier banged his sword against his shield in acknowledgement.

"To arms!" Vargus shouted.

Liam heard a chorus of whistling and staccato thumps as arrows started flying from both the north and south at their makeshift fortifications. He heard the splashes as a few arced over the walls. He was relieved to not have heard any screams from the initial volley.

"Felerin, fire now!" Constance shouted over the cacophony of arrows thudding into wooden walls. They anticipated that living dead would be involved. Felerin was set up right next to a campfire with several cloth-wrapped, oil-soaked arrows, but Liam couldn't afford to focus on that. His worst fears were confirmed.

Even as he was running to join Vargus, he saw the three goblins with skin as dark as coal sprinting through the field. Wights. Just like the little dead girl, Claudia, who attacked the night before. He never got a chance to appreciate how fast a wight could move. Compared to the shuffling of the sickly pale ghouls, the wights moved with a fluid grace.

Vargus stepped forward, blocking the entrance to their camp just as the closest wight leapt for it. He took the entire force of the charge on his shield. The small corpse was supernaturally dense. Vargus cried out in pain and slid nearly two feet from the force of the impact.

Liam watched in horror as a second oily black wight crawled its way through the gap. His heart raced as he rushed forward to engage it, locking his shield as close to Vargus's as he could. He felt the heavy impact as it slammed both arms repeatedly against his shield. "More torches. We need someone back here with torches!" he shouted, struggling to keep his shield in position.

Vargus stabbed at the undead goblin from beneath his shield and it looked like he was having some success. Liam hadn't been able to get his body turned to the side behind his shield, and holding the wight off was getting increasingly difficult. It was just too strong for him. He cried out as he tried to push it back, but as he strained, it got its hands beneath the shield.

It reached out and sliced its claws across his thighs. He coughed as freezing cold raced through his body, knocking the wind right out of him. It was like getting punched in the solar plexus. He struggled and gasped, trying to regain his breath. That moment of weakness was all the wight needed to press its advantage. It surged forward beneath the shield, its unbelievable weight slamming into his hips.

Liam felt like his heart would burst out of his chest as he fell to his back. The thing started clawing and ripping at his belly. His chainmail slowed the claws down, but he could feel pain and wetness in a few places already. It would only get worse. He looked around franticly. Vargus impaled his, but his blade appeared stuck. He was desperately struggling to rip and twist his blade free as the third inky black corpse leapt into the camp, slamming into the veteran soldier's legs as it clawed at him. Joshua had one hand braced against Vargus's back, and Liam saw a warm golden white light pulsing where Joshua touched the soldier.

Liam let his sword go and grabbed his shield with both hands. He slammed it down onto the undead goblin's head again and again as he begged his battlemagic to strengthen his muscles enough to keep the wight from ripping his innards from his body. He felt his chainmail splitting and tearing. Liam felt his skin rip and bleed. He screamed and kept slamming his shield into the thing over and over, hoping that the wight would falter before he did.

He looked over to Vargus, praying that there'd be help from the grizzled veteran, but things weren't going much better for him. Vargus was knocked down also. It looked as if the impaled wight was failing. It twitched and moved a little, but it mounted no attack. Both of the undead goblins were on top of Vargus, though. Liam knew that it'd be all but impossible for the man to move under that much weight, and the unwounded wight was working its claws into the gaps of the veteran's armor.

Liam heard shouting and saw flashes of orange light. Was someone near him with a torch? He cried out as he felt the chainmail over his stomach finally fall away. If he could turn on to his side, he'd at least have some armor again. He desperately kept slamming his shield into the wight as he tried to roll to the right. He kicked his legs and twisted with what little strength he had left and rolled to his side. He was facing Vargus. He saw the old soldier frantically punching at the wight that was holding him down. The other one wasn't moving anymore. Sadly, Joshua wasn't moving either. He was laying on his back, with one eye open and a slender arrow protruding from the other.

"Hold on, brother," screamed Conner as he dove and then crawled to him. Liam saw that his brother's right hand was pulsing with a faint white light. Liam's breathing was weak and labored, but he felt better almost immediately when Conner touched him. The wight was still on him. It was clawing at the armor on his side. The creature was moving so slowly now, but Liam didn't think it would be long before it would rip into his side.

Russell entered Liam's field of vision. The boy was holding a small jug, and cautiously moving between the two downed warriors. He poured the contents of the jug over both of the wights as carefully as he could with his shaking hands. He must be terrified, thought Liam. Hell, everyone should be terrified.

"Ellie! Make fire. Do it now!" shouted Conner.

A tiny puff of fire sprung into being on top of the wight that was attacking Vargus. The fire quickly danced across the oil coating its back before erupting into a raging inferno. The wight twisted and writhed, and Liam felt an intense blast of heat as the wight on top of him also caught fire. It clawed at him one more time before it fell off of him to sputter and burn.

23
Malcolm

Malcolm flinched. He felt the wooden barrier vibrate against his back as arrow after arrow slammed into it. The goblins were attacking. Deep down, he knew why they were attacking. He could feel the presence of the other spirit. He rose to a crouch so he could see the group of advancing ghouls and goblins. He squinted and, despite the darkness, saw it.

Wispy shadows danced within one of the goblins in the forward group. Surprisingly enough, it wasn't one of the more heavily armored ones. The feeling grew stronger as Malcolm became certain of what he was seeing. There was a spirit within that goblin. It was like him, and he could feel it. It looked right at him and flashed him a wicked smile. It could feel him as well.

"*Yes, it can feel you. Its spirit is strong, and it wants to get stronger,*" said the voice inside his head. "*This entire attack was never about some damn fruit. Why do you think the old man sent us out here? He knew what we'd find.*"

Malcolm didn't want to believe it, but it was hard to argue. He could've studied much more efficiently back at the Citadel. It was no coincidence that his new knowledge proved important up here, given the presence of the goblin necromancers. The Chancellor spoke of being able to see the future in his dreams. The spirit was right. Arronhelm knew what they'd find up here on this farm. 'What do we do about it?' he thought.

"Why, we kill it, of course. We do the same thing to it that it wants to do to us," whispered the voice in response.

Malcolm watched Felerin send burning arrows dancing across the night sky at the ghouls shuffling toward them. She missed with the first two, but her third shot struck one of the ghouls right in the chest. The fire spread rapidly across its body. The other ghouls lurched to the side, away from the burning one. They were being directed to move away from the fire.

Shouts came from behind and Malcolm spared a second to look. Both Vargus and Liam were standing together with their shields locked. They were being attacked by wights. Arrows kept thumping into the makeshift defensive walls all around Malcolm, forcing him to crouch. He saw an arrow strike Jonin in the arm.

By the time he turned back to the forward group, the first burning ghoul was no longer moving, and Felerin managed to ignite a second one. The other two, however, were crawling in the water of one of the irrigation trenches. The rest of the western group of goblins were advancing much more quickly now. Malcolm estimated that the goblins were twenty yards away, and the ghouls only half that distance.

Constance seemed calm as she watched the group advance. "Darach and Attia. Stay here and deal with the ghouls when they arrive. Felerin, start picking off their archers. We want them to run once their command group falls." She sprinted out of the encampment without another word, past the burning ghoul and the other two that were crawling. It took her only a few seconds to make it to the goblins.

Constance moved like lightning! She fought like Attia did, spinning to avoid strikes and to add power to her swings, but instead of a single long blade, she wielded two shorter blades, one in each hand. The first goblin to engage her chopped downward with its halberd. She side stepped it and spun, one blade cutting cleanly across its neck, while the other blade lashed out and down, causing a nearby goblin to yelp in pain as a deep cut appeared across one of its thighs. She was moving between and around them so quickly that the goblins were having difficulties lining up their own attacks.

"*Excellent,*" the voice gloated. "*She'll do the work for us...*" Malcolm shut the voice out as he felt the rage building inside him. He felt used and dirty. The goblins only attacked to get at him. The deaths of Tessa, the farmers, and who knew who else by night's end would be on his hands. Deep down, he knew it wasn't his fault. How could he have known? Still, he wasn't going to gloat about it.

"Here they come," grunted Darach, taking a few steps back from the entrance, making room so that both he and Attia could act. The first ghoul through was the one that was burned. It used an irrigation trench to extinguish itself, but it looked absolutely grisly. Scorched, bubbled flesh hung in lose patches from its torso, and its seared innards reeked horribly. It didn't make it too far, though. Darach was ready, and a single swing of his pole arm put an end to the horrific creature.

The other two shuffled in behind the first. They moved deceptively fast when they lunged forward. The first was on Darach before he recovered from his swing. Malcolm saw frost form on the soldier's armor where it grabbed him. The man gasped, unprepared for the freezing paralysis the ghoul's touch carried with it.

The second one lunged at Attia, but she danced back and thrust her blade out as it closed on her. Her sword bit into the ghoul's abdomen, but the thing kept walking forward. It reached out, swinging at her. She ducked beneath the swing and sprung back, pulling her blade free. Attia continued her motion and spun, drawing her weapon in a long, wide arc that cut a deep river into the thing's belly.

She was slowing down rapidly. She seemed to be tiring. Malcolm assumed that she was relying on her magic to keep herself from being touched. He didn't know how long she'd be able to keep it up.

Fortunately, she didn't need to. Jonin ran into the ghoul, screaming. He wrapped his arms around its waist and tried to pull it to him, not understanding its supernatural density. Its claws raked across his shoulders and neck, spilling arterial blood almost immediately.

Malcolm didn't think the farmer wanted to live. His family and his life's work were gone. He probably wanted to die up here on the farm, with the rest of everything he ever knew. His sacrifice gave Attia the time she needed to get into position and line up her swing. She hit the ghoul squarely in the back, right beneath its ribcage. Her blade sliced it cleanly in two. Its top half fell to the ground and Jonin's body landed right next to it. Neither would ever move again.

Darach cried out for help, and Attia raced to him. The soldier managed to work the point of his pole arm into the chest of the ghoul, and he wedged the butt end of his weapon into the twisted trunk of a Ganna tree. As he back pedaled away from the ghoul, it impaled itself on the weapon. That didn't stop the living corpse, though, and Darach was now nearly pinned with his back against the tree. The pole arm held the ghoul still, so once again, Attia could take her time lining up a swing. She hit it in the back, right beneath the ribs. The ghoul was cut cleanly in two.

With the ghouls dealt with, Malcolm checked on Constance. Something within him wanted him to watch. He knew what that something was. His head was aching from the effort of blocking out its words, so he relaxed and let it return to the forefront of his mind. "*She's fighting it. Can you feel the goblin drawing upon its strength*?"

Constance had dealt with all five of the other goblins by the time Malcolm got back into position to watch. The ground around her was littered with sickly yellow blood and dead goblins, but she didn't even have a scratch on her. The remaining goblin wasn't alone. Malcolm saw two bodies of swirling darkness on either side of the goblin necromancer.

"*Wraiths,*" whispered the voice. "*He's brought wraiths across to keep her at bay. If she gives him too much time, he'll force those wraiths into the bodies of the dead, and they will rise again as ghouls.*"

Malcolm watched as both of the spirits dove towards Constance. The way in which the wraiths gracefully floated and swirled as they moved was both terrible and beautiful. One passed a long slender arm of shadow through her and she cried out in pain. She was quick enough to roll sideways and avoid the other. Both wraiths immediately adjusted and pursued her, but she was fast enough to sprint in and execute cuts with both of blades against the goblin before the wraiths could get to her again.

The first cut hit the goblin in the shoulder. Her sword sliced deeply, painting a line of yellow as the wound instantly gushed blood. The other cut looked to catch the goblin lower, right above the waist, but it never hit the mark. Constance's blade held in midair, her cut stopped by an invisible force. Malcolm felt a brief pulse of spiritual energy. It felt as if his heart skipped a beat.

"*You feel it, don't you?*" the voice asked. "*She got to him before he could coax his wraiths into the dead. He's beaten. The spirit is using what power it has to protect its host.*"

Are there limits? Can it keep doing that? What else can it do? Malcolm's mind was racing with questions now. Were these things he'd be able to do? His heart skipped another beat, and then another, as Constance struck at the goblin necromancer with both blades. Both strikes were deflected by that invisible force again.

"*There are limits to everything, boy,*" whispered the spirit. "*Costs as well. Your friends and all these farmers... consider the lives they lost the cost for what we're about to gain.*"

The wraiths gracefully swung their long, thin shadowy arms at Constance, but the Pathmaker fluidly danced and moved out of the way of each. She was letting her magic guide her out of the path of the wraiths' icy touches. All the while, she kept striking at the necromancer. Another attack was magically deflected, and then another. The next swing, however, passed through the goblin. It was as if his flesh became an insubstantial mist, or something like the spirit-stuff of the shadowy wraiths. At the same time, one of the two wraiths melted into nothingness.

"*The spirit is too exhausted to protect him now. He's been forced to rely on his necromancy to save him from that strike, but the effort tired him. He lost his focus, and the Astral reclaimed one of his precious wraiths,*" the voice gloated.

With only one wraith left to harass her, Constance all but ignored it. She struck again and again at the goblin. Her first few swings passed through it without so much as leaving a mark as it protected itself with its magic, but eventually, the goblin became too exhausted to do even that. The second wraith faded back into the Astral, and Constance's cuts started to leave marks. The goblin necromancer screamed in pain as

Constance ran it through with both blades. It stood there for a moment, not looking at her, but at Malcolm, in shocked disbelief before it fell.

A cloud of white mist burst forth from the goblin as it hit the ground. The cloud didn't blast out in all directions as it had with the boar. Instead, it coalesced into a tight, thin stream that flowed directly to Malcolm. The mist struck him in the chest. It passed through his bones and flesh like they weren't even there, and Malcolm felt pure ecstasy, his heart racing as he felt the spirit within him exalt and grow.

"*Oh,*" said the voice in Malcolm's head after a few moments, "*you'll need to go through its possessions. It has something we'll need if we're to further your training.*"

24
Felerin

The goblin archers broke and ran even before the last of their western command group fell. Felerin shot four of the archers on the northern flank. While the goblins' arrows were weak and poorly aimed, most of Felerin's shots were deadly accurate.

Constance was what truly broke their spirit. She charged their leadership team, alone, and immediately started dropping them. Felerin hadn't been able to spare more than a few glances over to that battle, but she noticed that five of the six goblins in the command team dropped within the first fifteen seconds.

The last goblin was stronger than the rest. It must have been the one raising all the dead, as it summoned living shadows to defend itself. That goblin likely had strong defensive spells. Constance was having trouble hurting it. In the end, though, it died like any other goblin. There was something odd about the way it fell to the ground, but Felerin couldn't quite put her finger on it. It was like a memory on the tip of her tongue that she couldn't coax out. She thought she saw some kind of white mist, but that couldn't be it.

Felerin found it odd when Malcolm later went out into the field and rummaged through the dead goblin's pouches. He returned with a small leather case. Vargus warned her earlier to expect some strange behaviors from the boy. He said the Chancellor was sending this boy on his own mission, and that no one was to interfere. Fortunately, most of Malcolm's friends were tolerant of the boy's strange demeanor. Poor Glenn was almost comatose ever since they burned his brother's corpse. She and Vargus could look the other way easily enough. Darach didn't seem to care about much, other than making it home in one piece, and she warned Constance about Malcolm on their journey out to the farm.

Cleaning up after the battle was hard on all of them. Losing Joshua was a complete surprise and made caring for the others more difficult. Both Vargus and Darach pulled through the fight with minimal wounds. Their armor protected them from the worst of it, and other than being exhausted, Constance was unharmed. Liam, on the other hand, suffered a series of nasty slashes across his abdomen. His intestines were exposed in one place, but fortunately nothing was ruptured.

Eliana and Conner came together as a relatively effective healing team. Conner's build was so slight and delicate that he needed someone to help him, and despite being on the shorter side, Eliana was surprisingly strong for a little girl. She grew up on a Ganna farm, so the overall thickness of her build made sense. The two of them tended to each person in turn. Eliana made small talk while applying herbal compounds to each wound while Conner used his magic to search for deeper injuries that needed more than herbal remedies to address.

Later that night, they burned their dead in a large bonfire out in the middle of the Ganna field. Felerin thought it might have been nice to burn Jonin over by the disassembled shacks that were his home, but no one wanted to brave the stench of rotting donkeys, and the shacks were closer to the tree line, so safety was also a concern.

The dawn brought a tremendous sense of relief. While no one expected any more aggression from the goblins, the morning sun made it a reality. They survived the ordeal. They loaded the extra piles of Ganna fruit into the second cart, leaving a little room on one side for Liam to sit. Conner demanded his brother ride back to the Citadel. Liam protested, insisting he was capable of walking. The brothers argued over it until Constance got fed up and ended the discussion, siding with Conner.

The first hours of travel were slow. Felerin was left with the responsibility of leading the caravan through the trails. Constance pulled Attia aside shortly after the group departed and the two of them went off together. Felerin knew they'd be working their way back toward the goblins' elevated city to assess how significant a threat the remaining members of the tribe would be. The Citadel would likely send a group to destroy the remnants of that tribe once the Black Tide returned to its hives.

The attacks made no sense to Felerin. The expedition's intent the entire time was to quickly harvest and leave. There would have been more than enough Ganna for the goblins. Even if there was some kind of bad blood with the farmers, that score should have been more than settled when the goblins killed the farmers. Yet they continued to attack. There had to be some other motivation. With any luck, Constance and Attia would figure it out.

They travelled in silence for the better part of the morning. It was a steamy day, the warmest of the season thus far, and the air was stiflingly hot beneath the thick forest canopy. Eliana started distributing Waterweed to everyone when it became clear the heat would only get worse. Felerin appreciated the gift.

Waterweed came from a small root plant that grew in the swamps to the south. A skilled herbalist could coax the plant to absorb amazing amounts of water, so much so it could be made into a gum that kept a person hydrated for hours on even the hottest of days.

Felerin blushed lightly as she watched Eliana walk away from her. She liked the girl. Maybe they could build a friendship, or something even stronger in a few years when Eliana was old enough.

Constance and Attia caught up to the group when the oppressive heat eventually forced Felerin to give the travelers a break. She left the carts on the path and led the group a couple dozen yards off the main game trail to a naturally occurring cold spring. The Pathfinders knew about many similar springs scattered throughout the forest. On a day like this, everyone appreciated the cold, clean water. Everyone except Malcolm, that is. The strange boy refused to get too close to the spring. Instead, he sat at a distance and watched, his eyes almost closed.

"Pathrunner Felerin," called Constance as she and Attia entered the small clearing with the spring. "I must commend you on your teaching. Pathwalker Attia's skills are well developed. She spotted seven of the eight traps we came across along the way, selected all the appropriate paths when given the responsibility, and she leaves barely a trace when she moves through the forest. I'm really quite impressed."

"Thank you, Pathmaker," said Attia quietly.

Felerin smiled at both her mentor and her apprentice for a moment before bowing her head.

"I think Attia can run," said Constance after a moment of deliberation.

It stunned Felerin. The passage from one rank to another within the Pathfinder order normally happened during the Gifting Festival, which was a three-day celebration that took place after each year's planting. Pathwalkers who wanted to graduate to Pathrunners had dozens of skills to perfect before they were even considered, and nearly half failed to earn advancement on their first attempt. She knew Constance, as a Pathmaker, had the power to bypass those requirements, but it was rare. "Pathmaker Constance. The Gifting Festival is two seasons away. She's done so well, but there are many challenges she needs to complete yet."

Constance arched an eyebrow and Felerin was worried that she may have gone too far in challenging her mentor. "These are trying times, Felerin. I need not see the girl stay awake for a few days or make a bonfire during the rainy season. She knows the paths. She takes her responsibilities seriously. She's fought more terrors in the past week than some of our Pathrunners have seen in their entire lives. Stars above, she's just a teenager and she survived Shivertusk!"

Felerin frowned. Traditionally, each Pathwalker who's looking to move up is assigned a mentor to live and work with for a full month prior to the Gifting Festival. There were so many lessons she wanted to teach Attia, but she couldn't counter Constance's arguments. She sighed in resignation and said, "I guess they aren't kids anymore."

Constance nodded. "Pathrunner Attia. You may choose any Pathmaker's fire to visit this evening to have your leathers dyed." She smiled and turned to Attia. "I would consider it an honor if you would choose mine."

Attia's eyes welled up with tears as she nodded. "Of course. Of course, I will."

"Excellent,' replied Constance. "Then we should keep moving. I think everyone has had enough of a break."

The return trip to the Citadel proved far easier than the trip out to the farm. All of the trails were recently travelled, and most of them with large carts. As a result, any trimming of roots and branches already took place. The animals already fled, and the spots too muddy for a cart were already identified.

Felerin was concerned about what she was seeing to either side of the trails and most especially in the branches above. Routes through the rainforest weren't restricted to the forest floor. Even more defined paths existed in the twisted web of branches that connected each tree to one another, eventually growing into canopy thick enough to block out the sun.

Felerin was cataloging all of the wildlife over the course of her travels. This was her fourth trip along these paths in as many days. Some of the animals she expected to pass were no longer there. She saw signs of disruption in the branches. It was as if some larger creatures passed through, making their own paths at the expense of the ones the native wildlife used for decades.

It was to be expected, of course. As the Black Tide continued to spread to the south along the Serpent, it forced anything that made its home along the great river to flee or die. It was troubling, though. Who knew what beasts would move south? Not all of them would return to their old homes and hunting grounds. Some would decide the hunting was far better in the south. Farmers tended to be easy prey.

Felerin continued to monitor the changes to the local wildlife as they journeyed south toward the Citadel. Over time, the thick forested regions gave way to more and more farms and clearings. Felerin normally felt relaxed and at peace when she travelled these lands, but there was no denying the growing dread she felt.

She reached up to her neck and idly touched her tiny glass pendant necklace. Glenn's parents gave it to her only a few days ago. She liked it, but she didn't deserve it. She failed. Caleb would never see his parents again, and although she saved Glenn, she knew it wouldn't be enough.

It wouldn't ease their grief. By all accounts, what she did to save the boy was heroic, but she should have known that Caleb would run. She could have been closer to him when the attack started, or she should have assigned Attia, or even Liam to look out for the boy. She failed Claudia the same, or even more. Claudia was just a little girl. Of course, she ran.

Her eyes stung as she let her fingers slip beneath the slender chain that held the pendant to her neck. No one ever gave her a gift like that. A pretty trinket. Everything in her life had a defined purpose. The idea of wearing something that didn't help camouflage, of wearing something simply because it was beautiful, never even occurred to her. She bowed her head and carefully removed the pendant. She didn't deserve it.

Felerin took a few steps off the trail and waved for the group to keep moving. She waited as the children and soldiers made their way past. Glenn was walking back next to the cart. She waited for him and stepped on to the trail to walk next to him. She walked quietly for a while before placing the tiny glass necklace in his hands.

"I'm sorry," she mumbled. "Tell your parents I'm so sorry. I wish I'd been able to do more."

25
Eliana

There were still a few hours of daylight left when the group spilled out into the enormous clearing housing the Citadel. Eliana felt utterly exhausted. Seeing all the carts spread out across the clearing, some filled with rice, others with Ganna fruit, made the exhaustion into something entirely worse. She was making herself feel good about the expedition by telling herself how important the work was. Seeing the scores of carts just like theirs in the clearing diminished their efforts. Eliana felt helpless and weak, and for the first time in quite a while, she questioned the wisdom of her professors. Why did they need to harvest that particular farm in the first place? One or two more carts of food wasn't worth the lives it cost them.

She walked alongside Conner in sullen silence. They were checking on Liam often. Conner claimed he needed her help to check the wounds, even though his healing magic told him far more about his brother's health than her skills could. He was so unsure of himself. He needed her for confidence, and that was enough for her.

They crossed a few hundred yards before they were directed to stop and wait with their carts until a quartermaster could inspect the contents. From the look of the number of groups standing around with full carts, Eliana thought it might be a few hours.

Their group dwindled over time. Vargus left to inform the Chancellor of their arrival. Felerin left with Glenn shortly after to find the boy's parents. Eliana didn't mind either of those departures. If this mission was so darn important as to merit putting them in harm's way, the least the Chancellor could do was stop them from having to wait in line, and she respected what Felerin was doing. Glenn shouldn't be forced to answer questions about what happened to Caleb out in that field.

Constance and Attia left next. They were heading to some bonfire for whatever silly ritual was involved in making Attia walk, or run, or whatever they called it. Eliana couldn't remember. She barely paid any attention to the conversation at the spring.

Finally, when Darach was the only adult left, he claimed to be suffering from flu symptoms. Eliana tried to offer him the proper herbal remedy, but he refused. She was sure he was faking his sudden sickness, but there was no sense in pressing the issue. Eliana decided it was better without the adults anyway. It meant the rest of them could talk openly while they waited.

"Why did we even need to go?" she asked.

"I know what you mean," said Conner. "Look at all those carts."

"They didn't need to send us. At least not out to that farm—"

"I'm sure the Chancellor had his reasons," interrupted Liam. "It's best not to question the chain of command. We'll need as much food as we can get if we're going to survive."

"Maybe you're right," answered Conner

"You know, we keep saying we will talk about all this crap, but we're never alone long enough to do it," said Russell. He and Malcolm were leaning against the other side of the cart. They were ever since the cart stopped moving. "So here we are. Just us, with no adults to get in the way. Let's talk."

"Shouldn't we wait? Attia isn't here," said Liam.

"Yeah. She's getting ready to go put on an animal head, dance around a fire and hoot like an owl or something," said Russell with a chuckle. "By the way, anyone else creeped out by the whole Pathfinder thing?"

Eliana giggled and raised her hand. A little bit of comedy did wonders to lighten her mood.

Liam smiled at the joke and nodded. "You're right, this is as good a chance as we're likely to get."

"Okay, then I'll start," said Russell. "I'm hoping Malcolm might answer this. So, anyone else notice white mist shooting out and going just to Malcolm?"

"What are you talking about?" asked Conner.

"At the end of the attack. After we burned the wights."

"Oh. I was on the ground, working on Liam's wounds," said Conner.

Eliana remembered that moment well. Conner was on his knees, trying to heal his brother. Liam was on his side when the wight erupted into flame. Russell, though, was facing the other way back toward the front of camp where the other battle was taking place. "The rest of us were all facing away, Russell. We didn't see it."

Liam grunted as he sat upright and scooted himself back in the cart so he could see everyone without having to turn too far. "Malcolm?" Liam waited for just a few breaths before clapping his hands in front of Malcolm's face. Eliana startled. She hadn't expected it, but maybe it was what was necessary.

"Sorry, I was thinking," said Malcolm. "What were you asking?"

"The white mist. I didn't imagine that, right?" asked Russell. "No one else seemed to see it."

"No. You didn't imagine it. It was there. It went straight into me. It felt," Malcolm paused a moment as if deciding what to say. "It felt great."

"Did anyone else ask you about it? Constance, Felerin and Darach were right there. And what about Attia?"

"Attia saw it. She knows. She just didn't want to bring it up. As for the others... it's almost as if they couldn't see it at all. Or maybe they just forgot about it right away?"

Eliana couldn't believe what she was hearing. Why had the mist just gone into Malcolm? Was everyone else too far away from it? No, that couldn't be it. Constance was the one who killed the goblin. "That makes little sense," she blurted out.

"None of this does, Ellie," said Conner as he placed his hand on her shoulder to calm her.

"Malcolm," started Liam tentatively, "I know a lot has happened over the past few days. I get that you have some secret training going on with the Chancellor, but we're worried about you. You're just not the same person anymore. We were all out there with you. First for the boar, and now this messy matter at the farm. It seems like we're likely to be there with you in the coming days. You know a lot more than you're telling us. I think you owe us an explanation."

Malcolm stood quietly for a moment as if he hadn't even heard the request. Eliana could see Russell getting emotional and angry until he slammed his fist into the side of the cart and growled, "Fire and smoke, you cock, Tessa died out there!"

"I know," said Malcolm, his voice barely a whisper. "I'm just trying to find the right words. The ones that won't make it all worse."

"Just say what needs to be said. Don't worry about us," said Liam, his tone gentle.

"I started seeing things after the boar. During that whole walk home, I was seeing shadows, or ghosts, but it was more than that. There was this blinding headache, and this voice. I was the only one hearing it, though. The voice was in my head."

Eliana listened carefully. She remembered walking with him and leading him through the woods that afternoon. His eyes seemed so wild, like he was seeing things. What he was saying now at least made his behavior make sense. She wondered if, sometimes, it was the voice speaking instead of Malcolm. It would explain how he knew things he couldn't otherwise have known. "Malcolm, is the voice still with you? Can you tell us what it is?" she asked.

"Some kind of spirit," he said, but he quickly started rubbing his forehead and temples as if in pain. "Soul, not spirit. There's a difference."

Eliana thought back to the conversation between Liam and Malcolm that she casually overheard the night before the first attack. There was something about souls losing themselves and becoming just spirits, and there was something else about bodies. A spirit in a body wouldn't get pulled back. She twirled the thoughts around in her head and suddenly, they made sense.

"The conversation out in the fields," she blurted out.

"Huh?" asked Malcolm, still holding his head. "We didn't have a conversation about this."

"No. You and Liam did. I just happened to overhear—"

"Eavesdropping? Really?" said Liam. Eliana wanted to respond, but surprisingly, Russell jumped to her defense.

"No, screw that! There's been too many secrets along the way. I'm glad she listened in. At least we're finally talking about it."

Eliana couldn't help but blush. She wasn't used to anyone defending her. She nodded her thanks to Russell before continuing. "You said that spirits were like what's left when the dead forget and lose whatever they were, but you also said that some spirits held on to their memories. I guess those... those would be souls. Do I have that right?" Malcolm nodded. All evidence of his headache was gone. He looked relieved. Maybe it was easier for him if someone else guided the discussion. "So, I remember you ending that conversation by saying that both spirits and souls can protect themselves inside a body. Is that what happened to you? Is that voice a soul?"

Malcolm massaged his temples, but he didn't look to be in pain. Maybe he was afraid the pain would return. "Yes. It was a necromancer. I've seen visions... glimpses of his life, I think. An army of walking corpses marching on a city in the forest, and an orb that felt like burning ice. The Chancellor sort of knew about it."

"What? How did he know?" asked Liam.

"He said he sometimes dreams about the future. He's like me. He has another soul inside him. He said it's not just us either. There are others."

Conner shot Liam a meaningful glance and asked. "You think Dad has one?"

Liam winced, but nodded. "Based on that story he told us about Shivertusk, probably. Gunther too."

Everything she was hearing enthralled Eliana, but she could see a person walking their way. She needed to keep the conversation focused. "Why did the Chancellor send you out to the farm, Malcolm? If there was mist, does that mean there was another soul?"

Malcolm sighed, but nodded. "The goblin necromancer. The Chancellor must have dreamt about it, or maybe he knew about it from before. It doesn't matter. I just know it could feel me. It knew I was up there on that farm. It was hunting me."

"Wait, why would he send you up there to get hunted?" Eliana asked, but she could tell that others were having stronger reactions. Russell looked like he wanted to scream, but it was Liam who spoke first.

"He didn't just send Malcolm. He sent all of us, and armed soldiers to boot. He sent us up there to get hunted, expecting our group to win."

Malcolm looked like he was in pain, and not just from a headache this time. His face was contorted with emotion as if he were fighting back tears. "I didn't know! He didn't warn me. I didn't even feel the soul inside that goblin until last night in the fields, and then only after the voice pointed it out to me." Malcolm looked around frantically. Eliana felt sorry for him. He looked so lonely and scared. "It doesn't matter," he said, continuing. "What you're all thinking, it's the truth. The goblins were never after the Ganna. All those attacks were just about it trying to kill me."

"Okay, I'll bite," said Russell, his anger barely contained. "Why? Why was it hunting you?"

"The white mist. It wanted to get stronger. Had they killed me, it would have been white mist flowing from me into it. Instead, it was the other way around."

"So, he sent all of us up there as bait so you and it could see who eats the other's soul?" asked Russell.

Malcolm paused for a moment to consider the question. "Yeah. I think so. There was something else," he said as he reached into his backpack and retrieved a small leather case. He undid a tiny latch and opened it. There were fifteen small glass spheres inside. Seven of them glowed with a faint bluish-white light.

"What's that?" asked Eliana. She never saw anything quite like it. The tiny glass balls weren't glowing in the same warm way gem powder would when it was infused with magic through alchemy, or runecrafting. The light felt distant and cold to her.

"I don't know," answered Malcolm. "The voice told me I'd need them to go further in my studies."

"So, that's what it was all about," said Liam. His tone spoke of finality, as if he were closing the discussion.

Eliana looked to her right and saw that the approaching person was much closer now. "You should put that away, Malcolm," she whispered as she turned to face the newcomer.

Eliana felt a mixture of relief and anger as she recognized the approaching man. It was the Chancellor. He was hustling, with what Eliana thought was a purposeful expression on his face. As he got closer and got a better view of the situation his expression changed to one of concern. "Is everyone all right?" he asked. Eliana winced. She knew that was not the right way to start the conversation.

"No," growled Russell. "Tessa's dead, you donkey cock."

Eliana blushed at Russell's use of language and she saw Liam and Conner exchange concerned looks. The Chancellor seemed sad, but otherwise unmoved by the outburst. "I see," he said with a sigh. "I owe you all an apology. You see… there's just so much to do… so many things to prepare, and just so little time—"

"You sent us out there to die," said Russell, interrupting. Eliana wanted to calm him down, but it wasn't her place. She looked to Liam imploringly, but he shook his head. He wouldn't intervene either.

"No," said the Chancellor. "No, that wasn't it at all. I don't know what Malcolm told you. I suspect both more than I'd like, and less than he should have." That particular phrase struck Eliana as odd. Malcolm seemed to need help sharing information. Was the Chancellor the same way?

"Oh, save it," continued Russell, unmoved.

"I'm afraid we no longer have that luxury, young man." The Chancellor smiled warmly at Russell for a moment before addressing everyone. "You should all go to your quarters and rest. There'll be so much to do before the Black Tide arrives. Your assignments for the next couple of days will be waiting for you in the morning."

"So that's it then? You're not going to tell us the damn truth?" asked Russell.

"I fear that I'll spend time with each of you in the coming days, but it may not be possible. There are many things to do, and very little time left with which to do them. I'll do my best, though, for each of you. You'll understand someday—"

"Do your best?! Like you did for Tessa, and all those farmers?" spat Russell, but the old man was no longer paying attention to him. He was chanting lightly, his hands tracing circles and patterns of azure light in the air in front of him. Eliana never saw such a bold display of magic before. It was breathtaking and beautiful.

The Chancellor continued to weave deeper patterns of light in front of him for a few moments before turning to Malcolm and extending his hand. "Come, child, we have work to do."

Eliana thought the intricately woven web of vibrant blue light looked much like a doorway of sorts. When Malcolm stepped forward and took the Chancellor's hand, there was a bright blue flash and the sapphire portal quickly collapsed and faded. When Eliana's vision recovered, she was surprised to see that both the Chancellor and Malcolm were gone.

26
Conner

Russell stormed off after the Chancellor left with Malcolm. Conner understood his frustration. He felt it too. No one was answering their questions, and now people were dying. What made it worse, was that his own father was keeping information from them. He hoped that the conversation in the Monastery about Shivertusk took his dad by surprise. Maybe now, after there was time to reflect, he'd be willing to share more.

Conner spent the better part of an hour walking his wounded brother back to the living quarters Liam shared with their dad. Ellie offered to walk with them and help, but Conner could tell she was tired, so he sent her away to rest.

The brothers barely spoke during the journey. Conner got the impression Liam was even angrier with their dad than he was. It was understandable. Liam's relationship with Dad was much stronger than Conner's. After all, they lived together. If Dad was like Malcolm and the Chancellor, it meant he hid that fact from Liam all this time. He hid it from Conner too, of course, but it wasn't the same.

Their father was dozing in a sturdy wooden chair as they entered the room. He was always a light sleeper. Him not waking when they opened the door told Conner his father must be truly exhausted. Still, they didn't make it more than a handful of steps before the sounds of their footfalls woke their dad. He smiled at first, but his expression changed to concern when he registered that Liam was injured and having some difficulties walking.

"What happened? Are you all right? Was there some kind of accident?"

Liam winced as he sat down in the closest chair. "The Chancellor didn't tell you, I take it? He changed our assignment, Father." The tone of his voice confirmed what Conner suspected. Liam felt betrayed by their dad.

'No one told me anything. He changed the mission assignments? Where did he send you?"

"North—"

"North?" their father interrupted. "How far north?"

Conner heard the concern in his father's voice. He squeezed his brother's shoulder and said, "Dad. He sent us pretty far. To a farm right next to a goblin tribe."

"What? Why would he—"

Liam cut him off. "You know damn well why he did it! The white mists. Malcolm's possessed, has a soul, or however you want to say it. He's one of you."

Their father looked stunned. He moved his mouth for a bit, but no words came out. He almost looked scared. Conner never saw him like that before.

"Your wounds... please tell me they aren't serious... is everyone else all right?" asked their father in a panic.

"No," said Liam coldly.

"Malcolm?"

"He's fine. Seven others are dead. The farmers. Their entire family, and a scared little boy, and a young girl, and our friend Tessa. All for what?"

Conner saw the pain and confusion on his father's face. Conner wanted answers as much as his brother did, but he couldn't blame his dad for the farm. His father's reaction made it clear he hadn't known about the reassignment. There were things he needed to answer for, but not that. "Why didn't you tell us, Dad?" asked Conner, hoping to change the direction of the conversation. "Malcolm started describing it to us. Whatever it is, we deserve some answers, don't we?"

Their father looked down and nodded.

"Are you like Malcolm, Father? Do you have a spirit inside you?" asked Liam.

"Yes. I've been this way since I was a little older than you, son."

"Why is this happening? Why now?" asked Conner.

His father cleared his throat and frowned before speaking. "There seems to always be seven of us. I don't understand why that is, but whenever one passes on, we eventually find another in the Citadel who has received the gift." He smiled sadly. "Pathmaker Aelith never returned from her mission a few months back. I'd held out hopes she was still alive, but if Malcolm has the gift now, I guess Aelith is truly gone."

"You call it a gift? Malcolm seems in pain all the time. He has constant headaches. He sees things that aren't there. How's that a gift?" asked Liam. While Conner appreciated his brother's questions, a pit was forming in his stomach. A sense of dread took hold as he reconsidered all the recent events from his new vantage point.

"The headaches have been there for all of us, but some had it worse than others. My head is hurting bad right now. Talking about it openly like this is difficult. I like to think of the headaches as a symptom caused by a difference in opinions."

"I don't understand," said Liam.

"A disagreement between what I want, and what the one inside me wants. That part gets complicated, and it's different for each of us. Let me try to explain," he said as he massaged his temples.

Conner kept running the Chancellor's words over and over again in his head. The Chancellor feared that he'd get the chance to spend time with each of them. The dread grew stronger. His hands started to sweat and shake.

"The spirit in me differs from the one in Arronhelm. It's different than the one in Malcolm. Each spirit at one time was a different person, or creature, I guess."

"Souls," corrected Liam. "Malcolm's was a necromancer. It made it clear that there was a difference. Spirits don't really have memories. Souls do."

Their father nodded. "Yes. That's exactly it. So, the soul inside of me has his own ideas, wants and needs. Sometimes, he and I disagree about what to say, or how to approach a problem. We have to work it out between the two of us, and the headache is one side effect of that."

"I still don't understand how anyone would call that a gift," said Liam.

"The soul inside of me was a tremendous light mage. I suspect, one of the greatest ever to have lived. He's taught me so much, so quickly. Where you learn your battlemagic through constant practice, and Conner learned his healing spells through books and scrolls, I just simply... learned. The soul taught me to command light in ways I never thought possible."

"Does it know its name, or who it was?" asked Liam.

Their father shook his head. "I'm not sure it really knows when it lived. Arronhelm spent a great deal of time searching the limited historical records that remain, trying to find the identity of each of our gifts, but so much of our history was destroyed when we lost our war to the demons. He's found some information for each of us, but I don't know if any of it matters. Whoever or whatever my gift was, it's different now. He and I are tied together. Whatever life he had a time long ago is gone. He shares my life now."

"But you have to know something about his life by now, don't you?" asked Liam.

Their father massaged his temple and nodded. "I know a little. I know that he was the guardian of a great city, in his time. Arronhelm tried to find out which city, but there were just too many possibilities, and too few history books left to narrow it down. I know he died using his magic in defense of his city. That's about it."

"That's all you know, Father? That can't be right," said Liam skeptically. "It's only been a few days for Malcolm, and he's already witnessed scenes from his soul's past. It talks to him. We could almost ask questions of it through him."

“What? It was never like that for any of us. I was gifted for nearly three years before I even got a glimpse.” Their father looked shocked at Liam’s description of Malcolm’s relationship with his gift.

“It’s true,” Conner added. “We all talked just about an hour ago, while we were out in the clearing. We talked until the Chancellor came and took Malcolm for more training.” Conner pushed his sense of dread aside earlier enough to focus on the conversation, but mentioning the Chancellor brought it all back to him, full force. He remembered the sadness on the Chancellor’s face as he spoke of how he feared he would need to work with each of them in the coming days. There were never more than seven with the gift in the Citadel. If new people were destined to receive it, those with the gift now would need to pass on. Conner felt the dread blossom into crippling despair. He tried to fight back his tears, but his breath caught in his throat. The tiny gag was enough to break his resolve, and once the tears started, there was nothing he could do to stop them.

“Conner, what’s wrong? Don’t cry,” his dad said with warmth and concern, as he pulled himself to his feet. “This is a good thing. Your friend has a great gift…”

“It’s not that, Dad,” sputtered Conner through his tears. “Chancellor… he said…” Conner didn’t want to say it, as if saying it would make it a reality. He wanted to just cry and leave it unsaid and maybe it wouldn’t happen, but he knew it was just childish, misguided hope. He took a shuddering breath as his father rushed to him and wrapped him in a hug.

“Said what, son?” he whispered.

“He said he’d be training more of us,” Conner said as he threw his arms around his father’s waist and squeezed as tight as his frail arms would allow. “Soon. He said soon.”

Conner’s dad said nothing for quite some time, but Conner could feel him tremble a bit. He could hear his father’s shuddering breath and racing heart. “All right, son,” he finally said as he broke the hug and took a step back, turning to Liam. Moisture filled his eyes as he continued. “Liam. I need you to sleep in the Monastery tonight. Tell them that, on my order, I need your wounds completely healed by morning. Request that Devin come see you. If he does, tell him I'm requesting protections for you."

Liam looked confused. "I don't understand, sir. Why do I need to stay in the Monastery?"

"I wanted to wait, but it seems time is moving too fast for all of us. Your Rite of Passage happens tomorrow morning. We need you healed and strengthened with a few protective spells to compensate for the damage to your armor."

"Yes, sir."

He turned back to Conner. "You should stay here tonight. We can spend some time together. We depart at first light tomorrow."

Conner's heart leapt. He wiped the tears from his eyes and smiled gratefully at his father.

27
Malcolm

"Try it again," said Arronhelm from his desk on the other side of the library with no windows, no entrances, and no exits. Malcolm always liked the whimsical stories the arcane sciences students told of hidden libraries that only mages could access. He never believed them, but he loved the idea. Now that he was in just such a place, he found that he hated the idea. He felt trapped, short of breath and claustrophobic.

His shortness of breath was less the result of the enclosed space and more the consequence of his newly earned knowledge. The 'Other', as he came to refer to the voice in his head, started bargaining shortly after they arrived in the library. It grew stronger and more assertive ever since consuming the white mists of the goblin. The Other was unsatisfied with Malcolm's progress. It felt he should study harder. More than anything else, the Other impressed upon him a sense of urgency. Everything was happening so fast. Malcolm had too much to learn in an impossibly short amount of time. The Other offered to help him learn, but there was a price to pay.

The Chancellor warned Malcolm against bargaining when he asked for advice, but the warning felt half-hearted. In the end, it was Malcolm's driving thirst for knowledge that swayed him to take the bargain. He understood that the Other likely saw that trait in him and exploited it.

Malcolm made sure the Other understood that this initial bargain was a test. If the price was too high compared to the gains, he'd avoid bargaining again in the future.

The Other helped him by filling his mind with the underlying language of necromancy magic. Where yesterday, it took Malcolm minutes to read a single paragraph in his tome, he could now skim through paragraphs and distill their essential meaning in a matter of moments. The cost was high, though. While his mind expanded, his body withered and waned. His breathing became weak and labored, and it felt as if he were always a touch out of breath, like he just finished running somewhere.

Malcolm knew there were other manifestations of his bargain. There wasn't a mirror in the library, but he didn't need one. He saw Arronhelm's reaction the moment after the change took place. He didn't care much about his appearance, and he didn't have parents to explain it to. Still, his friends and teachers would notice. He needed to be prepared to have some kind of explanation at a minimum.

"You were close last time," said the Chancellor encouragingly. "The first step along a path is often the most difficult one to take, child."

Malcolm looked down at the tiny glass sphere filled with swirling blue-white mist. He tried again to reach out to it with his mind. He learned from the tome that the spheres were called Soulstones. They were created with a rather simple spell. After his deal with the Other, Malcolm found it easy to commit the spell to memory.

The difficulty in making Soulstones stemmed from the need to find a fresh enough soul to imprison. When something dies, its soul crosses over into the Astral and remains near its body. The soul only remains for as long as it retains the personality and memories it had in life.

The Astral strips these things away, in most cases, very quickly. Once a soul surrenders any semblance of what it was in life, it becomes a spirit. The type of spirit a soul becomes is based on how long it held on to its identity after death. Souls that fail quickly, become shadows, while stronger ones become wraiths, apparitions, haunts, or in rare cases, ghosts.

The tome recommended trapping the souls of recently slain humans or other intelligent species. The souls of animals and other simple creatures generally eroded too rapidly to be useful for Soulstones.

Fortunately, the leather case he took from the goblin necromancer held fifteen of the glass balls. Seven of those spheres still had souls within them. With any luck, that number would be down to six soon enough, Malcolm mused.

He squinted and saw the shadows within the Soulstone dance around and through the glowing blue-white mist. He felt the soul more and more. It was responding to him. He felt it move around in the tiny sphere in accordance to his thoughts and wishes. Malcolm smiled. "I've got it, Chancellor!"

Arronhelm nodded. "Well then, child, let me see where that puts us on this chart." The Chancellor mumbled as he moved his fingers over a spread-out piece of parchment on his desk. "Ah, I see. Now that you have its attention, you can freely pull it out of its stone. Once out of the stone, the Astral reclaim it. Does that sound right to you?"

Malcolm nodded. He understood well enough, but the Other warned him of potential dangers. He needed Arronhelm to understand the process as well as he did. "Yes, Chancellor. The soul doesn't belong in this world. The barrier between worlds will weaken as the soul fights the call of the Astral. There'll be a moment when the Astral pulls this soul across. In that moment, I'll be able to bring a spirit from the Astral into this world. An exchange."

Arronhelm nodded as he tapped the parchment lightly with his fingers. "This chart has many warnings scribbled on it. I know a great deal about magic, child, but this is rather outside my experiences. Why do this? What do you gain by pulling a spirit into this world?"

"Spirits mindlessly attack the living, Chancellor, but necromancy allows me to give them purpose. I can direct them to attack my enemies, or, once I learn how, use them to reanimate the bodies of the dead so they can become even stronger weapons."

"I see. And the dangers?"

"Some spirits are stronger. Some places have far more spirits than other places. There's no guarantee that the spirit I call will be the one that crosses over. Something stronger or altogether different may cross the barrier. If I'm unprepared or unable to control what comes across... it could go badly." Malcolm didn't feel a need to explain in more detail. He said enough to ensure that Arronhelm knew the risks and was prepared. He felt no reason to delay things further. "I'm ready to try when you are, Chancellor."

Arronhelm shook his head and started chanting lightly. He traced intricate patterns of sapphire light in the air around him. This time, though, instead of forming a gateway, the sigils of light tightened and collapsed in on themselves. Each formed a tiny, brilliant blue star that spun in orbit around the old man. There were four of the vibrant stars when he was finished. Malcolm knew there were many different spells in wizardry that enhanced the potency of a caster's magic in a variety of ways. He suspected the blue stars were the product of such a spell.

"Well, that went rather well, I must say. I'm more than ready, child. You may begin."

Malcolm rolled the Soulstone around in his fingers for a moment as he focused on the soul inside. The soul immediately responded to him, and Malcolm found it easy to draw it out of the stone. It expanded as it left its glass prison, until it was the size of a small child.

Malcolm saw it as a moving shadow when he squinted and used his special sight, which he now knew was called Spectral Sight. The soul was otherwise invisible. It began to struggle almost immediately. It didn't belong in this world anymore, and the Astral was determined to reclaim it. Malcolm watched as other spirits swirled and gathered around it. They could sense the barrier between worlds softening. The soul swirled in anger as it slowly, inexorably was drawn out of this world and into the Astral.

This was the time to act, and Malcolm didn't hesitate. He saw the spirit he wanted to bring across. It was small, merely a shadow. He called to it, projecting his thoughts and will into it as the tome instructed him to do. He saw it respond. At the same time, though, other spirits near it responded. In the blink of an eye, two larger spirits charged the breach between worlds. They were wraiths, just like the ones the goblin necromancer called. Malcolm tried to release his call on the shadow, but it was too late. The wraiths followed it like a beacon right to the weakest point, the spot where the soul was being pulled into the Astral. They no longer needed the calling to try and cross. He watched as they forced their eerily long, shadowy arms through to pull themselves across to this world.

"Chancellor!" shouted Malcolm as he fell backwards, away from the point where the wraiths were coming through. He felt a blast of chilling air as first one, and then another forced themselves through. Unlike the soul, the wraiths were at least visible to the naked eye as tall, slender wisps of swirling shadows. They didn't have legs, so to speak, but rather floated and danced, much like a piece of parchment did in a swirling wind. Malcolm scooted back from them. While he hadn't intended to call them, they were here because of his call. The Other discerned what he was thinking, or perhaps it was the Other that gave him the thought in the first place.

"*Yes, if you're strong enough, you may still master them,*" it whispered to him.

"Get back," shouted Arronhelm. He rose to his feet, his hands already sparking with electricity as he crafted his spell. Malcolm needed to try, though. Arronhelm wouldn't always be there to save him. He concentrated and forced his thoughts and will into the closest of the wraiths. He suddenly felt as if someone poured ice water down his back. Shocked, he exhaled sharply and was surprised to see his own frosty breath. At the same time, the wraith stopped moving entirely. Malcolm felt a sense of exhaustion slowly building, but he knew he mastered the wraith. He could direct it if he wished, although the fatigue would build rapidly. More importantly, he could send it back. With merely a thought, he forced the wraith to turn and move back towards the breach. The Astral reclaimed it, and in an instant, it was gone.

Malcolm was so distracted with his own battle, he completely ignored the other wraith. It surged forward, swinging its eerie, whip-like arms at him. It barely made it a step before a thick, blinding blast of lightning struck it. The wraith floated, paralyzed in the air for a few moments as white-hot electricity danced around and through it. Malcolm closed his eyes for a second to block the brightness of the lightning. When he reopened them, the wraith was gone.

"Well, wasn't that exhilarating," said the Chancellor as he clapped his hands. "I'd call that a most successful test indeed!"

Malcolm shivered as he climbed to his feet. "That shouldn't have happened. I tried to call a weaker spirit."

"Nonsense, child. That's precisely what should've happened."

"What? Why? I messed up."

Arronhelm laughed. "You learned to use a Soulstone, and you overachieved on your very first summons. You called two spirits, and I suspect both were stronger than the one you wanted. You even managed to control one long enough to send it back." Arronhelm smiled, clapped his hands again, and actually giggled. "You can call that a mistake if you wish. I call it excellent progress!"

"I was trying to call a weaker spirit. Those wraiths came across instead. I didn't time the transfer well enough, or my call to the shadow wasn't strong enough. What if you hadn't been—"

Arronhelm cut him off. "None of that! I won't have such a breakthrough sullied with worries and what-ifs. Now, are you injured?"

Malcolm sighed. "No Chancellor. I'm tired from the spells, but I'm unharmed."

"Good. I have something I'd like to show you," said the Chancellor as he gradually wove patterns of blue light in the air. The sigils twisted and grew together into a doorway. Malcolm was already walking toward the Chancellor, so the old man didn't even need to reach out for him. There was a brilliant flash of blue light as the spell completed. Malcolm momentarily felt as if he were falling, but he'd felt this earlier in the day, so this time he was prepared.

A moment later, Malcolm was standing with Arronhelm in a long hallway. There was a closed door immediately behind them. The hallway stretched out in front of them for fifty feet before it dead-ended. He didn't recall ever being in this hallway. There were no other doorways, furnishings or side passageways. The only feature of interest was a large painting mounted on the far wall.

Malcolm saw the painting vividly, despite the distance. It depicted a noble white horse, with a mane that looked to be spun from slender strands of sun-kissed gold. A long, silver horn stretched out from the horse's forehead. There was a background, but Malcolm barely registered it. The horse was so incredibly vibrant that it glowed. It was as if its majesty was so great that it pulled the color and light out of everything else around it.

Malcolm's heart pounded in his chest. He could feel the painting calling to him. His head started throbbing. He burst into tears as he walked towards it. It took him a moment to recognize that the emotions he was feeling weren't his own. Those feelings belonged to the Other.

"Please," the voice implored him, *"let me touch it?"*

Malcolm continued to walk toward the painting. It seemed to look at him as he got closer. He looked back at the Chancellor, but the old man merely smiled and nodded. He felt a warmth wash over his body as he got even closer. He reached out. He was only a few steps away when he heard himself speak. The Other was controlling Malcolm's mouth, speaking through him.

"I tried. We tried."

"I know," came the response. It was ethereal and musical. Beautiful and terrifying. Malcolm somehow knew that only he and the Other were hearing it. Tears poured down his cheeks. *"You did everything you could, dark one. You were betrayed. We all were."*

"I should have known!" Malcolm was sobbing openly now. He took another step. His hand was only inches away.

"You couldn't have known. I told you then that it wasn't over. It took me so long to find you and the others. To bring you back to me."

"Why? I don't understand."

"To save us. To make it right again," the beautiful voice said.

Malcolm's heart felt like it would burst as his hand touched the panting. It was warm and electric. It filled his weakened body with energy, and it filled the Other with joy. The swirling emotions within him crescendoed to a maddening intensity.

"Let me show you. Let me remind you," said the voice of terrifying beauty.

Malcolm shut his eyes. His nostrils were filled with smoke and the fetid stench of the dead. He was in a smoldering city. An endless horde of twisted, shuffling corpses staggered down the streets. He knew this was the same army he saw in his visions earlier. Just as he knew they served him then, he knew they served him now. There was a tower off in the distance. They were all making their way toward it.

He looked to his left and saw the Unicorn in all her splendor. She stood easily seven feet at the shoulders, and her eyes glowed like molten gold. The ground below shook as enormous trees, and creatures of earth and stone walked behind her. The air above was filled with thunder. A battle in the night sky raged on, as terrifying winged demons hurled gouts of flame at majestic thunderbirds that trailed lightning from their wings.

Malcolm smiled. They were winning. They took the fight to her very doorstep, while the others all ran away and tried to hide. The Demon Queen was stretched too thin, and what forces remained couldn't stand against the combined forces of both nature and the dead. Gaea was shattered. The world suffered, but the healing would start today.

Malcolm heard a deep whooshing sound above and behind him. He turned to see a pair of portals of swirling darkness form. The neverlings and their pathways in and out of the Astral. They were early. They weren't to be involved until the tower was taken. Malcolm spun to face the twin portals as the night terrors emerged.

They were massive and horrific, each crafted and built from the living flesh of a dozen or more people. Human arms and legs, misshapen and twisted together to form limbs thick and powerful enough to propel the two-ton monsters. There were eight of the beasts. Each one roared and fixed its baleful gaze on him, and in that moment, he knew he'd been betrayed.

Malcolm opened his eyes and pulled his trembling hand back from the painting. His heart was still racing, and he could feel the tears drying on his cheeks.

"You wanted to know what called your spirit to you. Whatever entity lives in this Painting did. It calls them all," said the Chancellor softly from close behind him. He must have moved closer while Malcolm was lost in his dream. "It spoke to you, I take it?"

Malcolm turned to face the Chancellor. He didn't need to say anything.

The Chancellor nodded. "I didn't see your vision, or hear what she said to you, but I understand, child. It was this way for all of us." Arronhelm held out his hand and waited for Malcolm to take it. "Come. We have a few more things to study yet tonight."

Malcolm's head was spinning. He nodded absently to the Chancellor, but all he could think about were the terrible visions he just witnessed.

28
Attia

Attia waited at the edge of the clearing as the group of three slowly made their way toward her. It wasn't dawn yet. They were on time, early even, but Attia was waiting for the better part of an hour. It was her first assignment as a Pathrunner, and she was eager to prove herself.

The messenger delivered word to Constance's bonfire last night during the celebration. The Commander requested Attia to be the guide for Liam's Rite of Passage. All the soldiers did it at one point or another. The runecrafters needed the heart of one of the local game animals to craft Attunement Runes. When complete, the runes would magically alter the shape and fit of the armor to perfectly match Liam's body.

It was tradition that each soldier killed and harvested the heart of the animal for his own armor. It was a test of sorts. Attia knew of a variety of animals that would work fine for the runes, including some prey animals, but most soldiers wanted to be led to predators. She assumed that it was some kind of badge of honor in their order.

Attia could get similar runes for her freshly dyed leather armor, if she wanted. Attunement Runes were valuable for anyone who wore rigid or heavy metallic armors, but they weren't nearly as important for leathers. Both Felerin and Constance opted for Runes of Concealment on their leathers instead, and she just assumed she would make the same decision.

She played a little hide and seek out in the forest with Constance the other day, while they traveled back from the goblin settlement. Constance could virtually disappear into the foliage right in front of her eyes. Her runes magically shifted and colored the camouflage patterns of her armor to match the surroundings, much like a chameleon.

Attia waved as the Commander and his two sons drew closer. The predawn air was damp, but pleasantly cool. There was a thin, ghostly fog clinging to the thick grasses of the clearing. It would burn off rapidly after sunrise, but for the moment, at least, it was beautiful.

She took a few seconds to adjust her pack. They would need to move fairly quickly. The Black Scar a mile away, but they needed to be there before the full heat of the day took hold or the hunting would be more difficult. Larger animals used the Scar to move through the thick rainforest, especially this time of the year. Everything would be moving south to escape the Tide, regardless of the path it was taking.

"Morning," called the Commander as he approached. He wore his broadsword across his back, but otherwise was dressed casually. Liam was the only one dressed for battle. His mail looked partially repaired, which was surprising. Attia assumed it would take days to repair Liam's armor, given the extent of the damage. Being the Commander's son definitely had its advantages.

"Morning, sir. Unless you have specific prey in mind, I plan on taking us to the Scar," said Attia.

"Nothing specific. The Scar will work. And call me Duncan," he said. "Come along, boys. We should get moving."

Attia waited for Conner and Liam to catch up before starting to navigate the web of trails that led out to the Black Scar. The Scar was used as a planting bed for several herbs requiring full sunlight, and a more root-rich soil than what could be found in any of the clearings close to the Citadel. The paths were well-traveled by the herbalists. It made for a swift and easy journey.

The group walked in relative silence for the first half of the journey, but eventually the silence gave way to the ordinary banter of brothers. Attia picked up from their conversation that Liam was healed overnight in the Monastery and that a Lifeshield and a Breakward were cast on him to prepare for this morning's hunt. Conner was impressed and went to great lengths to describe to his brother how the spells worked. Together, they would toughen and protect his body from the first attack to slip cleanly past his defenses. Conner provided other details and variables, but Attia decided not to focus on them. Her role was to safely guide the group. She couldn't afford to get too distracted.

It took them an hour to make it out to the edge of the Black Scar. The destruction was breathtaking to behold. The Scar was fifty yards from one side to the other. At one point, it'd been dense rainforest, but something ripped through it, uprooting and shattering trees. The Scar extended as far as the eye could see in either direction. Over the years, the fallen trees had hollowed out or rotted, but a tangled webbing of thick earthy roots remained. New, young foliage tried to grow from the silt of the fallen forest, only to be trampled before gaining purchase in the shattered soil. Over time, as more and more of the forest's larger creatures took to using the Scar, the bigger trees simply stopped trying to grow. Without the canopy to block out the sun, more traditional plants grew. Nothing with soft leaves ever survived long, though, as each year, the Tide came and stripped everything down to the bark.

Attia smiled to herself as she realized that right here and now, she was seeing something entirely new. The Tide was taking a different path this year. All the foliage in the Black Scar might survive this year. With a second year of growth, who knew what could happen. Maybe some of these plants would grow strong enough to survive or even flourish.

"It's amazing, isn't it?" said Duncan as he crouched down at the edge of the tree line.

"What do you think did it Dad?" asked Conner.

"No one really knows. It crosses so many miles. All the way from the savannah down to the swamps, but it doesn't extend into either. It just doesn't seem possible to me that some enormous beast could have done it. I've seen giants, heffaphant, and even drakes move through this forest. I don't care how big something is. Uprooting trees slows anything down. To have been able to do it over the course of miles?" Duncan shook his head as he motioned for both his boys to crouch down.

"What about a dragon?" whispered Liam.

Duncan frowned. "No one's seen one for ages, but I still don't think so. I mean, maybe it could've flown over the forest, spitting fire."

Attia found the topic tiresome. The Pathfinders spent a lot of time traveling the Scar. She heard conversations and debates about its origin more times than she cared to remember. "The forest would have burned in other places. Even if it were during the rainy season, some fire would have spread, especially if it came from the skies. The canopy connects everything."

"All right. What do you think, then?" asked Conner.

"I walked the full length of it a few years ago. It's one of the things every Pathfinder does as they learn. It's strange. The Scar maintains this width across the entire distance, never growing or shrinking more than a yard or two. No fire would burn like that. A great machine of war perhaps? Something from the time before. When we were still fighting."

Duncan nodded. "Possibly. It's also possible that it could have been something beneath the earth. Something primal, or elemental that moved close enough to the surface to uproot everything as it passed."

"I guess we'll never know," said Liam.

"Don't be so hasty, son. I know in my bones that this rainforest is special. It's filled with history, magic and mysteries. But you're special too. All three of you. What happened to Malcolm wasn't an accident. Only a fool can look at everything that's happening right now and ignore the connections."

His words stunned Attia. Had Conner and Liam talked about it with their father? It wouldn't be hard to imagine, but how much did he really know? "Malcolm, sir? What happened to Malcolm?" she asked.

"He knows," said Conner quietly. "We'll fill you in later."

Attia started to answer but stopped herself as she saw a bit of motion off to her right. She held up a closed fist to silence everyone and crouched even lower. There was a silhouette off in the distance. It gradually approached, growing clearer until its shape was unmistakable.

Duncan whistled softly. "That's an awfully big bear, son. You sure you don't want to wait for something else?"

"It's meant to be, Father."

"Does he have to do this alone, Dad? I mean, it doesn't make a lot of sense," said Conner.

Duncan shook his head. “Well, tonight at the feast, the story will be all about how Liam bravely killed the bear in single combat, but between the four of us, of course you and Attia are going to help your brother.”

“Stars above, Father! I won’t cheat. I can’t believe you’d even suggest it!”

“Who said anything about cheating? The tradition isn’t for each soldier to come out and kill a powerful beast in single combat. Do you have any idea how many soldiers we’d lose that way? No. The real tradition is a small team comes out here to hunt and kill an animal, but the story is always about the brave, triumphant, solo battle.”

Attia snorted as she turned towards Liam. “Seriously, you never knew?” she asked as she loosened her sword free from its sheath, just enough to draw it quickly and easily. She would have preferred Liam to wait for easier prey, but it wasn’t her decision

Liam blushed. “No. I always thought... I mean.”

Duncan put one hand in front of his mouth to muffle his laughter. He slapped Liam on the shoulder with the other. ‘Oh. This is priceless. It never gets old. It only works about half the time. A lot of the young soldiers get tipped off.” He stopped speaking for a moment. Attia thought she saw his eyes welling up. “This has been a perfect morning. I loved spending it with both of you boys. Please don’t ruin it all by getting yourselves killed.”

29
Liam

Liam's pulse raced as he made his way down into the Black Scar. His boots sunk in the soft loamy soil, and he nearly tripped while working his way through the roots. "Be careful, you two," he warned.

"We'll be fine," whispered Attia from right behind him. Liam was amazed at how easily and quietly she moved over the treacherous ground. "Set up in that hollow?"

Liam saw the area she was suggesting. The ground dipped a few feet lower into a very shallow pit of sorts. He could see some broken roots poking out along the edges. He nodded and started carefully making his way there. There would be far fewer hidden roots for him to contend with in that pit, and once the bear was at the lowest point, he'd have the higher ground.

"Hurry, son, it's coming!" shouted his father.

The bear huffed and growled as it approached. Liam made his way into the shallow pit and found his footing. His movements aggravated the bear. It raked its claws against the ground, cutting deep rivulets into the soil. Its massive body shook and rippled as it rocked its head back and forth and roared. Frothy white drool splattered the ground. Liam's heart pounded in his chest. He set his stance sideways behind his shield but kept his body loose. If it charged, he wanted to quickly yield ground to it. The bear was smaller than Shivertusk was, but the sheer thickness of its body was terrifying. So much fat covering so much muscle.

"Stay back, both of you," he shouted as the bear rushed forward. Liam needed to move freely at first. The initial contact could make or break the fight. Liam felt his adrenaline flow as the beast drew closer. He focused his attention on his shield, letting his battlemagic help angle and guide it. The bear's strikes would be far too powerful against chainmail armor for his limited magic to do much to protect him. He'd have to concentrate on keeping his shield in front of him and hope that the spells the healers placed on him would be enough to save him, should the beast land a clean swipe.

The bear paused for a brief second at the top of the shallow pit to roar again before bounding down into the hollow. The speed at which it covered ground amazed Liam. He back pedaled, hoping against hope that his brother heeded his warning. The bear kept rushing forward, but Liam backed away at an angle to the bear's charge. It couldn't stop its momentum quickly enough to drive its mass into Liam. Instead, it threw a claw out in a deadly, sweeping arc. Liam caught the tremendous force of the blow with his shield, and fortunately, the angle was perfect. He felt burning pain in his arm and shoulder, but he kept his footing. Most importantly, the bear was positioned in the lowest part of the shallow pit.

"Now, Attia. Circle to its flank! Conner, right behind your brother," bellowed his father from off to the side. Liam felt comforted by the fact that his father was watching and directing things. It meant that he'd be able to focus on the bear. It turned to face him, and Liam extended his sword to keep it at bay. He knew he had little hope of cutting through all that fat, swinging his broadsword one-handed, but he could still stab at the thing.

The bear swatted at the side of the sword with its other claw and Liam nearly lost his grip. Man, this thing was strong, he thought. He felt his brother brace a hand on his back, and waves of cool, soothing energy washed away the pain in his arm. At the same time, Attia gracefully spun past the bear on her way to its flank. It bellowed in pain. Her sword cut through the fur on its shoulder, leaving a crimson river as blood poured from the wound.

Liam didn't think her cut made it to muscle, but it drove the bear into a frenzy of anger regardless. It whipped its head around to face Attia, but she kept circling behind it, forcing it to move its feet to turn, exposing the side of its neck to Liam. He leaned in and drove his sword into its shoulder. The fur and fat were hard to get through, but he hit muscle and bone. It roared and swung its arm back at him. Fortunately, Attia moved to the correct flank. Even as the bear turned toward her, Liam kept his shield between him and the bear.

The backhand swing was incredibly powerful. It struck him squarely, driving his shield back into his body. He felt his ribs flex, and he might have collapsed in on himself from the weight of the blow, but the warding spells sprung into effect to absorb the impact.

Attia spun around, drawing her blade in a wide arc. Backhanding Liam slowed the bear down. It helped Attia to get the distance she needed to add tremendous power to her swing. She cut into the meaty part of its thigh, her magically sharp katana slicing through both fat and muscle. Blood flew from the wound. The beast cried out in pain as it frantically and turned to face whatever hurt it so. Attia danced back and away. The clever girl was forcing it to chase.

The bear lunged forward in a half-staggering limp. Liam thought it might have caught Attia off guard. She was no longer trying to spin or attack it. Instead, she focused on keeping away from it. It was dead set on her, giving Liam its back. The time for defense was over. He let his rage build as he focused his magic and energy on precision and power. He shouted and charged in, driving his sword into the bear. Liam barely felt the tough hide or the inches of thick fat this time. He put his full strength and body weight behind his sword as he drove it deep into the animal. The bear's momentum carried it forward, ripping his sword from his hand.

The animal was forced to slowly limp now. Liam's sword pierced all the way through its thigh and into its belly. The fact that the sword was still lodged in its leg made movement even harder. It huffed and spat as it tried to amble forward after Attia, but she was far too fast for the hobbled bear.

"Take your time, Attia. Stay ahead of its spin," his father shouted, but it wasn't necessary. Attia got in position and started her attack. She was to its side as it was still trying to turn. She ran past it, her blade out and low. Attia brought it up as she moved past its thighs and spun to finish the slash after the katana already cut into the bear's fur. The result was a deep muscle cut right across the front and outside of the bear's thigh. With one leg disabled by Liam's sword, and the other cut deeply in two separate places, the bear fell.

"Get away from it now. All three of you," his father warned as he walked out toward them. The bear's breathing was labored, but it was still dragging itself with its powerful front legs. It was still dangerous. Liam saw Attia work her way back out of the shallow pit. He backed away from the bear. He trusted that Conner was already at a safe distance.

"Shouldn't we put it out of its misery?" Liam asked as his father walked up next to him.

"You should be the one to do it, son," he said as he handed Liam his own broadsword.

The sword felt so light and balanced to Liam. He practiced with his father's sword a few times in the past, but the feel of it always surprised him. The blade was covered in layers of Runes that made it faster, sharper and lighter, but none of that would help if he got sloppy and let the bear take him off his feet. Liam heard cautionary tales of soldiers underestimating a downed opponent before. He didn't want to become such a tale himself.

He approached cautiously from the side. The bear tried to turn, but it was slow. He watched Attia out circle it before, so he kept moving, forcing the bear to keep trying to spin around. It didn't take long before it tired and simply stopped trying. Its breathing was heavy and wet now. Both of Attia's deep slices were still bleeding. When Liam was confident the bear would stay still, he stepped forward and plunged his father's broadsword into its neck. It sunk in much more easily than his own had. The blade might have been sharp enough to sever the bear's spine, but he wasn't certain. This wouldn't be as quick, but he knew it would work. "Thank you for your sacrifice," he whispered to the bear.

"Well done, son. Well done!"

Liam took a deep breath, soaking in the moment and basking in his father's praise.

30
Eliana

It was after sunrise by the time Eliana made it down to the clearing, and Silver was already out there, working with a small team. Silver was the most skilled natural mage in the Citadel, and like Eliana, she dedicated herself to all four elements. She was both Eliana's teacher and her idol.

She was beautiful in her white robes and long platinum hair, despite the vibrant green and orange parrot that sat on her shoulder. Eliana didn't care for that rude bird one bit! Every time anyone would make a mistake in class, the parrot would be the first to point it out. It was unsettling. To make matters worse, while the bird seemed to only have twenty words in its vocabulary, at least half were vulgar.

Silver was a joy to watch work. She coaxed the earth to split open with ease. She crafted long, deep trenches in the ground out in front of the Citadel. A full team of diggers would need hours to move so much earth, but she did it in minutes. Other natural mages pitched in to help, and Eliana tried as well, but she quickly realized her magic was far too weak to make a meaningful impact. She could get the soil to dig and shape itself, but she couldn't come close to the sheer volume of earth everyone else was moving. Her cheeks flushed with embarrassment. She thought she was better at it. Seeing this just showed her how much she needed to learn.

Eliana thought the design made good sense. Wide moats would be dug out from either side of the Serpent at an angle. The moats were to carry water past the Citadel and cut back into the river on the other side. This would create an island around their home. All the loose earth from digging the trenches was to be used to reinforce the walls within the moat, and to make short protective barriers all along the outside of their island. The original idea was for runecrafters to place some protective runes over everything, once the moats and walls were built, but it didn't look like that would happen anytime soon.

Most of the runecrafters were working to the north of the moats. They were crafting long bands of Runes of Protection against Insects on each side of the Serpent. If the runes were written correctly, and the magic within them was strong enough, they would form barriers the giant ants couldn't cross. The Black Tide would be forced to flow out and around the runes, drastically reducing the number of insects trying to cross their moats.

The real work for the rest of them started once Silver and her team finished carving out the rough shape of the moats. Using magic was very tiring, and the effort involved in cutting the initial trenches took its toll. Expanding the moats and packing all the loose earth into walls and berms fell to teams of people working with shovels. Eliana, like most of the children, was too small to work down in the trenches. Instead, she worked on the walls being built around the perimeter of their island.

Exhausted, Eliana spread more Aloe Paste over her arms and the back of her neck. Hours of packing earthy mud into tight walls proved hard work. She couldn't avoid the stifling heat of the day, but she could prevent herself from getting sunburned. She remembered being excited earlier in the morning when she saw she was assigned to moat and wall construction, but four hours later, she felt defeated and demoralized.

The excavation of the western moat was nearly complete. They were just widening it now. Once it was perfect, they'd collapse the small remaining sections of earth blocking the river. Water would flow in, completing one half of their moat. When the whole project was complete, they'd have a fifteen-foot-wide circular moat of fast-moving river water surrounding the entire Citadel, spanned by a few removable bridges.

Eliana thought there was maybe an hour of work left down within the western moat before they'd be ready to flood it. With little left for her to do, she decided it was a good time to take a break. She could've started working with the earth from the eastern moat, of course, but she hadn't seen any of her friends all day. She decided to try and find them instead.

Groups of people, working at various tasks, filled the clearing. She passed a makeshift logging camp where wood was being reduced to kindling, soaked in oil and wrapped in cloth. They would spread that around the outsides of the moats to create yet another deterrent for the ants. Most of the camps she passed, however, were processing food. She walked from camp to camp as she made her way to the west. She was about to give up and head back when she spotted Russell.

He was in a small camp with a group of mostly women. Some were working as a team to thresh countless bundles of rice. Some walked over the bundles, while others beat the bundles with sticks. The last couple of people collected the rice and swept it over to a large area of stones to dry. Eliana thought the stones were warmed by magical means, as she could see the heat coming off of them, but no obvious fire source.

"Hey, Mom. I'm taking a little break," Russell said as he saw Eliana approaching. He didn't wait for a reply. He just got up, left the camp, and walked over to her. "Hey, Ellie, you're all covered in dirt, mud and whatever that paste you use is."

Eliana smiled. "Aloe. It's made from the Aloe Reeds that grow along the—"

"Look, I don't really care what it is. I could throw some rice on you, though, if you want. It'd make you look even more miserable," he said with a grin.

"I was so looking forward to working on the moat, but now I just want to collapse somewhere and sleep."

"I'm sure you can stay over here and help with the rice if you want. I think there are a bunch of camps working on Ganna fruit to the south a ways if you'd rather do that."

"I was going to head over there in a little while, actually. It looks like a lot of the southern farmers have been showing up throughout the morning. My parents might already be here, but I wanted to wait until I was sure everyone coming today was already here, you know?"

Russell thought about it for a moment before nodding. "Nothing worse than looking for them before they got here, and then having to go back to work, wondering if you missed them?"

Eliana beamed him a smile. It was a small thing, but it felt so good to be understood. "Exactly!"

"Speaking of families, I saw the Ericksons about an hour ago. Attia was with them too. They saw me and stopped over to talk for a minute."

"Liam and Conner?"

"And their dad. They were coming back from hunting a bear. They were carrying a pole between them with strips upon strips of meat. I mean, it must've been a really big bear."

"Huh," said Eliana, a little surprised. "Would've been nice to have been included in that."

"What, you aren't enjoying playing in the mud?" Russell laughed. "It was some kind of trial or test for Liam. Something all the soldiers do. Attia was only along because, apparently, no one can find anything around this blasted place without a Pathfinder."

"I know," she said dejectedly. "I just thought we were all friends. Would've been nice to have known about it."

Russell shook his head. "Liam made it sound like their dad just sprung it on them last night. He said there's going to be a feast up in the Smithy later tonight to celebrate the hunt. We're all invited."

Eliana was relieved. Maybe she was wrong to have felt left out. It was something that happened to her so many times in her life. It was natural to think it would happen again. People just didn't seem to like her. Maybe she was difficult at times, but she was a good person. She deserved to have friends, just like everyone else.

"All right then," she said. "Do you think anyone would mind if I spent the afternoon with my parents instead of working in the mud? I planned on having dinner with them, but if we're invited to Liam's feast, I really want to be there."

"Are you asking me for permission to play hooky?" asked Russell, grinning ear to ear. "No one will miss you out there moving mud around. Go be with your parents. I'll see you at the feast tonight."

Eliana smiled her thanks to Russell. She knew how Russell would answer before she asked the question. She even felt a touch guilty for needing him to tell her it was all right to spend time with her parents instead of working on the walls. It was so absurd. They were fighting for their lives tomorrow. Of course, she should see her parents today.

She worked her way to the south, assigning each camp a number and an identifying feature as she passed it. It was easy enough for her to do, and it would make searching every camp for her parents much simpler.

She found her parents in the camp she labeled fourteen, yellow pants. It was an easy name for her to come up with as it was the fourteenth camp and there was a woman with brightly stained yellow pants. The silly naming game was just something she was doing to keep her mind occupied as she searched for mom and dad. It didn't matter anymore.

"Look, Grace. It's Ellie!" said her father as he saw her coming. Both of Eliana's parents were dressed in simple linen clothing, dyed brown, with their hair tied back in tight ponytails. They were farmers, and successful ones at that. Everything about their dress, their bodies, and their demeanor seemed to support that. Even as she approached, neither of them stood. They continued to inspect the seals on the Ganna fruit, but with just their hands now, instead of their eyes.

"Ellie, look at you! You've grown so much this season. What do they have you doing, all covered in mud like that?" asked her mother. Eliana knew she was just making light conversation, but it felt good, nonetheless.

"Building walls, but that's not important now," she said as she rushed into camp and threw her arms around her mother, hugging her tight. "I've missed you two! So much has been happening."

"Don't worry. There'll be time to talk on those things later," said her dad. "Your mother and I are just glad to see you."

"But what if things go badly?" Eliana planned on being brave and strong but being with her parents again reminded her how much she needed to be comforted. She was scared, but her parents were here now to tell her everything would be fine. "I'm scared."

"It's all right to be frightened, sweetheart," whispered her mother gently. "Stars above, we're frightened too, but it don't change nothing."

"Your mother and I have a gift for you," said her Dad. "We were planning on giving it to you next planting season, but with all that's happening, I think we can give it to you a bit early."

Eliana was stunned. Her parents worked so hard to let her be away from the farm as much as she was. She didn't deserve special gifts. They did. "It's not necessary, Dad. You two already work so hard to let me stay here and study."

"Nonsense, you're too darned smart to spend your life on the farm," said her mom as she reached into the pouch at her side and retrieved a tightly rolled piece of parchment. "Yer dad made it himself anyway. It didn't cost nothing."

Her father smiled. 'I raised all the eels myself. Your mom went out and found me enough Camphor Berries to stay up long enough to write the darn thing. I'm a little too old now to be staying up for a few days straight to pen a scroll."

Eliana's heart skipped a beat and her eyes welled up. Most farmers knew a smattering of natural magic. Mastery of even the simpler earth and water spells made farming much more efficient. Farming was handed down from one generation to the next, mother to daughter, father to son. The earth and water magics they used to help them farm were passed down as well.

Her father grew up fishing the lakes and waterways of the deep swamps. He never learned to control the earth. He learned to work with the winds instead. It was one of the things that made it so hard to be away from her parents. Magic, on most farms, was a responsibility shared across a full family, with each person able to devote small bits of magic toward tending the soil. While both of her parents could work with the water, her mother was the only one on the farm with knowledge of earth magic.

"You shouldn't have!" she said, but she was already unrolling it to read it. Spells could be learned in a variety of different ways, depending on the school and the type of spell. Many of her natural spells were taught through scrolls. Like in runecrafting and alchemy, gem powders were used as a vehicle to store eldritch energy. Other reagents and components were combined with the gems to make an ink. Hours or even days were then spent actually writing on the parchment, but once complete, the scroll was a truly magical thing. It was like distilled knowledge. It would take her just a few moments to read the scroll. When she was finished, the parchment would be blank, but the knowledge it taught would be hers forever.

"I trust you know what spell it is from your father's description of what was involved?"

"Yes, Mom. It's Lightning. May I read it?"

"Of course, sweetheart. Just make sure not to shock yourself. It's a bit advanced."

"I know, Mom. I'll be careful," she said quickly. She began reading and her heart swelled with joy as she felt the knowledge race into her mind. The movements, gestures and words were all laid out in beautiful simplicity, held in the tight magical script her father spent days writing for her. It meant even more to her to know he wrote it. Just as her parents taught her to farm, they were teaching her some of their magic as well. It was as it was supposed to be.

She lost track of time as her mind adapted and built a complete understanding of how to produce lightning from thin air. She closed her eyes for a moment as she processed it all, and when she opened them again, the parchment was blank. Her face melted into a warm smile. "Thank you so much!"

"Oh, don't bother on it, Ellie. You've got some time to sit, talk and farm with us, or do you have other things you've got to do?" asked her father.

"I've something I need to do later tonight, but I have a few hours right now," she said as she sat down on a stool between her parents and picked up a piece of Ganna to inspect. As much as she was terrified of the Black Tide, the simple act of farming with her mom and dad was comforting.

31
Russell

Russell found the smells of sweat, roasted bear and smoke from the forge fires pleasant. They paired surprisingly well. It could've been that he was on his second glass of garn, of course. He rather despised Ganna fruit ever since living through the nightmare at the farm, but it was hard to dislike garn. He only had the spiced Ganna wine a few times. It tended to go straight to his head.

A pair of long tables were set out in the middle of the room and one of the forges was converted to a makeshift oven to cook the bear. Russell guessed the soldiers hosted all their celebrations up in the Smithy, as most of the soldiers and blacksmiths knew one another. They even seemed to like each other.

He, Attia, and Eliana didn't know many of them, but the Ericksons were good hosts. Liam was the guest of honor, and therefore sat at the head of the table with his father. Conner sat across from Russell and a seat was left open for Malcolm, should he find time to attend. Russell doubted Malcolm would.

Russell watched with amusement as Liam told the harrowing tale of his narrow victory against the ferocious bear for the fifth or sixth time. He was a horrible liar. Attia and Conner already filled Russell in on what really happened. Russell wondered why they even bothered to lie about it. There were forty or so people in attendance. Most were older soldiers who'd already been through their own Rites of Passage. So, if everyone knew it was a tall tale, what was the point?

"He's such a shitty liar," Russell said as he finished off his second glass, hoping someone would come by and refill it.

Vargus grinned at him from across the table. "He's truly piss poor at it, ain't he?"

"What's the point, though? If everyone knows he didn't kill it alone, why bother lying?"

"Leadership practice," grunted Vargus. "A good leader has to be a good liar. Tellin yer troops they're likely gonna get a spear to the guts or an arrow to the balls don't really work well for morale. Besides, some folks did a solo kill for their trial." He nodded toward a giant man, with a lion's mane of a beard, sitting next to the Commander by the head of the table. "Well, Gunther did at least. In my book, that lets the rest of us pretend."

"Dad didn't?" asked Conner, a bit surprised.

"Nah. Yer dad's a smart one. He don't take dumb risks. That's why he's Commander and not Gunther."

Russell held his glass out as a man passed with a flagon of garn and was rewarded with a refill. He saw men loading generous slabs of meat on to a serving platter and his stomach growled. The mixture of seasoned rice, squash, and onions set out across the table was good, but he was looking forward to tasting the bear.

"Can I have everyone's attention?" shouted the Commander, rising to his feet.

"Until they finish serving up the meat, not a moment longer," grunted Gunther to a chorus of laughter.

"Fair enough," said the Commander as he held his glass up high. "A toast, then. To Liam and Conner..."

"And the Pathfinder girl who prolly killed the damn thing," added Gunther with a cough.

"To my sons," the Commander continued, loud enough to be heard over the laughter. "I've never been prouder as a father than I was this morning, seeing both of you face such a big challenge." He smiled and clinked his glass with Liam's before continuing. "And to all of you. I couldn't wish for a finer group of soldiers to lead."

Vargus leaned across the table. "See what I mean? He's a much better liar. Gunther would have called us out for the bunch of miserable piss pots we are."

"Oh, get on with it, Commander," shouted a soldier from the other table. "The best part of a toast is the part where we all drink!"

The Commander flashed the man a grin and took a drink from his glass. The room erupted into a chorus of cheers and the sounds of fists banging on hardwood as the men drank and celebrated. Liam's father slapped his son on the shoulder and sat back down. He was smiling, but Russell didn't think it was real. There was something in his eyes, or maybe it was how the smile vanished as he surveyed the room. The Commander appeared troubled.

The bear was soon brought, and everyone was given a portion. Russell found it to be on the tough side, but good, nonetheless. He discovered it was best when mixed into the rice with a little garn poured over it. Now that the celebration was fully under way, there were more people walking around with flagons of the fortified Ganna fruit wine. Using it as a sauce for his food allowed him to get his glass refilled more often. It was a brilliant plan.

"Is this how it always is, Vargus?" asked Conner.

"When we celebrate, and when we mourn," he said as he winked at Russell and poured some wine over his own rice. "But no, not all the time. Life's hard for all of us, one way or another. There's always work to do. Helps to have moments like this from time to time."

"We don't do anything like this in the Monastery. It's always so quiet."

"So, drink quietly?" added Russell. Conner shot him an angry glance, but he didn't care. It wasn't his fault that Conner was whiney and unwilling to take his good advice.

"It's not the drinking I miss," said Conner.

Eliana smiled and put her hand on Conner's. 'It's all right. Russ was just making a joke. We understand. Let's just enjoy tonight."

Conner heeded Ellie's advice, because it wasn't long before he was laughing and smiling again. As the night wore on, Russell decided that

Attia needed to be the next target. The girl was always so damn serious, and tonight was no different. She wasn't laughing. In fact, she was looking rather concerned. Russell followed her gaze and saw Constance crouching between the Commander and Gunther. When did she sneak in, he wondered? The two men were leaning in so that the three of them could discuss things quietly. Liam and a few others near the head of the table were paying attention and trying to listen.

It didn't take long before more people noticed. The room got progressively quieter as everyone took note of the Pathmaker speaking with the Commander. With the Black Tide coming, Constance would only bother him at his son's celebration if she had bad news. The mood and feeling in the room quickly shifted from happiness to dread. It left Russell feeling off balance and a little sick.

The Commander cleared his throat and frowned as he climbed to his feet. "I'm afraid I have some troubling news, but from the looks on all your faces, you've already figured that out. What we tell you here stays in this room... at least for now. I haven't decided how to tell the rest of the Citadel yet, and I need a few hours to think it through. Can I count on all of you for that? We can't afford a general panic."

He paused for a few moments until there was a general murmur of agreement throughout the room. "Go ahead, Constance. They're all soldiers. You don't need to pull any punches."

Constance rose from her crouch and spoke. "We've been tracking the progress of the Tide as it moves. Initially, it travelled slowly down the Serpent. We hoped to have four or five days yet to finish our preparations, but things changed for the worse yesterday."

Russell didn't like where this conversation was going one bit. He took a drink to calm his nerves, but it didn't seem to help. He took a second drink. Maybe that would help.

"The Tide is moving quickly now. We've tried to get close enough to see and understand what's happening, but it's been difficult. We kept track of it early on by watching from the other side of the river. That ended when the Tide came across a collection of downed trees that formed a natural bridge across the river."

"There's never been any such bridge. Trees wouldn't just fall like that," Attia whispered, but loudly enough that Constance and a few others heard.

"I know, Attia," said Constance as she held up a hand to quiet any other discussions. "The Tide used the bridge to spread out. It sent some of its mass to the other side of the river, forcing us to move in front as opposed to alongside of it. That's when we started noticing other fallen trees in critical areas. Places where the tide would be too constrained or delayed were cleared of obstacles. Tributaries and other waterways that would be difficult to cross now had bridges."

Russell could see the dread and fear written on everyone's faces. The Black Tide was horrifying as a mindless manifestation of nature. The thought of it being guided and helped by something both intelligent and powerful enough to knock down trees to make bridges brought the terror to a new level.

"We stationed Pathfinders farther down the river to watch some of the places we knew the Tide would have difficulties passing. There are hippos in the river, and a few drakes that nest alongside the water. We hoped that maybe some of the larger animals were knocking over trees in their haste to get away from the ants, but what one of our Pathfinders saw, or actually didn't see, confirms our worst fears."

Constance looked to the Commander as if she wanted permission to continue, and he nodded to her. "Pathrunner Arick was watching where Relersin Creek empties into the Serpent. It's fairly wide and runs fast at that spot. He hid up in the trees a fair distance away. He saw one tree and then another uproot itself and fall across the creek to make a bridge. When he investigated further, he found deep, clawed footprints by the fallen trees, and punctures in the trunks from where claws gripped the wood."

"Stars above! What kind of monster can do that?" asked a woman from the other table in a hushed tone.

"We're not certain. It's possible that—"

"Come on now, we're not frightened children," said Vargus, interrupting her. He held both hands out in front of himself and looked to the Commander, pleading.

"All right," said the Commander. "I owe you the truth." He sighed. "Invisible in broad daylight, and strong enough to pull trees from the ground with ease. I wish it were otherwise, but the only things that I know of that can do that are the Demon Queen's Guardians. And with both sides of the river to cover, I'd wager we can count on at least two, if not all three of them." The room got louder as the soldiers absorbed what they were told. Russell thought he heard real panic and fear in some of the small conversations that suddenly sprung up all around him.

"Quiet down, now!" said the Commander. "A few of us have faced the Guardians before. We survived back then, and we're much more powerful now. No, I don't expect them to engage us directly. They're using the Tide as a weapon for a reason. When the Tide is here, they'll keep their distance. Maybe they'll counter some of our spells, but we'll have no shortage of protections. There's a reason the Citadel still stands."

"How long? How long until the Tide hits us, Chief?" asked a bald soldier with huge bushy eyebrows.

"Not tomorrow, Garrison, but near sunrise the next day," said Duncan.

"And the other Pathfinders? You'd said there were others stationed along the river, Pathmaker," asked Attia.

Constance flinched at the question. 'We've yet to find their bodies, but the other three never reported back. Silver sent her words out along the wind to each of them. Her spells couldn't find them either."

Vargus grabbed a flagon and filled Attia's glass. "We drink some when we celebrate. We drink more when we mourn."

Russell held out his glass and Vargus refilled it. If tomorrow was one of the last days for all of them, he might as well enjoy this one to the fullest. He looked around as he took a deep drink and was satisfied to see many others arriving at the same conclusion.

32
Arronhelm

Arronhelm smiled sadly while he watched Malcolm study. It cost Arronhelm so very much to prepare for him. Tomes on the subject of necromancy weren't common, and with so little time, Arronhelm didn't have the luxury of being careful. He was glad he did it, though.

Malcolm was amazing. The boy already read more than half the books he gathered for him. Ever since Malcolm made that deal with his spirit, his progress was phenomenal, but the deal withered him. It was a trade Arronhelm would've gladly made himself, were he offered something similar.

It was impossible to keep up anymore. The dreams were coming too rapidly and Arronhelm was simply overwhelmed by it all. He stopped sleeping for a time, but it merely caused the visions to bleed into his waking reality. He understood, he truly did. Dreams were how the soul guided him and helped him with his work. There was so much the soul needed to show him yet, but they were nearly out of time. He felt like he was constantly running, but never fast enough. The boundaries between dreams and reality were rapidly fading for him.

He was the Architect. He accepted and even embraced that purpose for his life. He and his second soul worked in relative harmony across the decades to prepare for the future. Working together, they built the

Citadel into a small, but powerful enclave, but his time was running out. He always knew, in his heart of hearts, that his tenure would eventually draw to a close. His role was to build and pass on a strong foundation to the next generation that followed him. Still, the reality of it was like a crushing weight on his chest. There was too much work yet to do. He felt like a failure. He desperately needed more time.

He never dreamt of so many new souls all at once. Sure, others, blessed with the touch of another soul, died in the past, but it was a rare occurrence. He hadn't been surprised when he dreamt of the soul of the necromancer. It merely told him someone would, or already had passed on. With Aelith losing contact so long ago, he assumed she died. The depressing reality of the situation only hit him a month later when he started dreaming of many other souls, all at the same time.

Decades ago, his visions weren't restricted to vague impressions of whatever new soul the Painting was calling. He used to receive vivid visions of who'd die and how it would happen. He promised never to give warnings or even talk about it. It was a terrible burden, but knowing who was destined to die made it easier for him to prepare for the future. He broke that trust with his second soul once.

He loved Emily so much. It was so very foolish of him to try and warn her, but he wanted to save his lover. The soul fought him tooth and nail over it. No matter how hard he tried, he wasn't able to find his words. The soul ripped and twisted everything to the point where he became unintelligible, and it only got worse from there.

The visions came next. The soul filled his every waking moment with horrifying, twisted nightmares. They crippled him and stripped him of his sanity. In the end, when he finally fought through it all to warn her, she didn't believe him. By that time, no one did. They all thought he'd finally gone mad. She died, of course. Just like he predicted. That was thirteen years ago, and his second soul never showed him who was destined to die ever since.

Arronhelm didn't need dreams to know who'd die this time. If his visions were true, it'd be most of them. He didn't need to wonder how either. The timing of everything was just too perfect. It would happen soon. The Black Tide might not kill them, but in one way or another, the arrival of the ants would set events into motion. He wanted to warn everyone of what was coming, but he knew the soul wouldn't allow it. Further, he knew it wouldn't change anything. All he could do was research each of the new souls as they were presented to him.

Of course, it was a fool's errand. Still, he desperately tried until even that became impossible. Leaving the Citadel was no longer a safe option for him. Whatever materials he gathered would have to be enough.

Arronhelm felt Chariden's siren call on his sixth trip to Derregain in as many weeks. Ordinarily, he never magically travelled outside of the Citadel more than once or twice a year. He knew the risks. The Demon Queen fought him on two occasions in the past. He knew how powerful she was. He understood she could send her Desires into anyone's heart, nearly anywhere in the world.

He knew she sent her insidious Desires to scour the world, searching for him. He was safe within and around the Citadel. The power of the Painting made sure of that, but Derregain was hundreds of miles away. Arronhelm had no protection there.

Arronhelm reasoned that even the Demon Queen's power must have limitations. He didn't believe her capable of constantly trying to capture his heart. She needed to know when and where to look, but the more often he magically traveled to Derregain, the more likely one of Chariden's agents would recognize him.

It hadn't felt like much at first. He just finished purchasing a rare history book about Silverhorn, an ancient order that had something to do with one of the new souls. Suddenly, he got the idea to go buy a crystal rose. He thought nothing of it. It was probably just something he saw in one of his many visions. It didn't need to mean anything to him, as long as it held meaning for one of the new souls.

The terror struck him the moment he walked into the glassworks store and laid eyes on their roses. He saw a vision of himself kneeling to present the rose to the Demon Queen. He saw her take it from him, and his heart melted with joy at her smile. He remembered the absolute horror he felt as the magic of Chariden's Desires flared to life. Her call was strong, and he struggled to manage the words and gestures to magically return to the safety of the Citadel.

He was a prisoner now. He could move freely within the Citadel, and in the surrounding forests and clearings, but that was all. The Painting generated some kind of protective shield that extended just shy of a mile from it in all directions. Even the strongest demons had a difficult time crossing it, and despite all her power, Chariden never managed to force her Desires into the heart of anyone behind the barrier's protection.

Sadly, Arronhelm discovered that with Chariden already inside his heart, she was there to stay. While the Painting could block the Demon Queen's compulsions, it couldn't remove any of those that were already rooted within.

It was easy enough for him to test. He walked out to a farm he knew lay just inside the barrier. He felt her siren's song again the instant he took that one step too far. He remembered how his heart sang and how his mind filled with glorious visions of her. He remembered wanting to cast a Flight spell and journey to be with her. It was difficult, but he resisted, but it was only a matter of time. He couldn't risk being outside of the Painting's protection, ever again, if he could avoid it.

The books he gathered thus far would likely be all there were. The professors could help the children with their studies, of course. The Citadel's teachers and libraries were equipped to teach most arts. It would only be the nature of the souls and their relationships to their hosts that lacked, and Malcolm was already teaching the others about that. The necromancer within Malcolm worked with spirits and souls all its life. It had a better understanding of it all. Maybe that's what the future demanded?

Arronhelm sighed as he watched Malcolm continue his studies. The boy was almost oblivious to the outside world while he read. Arronhelm wanted to warn Malcolm about what the next few days would bring. He wanted to protect him, but who's to say that warning him would even help? Maybe if he let Malcolm read for just a few more hours, the boy would learn something to protect him and the others far better than any warning could.

The Tide would be here in just over a day. Arronhelm heard about the new estimated arrival time from the Pathfinders. It was troubling, but it wasn't what scared him. The fact that the Tide was being escorted by what could only be the Demon Queen's Guardian demons tied everything together.

Chariden must have made a deal with the spiders to get them to remove their webs. That sent the Black Tide directly at the Citadel. The Guardians were likely the only demons she controlled that were strong enough to move through the Painting's barrier, so she sent them along as escorts. It meant that they'd be present while the Tide was upon them. The Guardians were incredibly powerful spell casters, capable of summoning aid from Hell itself.

Arronhelm was certain the attack would be deadly. It would be brutal enough to force many of them to sacrifice themselves. All he could do was hope their sacrifices would be enough to keep the walls of the Citadel standing, and the precious Painting safe. For him, it was simple. He'd protect the Painting or die trying. The alternative, for him, was far worse than death.

33
Conner

"We'll have your team responsible for the area between posts seven and eight," said Conner's dad to the assembled group. Conner was tired. He drank too much at the celebration, and what little sleep he got was plagued with nightmares. He suspected everyone else felt much the same. Still, the work carried on.

"Your only job will be keeping the ants from making it on to land. We've engineered seven reservoirs with gates we can open to flood additional water through the moats. With any luck, we'll be able to flush the moat out into the Serpent a couple of times throughout the morning. Make no mistake, there'll be millions of ants passing by us. A lot will try to cross. Some will manage to pull it off. The reservoirs are only there for emergencies."

"Is it even possible for the ants to cross moats this wide, sir?" asked Liam.

"Regrettably, yes. Remember, the Tide makes its way all the way south, well into the swamps. They're no strangers to crossing rivers and streams. Once some them get a hold of the shore, others climb on until they build themselves into a bridge. They'll do the same thing here."

Conner looked over his team. Vargus was assigned to them as a guard, which brought Conner a sense of relief. The old veteran was a fearless fighter, and he already knew Conner and his friends. A second soldier, a thin man with facial features resembling a weasel, was also assigned to protect them. His name was Wayne, and Conner already disliked him. While the man never refused an order, he seemed to take pride in asking questions about everything to the point where it was often just quicker not to involve him. Conner's dislike of Wayne was balanced by his deep admiration for Nora, the young woman assigned to provide medical support. She was one of the more accomplished healing students within the Monastery. While Conner's skills with countering toxins were limited, she was quite good at it.

"If things go well, the Runes of Protection will divert most of the Tide off to the sides," said his father. "The ants that trying to cross our moats should only be those that curl back in and around the runes. Again, that may end up being tens of thousands over the course of the morning, but the goal is to get the Tide to turn. We need to get its momentum flowing out to the sides of us."

Conner yawned and looked over at Liam in his new suit of plate armor. Their father gave the bear's heart to the runecrafters before the feast and ordered them to work all night, if need be, to carve the necessary symbols into the metal to complete the Attunement Runes by morning. The result was a suit of plate armor that moved with the fluidity of chainmail. Liam looked strong and confident in the armor.

Most of his friends appeared confident to Conner. Even Ellie and Russ, who were equipped with glorified brooms for pushing ants back into the moat, seemed to accept and embrace their roles. Attia received a combat assignment that left her free to kill any insects she wanted to. Wayne protested, saying it was unfair that she was given flexibility when he wasn't, but Attia certainly appreciated the freedom. Conner was pleased with it too.

If there was an exception, it was Malcolm. The Chancellor walked down with him about midday. Malcolm was wearing the tan robe he wore out to the farms, but he carried a staff as well now. Conner thought it was a bit overstated until he realized that his friend needed to lean on the staff often. Malcolm looked so different than he did just a few days ago. His skin looked thin and brittle. Conner could see faint blue veins beneath the skin all across Malcolm's face, and his eyes were bloodshot.

He looked weak and frail. Conner didn't want to point it out, and as it turned out, there was no need. Russell made sure Malcolm knew he looked like shit.

"There are thirty teams spread out around the circle, each with a section of moat to protect," his father said. "If bad things happen, just know that you're not alone. Call for help, but understand the path leads both ways. If a nearby team gets overwhelmed, I expect you to help out. Remember, our strongest fighters and casters will be stationed in the center. We'll see if any area is having issues. Help will always be close."

A large, elevated platform had been built in the center of their island. The command staff and several small, but powerful teams would observe from there. They'd move into action if needed. Conner hadn't been able to watch Constance in battle against the goblins, but he heard she cut through them in a matter of seconds. She'd be up there, and so would Gunther, Solen, Devin, Silver and several others who were regarded as legends within the Citadel. His dad would be leading them all.

Conner's father turned and pointed to a group of robed figures off in the distance. They were kneeling in a loose circle around one of the pylons that supported the weight of the Citadel. There were dozens of pylons, but only the four corner pylons had staircases that led up into the first level of the structure. "We're surrounding each of the stairways with its own set of Runes of Protection. If there's time, we'll have the runecrafters make a few other sets of runes, but just be mindful of them. Even if your entire area gets overrun, you can fall back to one of those circles of runes for safety."

Conner felt bad for the runescrafters. Yesterday morning, he saw them out working on the two massive sets of runes that stretched out from either side of the great river, the Serpent. There were a couple of them out there still, applying a few finishing touches to ensure that the magic held against the Tide. Others were pressed into service to finish his brother's armor. Conner was sure that some of those who worked all throughout the night were the same people who were kneeling and rushing to craft Runes of Protection around the staircases. It seemed to be endless, thankless work.

Conner's dad cleared his throat and frowned. "Let's talk about the ants themselves. I'd like to pretend that everything will go smoothly, but I think we all know that's not how the world works." His father walked a little closer and crouched down near the group so he could talk softly. "They'll range in size. I don't think I've ever seen one under two feet long make it this far south, and most of them will be considerably larger. The bigger they are, the stronger they'll be."

"I've seen ants drag things ten times their size. Are they as strong as regular ants?" asked Eliana.

"Good question, and no, not quite. One of the bigger ones might be able to drag a person along by itself, but in my experience, that's not what they like to do. These ants will have incredibly strong jaws. They'll have a tough time crushing plate armor, but if someone were to get knocked down..." He frowned. "Let's just say I've seen it happen before."

"The poisons, Dad?" asked Conner. He saw many ant bites and stings, working in the Monastery. Poison was always involved.

His father nodded. "All of them carry a little venom with their bites. I'm not going to lie. It hurts like hell, and it may slow you down a touch, but just don't panic. It's not the kind of poison that will stop your heart or anything like that." Conner wanted to direct his father to the stronger poisons, but his father held up a hand. "There'll be some ants with actual stingers. Their poison is a bit stronger. Actually, I'm going to say that it's a lot stronger. A clean hit from one of those will make your arms and legs lock up and spasm. You'll be lucky to make it more than a couple dozen steps before you fall over."

"Well, that sounds fun," said Russell sarcastically.

"Each team is being supported by a healer who'll counter that poison, should anyone get stung. Nora is here for your team. Conner, are you able to cure that too?"

Conner cured it in the past, but only with teachers there to guide him. "I don't think so, Dad. I mean—"

"He can, sir," interrupted Nora. She smiled at him. "If he needs to, he'll be able to." Conner wasn't sure he agreed with her assessment of his abilities, but it felt good to hear her praise. Nora was smart, popular, and pretty. All the boys in the Monastery wanted to spend time with her. He couldn't help but smile at the thought that she had faith in him.

His father nodded. "All right. Then the poison won't be much of an issue for this team. Nora and Conner will assist if anyone gets stung too badly. Really, it all comes down to everyone staying on their feet and being smart. Those of you with brooms will be doing the most, I hope. Keeping an ant from getting over the wall and on to land is just as good as killing one. "

"As for killing them, sir. Is there anything we need to know about?" asked Liam.

Their father shook his head. "They're really tough. I think you and Vargus will have your best success slicing down between body segments. Cripple the things and leave them. Wayne, your mace will either work great or not at all. It's heavy enough or it isn't. I think you'll figure that out pretty quickly. "

Wayne looked like he wanted to ask a question, but Vargus growled at him. Conner had to fight to hold back his laughter. The old veteran literally growled like a jungle cat at the weasel-faced man. "Father," Conner started, more to distract himself from the comically pained expression on Wayne's face than anything else, "if the Tide is here before dawn, what do we do about light?"

His father smiled. "Good thought. The numbered posts will all have torches, and we'll be lighting the oil and timber that's been spread out on the other side of the moat. We should get a good amount of light from that. Expect a lot of magic, but if for some reason, it's just too dark," he said with a grin, "I'll take care of it."

Conner suddenly wanted to hug his father. The feeling was powerful and unexpected. He knew it wouldn't be appropriate. His dad was the Commander. He was responsible for getting the entire Citadel ready to face something truly horrifying. His dad needed to project confidence and strength, but it didn't make Conner's feelings any less real. "All right, Father," he said softly. "I won't worry about the lights." What Conner meant to say was that he was worried about his dad.

His father smiled and nodded at him as he rose from his crouch. Maybe he understood, Conner thought. "I have a lot of other teams to prepare, and the day's grown long. Dusk will be here before we know it, but I wanted to spend what little extra time I had here. This is the youngest team, but I have faith in all of you. Now, finish preparing the area, but don't waste any time. Everyone's tired, and we'll be waking people and getting them out here well in advance of the Tide tomorrow. If you're going to sleep at all, now might be your best time."

Conner's father regarded each of them for a moment. He looked at Liam last. "You'll do well today, son," he said with pride before turning and walking purposefully away, towards the next team. Conner's heart skipped a beat as he fought back the tears. He needed to be told that he'd do well too. Most of all, though, he wanted his father to stay. What if this was the last time he saw his dad? He wanted to run after him to spend just a little more time, but Liam turned to him and gently shook his head. Conner saw the same emotion in his brother's eyes and he understood. His father had a tremendous responsibility.

"You heard the Commander," said Liam to the group. "Finish up here and get some rest."

As much as it hurt, Conner had to let his father go.

34
Eliana

The morning air was cool and damp, but Eliana's shivering had little to do with the weather. She was terrified. She heard the Black Tide from the moment she reported to her post a half an hour ago. It sounded like the roar of a waterfall, but it had a higher pitch. The sound was soft at first, but the volume gradually grew. Now it was more of a sickening drone, and it'd only get louder. The vibrations were worse than the sound, though. It was still almost an hour before dawn, and she could already feel the movement of the Black Tide.

The passage of time grew into its own horrifying monster, as the vibrations and the sounds continued to inexorably surge in power. Eliana saw that she wasn't alone in her misery. Her friends were huddling closer together for comfort and camaraderie. Everyone knew the Tide was on their doorstep. They simply couldn't see it yet, and their imaginations were making the worst of it.

The shouts came shortly before dawn. The sky was just starting to tinge with hints of red, orange and gold from the sun that would soon peek its head over the tree line. A few brilliant, but small spheres of light shot up and streaked across the sky, until they slowed and stopped high above, casting the clearing in an eerily delicate, silvery light. The shouts that followed were louder and Eliana thought they carried a sense of fear and desperation with them. Maybe that was just how she felt.

She was short, and with everyone in front of her, it was difficult to find a position where she could see, but Vargus took mercy on her. He reached down and effortlessly lifted her up on to his shoulders. At first, she wasn't quite sure what she was seeing. There appeared to be a strange, shimmering liquid spilling out of the trees on the far side of the clearing. To her, it looked almost like the forest itself was bleeding, but instead of a rich red, the blood was ebony, with silvery highlights from the light of the Flare spells.

More and more of the liquid poured from the edges of the trees. It came faster and faster, and as the front of the shimmering, chittering mass of darkness oozed across the clearing, Eliana saw them. Ants. So many ants! Skittering and crawling over each other, the ones in front racing forward so as to not be trampled by the ones behind. The sight of it was maddening. Eliana wanted to scream. She thought she heard others cry out, but she couldn't be sure. The droning cacophony of the surging mass of insects devoured all other sound.

And they just kept coming. In her imagination, she thought the ants would sweep down, hugging either side of the river, but this wasn't that at all. This was much worse. The ants stretched out as far as her eyes could see. They started pouring into the clearing from the sides as well, all racing to fight their way out of the thick forest to open ground. She put her hands over her ears and started to cry.

Vargus squeezed the tops of her thighs. He must have felt her sobbing. It was comforting, and it brought her back from the edge of the pit of dizzying fear. It would've been so easy to have been just a frightened little girl in that moment, but she worked too hard, and had too much to lose to give up like that. She thought about her parents and wondered what they'd think. They raised her to be strong! She wished they were stationed here with her, but the Commander had them working as part of a team near post twenty-four. She knew that they'd be critical to the success of that team, just like Vargus and Nora were to hers.

There was a sound, much like lightning striking a tree, as the first of the giant ants crashed into the magic of the Runes of Protection on either side of the Serpent. The barrier fields created by the narrow, nearly two-dimensional, oval patterns of runes flashed and sparked. Crackling bolts of amber energy started dancing rapidly around the barrier fields. As more and more ants slammed into the fields, the bolts of energy combined and thickened, until the entirety of both fields pulsed and glowed. They looked beautiful to Eliana. From this angle, the Runes of Protection looked like giant panes of glowing amber glass, each only climbing to a height of ten feet, but stretching out more than a hundred feet away from the river on either side.

The droning cacophony of the swarm rose in both pitch and volume as more ants were driven into the magically impenetrable fields. The mass and momentum of the Tide kept forcing ants into the Runes of Protection. Thousands upon thousands of insects were crushed as the Tide mindlessly pushed its bulk against an unnatural force it was simply incapable of understanding. Eliana saw the darkness growing against each field as the bodies continued to pile up against one another. Would the Tide just keep crushing itself until the piles of its own dead stacked up high enough as to allow the ants to flow over the magical walls?

The river darkened as the dead insects liquefied and drained off into the river. A swarm of live ants started spilling into the Serpent, deflected and pushed off to the sides of the barriers by the unrelenting pressure of the Tide's forward momentum. Eliana watched as the dams redirected countless wriggling, chitinous bodies off into the moats flowing around the Citadel.

The water was running fast, but it didn't take long before a few ants latched their jagged legs into the earthen walls of the channels and berms. Once an ant gained purchase, others crashed into it and held on to its body. Sometimes, the force of the impact would dislodge it, but other times, the ant would hold on long enough for others to attach themselves, building a bridge for yet others to climb upon.

Vargus gently lowered her to the ground as Liam moved off to the left. Eliana saw a place to the north where the ants caught on to the wall and formed a living ladder that others were using to escape the moat. They were pouring out and over the wall! Once on land, they scurried in all directions. Many were heading towards them.

"To arms," cried Liam as he moved to engage the charging insects.

"Ellie, help me," shouted Russell. She looked over and saw him leaning over the short wall, frantically pushing down with his broom.

"Coming!" she answered as she grabbed her own broom and raced over to the wall next to him. There were two ants holding on just above the surface of the water. One was trying to climb, but Russell was pushing back against it. She swatted at it, but as she did, two more ants that were being swept downstream, caught on to its body and forced their own legs into the wall. With four of them now anchored together, they were simply too strong for Russ and her to dislodge.

Russell started slamming his broom into the legs of one of the ants. "I can't knock them off! It's no use!"

"Hold on," shouted Eliana as she dropped her broom and placed both hands on the short defensive wall. She chanted quietly and pictured herself digging into the earth. In her mind's eye, she imagined the earth gently parting to allow her to move through unhindered. It took only a few breaths to picture her hands tunneling like worms through the side of the moat to a place right behind where the ants anchored themselves. She felt her natural magic responding. It flowed through her into the ground. The energy moved to where she directed it, pooling in the wall right where she envisioned. She started to gently blow, and the earth responded to her wishes. It started to loosen and fall away, slowly at first, but as Eliana blew faster, the earth fell away more quickly. The ants scrambled and tried to dig their spikey legs in deeper, but it was no use. A sheet of earth a few inches thick slid into the moat and took the ants with it.

"Thanks," said Russ. Eliana nodded. She felt a wave of exhaustion wash over her and she leaned against the wall for support. Her spell worked, but she realized she could've done it more efficiently. With the immediate threat cleared, she looked further up the moat at the massive ball of ants forming a living ladder. She wondered if she could dislodge them just as easily. She needed to get over there somehow, though, and she didn't think it was safe.

Both Liam and Vargus were engaged with a group of giant ants. The insects moved so chaotically that she couldn't quite tell how many there were, but she thought it was at least six. Both of the soldiers were crouching and trying to use their shields to bash at them. She saw dismembered ants on the ground between the two, so it seemed they landed a few strikes with their swords as well.

She looked back at the ball of ants in the moat. As she considered how much energy it would take to control the earth from this distance, she noticed the water in the moat start to churn and swirl. It looked like a whirlpool at first, but it rapidly took shape as more and more water was drawn into it. One of the stronger natural mages was making an elemental, she realized. Eliana studied the principals involved, of course. She just made the earth respond to her magic. With more magic, she could've shaped the earth into a living force of its own to fight for her.

The water elemental twisted and spun. As it did, it whipped heavy tendrils of swirling, condensed liquid around it. They looked like watery flails as they crashed into the ants over and over again. The strikes didn't appear to faze the insects at first, but it only took a few moments before Eliana saw damage being done. The ants shrugged off most of the swings without moving, but one out of every couple would land with enough force to crush or partially dislodge an ant from the others. The elemental spun faster and faster, and as it did, more and more ants were killed or knocked free from the ball. Eventually, so many ants were killed or broken that the tight ball of bodies collapsed and fell away from the wall of the moat to be swept downstream.

She looked back over at Liam and Vargus as they continued to fend off the insects that made it onto land. A few soldiers from the other group joined the battle, and it looked to Eliana that the fight was well in hand. Only a few of the ants were still moving full speed. Most were missing legs or body segments. Eliana saw the bodies of a few people scattered on the ground near where the ants climbed out of the moat. They were probably taken by surprise. It could've easily happened to her team too, had Russ not been paying attention and called for help.

Eliana turned to scan the other camps. Her heart raced as she saw the team around post twenty-four. They looked calm and relaxed. She sighed in relief. Her eyes were drawn next to the main platform. Silver's hands were raised above her head. Eliana saw slender rivers of lightning dancing between Silver's hands and a churning cloud, coalescing high in the sky above her. It was another elemental, but one made from wind instead of water. Silver lowered her arms and pointed as she completed her spell. Lightning coursed across the cloud as it flew out over the roiling ocean of ants.

The swirling wind elemental flew out past the river and the Runes of Protection to join four others just like it. They all swept down over the ants, and where they did, lightning and violent winds sent burning insects flying everywhere. The destruction of it all was breathtaking. Eliana studied and read about all forms of elementals but seeing it in person was a completely different thing. She felt confident for the first time all morning. The ants were terrible, but the magic of the Citadel was stronger!

Her feelings of elation were short-lived, however. Out of nowhere, one of the elementals shattered. One moment, it was raining destruction and devastation across the field of ants, and in the next, it blew apart, scattering itself across the predawn sky. Eliana watched in mute horror as a second, and then a third elemental followed suit. The remaining two survived for a few more seconds before they too dissipated into nothing but harmless air.

Eliana knew that it couldn't have been anything the ants did. An elemental could certainly be damaged and destroyed, but not like this. Her heart sank as all other possible explanations faded away, leaving her with only one.

The Demon Queen's Guardians were hidden out there, somewhere.

35
Attia

Attia was exhausted, and from the position of the sun, she doubted it was much later than eight in the morning. Her ears ached from the constant incessant droning of the insects, and her left thigh burned from where she was pretty badly bitten by one of them. She felt fortunate to be alive. She couldn't help but smile.

The Tide crashed into the Runes of Protection right around dawn. At first, it looked like the runes wouldn't hold against such a tremendous force, but miraculously, they did. The Tide kept pounding into the magical walls, crushing thousands and thousands of ants to death. The piles of their dead trampled bodies formed ramps of sorts. It looked like the ants might have been able to stack up enough of their dead to cross over the tops of the walls, and if not for the natural mages, they would have.

Attia never saw a wind elemental before. While the Pathfinder order taught natural magic, air was rarely selected as a specialty. For her part, Attia learned the element of earth, although she wasn't very good at it. After seeing the power of the wind elementals, she regretted her choice.

The natural mages sent storm after storm out over the endless field of giant ants. The storms never lasted long. Something was out there, destroying the magic, but the natural mages kept sending new ones.

They used the elementals to blow apart the piles of ant corpses before they ever got so high that the Black Tide could flow over the magical walls.

Over time, as more of the ants followed the walls away from the river, The Tide started to redirect itself. The ants never stopped ramming into the Runes of Protection, but after an hour, the majority were flowing out and around the magical walls.

Even with the Tide being pushed out and away, there were just too many ants out there. Many went right on past the Citadel, but others worked their way back in towards the moat. The fires along the far sides of the moat were lit, and that kept the ants away for a half hour or so. The fires eventually burned out, and the ants started to look for ways to cross the moat.

The design of the reservoirs and moats worked well. If the ants were trying to cross in ten different places at a time, nine of the ten attempts failed. Still, the ants were making it across with regularity, which led to constant battles all across their tiny island.

"Incoming!" cried Wayne. Attia turned to face the threat. A small swarm of ants were racing at them from back by post nine. The two teams to the south of them got overwhelmed earlier in the morning. Each team lost enough of their members that they were forced to combine into a single stronger team. This left the region between posts eight and nine poorly defended.

"We need help," called Attia as she moved back a few paces from Wayne, readying herself. There were more ants in the swarm than she thought they could handle, and to make matters worse, more were flowing over the wall by post nine.

"This is going to be shitty," said Russell as he waved his torch a few times to fan its flame back to life. Both Eliana and Russell abandoned their brooms in favor of torches over the course of the morning. Attia's long curved sword proved good for swiftly crippling the giant ants. Instead of wasting time on a second strike, she took to moving on to a new target and leaving the crippled insect behind for either Russell or Eliana to burn. They got comfortable working as a unit, but the number of ants that were coming was far greater now.

Attia moved off to the right, away from the moat. She wanted more room to work with, and she found that Wayne's shield was much more effective when he could keep the wall and the moat on his other flank. Further, it gave Nora a safe pocket behind Wayne in which to operate without the risk of being cornered by the ants. Attia spared a glance back the other way. Vargus, Liam and Conner were dealing with a group of ants that charged over from another breach. Malcolm was making his way over toward her group. She didn't know what he was capable of, but any help would be welcome at this point.

The ants rushed forward, converging on Wayne. He swung his shield low and smashed his mace down on the head of the first ant. It was on the smaller side. The mace broke through the chitin plating covering the creature's head. It crumpled to the ground, but as it did, two other ants ran over its body and snapped their jaws at Wayne. The soldier drew back from one set of pinching jaws, but the second set got a solid hold on his arm.

"Fire and smoke! Someone get it off me!" he shouted as he tried to shake it free from his arm. It was far too strong, and to make matters worse, it was heavy enough to prevent Wayne from straightening up his stance while it held him.

"Help him, Russ," yelled Attia as she lunged forward and spun, swinging her sword in a low arc. She felt her blade cut through the legs of one insect, but its chitin was jagged and strong. Her blade twisted in her hands just enough to prevent her from cutting into a second ant. Attia recovered from her lunge by somersaulting backwards. She was back to her feet before two charging ants got close enough to bite. She swept her blade down at an angle and caught one of the two perfectly, slicing it in half.

Another half dozen ants charged. Wayne was nearly immobilized now. Three ants made it past his guard and crunched their powerful mandibles down on his armor-plated thighs. Russell leaned in and burn the one free from Wayne's arm. It allowed the soldier to swing his mace again, but even as he connected and killed one, another rushed in to take its place.

"Get back, Russ," Attia shouted as she sprung forward, frantically slashing at the pack of insects that were converging on Wayne. She cut the head off of one, which earned her the attention of two of the six charging him. Attia was only wearing light leather armor. With four or more ants focused on her now, she couldn't risk getting caught. She relaxed and prepared her balance magic before somersaulting backward again, right past a charging ant. It bit at her, but her magic helped accelerate and guide her acrobatics in such a way as to avoid the bite and gain her some precious distance.

Attia shifted her wounded left leg back and sunk into a defensive crouch. Five ants scurried toward her. If she gave up more ground, however, the ants could shift in behind Wayne. That would likely be the end of him, and maybe Nora as well. Attia couldn't let it happen. She slashed her sword out in a quick draw cut and hit one of them in the side of the head. It died instantly, crashing to the ground in a twisted tangle of legs. The others rushed forward, and Attia started to panic. She heard Malcolm chanting, though, and out of the corner of her eye, she saw the shadows swirl and grow into a floating silhouette.

"Help!" screamed Wayne, but Attia had her own concerns. An ant sprung forward and snapped its jaws at her. She tried to turn and shift back a step, but she was too slow. A searing, stinging pain erupted across her calf and shin as the ant's jaws crunched shut around her forward leg. She slashed down and separated the thing's head from its body, but when she stepped back, she found herself slowed. With its mandibles still closed around her leg, the dead ant's head hung from her ankle like a ball and chain. It wasn't too heavy, but it hindered her movement, which was something she couldn't afford.

A wispy figure of swirling darkness floated in front of her. It had long, slender arms that spun around it like whips or ropes. The moving darkness drifted right into the ants, passing through two of the remaining four that were converging on Attia. They stopped moving in response to the wraith's touch. Frost and ice spread out over their ebony carapaces as all life and warmth was drawn from their bodies. Attia felt the cold of the wraith as it passed close to her. She shivered and watched it gracefully, but eerily move through the other two ants. Once again, their carapaces frosted over, and they quickly stopped moving.

"Hold them off with that thing as long as you can, Malcolm! I'll help Wayne."

Attia turned toward Wayne just in time to see a large ant climb out of the moat right next to him. "Watch out!" she screamed, but with three other ants holding his legs, there wasn't much he could do to get out of the way. It sprung at him, curling its abdomen forward as it did. Its stinger struck Wayne right above the thigh, an area of his armor that wasn't fully plated. The man screamed as the ant crashed into his body. Its weight and the pushing and pulling of the three on his legs were enough to knock him to the ground.

Attia watched in horror as more insects climbed out of the moat where the first one did. Wayne screamed. The ants let go of his legs and crawled on top of his body, their mandibles biting at the less armored parts of his body. Attia knew the reality of the situation. The poison from the sting was already arresting the poor man's movement. There was nothing she could do for him.

She could save Nora, though. "Run, Nora!" she shouted.

Attia sprung forward and swung her blade at the pair of giant insects that just climbed over the wall. Nora stood there, screaming and watching as an ant bit Wayne right in the face. Its mandibles snapped together with a sickening crunch. Wayne's teeth and jaw simply shattered from the pressure. "Run, damn you. Run!" Attia screamed.

More ants climbed out of the moat, as even more made their way over from post nine. They were being overwhelmed! Attia moved between Nora and Wayne. She heard the woman whimpering and repeating, 'I'm sorry,' over and over again, but there were too many insects converging to spare Nora much time. Attia swung her blade and extended her arms out fully. She cut one ant in half, but instead of stopping her cut, she continued her spin until her forearm made contact with Nora's side. She rotated further, gently pushing the woman in Malcolm's direction.

"Nora, go to Liam," she heard Russell shout. Attia had to trust her friends would keep the girl safe. She couldn't spare even a moment of her attention to look. Fortunately, the ants that worked their way over from post nine stopped and joined their brethren tearing at Wayne's body. The ants climbing up over the wall right here, however, started advancing on her. There were so many. She didn't think she could keep them all at bay, and with more pouring out of the moat by the moment, she knew their position was lost.

"Malcolm, Russ, everyone.... Fall back!" she shouted as she retreated, swinging her sword to slow down the rush of the advancing ants. She spared a glance to her flank and was pleased to see seven or eight frozen ant corpses, but she saw no sign of Malcolm's ghostly ally anymore.

"One step ahead of you," shouted Russell from somewhere behind her.

Attia was relieved to have no one else to worry about. At least a dozen ants climbed up out of the moat and they were spreading out to surround her. Her stomach turned and her heart skipped a beat as she realized that she was cut off from her friends. She could still retreat toward the platform, but the ants were now in front of her and to either side.

Attia panicked. She retreated faster and looked around, desperate for help, but it didn't look like any help would come. Everywhere she looked, she saw the same scene. Small clumps of defenders, frantically trying to slow the flow of ants on to the island. Many of the posts looked undefended. Attia didn't want to think about what might've happened to the teams assigned to defend those now abandoned posts.

"Well done," came the calm voice of Solen from behind her. Relieved, Attia took another gliding step backwards as her teacher moved out in front of her, a sword in either hand. The ants pressed from everywhere, all at once, but compared to Solen, it was as if they were moving in slow motion. Both blades thrust forward like striking serpents, each cleanly impaling a giant insect. As the ones moved in from the side, he twisted and spun, and with each spin, one of his swords cut with deadly precision. Attia couldn't tell if Solen was dodging on his own or letting his balance magic move his body for him. She suspected it was a combination of both, but each dodge was accompanied by a strike, and each strike crippled or killed an ant.

Cleared of immediate threats, Attia took the time to cut the ant head free from her ankle and check up on her friends. Vargus and Liam were fighting a pitched battle to the north, but Malcolm, Ellie, Russ, and Nora were with them now. Everyone was safe. She looked back to Solen and was amazed to see he'd already cleared his way to the wall. Eight ants lay dead or dismembered in his wake, and he showed no signs of slowing or stopping.

With a clear path, Attia advanced behind her teacher. She knew he didn't need her help to kill, but he might need the longer reach of her sword to dislodge the ants from the wall of the moat. Solen sensed her and understood her intent. "Good girl. I'll kill anything that climbs up. You cut them free from the wall," he said in a remarkably calm voice. Attia was astonished. The man was moving so incredibly fast, yet he wasn't even breathing heavily!

She ran to the moat with no regard for the chaotic ants. Solen was killing them within seconds of them clearing the wall. Peering over the edge she saw that was a single massive ant anchored into the wall that the others were catching and climbing over as the current swept them by. It was high on the wall. With a single slice, she neatly cut through four of its legs. It fell backward into the rushing water, its back legs twisting and breaking as the current swept it away.

"Good work," said Solen. "Let's help your friends with their fight and then support other groups. The Black Tide is only partially past us. We need to hold on for maybe another hour. We can't afford to get overrun again."

Attia nodded and started to move over to Liam and Vargus when she heard a shattering sound. It was as if twenty fine crystal goblets were all thrown to the ground at the same time. She looked up to see the Runes of Protection on the eastern side of the Serpent flash brightly before the glowing field of amber simply melted away into nothingness. With the barrier gone, ants flooded into and along the moat.

"We're in trouble," said Solen as he took off sprinting toward the surging swarm.

Attia's heart pounded and her mouth felt dry as she tried to fight the fear that threatened to overwhelm her.

Solen was right. They were definitely in trouble.

36
Malcolm

Malcolm heard the sounds of runes breaking many times throughout his studies, but he never heard anything like this. In the past, it was always the sound of glass gently cracking or fracturing. This was so much more and so much worse.

"*I warned them*," said the Other as Malcolm watched the enormous set of protective runes melt away. "*The demons taught us runecrafting in the first place.*" Malcolm wanted to question and learn more from the Other about that point, but this was neither the time nor the place. He was already exhausted from calling and controlling the wraith for so long, and things weren't getting any easier.

"Gather on me," shouted Vargus. "We guard our section of ground best we can. Liam and I protect either side of the group. Attia, you try and cut them down as fast as you're able. Russ and Ellie, brooms or torches. I don't give a shit as long as nothing comes out of that bloody moat near us!"

Malcolm shuffled toward the spot Vargus directed him to. Attia was the only one who wasn't with them, but she was on her way.

Malcolm squinted to shift his vision to Spectral Sight. He did it routinely now. He saw the wispy tendrils of shadow trailing Solen as the man sprinted north, past the group, toward where the ants were already pouring out from the moat. The shadowy soul within Solen seemed to grow and swell for a moment as the man stopped and waited for the first ants to make it to him.

"He and the soul have made peace. They'll hold that space together, or die trying," whispered the voice of the Other.

Malcolm wondered what his spirit saw. Could the Other see and interpret things in how the shadowy souls flickered and moved within their hosts?

The first ants that converged on Solen died within seconds. Malcolm witnessed the man's speed when he saw him defending Attia just a few moments ago, but something was different now. Solen was even faster. He wasn't waiting for the ants to strike at him and counterstriking like he did before. He was killing them before they got close enough to bite at him. His blades moved so fast, they became a deadly blur.

"Shouldn't we go help him?" asked Liam.

Attia shook her head. "We'd just get in the way, and we've our own problems to worry about," she said as she pointed to a different area where insects were climbing up and out of the moat. The first couple that emerged scuttled to the south, away from them, but the next group raced in their direction, and others followed.

Malcolm lost count as he watched ant after ant climb out of the moat. By the time Vargus stopped the first couple with a slam of his shield, there were a dozen or more on the way, and it didn't look like there'd be any way to stem the tide. Malcolm reached into his pouch, gathering one of his Soulstones. He rolled it between his fingers.

"You're much too tired to try that," warned the Other, but Malcolm's mind was made up. The warning was pointless. He wouldn't heed it.

If I die, you die with me, he thought. So, help me or don't. The choice is yours. His head pounded and his vision darkened as his spirit fought against him, but the pain and blurry vision faded quickly.

"I'll help, but understand, there's always a price," the Other responded, and as it did, Malcolm felt his exhaustion fall away from him. He felt strong and reinvigorated.

Malcolm coaxed the soul from the stone with ease, and the spirit world, the Astral, immediately tried to pull it across. There'd been so much death this morning that the barrier between worlds was already weak. Swarms of spirits gathered on the other side, ready to come across, but Malcolm learned much from his earlier summons. He identified the spirit he planned to call before releasing the soul from the stone this time. The transfer was quick and almost seamless. The Astral world pulled the soul Malcolm freed across, and at the same time, Malcolm drew a shadowy wraith into this world.

"Move," warned Attia as she stepped out in front of Malcolm and spun low to the ground. Her blade sliced through the legs of one ant and continued to cut a deep gash along the side of another. Malcolm saw more insects surging in to bite at Attia before she could recover.

He shivered and his teeth chattered as he forced his will into the wraith he just called. It felt much easier to him this time, now that he knew what to expect. He directed it forward with his thoughts and it responded without a moment's hesitation.

The wraith floated and danced forward, spreading frost and ice across the glistening chitin of the pair of insects trying to catch Attia. They stopped moving almost immediately, which forced the others to crawl over them. The delay granted Attia more than enough time to regain her stance and start her next flurry of attacks.

Malcolm needed to trust Attia to handle the rest. He was already feeling his fatigue build. He concentrated and the wraith responded by drifting out and away from the group. Malcolm fixed his gaze on the place where the ants were escaping the moat and the wraith obeyed, floating in that direction.

Malcolm shivered again. The exertion was causing him to sweat, but the icy chill from controlling the wraith nearly froze the moisture on his skin. It was an odd sensation, but one he thought he'd get used to it in time. The wraith was fast. It made it to the moat in mere seconds, freezing a few ants as it got into position. Malcolm smiled as it started spinning and casting its whip-like arms of shadow down at the ants climbing up from the moat.

"*Good,*" praised the Other. "*Easy now. The wraith is where you want it. You don't need to guide it so much now. It knows full well how to feast on life and warmth. Just concentrate on keeping it in this world. You'll tire much more slowly.*"

Malcolm took a deep breath and relaxed, doing as the Other instructed. He was astonished at how much easier it felt to him. He still felt the fatigue building within his body, but it grew so much slower this way. "Why didn't you show me this earlier?" he thought. He felt needles of pain behind his left eye and in both temples.

"*Knowledge is earned, boy! It's never given!*" hissed the Other.

Malcolm sighed and nodded, but the headache didn't soften at all. In fact, it got worse.

"*You've always known this. It's why I chose you over the others. I could see the tragedy in you. The loss of both parents. It was written across your soul, but instead of wallowing in it, you used it to drive your studies. Don't make me regret my decision, boy!*"

Malcolm felt the sharp headache soften and fade, but instead of making him feel better, he felt worse. He couldn't help but worry about the Other's growing strength and power. The soul wasn't wrong. Malcolm used the pain of his father's death to drive him farther in his studies. He was an average or even poor student before. In the year following his father's death he clawed his way to the head of every class he was involved in. But if the Other knew all of that even before possessing him, how much did it know about him now? Would he ever have a private thought again?

The sounds of battle intruded, forcing his attention back on to the matter at hand. Attia was working hard to keep a half dozen ants at bay. Liam shifted in her direction to give her a solid flank to work with, while Vargus appeared capable of covering himself. It was the battle to the north that surprised Malcolm the most.

Solen stood alone as countless ants continued to race across the moat as if it wasn't even there. There were hundreds of broken insect bodies littered and strewn around the small man. Solen seemed a little slower than he was before. He was no longer killing the ants before they lunged at him. At this point, he was spinning and twisting to avoid attacks, and killing the attacker in the same smooth motion.

When the Runes of Protection shattered, Malcolm suspected that enough ants flooded into the moat to form a dam or bridge of sorts out of their own bodies. He saw spinning spouts of water rising out of the moat to strike at the ants and their makeshift bridge, but the elementals were collapsing and shattering into meaningless spray almost as quickly as they were being created.

The magic that was binding water into elementals was being countered. To Malcolm, that meant that at least one of the Guardian demons was close. At the feast, the Commander said the Guardian demons were often invisible, but maybe they would be visible to him in the spirit world.

He squinted, engaged his Spectral Sight and scanned back and forth. Although the Other remained silent, Malcolm got the sense that it approved. He immediately felt the chill in his bones grow stronger, and the mounting feeling of exhaustion accelerate. He was still maintaining the wraith over by the moat. Using his Spectral Sight at the same time made that maintenance more taxing for him.

Fortunately, it didn't take Malcolm long to locate it, or rather, them. There were two forms floating in the air out over the ants. Malcolm wasn't comfortable judging distances with his Spectral Sight, but he got the impression they were close. In the spirit world, each of the floating forms had a small collection of twisted, tortured spirits swirling around it. One of the forms faced the moat, but the other was drifting toward Solen. Perhaps it was just the icy exertion of maintaining the wraith, but Malcolm's blood went cold.

"Solen, watch out!" Malcolm screamed. He felt warmth creep back into his bones as his wraith was drawn back into the spirit world. He'd lost his concentration. He only hoped that the wraith did enough damage to stop or at least slow the flow of insects on to their island.

"He can't hear you, boy. Even if he could, there's nothing you can do. He chose this battle," whispered the Other.

Malcolm had so many questions about what he saw of the demons when he viewed them in the spirit world, but there was no time to waste now. He heard a thunderclap and a whoosh of air as a thick bolt of shimmering force fired down from the sky around where Malcolm thought he saw one of the demons. It struck Solen in the arm, knocking the man to the ground.

Solen sprung back to his feet, but another bolt raced down, hitting him directly in the chest. The bolt struck with tremendous force. Malcolm thought, based on the way the man fell, that his ribs had been all but shattered. Still, Solen staggered back to his feet in time to evade and counterattack the next wave of ants, but he was much slower now.

"We have to help Solen," shouted Malcolm desperately, but even as he did, a third bolt of force ripped across the morning sky. This one shattered the man's thigh as even more ants leapt at him. Solen, despite his shattered ribs and femur, miraculously evaded and killed many of those that leapt, but this time, some of the insects got on top of him. Within seconds, others rushed in and crawled over him, and Malcolm knew there'd be nothing they could do to help the man.

Within moments, hundreds of ants washed past where Solen fell, flooding on to the island. Malcolm watched, stunned, as the defenders holding the closest camps were swarmed. They didn't have a chance. People in the next camps broke ranks and tried to run. No one was even trying to slow the ants down anymore. Everyone was running for their lives!

"Fall back! We need to withdraw!" shouted Vargus.

"I'll cover our retreat as best I can," said Attia as she moved a few steps to the north.

Malcolm knew he would be the slowest, so he started moving as quickly as his weakened body would allow. Vargus and Liam were keeping the path clear in the front, and to Malcolm's satisfaction, no ants were escaping the moat in the area he sent the wraith.

"*The platform,*" whispered the Other. "*Look to the platform.*" Malcolm was already straining to keep up with his friends could, but he couldn't resist turning to look for a few moments.

Arronhelm and the Commander were facing each other. They were yelling at one another. Both seemed to be pleading with the other. Gunther, Silver and everyone else was gone. They were likely responding to other troubled areas across the island. It was just Arronhelm and the

Commander left on the platform. Malcolm shifted his vision over to his Spectral Sight and immediately understood what attracted the Other's attention.

The Commander's spirit was spectacular to behold! It was glowing, brightly and beautifully. It flowed over and covered the man in what looked like an almost loving embrace.

"*Duncan and his spirit,*" the Other said. "*They've made their peace, but Arronhelm can't accept it. He doesn't want to lose his friend.*"

37
Liam

Liam scanned the area for threats as he marched forward. There was a good distance to go before they'd be to the safety of the protective runes surrounding the nearest stairway, but putting any amount of distance between them and the moat made them safer. Liam's biggest fear was the surging mass of ants sweeping down from the north. The moat failed, and although most of the Black Tide passed them by earlier in the morning, there was still a nearly endless supply of insects out there, waiting to overrun them.

A pair of ants scuttled forward at Liam from the right, forcing him to turn all the way around to get his shield in position to block the charge. He stabbed out alongside his shield and broke through the chitin of one, but both of the charging ants were on the larger side. He was worried they might have stingers.

"Attia. Two to clean up," he shouted. He held his position as everyone else passed behind him, and then pivoted and backpedaled, keeping both ants distracted and at bay with his shield until Attia was close enough to attack. She struck swiftly, taking the legs from one, and removing the head from the other.

"Conner... Liam," called Malcolm. "The platform. You... you need to see your father!"

There was something in Malcolm's tone that frightened Liam. His heart skipped a beat as he turned and saw his father and the Chancellor arguing. His dad looking and pointing toward the place where Solen fell. Thousands of insects flooded that space, and there was no end in sight. There was still an ocean of the accursed things out there beyond the moat. Liam sighed. He knew the battle was lost.

There was a change on the platform. Whatever argument they were having stopped. The Chancellor nodded, stepped forward, and hugged Liam's dad. Light began to slowly build and spill out from his father's fingers, eyes and skin. It was subtle at first, but it built quickly. The light was white and pure, but for all its warmth, there was a sense of foreboding to it. Liam felt sick.

"Dad," screamed Conner. "Dad... no! Whatever you're going to do, don't do it!" Conner wailed, sprinting toward the platform.

"Conner, stop," yelled Liam as he took off after his brother. Most of the ants were to the north, but many teams, all across the island, already abandoned their posts and were running toward the stairways. Their morale was broken. This made it much easier for the insects to move across the island, and Conner was so focused on their dad that he was oblivious to the dangers all around him.

The light cascading forth from their father kept growing in heat and intensity as Liam chased after his brother. An enormous ant was charging in from the side. Liam shouted a warning as he sprinted toward the thing, but Conner didn't react. Liam dove at the giant insect, hitting it broadside with his shield right before it was close enough to leap at Conner.

The light on the platform grew to an incredible, searing intensity. Conner stopped running and staggered back a step, holding a forearm up to shield his eyes. All around, people were turning and staring at the sphere of nearly blinding light expanding out from their father.

The ant recovered and was turning back toward Conner as Liam worked his way to his feet. He staggered forward and got his shield in between his brother and the ant just as it rocked its abdomen forward and tried to sting. The lance-like stinger deflected down, off the shield, and stuck into the soft earth.

Liam slashed downward with his broadsword, severing the stinger from the ant's abdomen. It hissed and lunged forward, swinging its head against the side of Liam's shield, knocking it to the side. With the shield no longer blocking, the ant snapped its mandibles shut on Liam's thigh. The thing's bite was incredibly strong, but the armor plating held. Liam reversed his grip on his sword and drove the point down through the ant's skull. It quivered for a moment, before falling to the ground, dead.

Liam grabbed his brother by the shoulder and started retreating to the safety of their friends. He saw sapphire lines being drawn in the air as well now, near his glowing father. Arronhelm was making a portal.

"We can't do anything!" he shouted. "We need to fall back," Liam screamed as he wrapped his arm around his brother's chest. Liam felt his brother fighting him, and he understood why. Liam's heart hurt so much. Conner's had to too. Both of them knew that this was the last time they'd ever see their father. Part of him wanted to let go of Conner. Maybe if both of them ran to their dad, they could convince him not to do this.

But Liam was a soldier. He understood that the battlefield was a living hell. He understood that you rarely, if ever, get to say goodbye. Liam sighed and kicked the back of his brother's knee, pulling him sharply to break his balance, making it easier to drag him away.

"Let me go! I want to see Dad!" Conner shouted, but Liam kept pulling him back.

"We owe it to him to survive this! You can't make it to him in time, Conner," shouted Liam. "Don't you understand? He's doing it to save us! Don't you dare take that from him!" Liam must have gotten through to him, because Conner stopped struggling. He went almost limp. He never turned. Liam pulled him back away from the platform.

The light got dizzyingly bright, and tight beams of light burst forth from the disappearing shape that had been their father. There was a flash of blue, and both Arronhelm and their father disappeared. A moment later, a blinding white light appeared out in the distance, deep within the ebony ocean of writhing ants. Now that it was much farther away, Liam could saw the light growing and expanding like a tiny, but intensely burning sun.

There was a flash of blue as the Chancellor returned to the platform, but the light of his magic was completely dwarfed by the rapidly expanding sun in the distance. Liam couldn't quite tell at what point the ball of light stopped expanding and started exploding, but when it did, it was absolutely incredible. Tens of thousands of ants were instantly incinerated. The blast stretched for hundreds of yards in each direction, throwing burning bodies everywhere. The rushing air and shattering force of the blast worked to disintegrate them, reducing them to dust and scattering them to the winds.

Liam coughed and gagged as the blast wave sent soot, ash and pieces of shattered insects all throughout the clearing. His eyes burned and he saw halos of gold and green anytime he closed them. His knees were weak, and his chest hurt as he staggered and dragged his brother backward toward where he thought his friends might be.

"He's gone," whispered Conner.

It surprised Liam that he could even hear the soft whisper. He thought an explosion and blast wave of that size would've been absolutely deafening, but there was barely any sound. What's more, the keening, droning cacophony of the endless sea of insects was all but gone. "I know, Conner," he said softly. "I know."

The passage of time no longer registered to Liam. He found the others at some point. It started raining, but the rainwater was acrid and mixed with fine ash. There were still hundreds of ants wandering across the island, but they were no longer organized or terrifying. Instead, they were aimless, confused, or even stunned. Whatever force was guiding them before was gone.

"All of you. To me, now!" came an insistent shout from off to his right.

Liam looked over to the see the Chancellor. He didn't know when the man made his way over to them. The Chancellor was tracing a pattern of blue light in the air. The sigils within this pattern were far larger and more involved than the others he saw before. Another portal. Liam assumed that this one needed to be more intricate because it was transporting more people.

He didn't really care.

His father was dead.

38
Cinderhorn

Cinderhorn sighed with a sense of amused resignation as the foul wizard opened a portal and delivered the glowing man somewhere out into the ocean of ants. He never saw a Fusion spell cast before, but he read about it. Devastatingly powerful, but absolutely suicidal.

This was all Erranaekis's fault! He was so desperate for a kill he wasted far too much energy bringing down that balance warrior. The ants would've eventually done it for them. Now, when they truly needed to stop a target, neither of them could afford to spend the energy to do it.

There was a tremendous, burning, acrid wind as the man completed his terrible spell somewhere out in the center of the Black Tide. Cinderhorn didn't need to turn around to know that virtually every living thing behind him was being incinerated. Tens of thousands of giant ants were being reduced to ash in mere seconds. What was left of the swarm was scattered, and Cinderhorn suspected the smoldering stench of so many dead would be enough to force the remaining ants to travel a different path. They'd do anything to avoid the killing field.

The Guardians were so patient and careful, all throughout the morning. They let the Tide do all the work, but no, that wasn't good enough for Erranaekis. With the Runes of Protection broken, it was only a matter of time. Had Erranaekis only remained patient, the two of them might have been able to stop the Fusion spell. Or better yet, they could have countered that asshole wizard and his blasted Portal spell. It would've been beautiful to watch the Fusion spell complete right where the light mage had been standing, directly beneath the Citadel. The massacre would have been glorious!

Cinderhorn frowned and silently flew off to the side to get a better angle. While he had wings, he rarely found reason to use them. He accessed far more refined methods of flight through his magic. The humans were retreating into their building. He didn't have time to dwell on the missed opportunity. He spent months researching the names and gathering the items of power necessary to summon the right allies from the Netherworld. There'd be no shortage of blood for the more basic summons, but he'd need to barter with the great elemental demons he planned to summon. He even managed to earn the Truename of a succubus.

"Our time is nigh, brother," whispered Erranaekis. "Once inside, there'll be no shortage of prey."

"Patience," whispered Cinderhorn. "We need to get inside first, and my summoning spells will take time. It'll take longer if the succubus refuses to lend me her power. She must be willing for the Gather spell to work. If she refuses, I'll be forced to rest. We may need to delay the attack..."

"The Queen won't tolerate delays."

Cinderhorn winced. He knew there'd be punishments for failure but pushing an attack without sufficient support was tantamount to Banishment. He was free of the Netherworld for centuries now and he had no desire to return. No one down there owed him anything anymore. Even a demon of his status and power could only hold a debt for a century. He'd have no allies or favors to call upon; but his enemies, of course, they'd still be waiting. Further, the preparations he was forced to make for this mission didn't go unnoticed in the Netherworld. He earned some new, powerful enemies quite recently.

"These people are still dangerous," cautioned Cinderhorn. "The balance warrior and their Commander were important, but among the least threatening on the battlefield. The old wizard's magic is dangerous now that he's desperate. Their healer knows a Banishment spell, Silver's grown in power since our last meeting, and Gunther is still what he's always been," Cinderhorn pleaded. "If the demon bitch dares refuse me, we must wait! With the spiders gone, we can encourage the Tide along this path again next year."

"They're vulnerable now. Two of their El'orin are dead, and the rest have spent themselves," countered Erranaekis. "Give these miserable wretches another year and they'll have corrected their foolish slothfulness. They'll defend this entire clearing with their pesky runes and moats. Whatever El'ominae is powering that disgusting barrier will be stronger too. It will have replaced their fallen El'orin with even stronger ones. Our window will have closed." Erranaekis drifted closer, speaking in a confident whisper. "So, once inside, how much time will you require?"

Cinderhorn watched the battlefield below as he considered the question. A few hundred ants recovered from the shock of suffering such huge losses. There were still a dozen or so battles taking place. Maybe a third of the defensive forces remained outside. Most were retreating. The doors to the inside were wide open and would remain that way for a while yet.

As much as he hated this plan, Erranaekis's arguments were strong. "It will take me the most time to summon the succubus. Assuming she permits me to Gather her power, I should be able proceed without rest. I've collected the names of seven of the elemental demons, at great personal cost, mind you. I can bring all of those across within a couple of hours. The basic ones will go quickly after that. There'll be no shortage of human blood to draw upon."

"You needn't remind me of your personal costs, we've all heard about it time and again. Poor Cinderhorn, always left to digging through cryptic texts, and always communing and bartering down below," hissed Erranaekis in a mocking tone. "I'm sick of hearing about it. It's time to see some results from your endless research. You have three hours. I'll have most, if not all of their protective runes disabled before then. Perhaps I'll even have time to do a bit of exploring."

Cinderhorn flushed with anger. Damn Erranaekis and his arrogant impatience! They talked about everything while escorting the Black

Tide. At every turn, Erranaekis was taking risks. He killed the Citadel's scouts and trackers when it would have been easier to just avoid them. He knocked over so many damn trees that it must have been obvious that the Tide was being guided and escorted. Most of all, though, he talked about how he wanted to find and kill whatever El'ominae spirit was protecting the Citadel.

"We all have our assignments. We're to take no additional risks," spat Cinderhorn.

"My assignments were to escort the Black Tide, help counter their annoying elemental spells during the assault, and clear out some of the protective runes within the structure," countered the arrogant demon.

"You were told to assist in the battle as well. Despite being weakened by the Tide, the human defenders will be strong," whispered Cinderhorn as calmly as he could. Inciting Erranaekis further wouldn't get him anywhere at this point. "Even if the Queen refuses to see it, you and I both know that the wizard's a seer. They won't be unprepared."

Erranaekis chuckled. "We're on the same team, brother. Of course, I'll be assisting. I just don't plan on joining the attack on the main gathering place when your army strikes. There'll be hundreds of pathetic men, women and children in their living quarters, cowering beneath their beds. How long do you think they'll let me slaughter their defenseless babes before they're forced to divide their forces and respond?"

Cinderhorn seethed with anger. "Fine. Do what you will, but summon your own damned aid! If I'm taking the risks, I'm benefiting from the full protection of my summons," he growled, hoping that by withholding aid he would force his ally to stick to the original plan.

"Fine, have it your way," Erranaekis snorted. "All the more glory for me."

"And more unnecessary risk for the both of us," pleaded Cinderhorn. "Just join me in the initial assault. We'll crush their leaders, and then take our time exploring, slaughtering and feasting."

"My mind's made up. Neither of us has dominion over the other. It'll be for the Queen to judge the weight of our valor."

"Or the height of our folly," said Cinderhorn with a sigh.

The argument was done. Wasting more time and effort on it was pointless. For now, he just needed to move forward and adjust. Cinderhorn returned his attention to the closest staircase. He noted the packs of tired people ascending the stairs. They were entering the building often, but there were still a few gaps. The demons needed those gaps to see into the building.

The outside walls of the Citadel were lined with an assortment of protective runes. Among them were multiple sets of Runes of Protection aligned to demons. Disabling them would take time and doing so would most likely trigger some kind of magical alarm. The better option was to magically transport directly inside the Citadel and avoid the runes altogether.

Unlike Arronhelm, however, the Guardians weren't able to teleport freely. Their spells required a clear line of sight. Once within, Erranaekis would be able to discreetly disable any runes that might prove troublesome to their attack. Returning to Nerreka wouldn't be an issue at all. The Guardians didn't require line of sight to transport themselves back to Chariden. She was the one who brought them to this world. They were inextricably bound to her. Unless Banished, they could always return to her.

"Soon, brother," Cinderhorn whispered. "We'll have the most time if we go after that next group. Are you ready?"

"I thought you'd never ask."

39
Conner

Conner's heart was racing and his head was spinning. His dad was gone. One moment, his father was on that platform, and the next, he was out there in that terrible field, with all those giant ants. He was glowing so brightly... so brilliantly. Conner desperately needed just one more night with him. There was more to say. There were just a few more hugs he needed, but it was too late. There was no more time for any of that. Dad was dead.

"Malcolm. Can you... you know," the Chancellor stammered. "Can you look and tell me who?"

Conner pushed himself back up to his knees. They were all in an enormous library. The room was generously lit by hanging bowls of Liquidlight, evenly spaced throughout the room. Several tables and chairs were scattered across the room, each piled with a chaotic assortment of books and parchments, as if each was the personal workspace of an equally disorganized mad scientist. All four walls were covered, floor to ceiling, with bookshelves. There were no windows, no doors, no entrances and no exits.

"Liam, for sure," said Malcolm as he looked around at everyone. "I think that's all."

"No, that can't be all. There must be two," said the Chancellor with a touch of agitation.

"I thought you said it sometimes takes a while. Maybe the second soul—"

"Just look again. I know the second one's here, boy," said the Chancellor.

Conner climbed to his feet before Malcolm came to look at him more closely. His friend's skin looked like that of an old man. It was unnerving, and Conner was glad Malcolm didn't spend much time studying him. Malcolm finally stopped in front of Attia. He stood there, peering at her for what felt like an eternity.

Malcolm sighed and said, "I think it's in her. I can barely see it. It's like it's hiding?"

"What are you talking about?" asked Attia, taking a step back. "What's in me? "

"Children," interrupted the Chancellor. "I'm so very sorry, but we haven't the time. Liam and Attia, please stay here with Malcolm. I'll come and get you when I'm able. The rest of you, please gather by me."

Conner was stunned. His father just exploded like a miniature sun! He needed answers. Right now, he needed his brother. He moved away from the Chancellor, shaking his head.

"Um, how about no?" said Russell. "There's never time, and shit keeps getting worse. Why are we leaving those three here in a room with no doors? Where are we going? What the hell just happened?"

Liam held up his hand. When he spoke, his voice was gentle and calm. "The ants were winning. Father sacrificed himself to save us. Solen sacrificed himself as well. They were both possessed like Malcolm. Now, I'm guessing we are too."

Russell shook his head. "What? That doesn't make any sense."

It all made perfect sense. Conner cried in his father's arms because he knew this would happen. "No, Russ," he said as he took a shuddering breath. "It makes sense. When one of them dies, another's made. Dad and Solen died. Liam and Attia are the new ones. Like what happened to Malcolm. Dad said there were always seven."

"Yes," said the Chancellor, a look of relief on his face. He smiled at Conner and there were tears in his eyes. "It's exactly like that."

"I don't understand. Am I supposed to understand any of this?" asked Nora. She looked exhausted and confused. Conner couldn't imagine how all of this must sound to her.

"Don't worry, Nora. I'll explain it sometime," said Conner. He felt slightly guilty that he was likely lying to her. "So where are we going, Chancellor, and why?"

The Chancellor ignored the question for a time. He suddenly seemed so small and frail. Russell cleared his throat after a few moments and Arronhelm shook free of his reverie. "Oh, I'm taking you down to the Great Hall. The wounded are being cared for down there. There's no shortage of work to do."

Conner sighed. He wasn't the only one in the Citadel who lost a loved one today. It was selfish to stay with his brother right now. He wasn't needed here, but he was needed down there with all the wounded. He nodded and walked over to Arronhelm. "All right. I'm ready."

Russell slapped the table next to him. "I want some answers before I'm going anywhere."

"Easy, lad," said Vargus. Conner wondered if Vargus somehow knew about the spirits. He was an older soldier, and someone the Chancellor trusted. Surely, he must know something.

Eliana gently touched Russell's shoulder, speaking softly. "Come with us, Russ. Liam and Attia need some answers right now too, and I'm starting to understand that it'll be harder for Malcolm to explain with all of us here. Besides, I want to help the wounded. I want to see Mom and Dad."

Russell sighed and walked over to the Chancellor. The old man was fumbling around in his robes. It took him a moment or two, but he produced an ornate broadsword in its scabbard. The Chancellor smiled awkwardly and placed the weapon on the nearest table. Conner was almost certain that an object of that size couldn't be concealed and contained beneath Arronhelm's snug robes.

It took him just a glance to recognize the sword as his dad's. The runes carved along the length of the blade gradually shifted from green to blue as they approached the tip. His father's sword was the only weapon Conner thought of as beautiful.

"I almost forgot," said Arronhelm to Liam. "Your father wanted you to have his sword. I hope it serves you well." The Chancellor smiled at Liam for a long time before shaking himself free from whatever thought he was lost in. "Now, Malcolm, I think you'll find all the research pertaining to the soul that chose Liam on that table in the far corner. I'm uncertain about Attia's, but there's a name and a few notes right here, next to the sword," he said, pointing. "One set of visions was incredibly cryptic, you see. I had endless troubles trying to decipher and follow its path. The soul inside Attia might be the cryptic one, given that you were barely able to see it."

The Chancellor didn't formally conclude the conversation. He just stopped speaking and started tracing graceful lines of intense blue light in the air. Conner knew that it'd only take Arronhelm a few seconds to complete the spell. Conner spent that time looking at his brother instead. Liam didn't immediately notice the attention. He was gazing somberly at their father's sword. He noticed eventually. Liam looked up a moment before the spell completed. He smiled sadly and Conner returned the smile, wondering if that might be the last time that he'd ever see his brother again.

Conner fell to his knees and threw up. The vertigo from the Portal spell didn't help, but it was really the sensory overload of the Great Hall that overwhelmed him. Whimpering, wailing, and sobbing filled his ears. The coppery sweetness of blood tickled his nostrils, but the sight of it all pushed him over the edge.

The Great Hall was converted into a crisis care hospital. Despite his training in the Monastery, Conner never saw so much trauma in one room before. Cots were set up to accommodate the wounded, but there was maybe one cot for every three people needing medical attention. As a result, people just found places on the ground to lie down and wait for care. Conner was prepared to deal with lacerations and allergic reactions, but he definitely underestimated the size and power of the giant ants.

There were people missing arms and legs. Others had open belly wounds and exposed viscera. There were rivers of blood, vomit and waste all across the hall. Soldiers and healers ran around, frantically trying to help those they could help, but things were out of control. Triage was a calculated and organized process. What was going on here felt like desperation.

"Ellie," gasped Conner as he worked his way back to his feet. "We have to do something."

"Good. It seems I brought you to where you're needed most," said the Chancellor with a touch of weariness in his voice. "You're to stay with the children, Vargus. If anyone tries to give you different orders, you're to ignore them. I'll return when I'm able."

"Easy enough," muttered the grizzled veteran as he scratched the scar on the side of his face.

"Wait. Where are you going now?" asked Ellie.

"There are still groups fighting outside. I need to make sure this doesn't get any worse." Arronhelm didn't wait for further discussion. He turned and walked toward the door.

"Let him go, Ellie," said Conner as he scanned the immediate area. Many of the wounded around him were beyond his skill, but there were some he could help. Conner pointed to one man with a nasty belly wound and moved to him. "Help me with some herbs please? And Russ, would you see about getting some bandages? As many as you can gather, I guess. There are a few people here I think I can help."

"I want to help, too," whispered Nora. Conner was relieved that she was shaking free of the terrifying and confusing events of the day. He didn't see what happened to Wayne, but he heard the terrible screams. It must haunt her, but she was a healer, and there were wounded people everywhere, desperately in need of her skills.

"Vargus, you work with Nora. Get bandages or do whatever she needs you to do."

Conner didn't wait for either Vargus or Nora to respond. He knelt down next to the man with the belly wound. He was pleased when Ellie knelt down next to him and started to organize her herbs. The man's injury wasn't all that different than the wounds he recently treated for his brother. This one seemed even easier, given there were no broken bones to contend with. Conner placed his hand over the wound and let his magic flow. The man winced at first, but quickly calmed.

Conner felt the pain-inducing toxin from the ant's bite, but he decided not to counteract it. Instead, he dedicated his energy toward making sure there were no hidden ruptures to the man's innards. When he was satisfied everything was safe, he willed his magic to gently close the laceration. It only took him a few seconds to stop the bleeding. Conner smiled. His skills were improving.

Emboldened by his success, Conner moved on to the next person. At some point, Russ returned with water and bandages, and with Ellie directing things, they grew into an efficient team. Conner treated whatever wounds he felt capable of dealing with. Ellie followed up with herbs to numb any lasting pain and prevent infections, and Russ bandaged everything up. Conner wasn't sure how long they worked. Time became a blur. Eventually, the exertion of using his healing magic built within him. He smiled and suppressed a yawn when Eli's parents found them and interrupted.

"Eli! We were so worried," called a woman dressed in heavy clothing as she rushed over toward them.

"Mom, Dad," shouted Ellie with tears in her eyes. "Are you two all right?"

"Arthur took a nasty bite," said the woman as she lunged in and hugged her daughter. Conner looked over at the man limping behind her. His face was contorted with effort. The wound was bandaged, but blood soaked through the cloth wrappings.

"Do you mind if I look at that?" Conner asked as the man got closer.

The man smiled, but shook his head. "Save your energy for those who have a greater need," he said with a cough. "I reckon you're already spent, and besides, Gracie smothered it in herbs. It bled more than I'd like, but it's all done with that for now."

Conner nodded and yawned. He didn't realize how much energy he spent and how many people they treated. He was exhausted. He tried to gracefully roll off his knees and on to his side, but he was too weak to catch his weight with his arm. He ended up sprawled out on the stone floor. It was cool and comfortable.

"I think I need a nap," he whispered to no one in particular as his eyes gradually closed.

40
Liam

Liam ran his fingers along the side of his father's sword again as he tried to process the events of the morning. The sword was incredibly light and balanced. He couldn't even fathom how much time it took the runecrafters to weave such tight, intricate patterns of magic into the blade. He always dreamt of owning a magical sword. Every soldier did. He just never imagined it would happen like this.

"Are you feeling anything yet, Attia?" asked Malcolm for what had to be the twentieth time in the past few hours.

"No. I mean, I don't think so."

"The Chancellor was convinced that both souls were here. I think I can see it in you when I look really hard. I don't know. Maybe it's just shy?"

Liam recalled his father's words the night before the bear hunt. "I think you might be right," he said quietly. "Father said it was something like three years before he got a sense of what kind of life the soul inside him lived. He was surprised about how quickly you started seeing visions."

Malcolm nodded. "Arronhelm says it's different for everyone. Some people have a harder time with it than others. I guess just be patient,

Attia. I just wish Arronhelm would've been able to find out more. The notes don't seem to make a lot of sense."

Attia sighed and nodded. "At least he found a name. Corin Enders."

"That's better than nothing," said Malcolm.

"Hi, Corin. My name is Attia. It's okay if you're shy. I don't do well with people either. I'm ready to talk whenever you want, though.' Attia blushed. Liam never saw that kind of reaction out of the normally stoic girl. It was a different, more vulnerable side of her. It became so easy as of late to forget how young they all were.

"How about you, Liam?" asked Malcolm. "Is yours trying to reach out to you at all? Did you feel anything when you looked through that book?"

Liam frowned. He felt something, but he didn't know how to express it. There was a dull thudding ache across his forehead and a feeling of tension in his neck that he couldn't quite shake. He was sure the book was the right one for the soul within him. He knew it the moment he read the title: 'The Order of Silverhorn, History and Speculation'. But when he started thumbing through the book, he felt as if the spirit wanted him to wait. The headache intensified the more he tried to move on from the horrific events of the morning. Liam felt best, while holding his father's sword and remembering. It was as if the soul was giving him time, or even trying to force him to remember his father. "I think it is, Malcolm."

"Excellent. Is it trying to speak to you? With me, I started seeing things right away. I didn't understand it at first, but I was seeing spirits. The soul within me spoke for the first time when I saw the ghost of Marcus. It was when I was passing that area on the trail with the drop-off."

"Right. Where you nearly fell," said Attia.

"And you caught me."

"That's where Marcus fell," said Attia. She hugged herself for a moment like she was cold. "I couldn't let that happen to anyone else."

"It wasn't your fault, Attia," said Liam. "To answer your question, Malcolm, it's not talking to me. It's kind of guiding me, though. My head hurts more when I try to do some things, and less when I do others. Does that make sense?"

Malcolm nodded. "Yes! That makes sense. What's it guiding you to do?"

Liam felt silly. He was worried he was being childish about his father's death. He didn't want to be like Conner, but he couldn't deny what he was feeling. Who else could he talk to about this if not his friends? "I think the soul wants me to grieve. Look, I know Arronhelm found the right book, but it doesn't want me to read it yet. My vision darkens and blurs when I try. I think..." Liam sighed. "I think it wants me to remember my dad. It wants me to think about how he sacrificed himself for us."

Malcolm winced and put a hand to his temples. Liam guessed the soul inside Malcolm took issue or otherwise reacted in a way his friend didn't want to share. It didn't matter. Liam knew he was right. He felt the soul inside of him approving of his interpretation. That's right, isn't it, Liam thought. You want me to remember him and his sacrifice.

Liam felt the pressure and tension in his neck grow stronger for a few moments before it simply fell away.

"*His sacrifice. It was beautiful,*" said a voice. It was barely a whisper, but Liam heard it clearly. "*Everything is about sacrifice. I've forgotten so much. I don't even remember what the struggle was about anymore. I just remember sacrifice. How hard we worked. How we died to protect... something.*"

Liam shivered and his eyes welled up with tears. He felt the pain and confusion in the soul's words. He looked back to the book and ran his fingers over the moldy leather cover. We should start reading this now, he thought. If you've forgotten, we should work together to remember.

"*Yes, we can start,*" it whispered.

Liam nodded as the tears rolled down his cheeks. He didn't know why it was so important to him that the soul, his Guest, celebrated his father's sacrifice, but it made his heart sing. Perhaps more than anything else, it was relief that he was feeling. The soul inside of Malcolm was a terrifying thing. It was a necromancer. It taught Malcolm to summon the dead. His Guest didn't feel like that at all to him. It felt warm and noble. He was so afraid whatever came to live within him would change him for the worse. He was worried that it'd be like how it was with

Malcolm, but it wasn't like that at all. His Guest was noble and honorable.

"It spoke to you," said Malcolm. "Just now, didn't it? I can see it better within you now."

Liam returned his father's sword to its scabbard. Ignoring his friends, he opened the book. He thumbed through it, trying to decipher how the author organized its contents. He half expected his Guest to guide him to a specific section, but when that didn't happen, he sighed, resigning himself to reading it from the beginning.

Liam felt the ground shake. At first, he wondered if he was having a vision, but a quick look at Attia confirmed it. The ground definitely shook.

"What's happening?" asked Attia.

"I don't know," said Liam, stepping back from the table and the old leather book. Suddenly, there was a sharp, deep crash from somewhere below them. The floor shook again, this time more violently.

"An explosion?" asked Malcolm. "The forges, maybe?"

Liam shook his head. "I don't think so. The forges are on the third floor. Even if we're on the fourth floor, that explosion sounded like it came from deeper than just one floor down."

"It didn't sound like it came from outside," said Attia.

"No. The building wouldn't have shaken like that if it were something from the outside," said Liam with a frown. He wished he knew where in the Citadel this hidden library was situated. He guessed they were most likely on the fourth floor, but that didn't help him understand what was shaking the building and from where.

There was another crashing sound and the ground shook yet again. The Great Hall, with its vaulted ceiling, was the largest room within the Citadel. Maybe something exploding in there would generate enough force to be heard and felt throughout the building? If something was going on in the Great Hall, it meant all the wounded would be right there at risk. Liam felt his heart skip a beat as the panic swelled within him. Fire and smoke! His brother was in the Great Hall!

"I think something's attacking the Great Hall!" Liam gasped as he looked around frantically for some kind of way out of the library. He saw a flash of blue light in the corner as Arronhelm appeared.

"Come to me now, children," the old man shouted.

"The Great Hall," Liam said in a tone of authority as he rushed to the Chancellor. "We need to help Conner!"

Arronhelm pursed his lips and shook his head. He started tracing familiar patterns of blue light in the air. Both Attia and Malcolm crowded in next to the Chancellor. Liam tried to process what was happening. Was Arronhelm shaking his head about going to the Great Hall? That couldn't be it. That didn't make sense.

"We're going to the Great Hall, right?" asked Liam while Arronhelm completed weaving his spell. Liam felt as if he were falling, and everything around him melted into pools of sapphire light.

41
Russell

The people closest to the doors never had a chance. The main doors to the Great Hall were built out of gorgeous hardwoods. They were heavy and covered with intricate carvings, but none of that mattered any more. The demons' initial assault reduced both doors to a cascade of deadly, burning shrapnel that ripped through dozens of people, instantly killing anyone unfortunate enough to be too close when the blast occurred.

Russell coughed as he worked his way back to his feet. He and his friends were fortunate. They were near the middle of the room when the doors exploded. Everywhere he looked, there were people running, screaming, crying, or dying. A woman on a cot nearby caught a large, jagged shard of wood in the side. Russell saw two other people right in front of him get hit by debris from the explosion. Life and death felt so random and out of control.

"We need to get out of here!" insisted Russell. Ellie was climbing to her feet, but Conner was crawling over to the nearby cot. Did he think he could save her? Did he even understand what was happening?

"Just give me a minute!" yelled Conner.

"Hell no! We've got to move now!" shouted Russell.

"Let me try to help her!"

Eliana finished getting to her feet and screamed. She was looking toward where the explosion took place. Russell wanted to look, but getting Conner moving was more important. He rushed to Conner and grabbed his hair. "Sorry, but we have to go," he said, pulling Conner's hair to guide the slim boy back to his feet.

"What're you doing?" Conner yelled as he started turning to face Russell, but he never completed his turn. "Stars above," he gasped as he caught sight of the entrance of the Great Hall. Russell looked, and his mind reeled at what he saw.

Unthinkable things were charging into the Great Hall through the gaping hole where the doors used to stand. The burning things were what Russell saw first. Massive dogs, with flames dancing across their backs, dripping glowing orange saliva that left smoldering pools on the ground. But there were two even larger burning figures behind the hounds.

Their faces were almost human if not for the enormous horns that curled out and up from their temples. Their resemblance to humanity ended there, though. Each had translucent, membranous wings and a long tail, tipped with a wicked looking spike. Flames danced all across their massive bodies, concentrating into raging balls of fire in each hand.

Russell watched in horror as one of those fiery demons casually tossed a ball of flame after a group of people trying to run away. The fireball caught up to them and exploded, bathing each in searing flames. Their dying screams joined those of others all across the Great Hall.

"Don't just stand there... Move!" shouted Vargus as he ran to them, Nora in tow.

"Where?" stammered Eliana. "How... where should we go?"

"Let's get to the wall over there," Vargus said, pointing. "We need to get out of the way."

A different demon caught Russell's attention. It flowed like oil across the floor as it moved close to a group of people who overturned several cots to use as cover. It pulled its liquid body together as it rose up, much like the water elementals did out in the moat. It didn't appear to attack. It just spun and swirled, but the people near it started coughing and clawing at their skin. Russell didn't understand what was happening until he saw water actually flowing out of those people. The fluid glistened in the air for a moment before racing into the horrifying demon, as if it were some giant sponge, capable of absorbing any and all liquid out of the area. Water continued to flow from the bodies of those poor people until, one by one, each of them fell to the ground, where they desiccated and died.

"Conner, Russ, move your asses now!" shouted Vargus.

Russell's heart pounded in his chest. He had to keep it together. He turned and pulled Conner along as he started running. Russell imagined the thing he just saw was ripping the water from his body, or that a fireball was chasing after him, and he found himself capable of running even faster than ever before. He made it to the wall, next to Vargus, Ellie and Nora. They were flipping over one of the heavy wooden tables.

"What the hell good is that gonna do?" Russell shouted. "Didn't you see what that sponge monster just did?"

Vargus moved out to the side and pushed both Conner and Russell to the ground behind the table. "Battle's nothing but a pile of shitty options. Take the one that stinks the least."

Russell climbed to his knees and peered out over the top of the overturned table. There were creatures spreading out all across the room, but despite that, he saw something that gave him a glimmer of hope. Gunther was standing strong! He was out in front of where all the demons were charging into the room. Silvery light flowed from him in all directions as he swept his huge two-handed sword around him in a deadly arc.

Two of the burning hounds leapt at him, spitting gouts of flame from their wicked maws. He cut the first one wide open with his swing. The other rammed into his side. Russell panicked for a moment, but the huge warrior barely moved. The hell hound bounced off the man. It tried to regain its footing, but it wasn't quick enough to avoid Gunther's next swing.

The pair of large, burning demons converged on the warrior, but Gunther was no longer alone. Other people were moving to support him. Both of the demons tossed balls of fire at Gunther and those who stood with him. A bald man in a white robe behind Gunther held up his hand. It glowed with a warm, golden light. Both balls of flame sputtered and faded away as the magic holding and binding them into powerful, explosive things was drawn away. Russell knew that those fire spells had been Dispelled. It was something he saw his arcane sciences professors do in class on the rare occasions students practiced offensive spells.

"That's Devin," said Conner. "He's the healer that leads the Monastery."

Despite his seven-foot height, the two winged fire demons were bigger than Gunther. They each swung their molten fists down at him while whipping their long barbed tails, much like a scorpion would. The demons were accurate with their strikes, but Gunther didn't give any ground. He swung his weapon out at the demons, forcing them to retreat out of the way.

All the while, Devin stood behind Gunther, quietly chanting. Both his hands began to shine with golden light as he pointed them at one of the massive fiery demons. It leapt back, hissing, but Devin's golden light coalesced and followed the demon's movement. It was as if the golden light became a living creature. No matter how the demon tried to dance and dodge, the light followed it. The demon slowed as more and more light surrounded it, until eventually the demon was enveloped by the light. It cried and wailed for a moment as the light surrounding it blazed into a blinding intensity, until suddenly both the light and the demon disappeared.

The remaining fiery demon howled and wailed as it saw the other Banished. "That one must die!" it shouted in a guttural voice, pointing at Devin. Several creatures back by the entrance to the room took notice, including one that seemed more confident and powerful than the others. That demon's facial features were catlike, and it had thick ram's horns stretching out from its temples. Its body shape was similar to that of the fiery demons, but its wings were dark and leathery instead of translucent, and there were no flames dancing across its body.

It extended one of its clawed hands towards Devin and sneered. There was a loud crash, and the air shimmered as a bolt of force blasted forth from the demon's hand. The bolt rushed towards Devin, but just like the fireballs earlier, it broke apart and faded before it could reach the man. There was a second crash and then a third as two more shimmering blasts of force lanced out at the bald man. The magic of the second was Dispelled before it could hit its mark, but the third one struck the bald man right in the chest.

Devin staggered back and fell to the hard stone floor, coughing. The fiery demon tried to leap at the stunned man, but Gunther charged forward and forced it to deal with him. Devin rolled to his hands and knees. He tried to push himself to his feet, but he never got the chance. The stone floor all around Devin melted into a viscous pool of mud for just a moment before hardening back into solid rock. Devin managed to pull his hands free from the muddy stone before it hardened, but his legs were trapped.

Russell saw another area of the stone floor ripple and melt into mud. The patch of soft stone began to move, slowly at first, but it rapidly accelerated. It moved across the room on a direct path toward Devin. The soft stone got taller as it got closer to the imprisoned man. It stopped moving a few feet away from Devin. It drew all the stone from the surrounding floor into itself. It only took a moment for it to grow into a towering monstrosity of earth and rock.

Its body was full of sharp jagged stones and its fists were blackened like obsidian. The thing had to be ten feet tall, and its eyes dripped molten magma like tears down on to its cheeks. Devin held his glowing hands in front of him as the thing crouched and struck down at him. The first and second blows crashed against a field of golden energy, but the third smashed into flesh and bone. Devin barely had time to cry out as the fourth blow smashed through his already broken chest, crushing him to death.

“Oh no, oh no,” stammered Conner. “No, no, no, it sees us!”

Both the enormous demon of rock and the fire demon were engaged with Gunther and the other soldiers. The fiery demon was spewing burning blood from several wounds, so Gunther was doing damage. Russell scanned the room, trying to figure out what Conner was panicking about and then he saw it. A thin stream of oily black ooze was flowing across the ground right toward their defensive position.

“We have to get out of here!” cried Russell. “We need to run!”

“No! We make our stand here,” spat Vargus.

“You don’t understand,” shouted Russell as he scrambled back along the wall, away from their makeshift barricade. He looked over and saw that the deadly ooze was getting closer. It was drawing the rest of its stream into itself and becoming a rapidly expanding pool. Russell felt heat and warmth splash his groin and run down his legs as the terror overwhelmed him. "Run!"

The pool started spinning, and a shape rose out of it. Russell couldn't bear to watch. He turned and sprinted. The battle wasn't just happening at the front of the room, though. There were a pair of strange, squid-like things anchored to the ceiling, striking down with hooked tentacles at a group of people cornered against the wall on the other side of the room. A man screamed as one of those hooks ripped into his back and tossed him carelessly up into the air where a dozen more hooked tentacles tore him apart.

There was another battle going on in the back of the room, where a pack of those enormous burning dogs were fighting a group of soldiers. They were spitting gouts of sputtering fire from their mouths, and the floor all around them was littered with smoldering corpses.

Russell stopped running. There was no place for him to go. He looked around, desperately searching for someone to save them. That's when he saw the woman in the white robe with her orange and green parrot.

Silver's hands were above her head. She was chanting and looking past Russell. Lightning danced between her hands, and even though they were indoors, her hair blew as if she were standing against a strong wind. More and more tendrils of electricity appeared, each arcing between her hands and forearms. Russell heard screaming from behind him, and as terrified as he was, he turned around. He had to see.

The monstrous liquid demon was spinning like before. All his friends were against the wall. Most were coughing, and both Eliana and Nora were clawing at their skin. Conner was surprisingly calm, though, with one glowing white hand held to his chest and the other to Vargus's shoulder. Russell didn't want to watch this. He had constant nightmares of muscles being fileted from Tessa's back. How would he ever sleep again if he saw all the water get ripped from his friends' bodies?

The air around the demon shimmered and sparked. The creature stopped spinning, and Russell saw it fix its searing red eyes on Silver. A moment later, a thick stream of blinding blue and white lighting surged through the air and struck the thing. The demon stopped moving, held paralyzed by the electricity that Silver continued to pour into it. There was a thunderclap as the stroke of lightning ended, leaving nothing but a smoking puddle of scorched ichor where the liquid demon used to be.

"Gather around me," shouted Silver, her voice full of confidence.

42
Attia

Attia gagged. It wasn't so much the vertigo from Arronhelm's Portal spell as it was the overwhelming stench of blood, entrails, and human waste. The four of them were in a long hallway, lined on both sides with evenly spaced doorways. They were in a residential area of the Citadel. Each door led to a set of sparse, family living quarters. Many of the doors were open. Others were shattered. Guts were splattered on the floor, and blood dripped from the ceiling.

"Where are we," whispered Liam.

"Where we're needed," said Arronhelm as he traced patterns of sapphire, crimson and amber light around him. Each sigil tightened and collapsed in on itself forming tiny stars that circled around the old man. When he was done, nine stars orbited him, most of them blue or amber.

There was a horrid screeching followed by a scream from the far end of the hallway. Liam took a few steps forward, but the Chancellor put his hand on the boy's shoulder. "Don't get ahead of me," he warned as he cautiously moved down the hallway.

"But someone's in trouble," said Liam in protest.

"They're already dead. Let's not join them," Arronhelm replied as he continued to creep down the hall.

Attia drew her weapon and ran through her breathing exercises as she followed the Chancellor. She heard more screams from up ahead, but for some reason she understood not to pay attention to them. They shouldn't be her focus. Her head ached as she looked down the hallway. The pain receded when she focused her attention on the walls. Or was it the doors?

"*Yes,*" she heard whispered from within her.

"Chancellor, the doors!" she warned. Arronhelm stopped moving. Just as he did, Attia saw the four doors closest to Arronhelm, two on each side of the hallway, shimmer and vibrate. Then, in the blink of an eye, they twisted and swirled, becoming something entirely new. Horrid, hooked tentacles lashed out into the hallway. The doors were no more. In their place, were black, oily, squid-like creatures.

"*Changelings. Demons that can take any form. Even human forms,*" said the voice in her head.

Having been warned, the Chancellor danced back and out of the way of the lashing tentacles. It would have been far worse had he taken a few more steps and been in between all four doors. Lightning was already coalescing around his hands when the changelings rushed out into the hallway. The closest one caught a blast of electricity in the center of its mass. It violently thrashed for a moment before collapsing into a pile of stinking black goop on the floor.

"Stay behind me, Malcolm!" shouted Liam. He took a step forward to stand next to Arronhelm. One of the three remaining creatures attacked him almost immediately. It held its body up with two of its tentacles, and lashed out with the other six, but its tentacles shifted and changed as it struck. Instead of striking as six individual tentacles, they melted together to form one thick, heavy arm that crashed into Liam's shield, knocking him backward.

The Chancellor continued to fall back as two of the things whipped their hooked limbs at him. All twelve strikes stopped short of hitting his body. A barrier of emerald green energy snapped into being in front of the old man. A Shield spell. While Attia's balance defenses helped her move out of the way of attacks, wizardry relied on barrier fields for protection.

The Chancellor took another step back. It left an opening for her. She was terrified of these things, though. They had so many ways to attack, and her armor was weak. Still, she felt a sense of calm wash over her. She didn't know what these things were, but the voice inside her, her Ally, did. Solen always warned her that hesitation was far more dangerous than action for someone with her fighting style. She fought her fear and acted.

Attia somersaulted into the gap and thrust her sword forward at the central mass of the closest of the changelings. She preferred to slash given how sharp her blade was, but this type of strike allowed her to maintain more distance. The changeling screeched as her sword bit into its oily body. It whipped its ropey limbs up into the air where they all melted into one single, thick tentacle before the demon slammed it down at her. Attia somersaulted backward in response. She felt her magic accelerate her movement, but not much. The floor cracked from the power the creature's attack.

The changeling leapt up and attached to the ceiling, its single limb melting and splitting into a collection of long, thin tentacles designed to impale. It never got the chance to use them, though. A bolt of lightning struck it right as it was getting in position. The changeling exploded as it died, showering the area in putrid, steaming goop.

Frigid cold washed over the right side of Attia's body. She didn't need to look to know Malcolm summoned something from the spirit world. She drifted a bit to her left to let the spirit he called move forward. Whatever it was, it was bigger and colder than the wraiths she saw him summon in the past. Its limbs were thicker and less wispy than those of a wraith, and it was faster.

She took a few steps back, allowing the spirit to advance down the hall toward one of the remaining demons. The changeling's tentacles thickened and became jagged and barbed. It thrust them out and through the approaching spirit.

"*An apparition,*" her Ally told her.

The apparition shimmered and faded a bit as the jagged tentacles ripped through it, but it never stopped advancing. The apparition leapt on to the demon. It didn't swing wildly like a wraith. Instead, it kept its arms close and moved its entire body to make its attacks.

"*Never let one stay near you. An apparition is a curse,*" her Ally whispered.

Attia didn't quite understand what it all meant, but the demon was struggling. It tried to get away, but the apparition was much too fast. It tried to slice and puncture with its shifting tentacles, but the shadowy spirit was always just one step ahead of it. All the while, the demon suffered icy touch after icy touch. The apparition was essentially smothering the demon. Attia shivered. It would be terrifying if something were doing that to her.

"A little help?" grunted Liam.

A changeling had two of its appendages wrapped around the top of Liam's shield and it was melting the rest of its attacking limbs into a single, wicked looking spike. The demon was leaking black ichor from several places where Liam cut it, but it didn't look like her friend could stop the attack that was coming.

The Chancellor was drawing tiny patterns of golden light in the air. Each collapsed in on itself when completed, but unlike the red, blue and amber stars that orbited him, these became completely invisible. She didn't think whatever he was doing would help Liam, and a quick glance at how heavily Malcolm was leaning on his staff confirmed that there would be no help from him either.

Attia moved alongside Liam and took a moment to assess her options. The demon was starting to make thrusts with its new spike. Liam was parrying the strikes into the wall along his right side, but it was only a matter of time before an attack snuck through. Attia decided the shield was the most important thing at the moment, so she carefully swung at the appendages that were wrapped around Liam's shield.

Her sword sliced through both appendages on the first swing, completely freeing Liam's shield. That can't be right, she thought. The changeling didn't even cry out in pain. Something was wrong. This was way too easy! It must've wanted her to come closer. Attia's heart raced as she started to panic. She tried to pivot and spin, but she was too slow. She tried to access her balance magic, but she wasn't calm enough.

Attia felt a searing pain in her front leg. She looked down and saw that the demon grew two new limbs to replace those she cut. They were both slender and covered with serrated barbs. One ripped its way deep into her thigh. The pain was maddening, but what was worse was the fact that the thing had her held in place. It immediately gave up its attacks on Liam. The large spikey limb it was using against Liam effortlessly flowed across the demon's skin until it was facing her. It was terrifying how this thing could rearrange its own body.

Attia frantically sliced downward at the jagged spike that impaled her thigh. She hit the appendage, but she wasn't able to slice all the way through it. She braced herself and got ready to parry the attack that was inevitably coming.

"Well, well, well. If it isn't Arronhelm and a few of his whelps," said a strange voice from down the hall. Its words could be clearly heard, yet it spoke in echoing whispers. Each echo seemed to come from an entirely different place in the hallway. It was so disorienting it made her head hurt.

Out of the corner of her eye, Attia saw whatever was talking enter the hallway. Somehow, she knew it was a being of great power. Her Ally must know something about it, she thought. Given her situation, she couldn't spare it any attention. The changeling thrust with its thick spike and she lurched to the side to get out of the way, causing her to rip and tear muscles against the barbed spikes running through her. Liam moved close and handed her his shield. He started swinging his father's sword with both hands, shouting with every swing. She knew he was using his battlemagic to enhance each attack. It was a gamble. She was grateful to him for trying.

Black ichor flowed from the creature as Liam opened a series of three deep cuts in the demon's side. It tried to thrust its spike into Attia one more time, but she used the shield to deflect the weak attack. She screamed in pain as the demon dissolved into black goop. The viscous liquid was burning hot, and the disgusting stuff scalded her skin as it exited her thigh.

"It's close isn't it?" said the echoing voice. "I think I can feel it. The El'ominae is in one of these hallways, isn't it?"

Between his leathery wings, and his eight-foot height, the demon that was speaking nearly filled the hallway. His facial features were a strange mix of a lion and a person and he had thick ram's horns sprouting from his temples.

"I know this demon. His name is Erranaekis. One of the Guardians," whispered her Ally.

Having destroyed the changeling it was fighting, the apparition floated down the hall toward the Guardian demon. Erranaekis smiled as he saw the undead spirit approaching. He held up a clawed hand that glowed with a warm, golden light. Malcolm coughed and wheezed for a moment before the Apparition abruptly faded into nothingness.

"Powerful necromancy for one so young, but easily Dispelled nonetheless," chided Erranaekis. He curled his upper lip into a sneer and rolled his tongue, smelling the air like a cat would. "El'orin," he hissed. "These whelps are the new El'orin? How marvelous! I can't even fathom how richly I'll be rewarded for destroying the El'ominae, its wretched children, and of course you, wizard."

"You overestimate your abilities, demon. You're outside of your domain. You're weakened. You're not even cloaking yourself," said the Chancellor.

"Power is finite. Sacrifices had to be made," said Erranaekis with a shrug that caused his leathery wings to rustle. "Besides, I so enjoy seeing the looks of terror on the faces of all the little lambs before I slaughter them. Invisibility tends to rob me of that delightful little treat."

Arronhelm walked forward until he was out in front of the rest of them. "Flee, demon. This is your last warning."

"His name is Erranaekis," whispered Attia.

The Guardian snorted and looked at Attia. His eyes smoldered with an angry crimson fire. "How intriguing. Perhaps I'll take you to the Queen, little girl. Actually, you're all welcome to come. Stand down while I find and destroy the El'ominae. In return, I'll spare your miserable lives and bring you before the Queen for Her judgment."

"You had your chance, Erranaekis," hissed Arronhelm, electricity dancing across his fingertips. "I gave you fair warning."

43
Eliana

Eliana never experienced anything like it. Her lips cracked, her throat ached, her eyes stung, and she felt a horrible, unquenchable thirst. She was alive, though. Thanks to Silver, they were all still alive.

"Gather around me," shouted Silver. Eliana wanted to cheer, but her voice was too weak.

"You heard her," grunted Vargus. The soldier pushed himself off the wall and took a few shaky steps forward, out past the overturned table they were using for protection. "I'll cover you. Get to Silver!"

Eliana grabbed Nora's hand and worked her way along the wall. Her legs were weak from whatever that demon did to her, but her strength was returning. Both Conner and Russ gathered behind Silver before Eliana and Nora made it there.

"Help us!" came the call from behind them. Eliana turned and saw a group of four people trying to fight off a pair of huge, burning dogs. There were corpses smoldering on the ground all around them, both human and demonic. A vicious looking squid-like thing with hooked tentacles was rushing along the ceiling at them from another direction.

"We have to help them," said Conner, but Eliana couldn't focus. Her heart was pounding, and her hands were shaking. There was so much death and chaos everywhere she looked, and her parents were somewhere out there. She needed to know they were still alive. Eliana had to find them! She wished they all stayed together as a group, but her mother insisted on trying to help anyone she could. Eliana desperately hoped her parents hadn't been close to the front of the room when the doors exploded. She saw people hiding behind and under tables along the far wall. Maybe they were there?

"Move child," said Silver, pushing Eliana to the side.

The gentle shove brought Eliana back to her senses. She couldn't save her parents. Both were more experienced spell casters than she was. If they weren't able to save themselves, Eliana wouldn't be able to change the outcome, but Silver could. That meant the best path forward was to stay with Silver.

The stone floor beneath the burning hounds rumbled and shook. Eliana heard Silver chanting quietly, and she knew her teacher was speaking to the stone floor. It was like what Eliana did to dislodge the ants from the earthen wall of the moat. This was much stronger magic, though. The stone floor buckled and cracked. Each stone tile broke into many jagged shards, before twisting and firing up into the bellies of the pair of hell hounds above them. One dog yelped and fell, its stomach impaled, and its neck sliced. The other bellowed in pain and limped to the side only to be cut down by a large man with a serrated sword.

There was a squawk. "Die bitches," said Silver's parrot.

The approaching squid thing dug two of its hooks into the ceiling and lashed out with its remaining six tentacles at the large man with the serrated sword. At first it looked like the beast was too far away, but the tentacles grew thinner and longer as they flew through the air. The tips twisted and changed from hooks to slender spikes. The man swept his sword across his body. He managed to knock most of the spikes to the side, but one struck him in the shoulder and another in the arm. He cried out in pain as the spikes twisted and grew back into hooks. The squid demon yanked its tentacles back, pulling the screaming man from his feet.

Eliana shuddered as she felt the electricity coalesce in the air next to her. As much as she wanted to watch Silver cast the spell, she knew it might blind her given how close she was. She turned away right as she heard the thunderclap. When she turned back, she saw nothing but steaming black goop dripping from the ceiling where the squid demon once was.

There was another squawk. "Damn right!" cheered the parrot.

"Get him up and get behind me," shouted Silver, pointing to the fallen man. "We need to make it to Gunther."

Eliana scanned the room and quickly found Gunther. It wasn't hard. Bathed in silvery light, he was standing alone now. There were bodies strewn all around him, but more of them were demonic than human. Two massive creatures of earth and stone stood against him. Each stood a full head taller than the gigantic man. They struck blow after blow, and while Gunther shrugged off some attacks, most of these were strong enough to force the man to parry and give up ground.

Silver started to stride toward Gunther, and the group followed her. Vargus fell in with the group as they passed him. There were some smaller skirmishes taking place throughout the room, but Silver was focused. She extended both hands, palms up, and chanted as she walked.

The earthen demon to the right of Gunther staggered back a step. Some of the larger sheets of rock forming the monster vibrated and cracked. Silver's chanting got louder, and chips of rock, dust and earth crumbled and fell away from the demon. It locked its dripping molten eyes on Silver and roared.

The stone floor beneath it buckled and split. Stones were falling away from the demon even faster as Silver raised her hands higher and continued her spell.

"The other one went underground. I can't stop it. It's coming your way!" shouted Gunther as he drove his sword into the earthen demon held by Silver's spell. With many of its rocky plates cracked or destroyed by Silver's magic, his sword cut deep and dislodged even more stones from the beast.

Eliana saw a rippling patch of softened stone racing across the floor toward their group. It drew in rock from the floor all around it as it moved. It grew taller and wider as it got closer, returning to its truly monstrous size right as it made it to Silver.

The demon struck down at Silver with both fists. She didn't move. Eliana wasn't sure, but she thought moving would've interrupted the spell Silver was using against the other demon. Surprisingly, the demon never made contact with Silver. Some invisible force stopped the fists a few inches away from her head. Eliana didn't understand how Silver did it. Natural magic didn't have a spell that did that.

"To arms you miserable wretches!" shouted Vargus as he rammed his shield into the thing's thigh and hacked up at its face. The demon barely registered Vargus's attack. It ignored the soldier and struck down at Silver again, but Vargus's purpose in attacking had never been to hurt the demon. Now in close, he slid around the demon and got in front of Silver with his shield.

Vargus dropped his sword and braced his shield with both hands. The weight and power of the demon's attack drove the man to one knee. He grunted in pain but climbed back to his feet in time to block the second strike. "What are you waiting for?" he shouted as he braced for the next blow, but the demon grabbed Vargus's shield instead. It ripped the shield away from him with ease and powerfully backhanded him with the return motion.

Vargus cried out in pain. The armor plating covering his shoulder crumpled like paper where the towering demon struck him. He was sent flying off to the right, landing hard on his stomach. He grunted and pushed himself back up to hands and knees, but the stone floor around him melted into a pool of thick mud for a moment before hardening back into solid rock. Vargus was trapped.

Silver's chanting was closer to shouting now. The demon punched down at her, and again its attack was stopped by an invisible force. Eliana wanted to do something, but she didn't think there was anything she, or any of her friends could do. She placed both of her hands above her head and tried to concentrate on her Lightning spell. A few sparks sputtered back and forth between her hands. She felt exhaustion wash over her. She was too young to try that spell, she thought. It wasn't going to work. Would it even hurt a demon of stone? The moment of self-doubt was all it took for the spell to spiral out of her control and fail. A jolt of electricity passed through her, leaving an angry burn on her right forearm.

Gunther was running toward them. The other earthen demon was nothing but a pile of dirt and rocks on the floor now, and Silver was finally able to stop her spell. The massive demon in front of her kept swinging its jagged obsidian fists at her, though, and whatever protective shield she was using was no longer working. To make matters worse, another demon was heading toward them. It had leathery wings and ram's horns. It was the one that knocked Devin to the ground with some kind of bolt of force or wind. Eliana thought it must be one of the Guardian demons.

"Eliana! Help me with Vargus," shouted Conner.

Conner was crouching next to the soldier. He was holding his glowing hand on the man's shoulder. Eliana didn't understand how she could help at first, but then she realized Vargus was still trapped in the stone floor. She wasn't sure she was skilled enough to work with solid stone, but it was worth a try. She ran over and knelt down next to Conner, placing her hands on the stone floor.

"If you can soften it up around my knees, I think there's a chance," said Vargus. "We've got to get out of here."

Eliana chanted and pictured her hands gently gliding through the stone as if it were soft mud. It surprised her how quickly her natural magic responded. Maybe the demon turning the stone to mud earlier made it easier for her. She didn't know, but she softened the stone holding Vargus, and the man easily pulled himself free.

Silver cried out in pain as the monster of earth struck her in the chest. She flew backward from the force of the blow, but never hit the ground. The winds held her up. Silver was hovering a few feet off the ground. Her parrot was still on her shoulder, hurling obscenities at the earth demon. Silver raised her hands and once again began chanting.

The earthen demon staggered back a step. Chips of rock, dust and earth crumbled and fell away from it. Gunther got in front of it and started hacking away with his heavy two-handed sword. It roared in anger and struck Gunther, but its attacks were slowed and weakened by Silver's magic.

Russell and Nora rushed over to the group, terror written across their faces. "Can we get the hell out of here?" Russell yelled.

"Yeah. We can't help 'em anymore," Grunted Vargus. "Did what I could, but my job is to keep you all safe. We're leaving."

The demon with the leathery wings and ram's horns moved off to an angle and held up its clawed hands. There was a whoosh of air, and then a billowing column of flame sprung into being, enveloping Silver completely. Eliana lost sight of her for a time. She was terrified, but the fire quickly sputtered and died.

"Finish the earth demon, Gunther," said Silver as she gracefully floated backward. The fire didn't appear to do anything to her. Her parrot wasn't even singed. "You'll find fire a poor choice, Guardian." Electricity was already dancing across her arms as she raised them above her head.

Lightning arced through the air at the Guardian demon. There was a flash of golden light right in front of it, and the lightning harmlessly dissipated. Silver sent another stream of electricity at it, but the same thing happened.

"Perhaps you're right," the demon said. Its voice sent shivers down Eliana's spine. It was musical, but in a disturbingly dissonant way. It sounded like a small chorus of voices, each speaking at a different pitch. The words formed chords that just weren't right.

The Guardian held up both clawed hands, and roared. The sound was a deafening, painfully dissonant chord. Eliana felt sick. Silver's arms whipped out to either side of her, and she arched her back. It didn't look like she had control over her own movement anymore.

"Your mastery of the elements is impressive. Literally dismantling my earth demons? I've never seen anything like that." The demon said, the tone of its voice almost gentle now. "You've truly inspired me. I wish I could spare you, but you're just too damn dangerous."

Patches of red started to appear on Silver's white robes. First, one by her belly, then another in her groin. The skin on her forearms ripped and split, and blood sprayed in the air.

"Run now!" shouted Vargus. "There! The door to the kitchens," he said, pointing as he ran. Eliana didn't need encouragement. Neither did any of her friends. Hopefully, her parents got out. They had to. She needed them, and they needed her.

"You work with earth, wind, water and fire," said the demon in its horrifying choir of a voice. "Flesh and blood are the elements I have mastery over."

Silver began to scream. Eliana didn't look back. Heart pounding, she ran away as fast as she could.

44
Malcolm

Two blasts of lightning surged forth, one from each of Arronhelm's hands. The miniature solar system of colorful orbs orbiting him sparkled as each spell completed. Malcolm knew from his basic understanding of wizardry that the orbs enhanced the speed and power of Arronhelm's spells.

There were two flashes of golden light in front of the demon, and the first blast of lightning harmlessly dissipated. The second slammed into the Guardian demon's shoulder, causing it to cry out in pain.

"My counter magic failed?" hissed Erranaekis in surprise, his whispered words echoing throughout the hallway. "Someone's been practicing. Impressive, but it's my turn, old man!"

The Guardian extended one of his clawed hands toward Arronhelm, and there was a series of loud crashes. The air all around the demon shimmered. Three blasts of force fired in rapid succession from the demon's outstretched hand. Golden lights sprung into being all around Arronhelm. The Dispel spells Malcolm saw him prepare just a few moments earlier intercepted the deadly lances of force, robbing them of their magic and power before they could strike.

"Did you really think you could best me with magic?" Arronhelm chided as he took a few steps forward. Liam was cautiously advancing along the wall to the right. Attia was trying to find a safe place to position herself, but she was limping, obviously in tremendous pain. Malcolm didn't think she'd be of much use in this fight.

Erranaekis roared in anger and charged down the hallway. Malcolm felt useless. He was exhausted from summoning the apparition. He wondered if the Other could restore his energy again like it had with the ants earlier in the day.

"*To what purpose?*" answered the voice. "*This beast is beyond you.*"

A barrier of emerald green energy snapped into being to deflect the impact of the Guardian's charge. Erranaekis clawed down at Arronhelm with horrifying speed. The demon's body was thick with muscle. Malcolm knew his own frail body would crumple from even a single strike.

Arronhelm twisted and dodged with surprising agility for a man his age and the emerald barrier flared up to take the impact of any blow that wasn't dodged. Bright blue electricity started dancing across Arronhelm's hands. The light grew in intensity until it was nearly blinding.

There was a crash of thunder as Arronhelm leaned forward and drove both hands into the Guardian's chest. The demon flew backward a few feet, howling in pain, his body smoking and smoldering where the lighting struck him. Erranaekis leapt forward in response, slashing at Arronhelm with both claws. The emerald barrier once again flared to life. It deflected the first impact but faltered on the second. Arronhelm took the powerful swipe on his shoulder. The force of the blow was enough to knock him into the wall.

"You're fading, old man," grunted the demon. "Power's finite, and yours is nearly spent. Without your magic, you have no hope of beating me," he said, moving to pin Arronhelm between himself and the wall.

The Guardian was clearly hurt. He was breathing heavily and his movements were slower. Even if Arronhelm's power was fading, the demon wasn't casting spells anymore either. His power must be nearly spent as well. Malcolm wondered again about how the Other replenished his energy earlier. This demon was well beyond his own skills, but what about Arronhelm's? Could the Other use its power to restore someone else?

Seeing an opportunity, Liam rushed forward and slashed at the demon's exposed back. His inherited sword carved a deep wound across the creature's back, cutting cleanly through the leathery webbing of one of his wings. Erranaekis howled in pain and spun around to face his attacker. Liam pivoted to get behind his shield as the demon leapt forward, punching with both of his massive fists, one high, and one low. Liam wisely took the higher of the two strikes with his shield. The lower punch struck him in the thigh. Erranaekis bent at the waist, driving his full body weight into Liam's leg. There was a sickening cracking noise, as armor plating bent, and bones snapped. Liam fell to the ground, screaming.

"I can do it, boy. I can restore the old man's power, but if I do this now, I probably won't be able to do it again for quite some time."

Malcolm didn't think there was much of a choice. The only way they were surviving this was through Arronhelm's magic.

"I'll do this for you, but I want your word. We have no hope of saving this world if we're forced to rely on others. There is weakness and betrayal everywhere, boy. From here on out, we do everything we can to avoid the charity of others. We carry our own weight. If we are given a gift, we insist on paying for it in one form or another."

Malcolm winced as he considered the bargain. He didn't understand how far the Other wanted him to go and he needed to be careful. The last bargain left his body frail and weak. He couldn't afford to agree to something he didn't understand.

The Other, sensing his need for clarification, continued. *"If we fall, we ignore the helping hands of others and climb to our feet on our own. If we're unable to, and we're forced to accept the help of another, we must find a way to pay that help back in our own way. We're too weak, Malcolm. If we have any hope of facing the challenges ahead, we must become stronger,"* said the Other.

Malcolm sighed. The Other had a point. The path of necromancy was one that would often isolate Malcolm from his friends and allies. He needed to be self-sufficient. "You have my word," whispered Malcolm, under his breath.

Malcolm's vision blurred, and his heart skipped a beat. Arronhelm nodded to him, electricity once again returning to his fingertips.

Erranaekis crouched, intent on finishing Liam off. Arronhelm released his twin lightning bolts directly into the creature's back. The blasts were small and weak. Malcolm suspected the Chancellor rushed his spells to get the demon's attention.

It worked, though. Erranaekis howled in anger and spun, swinging both of his claws in a wide arc as he did. Attia, who was carefully moving into position, fell backward to avoid being hit. Both claws slammed into the emerald barrier of Arronhelm's Shield spell.

"No!" Erranaekis roared. He swept his arms around, painting slender streams of darkness that lingered and hung in the air. It took Malcolm a moment to understand. Erranaekis was painting a doorway, much the same way Arronhelm did when he used his transportation spells.

Arronhelm held up his hands, both glowing with warm golden light. The doorway of darkness that was forming in the air shimmered and faded, its magic rendered inert by the Chancellor's own magic.

"Damn you! This isn't over," hissed Erranaekis as he retreated a few steps. Arronhelm wasted no time. He moved his hands in a circular pattern. A vibrant sphere of swirling, golden, amber and white light appeared between his hands. It was almost as if he were sculpting it. Erranaekis turned and ran, but it was too late.

A thick beam of seething energy burst forth from the sphere of swirling colors. It struck Erranaekis flush in the back. The Guardian fell forward, roaring in pain. Golden fires swept across his entire body. His wings melted away first, but the golden fires continued to eat away at him, devouring all they touched. It only took the spell a few seconds to reduce the Guardian to ash.

"It's over for you," said Arronhelm with satisfaction. "But sadly, it's not over for us. There's still fighting going on in the Great Hall. Thanks to Malcolm's aid, I have the power to get us there."

Liam cried out in pain as he used the wall to work his way back to his feet. "Conner. I need to help Conner." Malcolm saw the pain etched across Liam's face. Liam had to be relying on his battlemagic to even stand at this point. He wished he could help his friend, but his weakness prevented it. Attia moved to Liam's side, her weapon sheathed.

"You can lean on me, Liam," said Attia as she wrapped her arm around his back. Her leg was still bleeding, but she didn't look like she was in pain anymore. Malcolm knew there were some spells to ignore pain in balance magic. Attia was likely relying on a spell like that.

"Chancellor," said Malcolm. "We're not going to be much use down there. Liam can barely stand. Attia needs healing, and I don't have the strength to summon anything."

Arronhelm nodded and started tracing familiar patterns of blue light in the air. Malcolm moved closer to him while Attia helped Liam over. The blue patterns tightened and swirled, forming a doorway as the now familiar sensations of vertigo swept over Malcolm.

The sounds, smells and sights of the Great Hall were overwhelming. The stench of burning bodies filled Malcolm's nose. Both Attia and Liam retched, but smells like these filled Malcolm's dreams most nights now. They no longer caused his stomach to turn.

The Great Hall was a smoldering ruin. The main doors were reduced to nothing but a few splintered pieces of wood hanging from twisted metal hinges. From how the bodies were scattered, Malcolm guessed the crashes they heard up in the library were the main doors exploding.

There were a few battles still taking place. Malcolm recognized Constance defending a group of people from a pair of those shape-changing squid monsters. She was staying as close to them as possible, forcing them to shift their attacking limbs into shorter weapons. It stopped them from whipping sharp spikes or hooks at the people she was defending. He looked, hoping his friends were among those being protected, but he didn't think they were there.

Gunther stood in the center of the room, fighting a demon that looked much like Erranaekis, except its skin had a deeper red tone to it. It was the other Guardian demon. He remembered seeing two outside, floating above the Black Tide.

"That one is named Cinderhorn," said Attia. The demon glared at Attia for a moment, right as she said it.

Raging patches of fire were burning on the ground all around Gunther. They functioned much like walls, limiting his movement. Cinderhorn appeared unbothered by the flames. It allowed him to engage and disengage from Gunther with relative ease. Each time Cinderhorn leapt in, he delivered a series of quick, but powerful strikes. It was impossible for Gunther to parry them all. Malcolm remembered how easily Erranaekis shattered Liam's leg through plate armor. Was this thing capable of doing something like that to Gunther?

Arronhelm chanted, and lightning crackled to life between his fingertips. The hairs on the back of Malcolm's neck stood up as he felt the energy build and build. Cinderhorn pounced again, and Gunther moved to the side, pivoting to defend himself, giving Arronhelm a clear shot.

All of Arronhelm's colorful orbs flashed as twin streams of electricity arced out at Cinderhorn. Both spells fizzled and broke apart into harmless static in response to flashes of golden light. Neither bolt hit the demon. Arronhelm's lightning did nothing other than alert Cinderhorn to the new danger, but maybe that was enough.

The Guardian demon swept his arms around himself, painting slender streams of darkness that hung in the air like lazy smoke. This was similar to what Malcolm witnessed before, but this time, the darkness came together faster, coalescing into a circular plane of translucent shadow.

Arronhelm raised his hands, glowing with golden light, attempting to counter the escape spell, but Cinderhorn quickly turned and dove through the window of darkness. In an instant, both the portal and the Guardian demon were gone.

Arronhelm scanned the room and sighed. His face contorted into a pained frown as tears started to escape his eyes. Malcolm felt it too. Nothing would ever be the same in the Citadel. Its farms were wiped out, its leaders were all but dead, and most of its families were now shattered and broken.

Malcolm squinted and was nearly overwhelmed by the sheer intensity of the spiritual activity.

"Once this battle is done, you'll have souls to capture. You're nearly out of Soulstones. You may not have an opportunity like this again," whispered the Other.

Malcolm winced. He wanted to lash out at the Other for being so callous, but then he remembered his most recent bargain. He nodded. The Other was right. There was nothing he could do for those who died here tonight. Trapping their souls and holding them for a time was a small thing. In many ways, it would be a gift. It would be a way to allow the dead one last chance to fight against the enemy.

"Chancellor," said Liam sternly. "I understand what you're feeling. I feel it too, but there are a few patches of fighting still going on. Let's help finish things off. We've lost too many already."

Arronhelm turned to Liam and nodded, electricity already starting to build across his fingertips again. "Thank you for that, Liam. I most certainly agree."

45
Cinderhorn

Chariden's eyes smoldered as she listened to Cinderhorn's description of the battle. The Guardian knew his Queen was prone to fits of rage. He knew she wouldn't celebrate what they accomplished in the assault. To her, it would be all about what she lost.

"We need him back! Find a way to summon him," said Chariden apprehensively.

"You know the rules..."

"Damn the rules!" she spat. "I'm the Queen. I was given the three Guardians to help hold this world."

"Erranaekis can't be summoned. Not for a century," Cinderhorn said as patiently as he could manage. Why was he the only one who seemed to respect and understand the rules? "We can bring him back, but only after his time has passed, no sooner."

"But he's a Guardian, not some pathetic imp. There must be a way."

"None of us are exempt from the laws of the Netherworld. Not even you, my Queen."

Chariden's tail swished in agitation and she began to pace. Cinderhorn felt her rage bubbling beneath the surface, barely contained. The loss of one of her Guardians made her vulnerable. The other demon lords and nobles would take notice. It would be seen as a sign of weakness. Some would more openly suggest that another demon might be better suited to rule this world.

"I need to call Nesharon back to us," said Chariden, still pacing.

"That would be unwise, my Queen. We already discussed this, remember?"

"Oh yes, I remember," said Chariden as she stopped and focused her smoldering gaze on Cinderhorn. "I remember wanting to send all three of my Guardians against the Citadel, but you counseled against recalling him."

"And I still do. Your treaty with the neverlings—"

"Damn the treaty!" she howled. "They shouldn't need my constant protection."

Cinderhorn sighed. Chariden was immensely powerful, but her anger and impatience often clouded her judgment. Nesharon's appointment to the neverlings was largely symbolic, but it was critically important, nevertheless. His constant presence within the neverling towers sent a message to the Vel Sathir that any attack would be considered an attack against the Demon Queen. Perhaps more importantly, his presence gave Chariden an easy way to monitor the neverlings and their activities.

"My Queen," Cinderhorn said cautiously, "it took decades of negotiation to get Nesharon in position. It is, of course, your right to call him back to you. The Guardians serve the Queen and no one else. I'm merely suggesting that there may be unforeseen repercussions."

"Your objections are noted, but he's been apart from us for too long. His time with the fleshcrafters needs to end. The Vel Sathir have all but abandoned this world, and the neverlings are far too cowardly to betray me."

Cinderhorn bowed his head, conceding the argument. Drawing attention to how willingly they betrayed the Dark Lord in the past would do little to sway her. No. He said his piece. Nesharon was cunning and wise. Perhaps he could dissuade her from this path.

"Tell me, Cinderhorn, do you think Erranaekis found it?" Chariden asked.

Cinderhorn considered the question. "I suspect so. Their seer, Arronhelm, wouldn't have left his allies twisting in the wind if he had any choice in the matter. He must have known Erranaekis would find the El'ominae. It left him no option, but to defend it."

Chariden took a deep, calming breath before smiling sweetly. Cinderhorn was worried. The Queen's rage was dangerous and difficult, but a gentle smile was always an overture to an unpleasant task.

"We need to know what Erranaekis knows. Please contact him and ask him for me."

Cinderhorn winced. It took him months to gather enough favors and secrets to pull off what he did in the Citadel. Finding where Erranaekis was trapped in the Netherworld would be time consuming, but not impossible. Getting him to divulge his secrets was another matter.

"It will take time, my Queen. I'll need to find where he's imprisoned before I can craft the right rituals to speak with him. He'll want compensation, I'm sure. It will be difficult to arrange."

"These are issues for you to deal with, my sweetest servant," Chariden purred softly. "That's why we need Nesharon to return. He can handle the day to day matters for as long as it takes. I want you free to devote your full attention to this." Chariden reached out and caressed Cinderhorn's cheek before whispering, "In fact, I insist."

Epilogue

"That was better. Do it again, girl. I don't think the wand absorbed that one, but you're improving," said Arronhelm as he skimmed through one of the dozen tomes scattered across his work bench.

"But we've been at this for hours, Chancellor," Eliana whined. "The wand only seems to absorb the bigger Lightning spells, and I get burned every time I try one."

Arronhelm looked up from his reading and smiled. "That's why Conner is here. He needs to practice his healing. This way, we accomplish both."

Eliana sighed. "I wanted to spend some time with my mom. She hasn't been the same since Dad..." Eliana looked down at her burned hands. "Well, since... you know."

Eliana's father died when the doors to the Great Hall exploded. He never had a chance. All told, nearly a quarter of the population of the Citadel died during either the battle of the Black Tide, or the demonic assault that followed. So many families were shattered and broken, but there was no time to mourn.

Two weeks passed since the Black Tide washed over them. It would soon start its journey back to its home, in the savannas to the north. Unless the Pathfinders and runecrafters found a way to coax it into taking another route, the Citadel would be forced to face it again. Then there would be the rainy seasons to contend with, and the prospect of rebuilding and replanting all the farms they lost. What scared Arronhelm most, was wondering what the demons were doing. The Citadel was weakened, and the demons knew it. They would strike again. The question was when and how?

"I'll strike a bargain with you," said Arronhelm. "Make your next Lightning spell bigger than any of your other attempts. Show me some progress and I'll let you go for the night. How does that sound?"

Eliana frowned. She raised her arms above her head and took a deep breath. Sparks danced back and forth between her hands. The sparks gradually lengthened into slender streams of electricity. Arronhelm saw the palm of Eliana's left hand turn red and blister, but to her credit, the girl didn't lose her concentration. She held her spell longer than any of her previous attempts before letting the lightning arc across the room to strike a small ebony wand, resting on a table in the corner.

"Ow!" she cried, gingerly touching her blistered hand.

"Let me look at that," said Conner. His hands pulsed with a gentle golden-white light.

"Thanks," said Eliana as she extended her hand to Conner. "I think the wand took the charge that time, Chancellor. It felt like it did, at least."

"It most definitely did, girl," said Arronhelm, grinning. By his estimation, the wand collected enough energy over the past few days to release eight bolts of Lightning. None of them would be large, but they would be much more effective than a broom for dealing with the Black Tide, should the Pathfinders or the runecrafters fail in their missions to divert it.

Arronhelm planned on giving the wand to Russell. Natural mages accessed electricity in a much different way than wizards. It would be quite some time before Russell could safely cast a Lightning spell, so the wand proved to be the perfect solution. Both Eliana and Conner honed their crafts while charging the wand with energy, while Russell gained access to a means of defending himself.

In hindsight, Arronhelm wished he remembered the old wand a few weeks earlier. He locked it in a desk drawer more than a decade ago. He relied so heavily on his ability to see the future that it never even occurred to him to look to his past for solutions.

The visions were coming less often now. Arronhelm knew that there was one more spirit on the way. He was certain of it. There were six distinct spirits stretched across his visions. Maybe the lack of visions meant the sixth wouldn't arrive soon. Then again, maybe his spirit already shared everything it knew and the sixth would arrive tomorrow.

"Once Conner finishes with your hand, you may leave me for the night, but I expect you both to use the time to catch up on your readings."

Conner pulled his hand away from Eliana's and all the redness and blisters were gone. "We know. We know," he said with agitation.

"They're all we have to work with, and they weren't easy to gather either!" snapped Arronhelm. Taking another trip to Derregain was dangerous for him. He was fortunate enough to have made it in and out of the city without succumbing to the call of the Demon Queen, this time. He knew of a handful of scholars and historians there that managed to accumulate or, more likely, recreate a great deal of research on the demons themselves. He purchased copies of everything they had.

Such books were incredibly rare. The demons were efficient and meticulous in their efforts to destroy most of humanity's libraries after the war. They went to even greater extremes to make sure any and all books describing demons, themselves, were destroyed. As a result, any kind of research about the demons and their capabilities was so rare as to be priceless.

"It's just that these books are so hard to make any sense out of," said Eliana as she gathered her things together. "Especially that language book you asked me to look at."

Arronhelm nodded. One of the books he purchased was a set of written communications between demons that was collected over the years. The historians and linguists who compiled it did their best to reverse engineer the language. They left hundreds of notations in the margins, but even so, it would still be exhausting to learn the demon's language in such a fashion.

He initially gave the book to Attia. The soul inside her seemed to know so much about demons, he thought it possible that it already knew the language. When they discovered that Attia couldn't understand it at all, Eliana was his next, best hope.

"Why don't I take a night or two with that one, Ellie?" asked Conner.

Eliana shrugged. "I'll give it another few days, I think. I don't give up so easily."

Arronhelm nodded. "Precisely why I gave the book to you. Now, please leave me," he said, waving his hands as if he were shooing away a fly. "I expect to see both of you, along with the rest of the group, bright and early tomorrow morning. As always seems to be the case, there is just so much to do, and so little time to do it."

Arronhelm rubbed his temples as he watched the two of them leave. He thought of them as children, but they all grew up so fast in the past month. They were far closer to adults than children now, and that was a good thing.

The knowledge and power of the souls the Painting called this time was unlike anything Arronhelm ever witnessed before. Attia's ability to see and recognize those demons, and everything Malcolm could already do, was astonishing. He couldn't wait to see what the others were capable of. Arronhelm was positive that this new group of souls was the future of the Citadel. There was no question about it.

The old man rested back in his chair and smiled. The sacrifices everyone endured were tremendous. So much suffering. So much death. Arronhelm knew his time was all but gone. He spent his entire life preparing to receive whatever souls the Painting called. Now that it was all finally coming together, though, it felt different.

Despite his exhaustion, Arronhelm felt joyful, energized and alive. This group of young adults was his life's work. They were strong already, and they were just starting to explore the depths of their potential.

For the first time in a long time, Arronhelm felt a glimmer of hope.

Acknowledgements

It's surreal to look back on all the gaming marathons I've participated in over the years. Summer days that melted into summer nights. Rolling dice, mainlining sugar and nicotine in basements, dinner tables, or wherever we got together to play. I never would have conceived of, let alone written this book, if not for the patience and participation of so many of my gaming friends.

I remember the endless player versus player battles between Nico and Howard. (A.K.A. Boomer) Campaign after campaign, Boomer betrayed his friend, but every time, Nico escaped through one desperate die roll after another.

I remember Graig Canter's Dice-Prison… an odd collection of plastic milk crates, where he exiled dice that failed to score acceptable numbers, until gravity, time and the general chaos of the basement allowed them to eventually fall to the bottom and escape to the precious freedom of the carpeted floor.

I remember Gary Canter setting his dice to graze out on the lawn, and more than one person blowing cig smoke over theirs to get them ready.

Over the years, the game took on a new significance in our lives. It was our way of keeping our group of friends together. The game became the anchor that tethered us to one another, occasionally calling us all back, once every few weeks, to spend an evening together. Rolling dice, arguing, cheering, drinking, and generally having fun.

As we followed different paths in life, people cycled in and out of the gaming group. Each campaign had a different cast of players, with different stories and different timelines, but we carried elements from each through to the next... adding history and life to what I hope will grow into a rich and nuanced fantasy world for all to experience.

Over the years, players moved away, most notably Matt Tetreault, Tracy Greiff and David Duewell. Tragically, others who played are no longer with us. We remember you often when we gather to play: Bill Keller, Chris Borgh, Gary Canter, and of course, Kelly Konkol. It's bittersweet to come together and form a game after losing a loved one. The loss is poignant, but it also reminds us of the many blessings we still have.

More than a decade ago, we gathered in some West Allis bar to discuss the campaign that would eventually grow into this novel. We needed a necromancer for this story, and Jason Haupt accepted that responsibility, creating Malcolm. Few adventuring parties succeed without both a tank and a healer. David Hoover, and Martin Tierney assumed those respective roles, giving us Liam and Conner. (Some day, Martin, we'll rope your brother, Joe, into one of these games. Until then, I appreciate his advice and encouragement.)

Graig Canter, and my late wife, Kelly, got more freedom in how they crafted their characters, giving us Eliana (although in the game, the character was Igglethorpe) and Attia. Nick Makarewicz joined the game later, providing the group with their wizard, Russ.

I think it was something I heard on Geekshock (a podcast) that finally convinced me to start writing. They were discussing a great fantasy author with an incomplete trilogy who was getting courted by one of the streaming services and it got me to thinking... With science fiction and fantasy content more popular than ever, what was I waiting for?

Writing slowly grew into a passion for me. I was blessed with an active group of beta readers who applied a healthy balance of deception, patience, flattery and drunken 6am emails to keep me going. I don't know if they planned it all out, but it's more entertaining, to me at least, to think it was all a coordinated effort.

Eventually, a targeted advertisement led me to Kathie Giorgio and AllWriters' Workplace & Workshop, LLC. The irony that it took a targeted advertisement to lead me to a place I literally drive past almost every day isn't lost on me.

This leads me to my final thanks for now, but before that, thanks Dan Byrne and Micah Gafford. Now, back to thanking Nona, Carrie, Mark, April, Angie and of course Kathie. The value of a good writing workshop can be, but shouldn't be overstated.

I have parents and others to thank, but I've already babbled on for too long.

It will have to wait until the next book.

About the Author

A classical pianist and marginal triathlete, JR Konkol is permitted to live in the sprawling home of four very large cats. He published his first table top RPG, *Of Gods and Men*, in the early 90s, and has been running games within that setting ever since. He recently returned to writing with the hope of sharing those stories with a wider audience.

Note from the Author

Word-of-mouth is crucial for any author to succeed. If you enjoyed *Citadel of the Fallen*, please leave a review online—anywhere you are able. Even if it's just a sentence or two. It would make all the difference and would be very much appreciated.

Thanks!
JR Konkol

CPSIA information can be obtained
at www.ICGtesting.com
Printed in the USA
FSHW011801280920
74228FS